The Last Benediction in Steel

Book II. The Serpent Knight Saga

By Kevin Wright

Quantum Muse Books

ISBN: 9798646809460

Also By Kevin Wright:

The Serpent Knight Saga

Book 1. Lords of Asylum

Tales of the Machine City

Book 1. The Clarity of Cold Steel

Others:

Monster City

GrimNoir

Swamp Lords

Dedicated to my big brother Greg.

…set out for the Terra Borza, *a wild country shrouded by the daunting heights of the Carpathian Mountains. Under the aegis of King Andrew II, as part of the* Drang nach Osten, *the Teutonic Brethren's overarching mission was to stifle the incursion of the eastern horde by seizing control of the high mountain passes.*

We were well-suited to do so.
—War-Journal of Prince Ulrich of Haeskenburg

Chapter 1.

THE SCARCE WIND had finally died, and so we drifted on in measured silence.

The watch was mine, and I sat half-awake. Or half-asleep. Perched at the tiller, slumped like a drunk at a tavern past last call, dreaming hard on the slosh and bother of golden brown from heady days of yore. So far gone. Lips cracked. Mouth watering. Stomach groaning. How many? Five days? No, four. Stephan'd caught that fish, that shitty little fish. All day long sitting there with pole and line. And then what's he go and do? My saintly brother?

The bastard doles it out piecemeal to everyone.

One. Single. Bite.

Not even a mouthful, but it was something, I suppose. Best bite I'd ever had. Better than Yorkshire baked pike.

I felt a tug on my shirt, cracked an eyelid, yawned. "Hmm…?"

I blinked. It was Joshua, Abraham's boy.

"Yeah … what?"

"Mister Luther," Joshua leaned in close, eyes serious, "I heard something."

"Yeah...?" I shook off my fugue.

"A-A boat, I think." He pointed off west. Or east. Or somewhere. "Over there."

Port.

A splash.

"Shit." Reavers. That tore me awake something fierce. Heard maybe a boat bumping against our cog. They'd come in the dead of the moon when only pinpricks of starlight and the vast expanse of milky night glowed above. Nigh on invisible. But I could smell the bastards. The stink of hard-tack and salt pork and cold iron.

I yanked Joshua in close. "Go get Karl," I hissed. "Double-quick. Then get below. Bolt the hatch." I shoved him off, scrambling through the dark.

I slid Yolanda from her scabbard as Karl materialized like a wraith.

"He found us," was all I said.

His assassins came first. The subtle ones. Naturally. Over the gunwale of the *Ulysses,* they came crawling like things spawned from the briny deep. Cold and silent except for the drip of water, the stretch of taut rope, the scuff of body across plank.

"How many?" Karl hunkered by my side.

"Too dark." I squinted. "Five?" I pulled my boots off, laid them aside. "Portside. Going for the bow."

"Yar." Karl stalked off for infinity.

I laid a hand to his shoulder, hardly able to see him even at arm's length as we snuck along at a crouch. The grit of sand beneath my feet bit through the numbing cold. But it gave traction. Stealth. Gave some sense to the ship's pulse that shoes'd deaden.

The assassins padded along the port side, near even with us. Five aboard had bounties on our heads. Me. Karl. My brother Stephan. Abraham ben Ari. Hell, even Lady Mary.

We passed the mast. Karl paused. "Stay low. Cover the stern." Then he vanished.

Dropping to a knee, I gripped Yolanda, licked my chops, waited.

A rattle sounded from the fore-hatch as one of the reavers tested it, jiggling it, trying to lift it. He'd find it bolted from below if Joshua was worth his salt. And he was. Then he'd call for an axe. I was fair sure he'd find one.

I wasn't wrong.

One, two heartbeats, the *whoosh* of Karl's thane-axe whipping — *thunk!* — then *"Mother of God!"* And screams tore out followed by frenzy. A hacking slapdash of steel and wood and pounding feet.

I squinted, trying to discern friend from foe.

"Die!" some blackguard yelled. "Bloody die!"

Karl failed to listen. He was an uneducated bastard. Couldn't read. Couldn't write. Could barely speak his own language let alone mine. A man of small ideals but hell and high water with that thane-axe of his.

I held post by the mast, waiting as Karl slaughtered the assassins.

Why wasn't I, Sir Luther Slythe Krait, the valiant knight, fighting along his side? Simple. "Mother-*fucker!*" someone screamed. One-against-five is poor odds unless it's pitch black. Unless *no one* can see. Then the one's a strength. Cause the one knows all he has to do is hit *anything* that moves. Anything that makes a sound. Anything and everything. Which was exactly what Karl was doing. A body crashed into the water. Feet pounded below decks.

Someone yelled from the stern hatchway. Stephan? Or Avar? It was muffled tight, and my focus lay elsewhere.

"Stay below!" I roared.

The yelling ceased instantly.

Shod feet clomped my way. I slid out from the mast, keeping low, aiming a blind cut that whisked a leg off an assassin. I turned as grappling hooks latched *thunking* onto the gunwale. The cog listed to port. More clambering up. Shit. En masse. And these weren't the assassins. These were the bruisers. Armor clanked and rattled.

I retook my post at the mast, using it for cover. Beside me, the legless blackguard lay dying. Loudly. Ostentatious bastard. His hand slapped on the deck as he reached for something. Warm-sticky oozed round my feet, between my toes, a repellent feel, but I relished the fleeting warmth.

Ahead, Karl was still hacking. Still killing. Still doing what he did.

"Please!" someone yelled. "*Mercy*—"

Karl gave it to him.

The *Ulysses* shivered. The port-side bruisers were nearing top. I strode to the gunwale and hacked over blindly, no finesse, not even aiming, just chopping wood free-form, taking some fucker in the face and dropping him into drink.

"*Thor's hammer!*" Karl roared from the bow.

Good. He was still alive.

To my left, a gauntleted hand slapped on the gunwale. I slid two steps and aimed another cut, wailing it along, sparking off armored shoulder and skipping into neck. Blood black as night spurted as I ripped and kicked, the blackguard gurgling back in plummet. Left and right, I struck as blots of black deeper than the dark surged over. Three. Four. Five. I skewered one, punching hilt-deep to sternum then kicked the legs out from under him. But he latched onto me, close as a lover, and we both slammed hard to the deck.

"God damn!" I yanked on my blade, but Yolanda was buggered-stuck through guts.

He kept kicking. Bucking. Fighting.

Another body splashed into the ocean.

"Bugger off!" I kicked and elbowed, shrimping in half, yanking Yolanda free of gut and gore and flailing limb. Rolling back, away, through a forest of pounding boots, someone kicked me in the flank, the head, slammed me back-first into mast. I licked out a cut, missed. Slung out a second, skimmed it off the deck, flicking off someone's foot.

"Krait!" Karl roared near. "Pray to your worthless God!"

"Already doing!" I spat back as his axe swooshed by overhead.

Two bastards wailed away, kicking the legless bloke, mistaking him for yours truly as some blackguard barreled into me. Through me. Yolanda nearly cut off my head, but I twisted her, catching only her flat. "Shit—"

"Oy! I got him!" A bruiser dropped across me, spasticating in madness, one hand gripping my hair by the fistful.

Twisting, I punched a quillon into the bastard's side. Ribs broke. He gasped. His dagger plunged, but I read it by feel and drove up into him, snaking a leg round his and shoving him back. Hard. Instead of my neck, his dagger opened my shoulder blade, suddenly all wet and warm and suffused by a sharp centric burn.

I clambered onto him. Smashed him. Bashed him. Pommeled him in the face hard, twice, teeth shearing off, caving in, breaking off at the roots.

He stopped moving.

Something *wuffed* past above. I dropped back atop top my new best friend as Karl strode past, whipping that axe faster than anyone had a right to. Don't know if he hit anyone, but the bastards scrambled for the sides as Karl roared, stomping forth like an mad tyrant. Bodies crashed into each other, into the hull of their boat, into the briny abyss.

Those that weren't screaming and drowning rowed off like maniacs.

In the aftermath, gasping, bleeding, cursing, I scanned the horizon. Still could make out nary a God-damned thing.

Behind, one of the bastards rolled over, groaning, whimpering, and spat teeth skittering across the deck.

Waves lapped against the hull.

"Y'understand, when yer on *watch*," Karl leaned his thane-axe against his shoulder and wiped his blood-spattered hands on his pants, "that ain't *all* you're supposed to do."

"But you're just *so* handsome." I batted my eyelashes then marched over to the poor son of a bitch dying in droves all across our deck.

"P-Please, mister." The poor son of a bitch raised his hands. Small hands. Trembling. Wasn't much more than a kid, truth be bare. "Th-They press-ganged me. Made me come. I—I didn't want to hurt nobody. Truly, I didn't."

"I believe you, kid," I said then did him the biggest favor of his short life.

...our battalion's duty lay bare: spread Christianity and civilization south into 'the Lands Beyond the Trees,' as it is called, a place of wayward faith and inbred paganism.

We sought to educate the savages, to convert them, to save their souls from the bowels of Purgatory. But we went with axe and hammer, sword and spear, fury and flame, and even at journey's outset, we kenned clearly the truth of the matter.
—*War-Journal of Prince Ulrich of Haeskenburg*

Chapter 2.

I AWOKE SCREAMING in the fetid dark. Swaying. Moving. Breathing. Fearing the worst. For a moment, I was lost. Sweat soaked my hair, my clothes, my hammock. I blinked... The hold of the *Ulysses*. The poor son of a bitch kid's pleading, sobbing, begging for his life, echoed through my mind, *Please, mister, I didn't want to hurt nobody...*

Every night now. Seven nights running. Soon as I laid back, closed my eyes, that damned kid, that damned night, those damned words.

I needed a new nightmare.

"You alright, Mister Luther?" Sarah peeked up wide-eyed from the far side of Abraham's makeshift cot.

Please, mister...

"Yeah, kid. Sure," I lied, rolling out of the hammock.

"Krait..." Abraham ben Ari coughed. His cot was little more than some empty boxes and barrels bound together with cord. Some flea-bitten blankets for a lumpy mattress. For all it wasn't, I still eyed it with leprous jealousy.

"Yeah...?" I picked the sleep from my eyes. "What is it, Abe?"

"By Jove," Abe coughed, "where are we?"

"No idea." I staggered up from the hold, shielding my eyes, and stared out back over the *Ulysses'* stern, at the rush of dusk clawing on strong.

The *Ulysses* rocked gently from side to side, slogging along, sluggish through the water, small waves lapping at its sides, nearly drinking over, as the town of Haeskenburg materialized out of the azure mist. Claustrophobic tiers of single-story cottages grew into two and three-story houses cramming the town's saddle-back lay. As a whole, the town had the aspect of a sad thing collapsed across its death-bed, crippled by consumption, dying by degree.

Good old Haeskenburg.

Said no one.

Ever.

"Any sign?" I hollered up through both hands.

"Nay, Sir Luther!" Chadwicke's voice echoed down from the crow's nest. "Nary a ship from here to horizon."

It'd been a week since the attack. A week of alternately backbreaking rowing upriver or fighting off tempests trying to dash us to pieces against rocky shoals. *Sploosh...* All to the intermittent piss-trickle of the bilge pump vomiting water. *Sploosh...* Karl was down there, waist-deep in frigid swill, freezing his arse off, working the lever back and forth, tireless as an automaton. *Sploosh...* The only thing keeping us this side of the surface.

"It's possible we lost him." Stephan angled the tiller underarm, steering the *Ulysses* upriver. Always upriver.

"Yeah ... possible." I rubbed my back against the mast, digging in like a bear against a tree. It was healing, but the stitches Stephan had sewn were tight. Itchy. Out of reach.

"You're going to tear them open," Stephan warned.

"What I'm trying to do."

"Slade's not going to stop."

"But like you said," I paused from self-mortification, fixing him through one eye, "maybe we lost him."

"You truly believe that?"

"Since when do I believe in anything?"

"A fair point."

I nodded at the tiller, and Stephan slid aside.

The fact of the matter was I *didn't* believe it. Not even a little. That grinning bastard was still back there. Slade Raachwald. Him and his pack of shit-heels and blackguards, still stalking us, just shy of sight and sound and aiming to creep up and knife us in the dark. He'd hound us til we put him in the grave. Or him us.

Stephan gazed toward Haeskenburg. "We need to put in."

I tightened my grip on the tiller. "We need to keep moving."

"We can't."

"We have to."

"We're out of food." Stephan wiped his lone hand on his pant leg. His other hand was gone. Lost. Another gift from Lord Raachwald, the Lord of Asylum and Slade Raachwald's own father.

"We're nigh on out of coin, so we ain't buying anything," I said.

"We can trade."

"Trade what?" I glared out over the black water. "Sickness? Misery? Cause that's all we have in abundance."

"The arms and armor the blackguards bore." Stephan untied a rope, drew it tight, fixed it with a belaying pin. He was getting adept using only the one hand. But that was Stephan. Grin and bear it and move onward. Me on the other hand…? "Good steel's always worth something."

"Good's a little strong." Three of the reavers had died on deck. Others had left behind weapons. Limbs. Dignity.

"Steel's steel."

"Hrmm…" He did have a point, not that I'd concede it easily.

"We'll simply have to scratch up some luck."

"Out of that, too." The *Ulysses* was riding so low I could practically touch the water. "The good kind, anyways."

"Then we make some."

"Sounds like work." I swallowed. Took a look behind. Shivered. "No. You're right. Slade's still back there. Somewhere. Best we keep moving. Put in at the next town."

"We put her through her paces." Stephan laid a hand upon the transom, running his hand along, feeling the grain of the wood. "And she endured. But she won't weather another storm."

She might not weather another calm, I thought, but didn't say cause I'm a stubborn prick. At best. So I just shrugged and lied, "She might."

"Abraham's dying of pneumonia." Stephan's eyes narrowed as he played his trump card.

Abraham ben Ari was an old business partner, employer, and for a short time, friend. Now he and his family were cargo. Back in Asylum, Lord Raachwald, had a long list of folk to have their lungs hacked from their back. Might be Abraham topped the list. Unless it were me.

"Tough way to die," I said.

"How would you know?"

I fixed him a proper glare, seeing for a moment the visage of a skeleton dying of consumption. "Had to watch you doing it once upon a time, yeah?"

"Aye, brother, that you did." Stephan brought the full bore of his righteous-might down upon me. "Just as his family's down there watching him die as you and I fence jibes? His wife. His daughter. The *one* son he has left to this world?"

"Jesus. Fucking. Christ." I hocked a lunger into the water, watched it bend to shreds in an eddy, twisting and swirling, then swore again beneath my breath and tore on the tiller, changing course toward good old Haeskenburg.

* * * *

WE GIMPED into Crimson Bay, bulging off the Abraxas River like a goiter off a dead beggar's neck. "Docks are empty." I craned my neck, squinted. Strange for a town that made its living off scavenging trade up and down the river. *Middle-men,* they called themselves, but it was scavenging all the same. "Not much to look at, is she?"

"It's so quiet." Lady Mary brushed her short brown hair from her eyes, offering a wide-eyed glare as she took in all of Haeskenburg. It didn't take long.

Lady Mary'd filled out despite our limited rations and was no longer the withered wraith I'd found haunting Coldspire Keep. Her hair had grown back somewhat, too. It was still short, but it was now *evenly* short. The Lord of Asylum had shorn it along with her hand. He'd had his reasons, not that they reeked of sanity. "No ships. No people." She crossed herself and muttered a prayer, which about summed up my opinion of the place. "Is it plague, do you think?"

"Yeah. *Jesus.* Plague.*" I gripped the tiller. "You still fixed on putting in?"

"Where *isn't* there plague?" Stephan sighed. "It's better than drowning."

"Less certain, maybe, but *better's* a strict matter of opinion," I countered. Stephan was right again, though. The prick. We were barely making headway. The *Ulysses* had nothing left in her. Except water. And Karl was probably up to his neck, pumping away, grumbling, blurting curses to the old gods. That, at least, brought a smile to my face.

"Abraham said one of his trade partners lived here," Lady Mary offered.

"'Lived' being the keyword." I counted on my fingers. "Plague. Abe's friend's probably a Jew. And this is Haeskenburg. That's three blows landed and we've yet to set foot through the breach."

Abraham and I had history and not the kind you think fondly on. I was the last person he'd have chosen to captain a ship bearing his family, but he hadn't had any choice. I owed him, owed him big, owed him more than I owed anyone, so I said, "Fuck it," then, "Drop anchor," and so we did.

* * * *

"I don't like this place." What I could see was not encouraging. A ramshackle scattering of abandoned hovels. Depleted. Hollow. Lost.

"You've been here before," Lady Mary said.

"Unfortunately." I felt for the dagger at my belt. "With my Uncle Charles, a long while past. Hunting a murderer."

"Did you apprehend him?" Lady Mary asked.

I stifled a shiver, a curse, memories. "No."

Lady Mary said nothing.

"Abraham's acquaintance is Lemuel ben David." Stephan dug his hook hand into the gunwale to steady himself.

I raised an eyebrow. "Abe's awake?"

"No. I let him sleep." Stephan shook his head. "But Ruth knows him as well. She says he runs a money-house in the Jewish Quarter."

"Imagine that."

"Do you know where it is?"

"Yeah. Over there." I pointed south along a jut of land called the Tooth, curling out round half of Crimson Bay. "Not much to it. 'Course, it's been a while."

"Do you know anyone here?"

"Well," I thought for a moment, "I knew a lass once."

"Rose of Sharon," Lady Mary pursed her lips, "you *'know'* a lass everywhere."

"I'm friendly." I shrugged. "And she was sweet. Wasn't much, truth be bare. We were just kids, practically."

"Remember anyone useful?"

"She'd be useful." But I considered a moment. "Used to drink with a knight. Sir Alaric. The lass's father. Hmm... He'd be pushing sixty or seventy by now. At least. And the harbor-master," I screwed my eyes shut, "Jacob, I think. No way he's still alive, though, not with the way he drank..."

Stephan nodded.

"So what's Abe need?" I asked.

"What's he need?" Stephan worried his hook at the gunwale. "He needs food. Hot drink. A warm fire. To be twenty-years younger. Have lungs clear of corruption. A heart that's not broken." He crossed himself. "He needs a miracle from God. Maybe two."

"The Good Lord pulling miracles for Jews now?"

"Wondering lately if he's pulling them for anyone."

"Blasphemous bastard," I smirked.

Stephan stiffened, muttering something beneath his breath.

I rolled my eyes. It was too easy with him.

"I'll go ashore," Stephan offered.

"No," I raised a hand, "you stay here. Apologize to God. Grovel. Confess. Scourge yourself." I swept the deck in a moment, eyeballing the lads, weighing in on who might be worth his salt in a shit town like Haeskenburg. Chadwicke or Avar? "You spell Ruth. Give her a chance to sleep. She needs it. I'll go ashore." I glanced over at Avar, a big raw-boned kid who looked like he might be good in a fight. "I'll take Karl and Avar."

Stephan pursed his lips. "Won't do Abraham much good if the town's razed."

"I'll go," Lady Mary blurted.

A frown darkened Stephan's face. "My brother said—"

"Just try and stop me." Lady Mary's hand balled into a fist.

"Ship-life vexing you, my lady?" I inquired innocently.

"No. It's you vexes me."

"Fair enough," I said. "You'll add a touch of class to this whole sordid affair."

"Excellent. I'll get my things." Lady Mary bolted off for the forward hatch.

"She's eager," I said.

"I don't like it."

"Yeah. Neither do I, but this is *your* idea."

"Aye. Yes. Fine. We need to get Abe ashore, though. Quickly. Quietly. Tonight if at all possible."

"I'll do what I can." I thought on our empty coffers.

Stephan glared up at the sliver of moon rising. "Are they friendly to Jews here?"

"Ain't friendly to anyone, brother."

…was the penultimate step upon the path which we five had set ourselves, to bring glory and honor to the good Haesken name which had fallen to so much ruin and disrepair…
—*War-Journal of Prince Ulrich of Haeskenburg*

Chapter 3.

HAESKENBURG'S STREETS spider-webbed labyrinthine up the hill, contorting left and right, doubling back, splicing off in three, four, and five-way intersections. The houses' second and third floor overhangs nearly colliding left naught but a slash of night sky above.

Beyond houses, there wasn't much to Haeskenburg, truth be bare, except the old Schloss hunkered atop the northern tor like some hunch-backed beggar. An old motte and bailey style fort. Stockade walls of pile-driven tree trunks lashed together. Sturdy but obsolete against machinery of modern warfare. Of course, we were as likely to find that here as folk with straight teeth.

"Should we try the Schloss?" Lady Mary squinted up at the gates looming through the mist.

I glared at Karl and he at me. "No fucking way," we said simultaneously.

I turned toward our present destination.

"What was it they called this place?" Lady Mary adjusted her hood against the rain.

"The tavern?"

"No, the town."

"Haeskenburg."

"No." Lady Mary tugged on her lower lip. "It was something … something else. Hmm? Is there a convent here?" Lady Mary had sworn off men, persistently, vocally, irrevocably, on numerous occasions, vowing to join the first convent we crossed. I had that effect on a lot of women.

"No," I answered.

She drew her cloak about her. "Good."

"They have a leper-house." I nodded toward the crest of Haeskenburg's southern hill. "Has all the amenities."

"All of them, huh?" Lady Mary frowned.

Old Jacob the harbor-master was no more. The shack he'd inhabited was long-since abandoned, along with everywhere else. A bloody ghost-town. The Jewish Quarter included. And Abraham's friend Lemuel was gone, too. Which left Sir Alaric Felmarsh, the last man on our list.

It was the fourth tavern we'd tried. The *Half-King*. It stood within a stone's throw of the Schloss's gates. A sign hung down, a crude painting of a king whose left half looked as though it'd been burnt in a fire, a mad slather of groping char splaying out to all points of the compass.

"C'mon. There's a light on inside." I pointed. "And watch your step."

A corpse lay in a puddle, not far from the *Half-King's* front door.

"Whoa—" Avar jumped back.

I squatted and clutched for a pulse at the dead bloke's throat.

He was about my age or had been, though not nearly so handsome. Fair clothes. Not the best, mind you, but probably a sight better than this town often saw. His face looked sunken, drawn, his skull prominent beneath papery skin. "Ain't plague." I glanced up at Karl. "Famine?"

"Who gives a shit?" Karl stood at the tavern door.

"Good point." I turned at a sound. "Hello…?"

A lady dressed in ragged finery slid from the shadows across the road, pulling a hood up as she skittered down the alley.

"Pardon! Oh, Madam—" Lady Mary raised a hand, "but could you tell us…"

Palms out to the wall, the lady glided along, splashing through the mud and into the far darkness, the sound of her sobs echoing long after she'd gone. Or … had it been laughter?

"Oh…?" Lady Mary's arm fell.

"Just as friendly as I remember," I said.

"What do we do now?" Avar inched back from the corpse.

"Well first, we raise the hue and cry." I glanced up against the soft curtain of mist. "Then cordon off the area."

"Form the *posse comitatus.*" Karl pulled out his thane-axe.

"Aye." I rose and drew Yolanda, testing her edge.

"Huh?" Avar's feet were dancing, eyes flitting from axe to sword and back again. "Wha—?"

"Next, we gotta notify his next-of-kin. Then," I met Avar's wide eyes, "it falls to us to avenge him. Hunt down his killer. Bring him to justice."

"W-What?" Avar scrabbled at the crossbow slung over his shoulder. "K-Killer? Murder? I thought you said—"

The grim line of my lips started twitching, trembling, and I let loose a smirk. Swallowed a guffaw. Karl rumbled, too.

"Just what in heaven's breadth is wrong with the two of you?" Lady Mary crossed her arms.

Karl and I glanced sidelong at each other. Snickering.

I shrugged. "Quite a bit?"

"Huh?" Avar latched onto the side of the tavern. "What—?"

"*Rose of Sharon.* They're jesting with you." Lady Mary rolled her eyes. "Bloody hayseed."

"Wha—?"

"C'mon, Hayseed." I dabbed at a tear at my eye and made for the front door, soft mud sucking at my boots. "You wanted to know what we do?" I slapped Avar on the shoulder. "What we came here to do. *And* we drink."

"But—"

"No." I shoved him onward. Ungently. Pointedly. Bodily. I was nigh on salivating at the thought of ale. "We're outsiders. We keep our heads down and noses out of the mud."

Lady Mary lingered by the corpse.

"Jesus…" Avar stared dumbly back. "Where in shades is everybody?"

"Who the hell cares?" I stood before the threshold. "Now, let's reconnoiter."

"R-Reconn…" Avar stammered.

"It's French for '*drink alcohol and fondle prostitutes.*'" I shoved him through the door. "Lady?"

Lady Mary covered her mouth. "Oh, my word…"

I crossed my arms. "You remember now, yeah?"

The cold rain fell.

"Aye," Lady Mary breathed as she brushed past, crossing herself, disappearing inside.

Folk had another name for Haeskenburg.

They called it *Husk.*

…travel with Father and three boon comrades, knights all, along with their own retinues.

We, the Haeskenburg Faction, as we have been come to be called, good-naturedly by some, less so by others, represent but a small arm of the greater body, comprised exclusively of Teutonic Brethren…
—War-Journal of Prince Ulrich of Haeskenburg

Chapter 4.

THE *HALF-KING* was a tavern not unlike a thousand others I'd frequented over the years, just dimmer, quieter, more desolate. But it was dry and it was warm and it was good to finally be somewhere, anywhere, that wasn't the stinking fastness of the *Ulysses's* hold. I felt her deck rolling beneath me still, that constant sense of motion, uncertainty, flux.

Hoping I could supplant that feeling with a true drunken stupor, I ordered a couple of ales and a whiskey. Avar laughed nervously at something Karl grumbled. Lady Mary merely gave the place the same slow sweeping glare of cool appraisal she gave everything.

"You folks ain't from around here." The barmaid set a pair of gorgeous flagons down along with a measure of whiskey.

"Luckily, no." I slid a coin across the table. My mouth began watering, my knees quivered, my heart pounded.

"Just watch yourself." The barmaid tucked the coin away to a place I'd never been but'd gladly go. "Town ain't what it used to be."

"Ah, you've a corpse lying nigh on your front doorstep."

"Oh lord." She wiped her hands on her apron and

hustled into the kitchen.

"Ain't what it used to be…?" I cradled my flagon, licked my lips, leaned in to inhale its rich scent. Beads of condensation sat still on its brim. Love at first sight, all over again. "Think maybe they used to have corpses *inside* the tavern?"

Lady Mary glared at my ale. "Was that the last of *our* coin?"

"Our?" I flipped a coin purse. "Fear not. Last of *his.*" I thumbed toward the front door with its corpse beyond, then took a hearty pull. Stifled a hefty groan, almost melting through my chair. "Wasn't enough to do us much good for lodging."

"So…" Lady Mary sat prim and proper. "Where is this justiciar?"

"Upstairs," I took a pull, "plowing the furrow of some whore."

"Plowing the furrow…" she echoed.

"Here." I slid an ale her way. "Take a pull. Sit back. Relax."

"How … er … long shall we need wait?"

"Barkeep says he went up just before we came in." I leaned back.

The tavern's walls were scattered with a variety of portraits. Men. Women. Children. All of different ages, shapes, economic strata. All done by a keen hand. An old woman's portrait, staid and imperious, glared out next to me, her wiry hair bound back, her gaze cold, haughty, appraising. Stifling the willies, I turned away.

"So…?" Lady Mary asked.

"So, he's an old geezer." I took another slug. "How long you hazard he's like to last?"

"I'm sure I wouldn't know."

"My guess? '*Not very.*'"

"How wonderful to be expert in such a variety of fields."

I grinned, raising my flagon. "Cheers."

Outside the window, an orange glow grew from down the far end of the row. Beyond the susurrus of soft rain came the chatter of voices, the bark of rasping laughter, footsteps trudging through the muck, and above it all … was it song?

"What is it?" Lady Mary asked. "Is … is it chanting?"

"Hmm…" I wiped the window clear. "Don't know."

"Can you see?" Lady Mary perched at my shoulder.

"Not sure." I squinted through the wavy glass. "Folk coming. Definitely. Something… A parade?"

"Rather late for festivities, is it not?"

"Depends what kind." I turned as a whore on her last legs hobbled past, dappling her liver-spotted fingers fey-quick across my back, coruscating shivers down my spine.

"What're y'all talking about, love?" A month at sea was telling. She had a gimpy leg, a lazy eye, and pox marks festooning her face, but none of those facts detracted from the beauty of her eagerness to consummate business relations.

"We were discussing these portraits." I held out a hand.

"Oh… Aye… Art."

"And art is all about eliciting feelings," I said. "Isn't that right?"

"Oh," the whore settled a crone claw on my shoulder and started groping me in earnest, "I know all about *illicit* feelings, love." She leaned in, whispering an impertinent question in my ear, punctuating it with the flick of her desiccated tongue.

I squinted in suspicion. "Is that even physically possible?"

"Oh, aye." She bit her lip and nodded slowly, coolly, confidently.

"Ahem, well," I cleared my throat, *"interesting.* And what be thy name, dear sweetest of ladies?"

"Wenelda."

I patted her knobby hand, "I'm so sorry."

"Sir. Luther." Lady Mary offered a glare Medusa might've envied.

"What's her problem?" Wenelda twirled a finger through her rat's nest of hair.

"Lonely. Aching. Miserable." I whispered behind raised hand. "Yearns to be in on our little … *arrangement.*"

"Well," Wenelda cackled, "I'd have to charge her double." What teeth she possessed were simply glorious.

"As would I." I turned a sober eye Lady Mary's way.

Seething, she rose from her perch, and for a moment, I feared she'd gaff me with her hook hand. But she'd shed it for the wooden one Karl had carved. She glared at, quivering, like some arcane alchemist seeking to transform it to flesh through will alone. Alas, it remained a hand. Exquisitely crafted, near indistinguishable from a real one, if you were cock-eyed, or drunk, or didn't know the difference between four and five.

"Look." Lady Mary jabbed me with her wooden fingers.

"Apologies, milady," I winked Wenelda's way, "but perhaps later. Urgent matters."

Wenelda curtsied smooth as a clockwork courtesan and lurched over to Avar and Karl who, I guessed, would be far more accommodating.

Outside, shadow-wraiths cavorted down the row, slithering across the Schloss's walls. Leading them, a stooped geezer in rags staggered along, barely able to grasp the edges of a massive tome attached to his neck by a collar and chain. One after another, bodies stripped to the waist began streaming past, rippling torches borne aloft. The chanting trembled the tavern rafters. Dust rained in rivulets.

Lady Mary leaned past, nigh on pressing her nose to the glass. "Monks?"

She smelled good. Better than Wenelda even. "Don't look like monks." I slid aside, out of the encroaching light, drawing Lady Mary as I did so.

"Unhand me," she cocked back her wooden hand.

"Easy…" I raised mine. "Don't want to entice someone with a brick who's itching for a face, yeah?"

The old barkeep came barrel-assing into the hall. "Wenny, Louisa, douse the lights—" She blew out a lantern. "Gentlemen, if you please." Wenelda launched off Karl's lap and blew out a light. I obliged by blowing out the one nearest me as the barkeep, barmaid, and Wenelda scrambled about pell-mell, dousing lights til we were sheathed in darkness.

"Karl." I nodded toward the front door.

But Karl was already by it, thane-axe in hand.

"Avar." I pointed to a side door.

"Wh-What—?"

"Stand by it," I hissed.

"Oh. Aye. Alright." He hustled over to it, a belaying pin clutched trembling in hand.

Upon either side of the street, twin lines of torch-bearers strode. Down the middle, stumbling through the muck, lurched a scrawny half-naked fella, a ring of thorns crowning his bloody brow. He looked like Jesus Christ headed for Golgotha. Sort of. The massive cross borne across his shoulders toppled, and he tumbled splashing after. Gawping, gasping like a fish, ribs straining against flesh, his naked chest rose and fell as he lay supine in the cold muck.

"Definitely not monks. Here," I patted my thigh, "you can see better."

Lady Mary ignored me.

Scrawny Jesus scrabbled to his knees, hands out as he shouted to the mob fast assembling. The Tome-Bearer staggered under his burden, dropping it open in the muck, eyes boiling with madness as he read, spittle flying, drool coursing, his high-pitched screech somehow melding with the mob chants.

"Jesus Christ," I muttered in awe.

Lady Mary didn't respond.

They were *all* dressed as Jesus.

"Please!" Scrawny Jesus's fingers interlaced in prayer. "Please! I beg you!"

"Flagellants," Lady Mary spat.

"Lunatics," Karl grunted.

"Yeah," I said, "that, too."

The chanting grew as some big bastard of a messiah barged his way through the mob, shouldering folk aside, a coiled scourge borne in one hand, a bottle of wine in the other. From his crown of thorns, blood eked lines down his broad mug, the legion of crimson trickles pinking his ragged beard, his hairy chest, his distended gut.

"I want to look away, but c'mon—" I held out an emphatic hand, "*Fat* Jesus."

"PLEASE!" Scrawny Jesus slithered like a wyrm, abasing himself before Fat Jesus. "Flay me, brother! *Flay me!*"

Lady Mary blanched. "Oh, my word…"

"What God-Son gets his arse so thoroughly stomped?" Karl rumbled.

Fat Jesus trudged forth, bit the stopper out of the wine

bottle, yanked it free, spat it aside. He and his scrawny doppelganger had a muted exchange before Fat Jesus raised his bottle overhead, roaring, *"The Body and Blood!"*

"This shit'd *never* happen to Thor…"

"The glory of God!" Fat Jesus upended the bottle, sloshing wine out over the two of them, flicking it in drizzles, christening the roaring crowd in a shower of spittled-crimson. Scrawny Jesus swayed on his knees, hands out, teeth bared in a rictus of ecstasy. When only drips came, Fat Jesus spiked the bottle into the ground, shattering it, showering Scrawny Jesus in shards of glass. "Flay yourself, brother." He cast him his scourge. "Do him proud."

"Yes!" Eyes glowing, Scrawny Jesus caught the scourge whipping round his neck. A cat o' nine tails of leather thong, bits of iron spike all knotted along its many lengths. Disentangling it, he took the handle in two hands, drew himself up, eyes closed in muted prayer, then whipped the barbed monstrosity back and over his shoulder, biting into spine. *Snap!* He yanked down. *Rip!* "Rrrrg…" Grimacing. Trembling. Teetering. "YES!" Then he did it again.

Snap! Rip! Grimace.

"YES!" the crowd roared.

"Just what the hell's wrong with you folk?" Karl asked.

"We've got a whole book about it," I said.

"Yer whole book's the *cause* of it."

"You ain't wrong."

"The Lord loves you, brother!" Fat Jesus roared.

The mob chanting to the caustic swish of laceration reached a fever pitch as Scrawny Jesus staggered to his feet, bleeding profusely, and stutter-fumbled his way onward, lurching to and fro in a drunken stupor, the mob jeering after.

Snap!

Thud!

Rip!

"*YES!*" They roared.

In a few moments, all the Jesus doppelgangers had fled down an alleyway, bodies pouring, pressing against one another, forcing themselves in, and the street was desolate once more.

"Holy shit," Avar breathed from across the room.

"You're half right, kid." I sat back, took a breath and a long pull.

"They left the crucifix." Lady Mary pointed towards Scrawny Jesus's cross wallowing in the swill.

"Yeah," I pointed at an empty puddle, "but they took the corpse."

...rigors of the road have indeed proved harsh, yet nary as harsh as the tearing of the caul of delusion I bore for him.

He wallows behind, head down, muttering, cursing, stumbling into camp hours after even the meanest servant has arrived. He scars the Haesken family name, weeping in his baser moments when he believes none can see.

Yet I do...

—*War-Journal of Prince Ulrich of Haeskenburg*

Chapter 5.

THEY GONE?" As the flickering torchlight faded up the row, the barkeep relit a lantern, waved out the taper, a trail of blue smoke twirling, then collapsed in the nearest chair with a pronounced, *"Oof..."* She picked up a mug and sourly eyeballed its innards. "Louisa, be a love and fetch me an ale and something stronger, would ya?"

Louisa hustled off.

Karl kept to the shadows, nursing his axe while Avar gnawed his fingernails.

"So," I called across the void, "what the hell was that?"

"Damnation? Ruin? The apocalypse?" The barkeep slathered a hand through her frazzled iron-grey hair. "Or the Lord Jesus, our Father? Take your pick."

Louisa returned with a pitcher and the shot of something stronger, but the barkeep proved strongest, wrestling it back with but a bend of her elbow. "Ahhh..." She wiped her chin. "Thanks, love."

"How long have they been here?" I asked.

"Hrmm..." The barkeep stifled a burp and patted her soft, prominent belly. "Excuse me. Not long. Nigh on a month. Maybe two." She filled the empty mug. "But too long. Double-edged sword, if you catch my drift?"

"No. Not exactly." I set Yolanda against the table. "They seem more of the single-edged variety."

"Well, y'see, plague's not taken root here as it has in so many other burgs," the barkeep said. "Somehow. Location. Luck. Grace o' God. What have you… Far as I've heard, we've not had a single case, whilst north and south up and down the Abraxas, towns've been laid to waste. Simply gone. Ghost-towns full of empty hovel and rotting corpse moldering away to wrack and ruin."

"Yeah," I said, "not like here."

"Aye." She smiled ruefully. "We've other problems, make no mistake. Always have, but plague ain't one of them."

"What's plague got to do with that lot?"

"I've no explanation for our luck, if that's what it be," the barkeep said. "Perhaps we're merely destined to die slower. Yet, yon lord of the scourgers claims it were by the grace of God *through* him that we been spared. You see'd that burly fella out there?"

"You mean Fat Jesus?"

"*Glurg*—!" The barkeep sputtered through her slug of ale. "Err, ah, yessir. Fat — ahem. Folk've taken to calling him the Nazarene. He's the one in charge of all that," she waved a hand, trying to conjure up a word—

"Shit-storm?" I offered.

"Aye. For sure. That works."

"Plague's been raging for well over a year," I said. "How'd he get people to swallow that one?"

"He yelled it loud, and he yelled it often." The barkeep shook her head. "Folk are so wont to misplace their trust."

"Folk are stupid." I took a measured pull.

"Aw, well, something like that." The barkeep rubbed her eyebrows slowly and Louisa started in on her shoulder with two practiced hands. "Ahh… Thanks, love. Still feeling somewhat rattled. Like walking on a floating log. Twisting every which way underfoot, all slick and bouncing, tough to get a grip." She let out a groan. "Ain't charisma keeps that rabble gaggling along behind like geese."

"No? He's practically bursting at the seams with it."

"No." She leaned in as though someone might hear. "It's what he can do."

"And what's that?"

"They say he can perform Christ's miracles. Cure the afflicted. Heal the wounded. Some even say he can," she lowered her voice, "raise the dead."

"*They* do say a lot."

Out of the corner of my eye, Avar grinned in rancid delight, "Oh my good gracious Lord," as Wenelda found a seat on his lap.

Lady Mary stared pointedly aghast out the window.

"And this Nazarene fella claims it's all their whipping and frenzying and passion-Christing that's keeping the plague at bay." The barkeep took a swig. "Now me? I ain't so sure of it."

"Says that they're keeping other things at bay, too," Wenelda cackled from Avar's lap. "Relax now, sugar," she crooned, rubbing his arm. "Let Wenny loosen all these knots."

Avar went flaccid. Well, most of him, anyway.

Lady Mary lowered her hackles, cleared her throat, took a surreptitious sip of ale. "What sort of things?"

"Begging your pardon, my lady, but the sort of things I don't want to be talking on." The barkeep crossed herself. "Sort of stuff no one wants to be talking on. Not on a night dark as this. *Jehoshaphat*. Them flailers see light in here…"

"They'll saunter in calling for women and song?" I asked.

"Nay sir," the barkeep's visage turned ashen grim, "not likely. I'm living on borrowed time as it is. Whorehouse and tavern *and* run by a woman." She crossed herself again and looked to the ceiling. "Mother of God."

"Can't be too careful."

"Aye. Got a few too many of the seven deadlies dwelling under my one roof. Y'understand?"

I raised my mug her way. "But two of my personal favorites."

"Heh, well, *they* ain't got no favorites. They only got them scourges and them torches, and they ain't shy on plying with the rough half of either. Mother of mercy. Burned down five houses last night on the east side."

"Why?"

"Expunging sin from the populace is what he's spouting."

"And what sins did the folk have?"

"Eh… Was a rumor one of them was harboring Jews." She swallowed. "Folk say the fire got out of hand. Conflagrated all the way down to the river."

"It'll do that."

"Aye, ain't no lie." The barkeep closed her eyes as Louisa dug into her neck. "Ooh, that's the spot, lass. Bless you. Ain't no Jews left."

"None at all?"

"No smart ones, anyhow. The Nazarene ran 'em all out. First thing on his list. Said they was an affront before the light of the Christian God. The crucifiers of our savior and all. Lucky the whole damned town ain't razed. After the Jews, they done the same with the taverns. Mine's the only still standing. Blessing of the Lord."

"Or cause the Schloss is a stone's throw up the road," I said.

"Aye. Or maybe that, too."

"Less competition," I offered.

The barkeep fixed me an eyeful. "Silver linings on maelstroms ain't often long term."

"Fair enough," I said. "And where's all the other folk? And what the hell's King Eckhardt doing through all this? Sitting around with his thumb up his royal arse?"

"The King took some folk into the Schloss at the outset," the barkeep said. "Got a tent city festering behind the stockade. But he can't fit the whole town in there. Not near even a quarter."

"And the rest?"

"Gone. Took whatever ships was moored. Made for somewhere. Upriver. Down. Anywhere. Others what were left? Hoofed it out of here, east, through the pass."

"They're probably all dead." Louisa shook her head.

"Best not linger your thoughts long on such matters." The barkeep patted her hand. "Pass is stoppered tight til May. Sometimes June. Sometimes beyond. Other folk we got living in abandoned houses, the mills, the guild halls, hiding round town. And there's a camp north of town, in the Grey-Lark Forest, and one up in the derelict old keep east of here."

"Why doesn't the King send out a sortie? Cut these bastards some crimson grins? Bunch of half-naked lunatics might scare a bunch of shop-keeps, but *fighting men?*" I swiped a hand out, knocking down legions of imaginary foes. "Sickles to chaff."

"Don't know. Don't make a whole lick of sense."

"So this Nazarene's the cock in the hen house."

"I'd say so, young man. Or the weasel."

"Talk about cocks and weasels?" Wenelda glanced up from the snaggle-toothed nuzzling she was doing at Avar's neck. "They hanged a priest two days ago. Scourged him raw first, too, I heard." She shuddered. Avar didn't seem to mind.

"A priest…?" Avar swallowed.

"Relax, sugar," Wenelda crooned softly. "There now. Sit back."

"Aye, folk're afraid to take him down." The barkeep frowned Wenelda's way. "The Nazarene deemed he hang til he rots."

"Lovely." Movement from the stairwell caught my eye. I nudged Lady Mary with an elbow. "Our quarry. Lasted longer than I'd have bet. Longer than me, anyways."

An old man fixed his cravat as he stepped into the hall from the stairwell. He kissed his hand and placed it against a portrait, holding it there as he swayed slightly to and fro, an empty tankard dangling limp from his other hand. His lips moved as he spoke low in the gloom.

"Pardon. Sir Alaric?" I was on my feet, sliding through the labyrinth of empty tables and chairs. "Sir Alaric Felmarsh?"

"Oy?" The old man turned, cleared his throat, glancing from side to side as though I'd caught him mid-thrust boning my wife. "Who is it now?"

"Sir Luther Slythe Krait." I offered a half-assed bow, rose, studied his lined face. He was short and stooped and old, one toe tickling the grave, the only thing of significance about him being the massive white sideburns slathered down to his chin from his barren scalp. A cracked reflection through a musty mirror twenty-some-odd years older than I remembered, but I was fair sure it was him. "You're Sir

Alaric, yeah?"

"Aye, sir." His hand settled on his sword hilt. "That I am."

"You went by Red way back when." I kept my hands up. Out. Open.

"Ain't been called Red in quite a piece." He rubbed a hand across his smooth pate. "All the reasons fell out some time ago. And what didn't turned to snow." He squinted at me, snapped his fingers, pointed, "Slythe Krait! Luther, aye? You were Charles's squire." He tapped his temple. "Out of Lankashyre. Never forget a name nor face, though sometimes it takes a mite to sift through all the rubble." He looked up. "And you've grown some, lad."

"Well, they say I'm quite gruesome."

I could practically hear Lady Mary and Karl roll their eyes — Avar was wholly occupied — but Sir Alaric laughed, a fair bit harder than my joke warranted, but then he was very, very old. "It's been, what?" Sir Alaric said. "Twenty … twenty-five years?"

"Give or take."

"Lord, how the years fly. You was but a lad." The twinkle in his eyes dulled. "Yer Uncle Charles…?"

"Passed on," I said. "Long while back."

"Hmm. Happens to the best of us." Sir Alaric smiled to himself and crossed his chest. "A good man he was, yer uncle."

"Yeah." Uncle Charles had been. And then some. Honest. Hard-working. Honorable to a fault. Probably a fair portion of the reason he was dead.

Sir Alaric glanced guiltily toward the stairwell. "Don't go jawing on to my wife, eh?"

"Long as you don't to mine."

"A fair bargain." Sir Alaric stomped forth all bandy-legged, and we shook hands. "Well met. Well met. So," he offered a winning grin, "what are we drinking?"

"Whatever you can afford."

"Grand. Dog piss all around." He slapped me on the back. "How'd you find me?"

I shrugged. "We drank here a few times is all. Drank a few places, truth be bare, but this is the only place still standing."

"Aye, old habits and all that..." Sir Alaric glanced over to Karl. "By the hound, I remember you, too, sir. That axe, most especially. She still sing sharp?"

Karl took a sip, nodded.

"Aye, sure and she does." Sir Alaric rubbed his hand together.

I introduced Lady Mary next but skipped over Avar as I was fair certain Wenelda was hand-jobbing him something fierce beneath the table. I didn't want to be rude.

"Well now," Sir Alaric, ever the true gentleman, also glossed over Avar, "how is it I can be helping ya then, lad?"

"Need a lay of the land. We've just shipped in, you see?"

"Hrmm..." Sir Alaric frowned. "Well, I'd think hard on shipping back out if I was you. Not upriver, mind. Plague's thick as a hill-women's back hair. Nay, nay. Head on out to the coast. East. West." He threw up a hand. "Pick a direction, but go."

"Why do you stay?" Lady Mary asked. "Aren't you afraid?"

"Me, lass?" Sir Alaric puffed himself up and beat his chest with a wizened fist. "The best swordsman in the seven kingdoms? I ain't afraid of nothing."

Lady Mary raised an eyebrow.

"Which seven we talking?" I queried innocently.

"Hah!" Sir Alaric slapped me on the shoulder, and I found myself grinning. "Some of the smaller ones, lad. Scattered over yonder. Probably never heard of 'em."

"Yeah. Sure." I shook my head. "Problem is, we're fixed on staying. At least for a short piece."

"Aye. Well then, I'd tread lightly, lad." Sir Alaric turned to the barkeep. "Oy, Sweet Billie, could you set me up a push and a shove?"

"Coming up, Red." Sweet Billie trudged for the bar.

Sir Alaric turned back. "What are you hauling?"

"Nothing but a few old friends in dire need of help. One's in a bad way." I held up my hands. "Not plague, mind you. Consumption. Seems odds are long he's going to make it."

"Hrmm…" Sir Alaric fingered his jaw. "Wants to die on dry land?"

"Under a roof. Lolling back. Feet by a crackling hearth."

"Don't we all? Hmm… Well, I suppose Haeskenburg's as good a place as any fer dying."

"We're a mite short on coin." I licked my lips.

"No matter." Sir Alaric waved a hand. "Only inn in town burned down. Might be you could squat? Plenty of abandoned houses idling away to nothing."

"If there's a section of town deemed safe?" Lady Mary leaned in.

"We're lucky the whole town ain't been razed." Sir Alaric shook his head. "Damn scourgers. You seen 'em, aye?"

"Yeah."

"Aye, quite the show." Sir Alaric's eyes twinkled in the lantern light. "And what is it you be wanting of me?"

Sweet Billie set down a flagon and whiskey tumbler.

"We need lodgings. Private. Safe. Tonight. Now, if possible."

"Safe, huh?" Sir Alaric took a pull. "Tall order."

"I've a drowning ship I'm willing to part with. Some arms and armor. Used, but newly acquired."

"Well, I'm no merchant to be haggling. Naught but a busted-down old law-man out of his league and on his last legs." He glanced at Yolanda's hilt. "Had a fine hand with a blade, if I recall. Still know which end to hold?"

"When I ain't sober."

"Well, then, lad," he set a coin on the table, "have another round on me."

…argued vehemently with the Hochmeister to order father to return, but he adamantly refuses.

I know not how much longer I can suffer his venomous presence…
—*War-Journal of Prince Ulrich of Haeskenburg*

Chapter 6.

ABRAHAM COUGHED OUT, a sharp seal-like staccato, jagging through the dim confines of the *Ulysses'* hold. Up to our ankles in sloshing water, Lady Mary and Stephan and I huddled round a table strewn with maps.

"Do you trust this Sir Alaric?" Stephan asked.

"Yeah, I do." I looked over as Abraham's cough died down. He hadn't gotten anything up, hadn't improved, but he was still breathing. Whether that was blessing or curse remained yet to be seen, though I knew where the smart money was. "Sir Alaric's a solid bloke. Always treated me well back when, and I was naught but a lowly squire."

"What of Uncle Charles?" Stephan asked.

"Uncle Charles trusted him. Wouldn't have dragged our arses halfway across the continent otherwise." I couldn't help but stare at the stretcher Abraham was destined for. My back ached just thinking of it. "Do I trust King Eckhardt, though? First off, I don't know him. So there's that. And secondly, he's a bloody king." My feelings on kings, lords, queens, or anyone with the power to grind folk under boot heel bent generally toward the negative. It was based on my long and varied history of getting personally and professionally screwed *over, under,* and *through* by those in power. I laid a crude map on the table and smoothed it out. "There's the old keep to the east."

"No one has dwelt there in years," Lady Mary said.

I glanced up. "You're only making my case stronger."

"We'll need to eat," she countered.

"Fine." I threw up my hands. "Why not hole-up in some abandoned house in town? Sir Alaric said there's—"

"And have that Nazarene maniac burn it down while we sleep?" Stephan crossed his arms. "When word gets out about Abraham—"

"Word?" I stabbed a dagger into the corner of the map. "Who's gonna squawk?"

"No one." Stephan set Abraham's copy of the Talmud across one of the map's sides. "But word always finds a way, brother. You know that. And as Lady Mary said, Abraham will need the clean water, food, and lodging Sir Alaric promised. Not to mention it would be better to have a palisade wall between us and this Nazarene character."

"That's debatable."

"That Abraham shall need to eat *and* drink?" Lady Mary frowned.

"No. The other one." I stabbed another dagger into another map corner. "Jesus, you've both lived with nobility."

"Have you lost all faith in humanity?" Stephan asked.

"Assuming I once had it?"

"And what happens when Slade finds us?" Stephan said. "Having allies against that fiend would prove a blessing."

He was right about that, too. Assuming our allies were willing to stand tall against that bastard-fuck. "I don't like it."

"None of us *likes* it," Lady Mary frowned.

I had nothing to say to that, nothing witty, anyways, so I just grumbled and pretended to study the map.

"So," Stephan straightened, "the Schloss is our best bet."

"For Abe." Glaring, I leaned in, lowered my voice. "Just to be clear, we're all going to risk life and limb on account of one man. One *dying* man, yeah? Cause that's what we're doing. Putting all our eggs in one basket, hucking it off the roof, and hoping for omelets."

"He's a good man," Stephan countered.

"Yeah. And good men die every day, brother. More often than not, that's the very reason."

"Then you might live forever," Lady Mary scoffed.

"Clever," I admitted. "But it still doesn't mean we should slit our own throats to join him—" I slashed a finger across my throat as a breeze blew in.

The hatchway was open.

I turned. *Shit.* Of Course. It had to be.

Ruth, Abraham's wife, stood atop the gangway. "Ahem, I…" She was a petite woman with long black hair, delicate, pretty in a plain way, under normal circumstances. And these weren't those. The toll our voyage had taken had left her a gaunt, wide-eyed, salt-scaled wraith somewhat akin to the rest of us, but worse. Ruth never slept, hardly ate what little we could fish up, and did the full tally of worrying for her three charges. She staggered to the bottom of the gangway, clutching the banister for dear life. "I merely wished to … to gather cloaks for…"

"Pardon." I stepped toward her as she clawed a pair of cloaks from a peg. "Lady, I—" I called after but she scrambled up and out and didn't look back. "Think she heard?"

"Does she have ears, brother?" Stephan deadpanned.

"Bite me."

"What is it you'd have us do, Sir Luther?" Lady Mary chimed in. "The ship is sinking. We have no food. And there are no other ships."

"Look here." I tapped a forefinger into the map. "There's a pass through these mountains. The Kriegbad. To the east. We could head round the town—"

"Snowed in til June." Lady Mary crossed her arms.

"So we bring shovels. Mattocks." I slapped the table. "Dig our way through."

They both glared at me.

"I told you I've a bad feeling about this place," was all I said.

Lady Mary scowled. "Perhaps you were expecting sunshine and roses?"

"I won't abandon Abraham or his wife or children," Stephan said quietly. "We owe him that. We owe *them* that." He looked me in the eye. "*You* owe them that."

I looked away.

"Say it."

"Fine. Yeah. Sure. I owe him. Owe him big." I yanked the two daggers from the map and let it curl its way back up to a foregone conclusion. "I know it."

"Then we make the best of it here," Stephan said. "For the now but with an eye to moving onward as soon as feasible."

"As long as *feasible* means *as soon as Abe's wearing dirt.*" I snatched a glance up the gangway, expecting Ruth standing there, glowering down, lips trembling, plotting justifiable homicide, but it was just an empty wind.

…once thought impossible, yet he scars the family name, the family honor, the family legacy.

I find I have grown to hate him…
—*War-Journal of Prince Ulrich of Haeskenburg*

Chapter 7.

THE KID WAS BOUND cruciform across a wheel as wide as I was tall. Its weathered grey wood had split in long gaping cracks. It looked to have stood there some time. The kid? Relatively new. He was pushing thirteen. Maybe. A ragged, bedraggled thirteen wrung clean of any of life's joy, compounded with interest by the more than usual fare. Half-starved. Filthy. Sick. The stark white of rib gleamed against vermilion as his back was excoriated lash by bloody lash.

The knight, the thug, plying the lash, knew his trade.

Intimately.

The sun peeked crimson over the horizon as we trudged single-file through the gates of the Schloss von Haesken. The gates, nigh on ten-feet high, like the rest of the Schloss, were unimpressive on a middling scale. They creaked, trembled, shuddered, yawning closed behind.

Not much to the Schloss, truth be bare. A lopsided three-story wooden keep off to the southeast, a stone chapel to the northeast, a barracks and stable south. Makeshift tents and litter choked up most of that yard, and it all stank to high heaven of humanity.

The wheel and the kid stood propped upright on a scaffold, front and center to it all.

"Oh, my dear lord…" Lady Mary stopped short.

"Just keep moving." I adjusted my grip on the makeshift stretcher. Abraham lay on it, wrapped in ragged blankets, eyes closed, snoring, oblivious. The lucky prick. "Stephan, for God's sake, don't—" I turned but it was too late. "For fuck's sake."

Stephan had abandoned our column, peeling off, marching for the crowd packed round the wheel. An attack of conscience. I read it in the set of his chin, his shoulders, his every movement as he strode with that quiet, dignified, refined purpose that so often caused us all to falter.

"Wanna switch spots?" I grumbled down.

Abraham didn't answer.

The crowd of wraiths stood at attention with bated breath, watching a show whose final act was etched in stone. The show was state-sanctioned murder. The cast were five knights and one doomed kid. The kid was a natural.

"Where's Stephan going?" Ruth blinked.

"To get us all killed," I answered.

A few heads on the edge of the crowd turned our way. Impotent, wild-eyed glares. Folk yearning for a target softer than the one earning their ire. Sometimes, a crowd rears up on its hind legs and if it can't gnaw an itch, it gnaws the next best thing.

"Stephan—" I bit back another ineffectual curse.

But Stephan was knifing through those simmering glares, pushing past bodies, toward spectacle's end. He glanced back, offered a nod then jostled on.

My brother, patron saint of all fuckers fucked or in the process of being.

I could see the kid's parents huddled off to the side. The mother was a mess. I couldn't blame her. Ruth gathered Joshua and Sarah, both crying, huddled to her side.

"Karl." I glanced back.

We set Abraham down.

"You two," I hissed. "Take him."

Avar and Chadwicke set down the sea chests and hustled forward. "Get him inside," I hissed. "Keep moving." I took a breath, loosened Yolanda in her sheath, ushered Ruth and her kids past. "Don't stop for anything." I set a hand on Karl's shoulder. "Get them inside."

Karl grunted something that might've been assent or regret and hustled along. The outskirts of the crowd parted before him which was a fair canny thing for it to do.

"Is it a death sentence?" Stephan hollered as he approached the scaffold.

Shit. I double-timed it, shouldering folk aside. "Pardon. Excuse me. Get the hell out of my way—"

"Eh…?" The thug paused mid-stroke, the lash whipping off blood and flecks of flesh. He set his tiny pig eyes on Stephan. Thug was a large man. Thick at the shoulder and neck. A man who'd worked at the pell a fair time and knew his trade. Which in his terms meant bullying, beating, and screwing over anyone lower than him on the lordly ladder. He cupped an ear. "What the hell you barking about?"

"I asked if the *child* was sentenced to *death.*" Stephan could be subtle when he wanted. This wasn't one of those times.

The crowd started to simmer and grumble assent though it didn't take to a boil as most of the folk present weren't as dumb and/or masochistically righteous as my idiot brother.

"Child? Wot?" Thug stuttered so flummoxed he vomited a jumble of sounds that could be construed neither as sentence nor word. A second knight, wearing an eye-patch, started jawing something in the big bugger's ear I couldn't hear and would've bet an arm and leg I didn't want to. The big bugger grinned at Eyeball, teeth lighting up in an ogrish grin. He pointed at my brother. "C'mere, you runty little shit!"

Silence from the crowd.

All eyes on Stephan.

Could've heard a pin drop if the ground wasn't churned mayhem. A rabbit darted from under the scaffold and bolted off. Jesus, even rodents were smarter my brother.

"What's the charge?" Stephan stood his ground.

"Huh?" Thug coiled the lash up, length by bloody length.

"What crime did the boy commit to warrant such a flogging? A serious crime, no doubt."

"None of yer business," Thug sneered artlessly as he stepped off the scaffold, dropping a yard and landing with relish and a thud. "And who the fuck are you?" He strolled forth, muck sucking at his boots.

Folk fought back. Away. Wholly abandoning their newfound savior.

I fought upriver through the current.

"Stephan!" I hissed, an arm's length away. "Bit your bloody tongue, and let's screw."

"Eh, wot?" Thug straightened, eyeballing me, feeling the texture of corded lash between thumb and forefinger. "Best listen to yer friend, boy."

Lady Mary appeared at Stephan's side and interposed herself between him and Thug. "Sir Knight, you are—"

Thug swept her aside with one meaty paw without breaking attention on Stephan. "Your whore always do the jawing for ya?" He glared down, hands opening and closing on that lash. "Don't like mouthy wenches." He smirked. "But I know how to keep 'em quiet."

The kid on the wheel sputtered red and gurgled something. No one paid him any heed except his mother, wailing by his side, picking ineffectually at his bindings. But all was suddenly dim, distant, sheathed behind a curtain of barbed menace.

"The lad's paid his debt, whatever it was, and then some." Stephan stood toe-to-toe with Thug if not eye-to-eye. Thug fair towered over him. Three other knights jostled forward, weapons clattering, each one dropping off the scaffold like turds from a horse's arse. Eyeball kept watch from on high.

The crowd was dispersing. Fast.

"Is he a thief?" Stephan demanded.

"Aye. A dirty rotten thief." Thug bumped Stephan with his chest, forcing him back. "And we flog thieves here."

"And you've accomplished that." Stephan pointed. "Look! Can you not see? Any more's a death sentence. It may already be."

The kid's head drooped, a bulbous knot at the end of a flaccid rope.

"You tryin' to educate me?" Thug bumped Stephan again. He was coming close to doing what he was going to. I could see it in the grit of his teeth, the clench of his jaw, the furrow of his lone cyclopean brow.

"I seek only to save a life," Stephan said. "What good is killing him? Who's to take care of his family in coming years should he die? Or with him a cripple?"

The crowd seemed collectively to pause its retreat and take notice of Stephan once more. From a safer distance.

"Shoulda thought on that a'fore he went stealing bread."

"A hungry belly overrules even the most law-abiding heart."

Thug opened his mouth in retort, but his gears ground to a halt. Public speaking, debate, rational thought … not this bloke's strong suit. Lady Mary clambered from the mud

51.

and made to push forward when I grabbed her elbow, pulling her behind. I caught her eye. Shook my head ever so slightly.

For once, she listened.

"Please. Sir Knight," Stephan's hook and hand came together in prayer, "allow me to see to his wounds. To treat them. I have some small modicum of skill. So that he might go on, heal, and further serve your lord throughout his meager days."

Stephan's eloquence was lost on the big dope, and I could see it coming before he did. Stephan's weakness? He sees the world through the eyes of a man of honor, compassion, loyalty. Like him. Which means two things. One: he thinks others see the world the same way. And two: he's always dead wrong.

Thug took his shot, raising the lash and bringing it down across Stephan's face, ripping a gouge from temple to jawline and blinding his left eye—

Except that he didn't.

Cause I shoved my idiot brother aside and caught the lash on Yolanda, short-blading her two-handed. The lash cracked to a halt around the blade, and I yanked it from Thug's grip, ripping the big bastard off-balance.

Now me? I see the world through the eyes of a shit. Of a man of cowardice and fear and dishonor. So I knew exactly what was coming. How it was coming. When it was coming.

A few in the crowd grew the stones to jeer.

Thug stood flustered at the loss of his toy and the catcalls from the crowd. He groped behind for his sword as I slid forward, snaked a boot behind his and shoved him back with the flat of my blade. He tumbled to the muck as Eyeball leapt from the stage and stomped forward.

The other three followed suit.

"Oy!" Eyeball hollered, drawing a curved blade. He wore an eye-patch with a red-eye emblazoned across it. A garish piece. He hissed low. "Back the fuck off."

"Greetings." I raised my guard and stepped back. I could've skewered the big knight, or at least hacked him crippled across the knee, but we were guests and manners were of the utmost imperative.

Thug scrambled to rise.

Disparate factions of the crowd continued jeering. Good to see a knight arse-end in the muck. Especially a shit-heel like him. Never mind the bloke put him there's no better.

"Stay down, you stupid shit." I tensed to swing.

More jeering. From the corner of my eye, I saw small-folk crouching to the ground, quick, sly, surreptitious. Gathering stones. Shit.

The big bugger stilled. Even through his ox-brain he knew I could end him with one blow.

"You're a dead one now, aren't ya, mate." Eyeball froze on Thug's far side. The other three skinned their blades, looking to Eyeball. Thug might've been the brawn of the outfit, but Eyeball was the brains.

"Enough!" a voice cried from behind. Sir Alaric. Karl was marching by his side then wasn't cause he was standing by mine. "Sir Madbury! Sir Krait!" The look he gave could've curdled milk. "Brother Miles! Stand down. By the hound, heel those pig-stickers. Stand down, I say! I'll not have comrades-in-arms at each other's throats!"

"Comrades..." I stepped back, lowering Yolanda. But I didn't sheathe her.

Von Madbury, the one-eyed blackguard, did likewise, though he was giving me a look I was fair sure mirrored my own. Minus the eye or strong, well-defined jawline.

"Gustav, get your arse out of the mud and give me a hand." Sir Alaric was up on the scaffold now, cutting the rope lashing the boy across the wheel. "Jesus Christ…" He caught the boy as he toppled forth limp as a doll.

His mother wailed. And with fair-good reason.

...settled within the lands were a backward folk, utilizing little better than stone tools for weapons.

They were subjugated swiftly, surely, absolutely...
—*War-Journal of Prince Ulrich of Haeskenburg*

Chapter 8.

THE OATH was brief. Perfunctory. To the point. The way oaths ought be.

Penitent, I rose and King Eckhardt Haesken the Third stepped forth, taking my hand in his, laying his other across my shoulder. He had nigh on two decades on me, was slender, drawn, careworn, and moved as though the very bones within him ached. An aura of frailty. Lines fissured out from around his eyes, and as he breathed, each breath came as a forlorn sigh of relief, as though he found rudimentary satisfaction in simply having managed to take it. He wore his cobweb-thin beard neatly trimmed, and his mantle was fine if tattered somewhat by age.

If I were a hedge knight then surely here stood a hedge king.

"The winter winds grind on longer than is just, cleaving into our rite of passage into spring." The King smiled wanly. "It is good to have your allegiance, Sir Luther, even if only a short while. As I recall, you are a staunch fellow and a fair hand with the blade."

The chapel of Saint Gummarus, patron saint of woodcutters and destitute nobility, was cold and poorly lit, a draft through a broken shutter singing a slow sad dirge bereft of lyric or harmony. Candle lights flickered by the shrine, by the table upon which lay the dead body of the youth who'd so recently been otherwise. Beyond, the mob hurled catcall and epithet along to the staccato rhythm of stones caroming off the walls and leaded roof. We all of us pretended to ignore it.

"You remember me, Your Majesty?" I said.

"Yes, Sir Luther, that I do. A long while past, to be sure, and amid a dark time," the King glanced at the corpse, "though it seems the light of memory shines brightest on those that are darkest. Were that it was not so."

His house sigil, a spiked wheel on field of blood, lay across his chest.

"Sir Alaric tells me you are a law-man to your king," he said.

"*Was*, Your Majesty. For a short span, a long time ago."

"And he says you are a good man."

"For a short span," I matched his wan smile, "a long time ago."

"Honest then, at least."

"When it suits me."

"Ahem. Sire," Father Gregorius stepped in, a slender man pushing thirty, prim and proper and in his best robes, his slick hair parted aside, "there yet remains the matter of the dearly departed." *Dearly* was a stretch, but I said nothing. "His family wishes to pray over him." He turned toward the door. "And the small-folk outside…"

A bastion of hoarse cries pierced the mounting wind.

"What was the charge?" The King picked at his sparse beard.

"*Charges*, my King. Multiple." Sir Alaric brandished a writ and adjusted his glasses, squinting, glaring at the parchment as though trying to set it afire through will alone. "Lad, could you?" He proffered the writ. "Dark as the devil in here."

"Yeah." I took it and ran a finger down a short list. "Multiple accusations of theft. Hmm. A loaf of bread, most recent. Poaching, as well, from the rabbit warren."

"Did the lad have a name?" the King asked.

"Walter, my King."

"Walter…" The King pursed his lips. "This was not Walter's first offense."

"First time *caught*, Your Majesty," Sir Alaric said.

"And had the lad anything to say in his defense?"

Yeah. *For the love of God, stop. Please!*

"Aye," Sir Alaric tucked his glasses away, "said it was to feed his ailing father."

I glanced at the corpse. Even before Sir Gustav had laid him open, counting his ribs wouldn't have been a chore. Kid looked like he hadn't eaten in weeks.

"Does he indeed have an ailing father?" King Eckhardt laid a delicate hand upon the dead lad's brow. It'd been gashed open to the skull.

"Aye, my king. He's in the tent city. An old lumber-jack. He helped build the Schloss's stables some twenty years past. A foreman. And he's sick abed with the consumption."

"Another one," The King sighed. "And what was the sentence to be carried out?"

"A flogging, my king."

The King ran his finger along the gash, pressing the skin back into place, a frown denting the straight line of his lips. "What happened?"

Sir Alaric sniffed hard. "One of the lads took too free a hand with the lash."

"By the book." The King grimaced. "Which *lad?*"

"Sir Gustav, my King."

"Gustav. Again." The King sighed. "And what have we to offer in the matter of wergild, Father?"

"W-Wergild?" Father Gregorius clutched his bible. "Your Majesty. You heard Sir Alaric. The boy was a thief. Caught red-handed."

"Even so." King Eckhardt finished smoothing out Walter's ragged scalp. "What have we to offer?"

"We have coin, Your Majesty," Father Gregorius said, "but think of the precedent. You'll have jack-a-napes pilfering whatever comes to hand with nary any fear of—"

I glanced over at the altar. Started counting the plethora of gleaming chalices lined up like a cadre of brass knights stationed upon it.

Father Gregorius read my thoughts, his eyes narrowing as he paused his protestations.

"A sentence of death is not uncommon for theft," Sir Alaric added. "Gustav was overzealous, aye. But you owe the family nothing. You offered them safety and shelter and in return—"

"I had their son slaughtered before their very eyes." The King gripped the end of his scraggly beard, his fist quivering, twisting, pulling so hard I thought he might tear it out. "Sir Alaric, have the seamstress stitch the lad's head up. It's an affront to my eyes. His mother should not see him so. It … it is the least we can do."

It wasn't the least, but it was damn-near close.

"Aye, my King." Sir Alaric rolled the writ up and tucked it away.

"We have erred." King Eckhardt wiped his hands on a handkerchief. "Overreached. Misapplied."

"These things happen," Father Gregorius offered.

It was a sad truth that, even in our current state of moral advancement, beating the shit out of children was still not an exact science. Someday though, through diligence, patience, innovation…

"What things?" the King turned.

"Mistakes, Your Majesty."

"Mistakes?" The King shook his head slowly. "And yet, we must do something to mitigate our mistakes, no? For we are a civilized people, are we not?" He turned to me. "Sir Luther, what would you counsel?"

"Me?" Jesus. My favorite thing, being put on the spot by a king. "Depends on how you want to play it, your majest—"

A rock struck the roof and rolled down, dribbling along the whole way. The screams from outside began to build again.

"Please." The King held out his hand. "Continue."

"Alright." I swallowed. "The smart thing'd be to gather your men and drive them all out. Today. Now. Having a shit-ton of pissed-off refugees squatting on your doorstep's a recipe for midnight visitations you're unlikely to forget."

"I've a dearth of fighting men as of late."

"Doesn't matter." I shook my head. "I counted five, yeah? How many more?"

"Eight. For a total of thirteen." The King patted his blade. "My son Eventine and myself are also trained in the knightly pursuits."

Sir Alaric winced as he scratched the back of his neck but left it at that.

Father Gregorius leaned in, "Your Majesty, I cannot stand here—"

"Good," I cut him off. "Counting me, I have another four to add to the tally. If you can arm us all—"

"These are my folk. My subjects. My responsibility." The King rubbed his throat. "I … I would wish to limit bloodshed."

I waved a hand. "We open the gates and come at them

from the keep. Rattle some steel. Crack a skull or two if need be. See who wants to stay and play. My guess? Long as those gates are yawning wide, they'll take the scenic stroll rather than widow's walk."

"Yet, I promised them shelter against the storm."

"And by *storm,* you mean this Nazarene blackguard running rampant through town, and not your own men, yeah?"

"Have a care, lad," Sir Alaric warned.

"But it stresses a point."

"It does, indeed," King Eckhardt said.

The priest touched a hand to the King's elbow. "A moment of weakness, Your Majesty."

"To turn them away…" The King swallowed, shook his head. "Nay. I would hold to that promise as long as tenable."

"Tenable, huh?" I winced. More like ten*uous.* But he was king. "Alright. Then you've two options. Either play it as the strong leader. Act like no wrong was committed. Say nothing. Admit nothing. Offer nothing." A hurled rock bounced off the stained-glass window of Saint Gummarus, but like the stout wood-cutter he was, he didn't break. "Or, you appeal to their heart-strings. Make a show of paying the family wergild. Admit the error." I didn't like this. I'd been hoping to sell-sword directly under Sir Alaric. Deal solely with him. Best if a king's not even aware of your existence. But giving them *advice?* You're flotsam to the current of their ever-changing whims. "The first'll send a clear message of strength to everyone under your aegis."

"Your highness," Sir Alaric peeked out a shuttered window, "we'd best—"

The King waved him off. "Go on, Sir Luther, and the second?"

"I'd advise the first, Your Majesty," I glanced up as a hunk of plaster rained down from the ceiling, shattering on a pew, "considering the, ah, recent weather."

"And the second, Sir Luther," the King's voice cracked.

"Can go either way. Fair and righteous or soft and weak. A coin flip."

"And you advise the first, even if here, behind closed doors, we know the truth?"

"A king who makes decisions based on truth and justice is unlikely to remain king for long." My hand was on Yolanda's hilt as a stone pounded the door. "That's been my experience, though the pool on that score's been harshly limited."

"What would you expect if it were your son?" The King raised a hand toward the door. "What if it were you out there in the cold? Your kin's blood spilt by an overwrought savage? And yours boiling. Seething."

"You start using me as a measuring stick," I laid a hand to my chest, "and I'll head out and start building a gallows."

"Kings traditionally receive the axe," the King corrected soberly.

"Fair enough, I'll fetch my whetstone."

"Proceed," the King said unmoved, "please."

"My own son killed?" I glanced at Sir Alaric and Father Gregorius, both watching intently. Thoughts of Abraham lying abed, all but one of his sons killed, flooded my mind. "Very well. If I were sober, I'd get drunk and grumble into my cups."

"And if you were drunk?"

"I'd do my damnedest to see the bastard killed my kid got worse."

King Eckhardt straightened as though his portrait were being painted. "I wish my decision to relay to my people that

I am a fair and righteous king."

A fair and righteous king? Well, there was a first for everything.

Another stone struck Saint Gummarus, shattering the head of his axe. Sir Alaric ducked aside as glass cascaded, tinkling upon the flagstones.

"The walls are thick." The King waved a hand.

"Yeah…" We wouldn't feel a thing when they toppled. "I'd start by flogging the ogre who killed the kid. Do it publicly. Do it soon."

"To quell the mob…" The King said.

"That a yes?"

"It shall be done," the King licked his pallid lips, "though, the *ogre*, as you say, counseled a similar sentence for you and your brother."

Father Gregorius crossed his arms, offering me the condescending appraisal of a high-hat prick. Not a smirk, per se. He wasn't that stupid. But I could read it there. Plainly.

"And what'd you say?" I met the King's gaze.

"I agreed you would need atone for your actions." The King waved a hand. "But, please, continue."

Atone… Visions of Stephan tied to the wheel as the lash descended supplanted Abraham in my mind's eye. I shook it off, dumbstruck a moment, wondering how fucked in truth we were. "And next," I looked to Father Gregorius, "there's coin to be doled?"

Father Gregorius met my glare with a wooden nod.

"What do the small-folk survive on?" I asked.

"We ration out what victuals we can spare," Father Gregorius said.

I glanced down at the corpse. *'What we can spare'* didn't look like much. "And how long are the stores like to last?"

"That depends…"

"On what?" I asked. "How soon you're willing to starve alongside them?"

"My kingdom is in dire straits, Sir Luther." The King glared hard. "Must we belabor the point?"

"Apologies, Your Majesty." I bowed. "Offer a wergild marker for whatever you deem the lad's life worth plus half. Half disbursed immediately and half in one year's time. And I'd offer something in the way of permanent shelter for the ailing father. Immediately. You've still a fair stock of quality lumber, yeah?"

"The corpses of trees, yes," the King said, "that alone we possess in abundance."

"Then have your carpenters build him a shelter within the courtyard."

"No, no, no, that is too much, Your Majesty, far too much." Father Gregorius was having a heart attack. Hopefully.

"Generosity to the poor," I deadpanned, "just like Jesus taught." I turned to the King. "Are your carpenters currently overtaxed with work?"

Father Gregorius tugged on his robes, snapping them straight. "Your highness, I strongly object—"

"Nay," the King raised a hand, "they sit idle. Not … not unlike the rest of us."

"Then they could use the work and maybe an extra ration." I ignored the priest, strenuously, giving Sir Alaric the hard glare. "And the odds of Walter's father surviving the year?"

"Eh…?" Sir Alaric did the mental math. "Not good, I'd guess, but I'm no physiker."

"And has the lad other family?"

"His mother. She's sickly as well. Not the consumption, but—"

"Alright then. Good. Mothers are easy. Construct a shelter to let the old man die in. After he passes, offer the widow work for food and shelter. Washing laundry, cooking, whatever." I nodded to Father Gregorius. "Have him negotiate it. Old ladies love priests." Even the shit ones. "Either way, she won't tarry. Not cooking and cleaning and trudging up the same hill to the same house her son's murderer lives in. And once they're both gone, use the shelter as a storehouse come next winter. Or an outhouse. Or whatever you need."

"Someone shall need relay this message to the small-folk." The King's gaze landed soberly upon me.

Father Gregorius pawed at the King, "Your Highness—"

"You have a powder-keg in your courtyard and sparks are flying," I said. "And you want some poor simple bastard to march out and kick it?"

The King pursed his lips. "I mentioned *atonement* before, Sir Luther, had I not?"

...the Haeskenburg Faction, myself, Elliot, Kragen and Ethel-Thrang, lead our first sortie yesterday into a pagan village. We converged upon it during the darkness of the new moon and set all the hovels ablaze.

It was lauded all around as a rousing success.

—War-Journal of Prince Ulrich of Haeskenburg

Chapter 9.

HELLFIRE BLAZED in the courtyard, the scaffold and breaking-wheel roaring aflame as the legion of the damned gathered for Mass. Their sermon was lit by flaming brands and proselytized through castigation and stone.

"Sure you want to do this?" I breathed.

Stephan looked pale. "This was your idea."

"It was the King's."

Stephan glared out a shattered window at the mob, for it was a mob now, gathered beyond, clotting the courtyard's center. Stephan nodded once. Succinctly. "King Eckhardt's on the level?"

"He's a *king.*"

"He'll do what he promised?"

"How the hell should I know?"

Stephan was breathing hard, chest heaving, nostrils flaring, glaring hard at the door, listening to the chorus beyond. It was a sound that got you moving. Unfortunately, we'd be moving in the wrong direction. "Just be ready with those shields."

"Sure," I banged a fist against mine, "to protect me."

"Yar," Karl grunted, "can't have such a dainty young lass getting knocked about in the squash." Whether he meant me or Stephan wasn't clear.

I glared Sir Alaric up and down. "You strapped, old-timer?"

"By the hound, I ain't going out there." Sir Alaric took a pull off a wine bottle, offered a tepid flourish, then bowed. "Apologies. I'm just here to see you on your way and lock the door after."

Karl grumbled something garbled but clearly and wholly negative.

"And what if it goes south?" I asked.

"*If?*" Sir Alaric shook his head, frowned, took another pull.

"Yeah. My thoughts, exactly. But you gonna be here to *unlock* it?"

"Rest assured," Sir Alaric saluted, "I shan't abandon my post except under the most dire of circumstances."

"Fantastic." I grabbed Stephan by the shoulder, shook him from his funk. "You ready?"

"Aye." Stephan blinked. "Yes."

"Good." I lit my torch on a candle then slid out the door. Stephan followed, hand on my shoulder, Karl trudging after. A screamed epithet echoed off the Schloss's walls. Followed by curses. Then the best part. Rocks.

"PLEASE!" Stephan raised his arms. "HOLD!"

"Sticks and stones, brother," I warned.

Stephan stood between Karl and me, our shields angled and raised, offering a slim opening through which Stephan might work his magic. Or get smashed in the face by a well-aimed missile.

The mob bent, morphed, twisted, coming around like some vast slow, yare-less war-hulk towards us, dripping bitter malice, a tall thin skeleton-looking bastard clambering to its prow.

"Get fucked!" Skeleton cocked his arm back then slung it forward, a rock whistling in its wake.

A blast as my arm absorbed what shock the shield didn't.

"Back up," I hissed to Stephan. "It's going sideways."

"No." Stephan shouldered through our shields. "Please! Wait! Listen!"

"*Jesus Christ*—" I made to maneuver ahead without lighting him afire.

"Hold!" Stephan marched forth. "I beg of you, hold! Listen!"

Rioters armed with rocks quelled an instant.

Skeleton stomped his boot, pointing, drool coursing down his chin, "Liar!"

"He hasn't said shit, yet." I met Skeleton's eye. "Give him a square shake." *Then* take aim. But I didn't say it as dripping sarcasm was often lost on mobs.

"Brothers! Sisters!" Stephan bellowed into the void. "Put aside your missiles. Please!"

"We ain't your brothers," Skeleton spat. "Ain't your sisters, ain't your anything, you pampered dandy!"

"Aye, it's true. My name is Stephan Krait. And indeed, I was born the son of a lord. But I, too, have known injustice." He pulled back his sleeve, revealing the caustic stump where his right arm ended. "And have suffered for it. I have made it my life's work to quell it!"

The mob settled at that, not wholly, and not Skeleton. "Then what in Hades you doing on their side?!"

Stephan pressed on. "I know what it is to lose. To starve. To—"

"Nooo!" Skeleton balled his fists. "He lies!"

"King Eckhardt offers the sire of the lad wergild. Housing and shelter as well."

"And what about his cursed murderer!"

"He is to be punished," Stephan announced. "Flogged. Publicly."

A chatter riffled through the crowd.

"And what of them who gone missing?" someone yelled.

"Aye, what's to be done for them?"

"Brother?" Stephan asked without turning.

"You got me," I whispered.

Stephan swallowed. "I'll speak personally to King Eckhardt about this—"

"Can you not see?" Skeleton screamed. "The son of a lord. What cares he for us? Can you not—"

Stephan trudged forth, marching across open ground until he was before the mob, until he was within it, eye-to-eye with Skeleton. Metaphorically, at least. Skeleton leered over him like a wizened scarecrow, his huge melon ungainly as an apple on a toothpick.

Shoulder to shoulder, Karl and I scrambled after. *Precipice*, a word that came suddenly to mind, and here we were lemmings scrambling pell-mell for it.

"You saw me this very morn?" Stephan asked. "Saw my brother?" He pointed to me as I skidded to a halt by his side. The scaffold and wheel stood somber and giant, mere echoes midst the burning silence. "You saw us here?"

"And what good would it do? Walter's still dead. And we're still starving."

"Times are hard," Stephan admitted.

"And about to get harder." Skeleton lurched forth and seized Stephan by the throat, or made to, anyways. Karl thrust his torch forth, freezing the emaciated giant in place while I stepped in and slammed him with my shield, knocking him onto his arse across the cold hard ground.

"Stop." Stephan raised his hand.

Karl lowered his torch. I scowled but restrained myself from putting the boots to him. Just like Jesus taught.

"Please." Stephan offered Skeleton his hand. "What is your name, good sir?"

"Fuck you," Skeleton rasped.

"What you said was just." Stephan pursed his lips. "I was not successful in saving the lad's life. Nay. I was too late. But I will say I risked my own life for his. I say this not because I fancy myself something of a hero. Heroes succeed. Triumph. I say it only because I wish you to see the truth of who I am." He laid a hand on my shoulder, quelling me trembling back. "I risked my life and would do so again," he turned to the mob, "for any of you."

I huddled behind my shield, keeping an eye on the mob, their hands behind threadbare cloaks, gripping hidden weapons. Karl was doing the same. If the mob decided to do what mobs do, it'd make little difference. A few seconds, maybe. A couple steps. A fair many would fall, yeah, but we'd be amongst them.

A chatter of accordance spattered through the mob.

"Who here thinks me a liar?" Stephan's voice rang out.

Silence only, but for the crackle of flame coursing through the night.

Skeleton scrambled on his arse backward, disappearing into the mob.

"I pledge this to you!" Stephan called out. "I shall parley with your king. I shall voice *your* concerns," he laid a hand to his heart, "which are now *my* concerns! And I shall dwell amongst you, bearing your travails, if you should have me."

Murmuring then at that.

"You mean it?" A woman shouldered through the mob. She was small, bedraggled, malnourished, but there was the glint of iron in her eye. "Truly now?" Her eyes narrowed.

"You'll speak with him? You'll stand for us? *With us?*"

"Yes," Stephan said, "I shall."

It's a funny thing, reading a crowd, a mob. There's little difference between the two, really, only intent, and intent's not always a thing you can measure, only sense. Some blokes'll kill you in a blink with a good-natured grin. Some can't mask the ire, have to let it pour free in horrific glee. But what can be masked by a loner is oft times impossible with a crowd, and that's what Stephan had quelled them back into.

He strode through them unafraid, grasping hands, introducing himself, nodding, talking, smiling. A few even patted me on the shoulder. A fair rousing moment, truth be told, but it was a sad state of affairs when he and I were the most popular blokes in town.

...tried to escape the conflagration, we slew them, one and all. The flames that throughout the night had scorched timber under aegis of dawn took to consuming the carcasses of pagan infidels.

Hochmeister Gaunt assures us a place in Heaven, seated at the right hand of...
—War-Journal of Prince Ulrich of Haeskenburg

Chapter 10.

I PULLED OPEN the door to see Abraham lying shivering abed, blankets up to his eyeballs, translucent as a drowned maggot. The hearth-flame seemed to cast little if no heat. But there were a roof and walls and shuttered windows, and it was dry. A thimble-sized pot of soup cooking. More than something to be said for that. Ruth hovered over him, laying a folded cloth across his forehead, pressing down with her palm, holding it there, her lips pursed in chronic consternation. Joshua and Sarah sat side-by-side at a small table. Joshua read a book while Sarah lay head down, cradled in her arms.

I eased the door closed, wincing as it creaked.

Ruth looked up, eyes glistening, filled with a mix of hope and horror. When she saw my face she abandoned the hope.

"You were expecting my brother." I straightened.

"What—" Ruth cleared her throat, fought to swallow, glaring all the while toward the window, "what became of that boy? The one from the yard?"

"What becomes of all of us." I licked my lips. "Eventually"

It was silent outside. Finally.

"Won't they—"

"They're all back in their tents, hunkered down with sore throats and raw souls." Hopefully. I nodded toward Abraham. "How's he doing?" But I already knew.

Ruth's pale visage darkened. "His fever's not yet broken. And I … I fear that it shan't." She didn't like me, and I didn't blame her. I'd killed her son Isaac back in Asylum. "Oy vey. It's best he's not disturbed." It hadn't been my fault. Or it had. Nigh on completely. But he'd been part of a cabal set against me, put me in a tight position, given me one of two choices. Him or me. I'd chosen me. "You should go."

"You need rest." I set an armload of blankets on the foot of the bed.

"I'm fine."

Ruth put me in mind of a sparrow, its bones so thin, so weak, so brittle.

"It's late." I could see she was cracking, fissures forming, moving in lightning-patterned jags even as I watched. Course, some of that might've been on account of me. "Lady Mary said she'd be along soon. To spell you." I lifted a blanket, offered it to the kids. "What are you reading?"

"The Talmud." Joshua tilted the book up.

"Still?" They'd been reading it aboard the *Ulysses*. The entire voyage.

"It's all we have," Joshua yawned.

"How many times've you read it?" I asked.

Joshua glanced at Sarah, still asleep, then started counting silently on his fingers.

"What *they* do is of no concern of yours." Hands balled into fists, Ruth marched over and ripped the blanket from my hands. "Just stay away from them," she growled. "Don't go near them. Don't talk to them. Don't even look at them."

"You hate me." I took a step back, hands raised. "I get it. Hell. I deserve it." I glanced at her children. "But you don't hate them, yeah? So what do *they* need?" My voice echoed dead in the close room. "What's Abe need?"

I could see the gears turning in her head, swallowing some retort no doubt lodged like a dry pine cone halfway down her craw.

"Tell me what you need and I'll go," I said.

"Joshie?" Sarah rubbed her eyes. "Mother, what…?" She stifled a yawn. "Oh. Mister Luther. Hello." Presumably, her parents hadn't told her that I'd murdered one of her brothers. And had a hand in the demise of another.

"Milady." I offered a bow.

"Go back to sleep, love." Ruth was kneeling by Sarah's side in an instant, rubbing her back, wrapping the blanket around her shoulders. "Close your eyes. Dream." She tucked the edges in around Sarah, hands shaking all the while. "We need more wood." She licked her cracked lips. "We need clean water. A bucket. As well as some linen. Strips would be fine. To… To clean him."

"Of course." I raised an eyebrow at the children. "Them?"

"Please," Ruth gathered herself up, "don't speak of them. Don't speak to them. Don't…" She nearly collapsed to a knee but caught herself, straightened, brushing a stray coil of hair from her eyes.

Sarah latched onto her. "Mother?"

"I'm fine, dearest," Ruth said.

Joshua latched on as well.

"Yeah…" I took a breath, nodded, swallowed. "Wood. Clean water. Linen." I turned to leave.

"*Krait*…" Abraham shifted in bed, his voice a low ghost moan.

"Abe?" I marched over. "What is it?"

He beckoned with a single finger, managing somehow to make it look exhausting.

"Sorry it took so long to check in with you." I knelt by his side. "Been a long day."

Tears brimming in her eyes, Ruth bit her knuckle.

"Where...?" Abraham struggled to sit up and failed, collapsing back in a gasping heap. "Where are we?"

"Haeskenburg."

"On the Abraxas?" Abraham asked quietly.

"Yeah," I said. "*That* Haeskenburg."

"Oh, my word. Yes. Yes." Abraham pinched the bridge of his nose. "Were you able to ascertain Lemuel's whereabouts?"

"Sorry, Abe. We tried. He's gone. Or dead. Or both."

"Dead..." Abraham echoed. "Ahem. Ruth, m-my dear, some soup, please, if you would?"

Ruth sniffed, smiled, wiped her eyes. "Of course."

"Relax." I held up a hand. "I'll get it."

"Why did we put in here?" Abraham asked. "Perhaps we might sail further—"

"It was here or drown." I kept my voice low as I ladled soup. "My vote was for drown." I shrugged. "I was outvoted."

"*Oy gevalt.* You should have woken me."

"If the angry mob couldn't, we figured you'd earned a stretch."

"Even so."

"Next time then," I conceded.

"What happened?"

"The *Ulysses* shit the bed." I handed Ruth the soup. Her hands were still shaking. "Got it? You sure? Good." Seemed she'd brook no other way. "She was sinking. I've got Avar and Chadwicke on it. Gonna dry dock her soon as possible.

Tomorrow hopefully. Heavy repairs." It was the smart move. Smart unless Slade Raachwald had tracked us upriver. Smart unless Slade saw her. Recognized her. Acted accordingly. Then we'd all be begging to drown.

Abraham blinked. "What is this place?"

"The Schloss von Haesken." I winked. "Nothing but the best, yeah? Pulled some strings with an old justiciar I know." I didn't tell him those strings were tied to an anvil balanced precariously above our collective heads.

"Hmm…" Abraham closed his eyes. "King Eckhardt is said to be a fair man, yes?"

"Yeah. Maybe." I shrugged. "I don't know."

Abraham forced air out. Breathing was a chore for him. A chore to watch. "And how is the remainder of our … situation?"

Ruth's eyes welled. "Everything is fine, my love—"

"The *Ulysses* is an apt metaphor," I cut in. No sense in lying. Not here. Not now. "We're in it and in it deep."

"You never were a liar, Krait." Abraham smiled wanly. "You might elicit too much joy in the delivering of harsh truths, but," he fought dry-mouth to swallow, tonguing the words out, "no liar."

"I've no joy in this."

Ruth cast me a glare and proffered a shaking spoon to Abraham's lips. "Eat."

"Thank you, my dear." Abraham sipped tepidly at the soup.

"You should go," Ruth said without turning my way. "Now. Please." She pointed with the spoon. "He needs … he needs his rest."

Abraham patted her hand and mumbled something I couldn't quite hear.

Ruth cocked her head toward his greyish lips, listening, eyes quivering in withheld tears. "Yes, my dear, of … of course."

"Krait."

"What is it, Abe?" I asked.

"Forgive me." Abraham dabbed his lips with the corner of his blanket. "And coin? How are we situated with coin?"

"I'm working on it."

"Did you—"

"I'm sell-swording for King Eckhardt." I shrugged. "Food. Lodging. Get us back on our feet. The lumber we need for the *Ulysses*. I just finished taking my oath. We're serving a warrant come dawn. And we've some gear to hawk if we can find anyone willing. Courtesy of our friends from Asylum."

"My dear," Abraham nodded a mite to Ruth, "can you fetch me pen and paper?"

"I—" She looked around the small room, hoping it might somehow materialize. She came finally to me.

"I'll add it to the list."

"Rest, my love. There's no need—" Ruth clutched his hand. "If you could simply clear this cough."

"No, no." Abraham took her hands and kissed them. "Of course, my dear, of course. I don't intend to leave you soon. But I have trade contacts here besides Lemuel. Hanseatic men. Merchants. Men who owe me. I think it time I called them in."

"These, contacts?" I raised a magnificent eyebrow. "They wouldn't happen to be Jews, would they?"

"Err? Yes, mostly." Abraham struggled to turn my way. "Why?"

Ruth glared hard my way, shaking her head. Fiercely.

"You   know   why,"   I   answered   anyways.

...conquest after conquest. It was a heady lust that burgeoned within even whence thirst had been quenched and hunger slaked.

But hence, there came the clan-holt.

—War-Journal of Prince Ulrich of Haeskenburg

Chapter 11.

WE WERE SERVING a murder warrant.

"Used to be they condemned criminals here, a generation past." Sir Alaric glared up through the cold dawn rain, shielding his eyes with a gloved hand, breath steaming, the ruins of the old keep looming like walls of a steep canyon, a legion of dark windows, empty eyes, watching down. Brown vines and dead vegetation encrusted a massive breaking-wheel propped up in the center of the courtyard. Not unlike the one in the Schloss.

"Hunting criminals. Catching 'em. Killing 'em." Sir Alaric wiped his chin. "Has to be done. A necessity. Chop off their heads. Hang 'em. Whatnot. But breaking 'em? By the hound. Hearing the deliberate snap of bone?" He shook his head. "Brings us all low."

"Sends a message, though," I said.

"Aye. We're barbarians, despite our best attempts at Christ's word."

"Now your King just beheads them or your ogres flog them rotten." I kept a hand to Yolanda's hilt. "You've come so far."

"Was an old Haesken family tradition," Sir Alaric said.

"Yeah?" I glanced at him sidelong. "Mine has ham every Easter."

Sir Alaric seemed suddenly consumed with knocking ashes from his pipe.

Tied off and staked down, a mishmashed muddle of tents and lean-tos huddled in close groups through the old keep's courtyard, silent but for the patter of rain against canvas. Eyes from within watched. I felt them but saw no one.

"Slow-cooked over a spit…" I kept my eyes to the tents, to the doorways, the windows. Had the sense that king's officers wouldn't be loved round here. Or anywhere else for that matter. "Basted in honey. Brushed on like paint." I swallowed. "Turning it round and round. Take all day." I glanced over to the kid. "Ever have it that way?"

"Eh? Huh? Wha—?" Young Parwicke stammered. I made him for nigh on par with the lad from the courtyard. From the slab. The crypt. "Ah … no, Your Majesty."

"Ain't a king, kid."

"Huh? Oh. Sorry." Young Parwicke's shoulders were up by his ears, hands fidgeting, eyes feverishly scanning the grey stone structures. "Ain't never had it that way." He looked like he hadn't had much of anything of late and for a fair decent stretch beyond. "Sir Luther," he added after.

"Too bad." I smacked my lips. "Sweet as candy."

A stone toppled from a fallen tower. I nearly shit myself. *Jesus.* Tried playing it cool. Karl caught it, though, and chuffed a rough sidelong rumble.

The kid said nothing, though, just glanced expectantly at Sir Alaric. It was his show. The weight Karl and I bore was trying to look big and scary. There was a certain freedom in being a base tool. No need for thought. Making decisions. Morality.

"What say you, lad?" Sir Alaric chewed his pipe.

"Aye, sir. That's it." Young Parwicke pointed. "Over yonder."

"The gaol?" Sir Alaric glared at a squat stone structure, a massive lock and chain crisscrossing its front door.

"Nay. Beyond. The old chapel." Young Parwicke jumped at a sound, real or imagined. He was one of many from the tent camp, but the only one we could find willing to spill. I'd hazard it'd make him about as popular as us but said nothing. We all have our reasons, and an empty belly was better than most. "C-Can I get my coin, sir?"

"Nay, lad," Sir Alaric strolled past him without looking, eyes only for the prize, "not til we've come to grips with our quarry."

"Uhh…"

I could see it plain as the pimples on his mug, Young Parwicke was itching to bolt then and there, payment be damned, but greed's a bitch and a bastard and a sticky thing all stitched inexplicably into one. A ponderous thing to bear, for sure, but even more so to set down.

Young Parwicke glared at the old chapel. "Ain't going in there."

I didn't blame him.

The old chapel rose crooked and gnarled, slathered en masse by an onslaught of ragged pine and bristling twig. Their tops were still green, but lower down was consumed by a riot of jabbing sticks devoid of any vibrance or joy or semblance of sanity. Where the trees began and chapel ended was difficult to say.

"Lovely." I eyeballed Young Parwicke. "Any folk squatting inside?"

He gave me a look that clearly stated, *Are you nuts?*

A bead of rain inched down my spine. *"He* still inside?"

"I…I think so." Young Parwicke offered a somber nod. "Saw him go in last night."

"Last night, huh?" An old oak door stood burst ajar, sopping with congealed rot. "So you really have no clue."

"Eh…?" The kid kicked a stone. "Nay, sir."

"Ever been inside?"

"Nay."

"Great." I turned to Sir Alaric. "By your leave?"

Sir Alaric blew snot out one nostril then waved me onward. He didn't seem one for pomp or ceremony.

I nodded to Karl. "Take a look round back."

Karl offered a sarcastic bow and trudged off.

"Sure it's our man?" I scoured the ground. Footprints, some going in, some out, scarred the muck.

"It's Rudiger," the kid answered.

"Alright. And what's he look like?"

"He's a … a big fella." Young Parwicke flared his arms out. "Not tall, mind, but stout. Wide. Dark brown hair. Sports sideburns that connect nigh on in a beard. Was," he screwed his eyes shut, "wearing a reddish-colored hat."

"He by himself?" I asked.

"No. Was with another fella and the Grey Lady."

"Grey Lady?" I said. "Like a noble lady?"

"Don't know," Young Parwicke said. "Was wearing finery. But all mucked up. Looked like it mighta been white or pink once."

"Fancy. What'd she look like?"

"Like hell." Young Parwicke picked at his lip. "Long hair all a-tangle. Light brown. Slender. Pale."

"No name?"

Young Parwicke shook his head. "Folk just call her the Grey-Lady. Wanders around town. Up here from time to time. Always talking to herself, laughing low. Giggling. Folks ken she's mad."

A vision subsumed me, of the corpse outside the Half-King, of the haggard lady leering as she glided down the alley, giggling. "And what do you ken?"

"I ken I give a wide berth when I hear her coming."

"Great." I took a deep breath, shook away the vision. "Tell me about this third fella."

"Kind of a funny-looking."

"How so?"

"A tall, hefty bloke. A big belly." Young Parwicke patted his stomach. "Like a lady with child. But with arms and legs like toothpicks. Balding and a grayed beard. Wore a brown homespun cloak."

"Know his name?"

"Nay." Young Parwicke blinked. "New fella come to camp. From the south side or so's someone said."

"Who said?" I asked.

Young Parwicke considered a moment then shrugged. "Don't know. Just someone."

"Right. Anything else?"

"Heard he was a brewer. Others say he's an old monk."

More drivel. "What's the word on Rudiger?"

"Used to be a miller, maybe, once upon a time. Folks ain't like being around him. Even talking about him. They ken him weird."

"Weird...?" The hair on my neck stood up.

Young Parwicke picked at his ear.

"Alright then, lad," Sir Alaric said. "Many thanks. You go hunker down yonder." He patted his coin purse. "We'll even up on our way out."

The kid didn't need to be told twice. He scurried off rat-quick, disappearing in the shadow of a blink.

"You playing games, old man?" I squared up on Sir Alaric, crossed my arms, gave him the hard glare.

"Eh?" Sir Alaric adjusted his cravat. "What?"

"Don't bullshit me," I said. "What'd our man do?"

"I told you already. Murder."

"Yeah…" Something was off. I could smell it. Taste it. "What is it about *this* murder? In particular?"

"Well," Sir Alaric scowled, "*murders* would be more apt. Few folks've gone missing, and Rudiger's the last one seen with more'n a couple of 'em. Folk ain't rushing to talk, though. Not in the open. Our Parwicke's a brave lad."

"Stupid," I corrected. "How many murders?"

"Enough."

"So he's good."

"Might not call it good, but, aye. Fella's proficient."

"And what about the *weird?*"

Karl appeared, trudging round the corner of the chapel, picking thistles from his beard. "Nothing out back but a trench-shitter by the curtain wall." He showed some teeth as he drew back the string on his crossbow and set a bolt within. "Couple old pictured windows. Narrow. Mostly busted out."

"Can he get out of them?"

"If he greases up."

"Well, let's hope he's no Dago." I gave Karl the lowdown then turned back on Sir Alaric. "And this Grey-Lady? What of her?"

"Warrant's for Rudiger." Sir Alaric shook his head. "Don't say nothing about cackling hags."

"And we're in it for the long haul, yeah?"

"Aye. Like the old days." Sir Alaric drew his sword. It was an old blade, nothing fancy, but serviceable, staid, not unlike him. "Blood and iron. Dead or alive. Him or us. You ready, lads?"

"No." But I stepped inside despite, Yolanda gleaming at the forefront. "But I'm freezing my balls off out here."

Inside, it was drips. Cold. Slow. Drips. Old pews sat hoary and cracked, all stacked in a pile in the corner. The saw-toothed edges of stained glass rimmed the empty windows like the jaws of some long-dead beast. Tree limb and root squirmed through the ceiling, the walls, the floor, upending slats and cracking mortar. A massive anvil stood immobile at the head of the room, as stout and immovable as Thor's *Mjolnir*.

"Used to be a cross set atop the anvil." Sir Alaric crossed himself.

"Old gods and the new," I said.

Karl hocked a wad.

I wiped Yolanda off with my cloak and laid her bare across my shoulder.

Karl stayed along the right, laying a gnarled hand atop the anvil as he passed.

I took the left.

"Stairs are over yonder." Sir Alaric lit a second lantern and handed it to me. "Round the far corner."

"You used to come here?" I asked.

"Aye, for Mass. Back when I had hair." Sir Alaric pointed with his pipe stem and stepped over a warped pew. "Stairs. Over there."

The stairs were in fair shape. Some dust. Nitre. A few cracks here and there.

"Footprints." Karl was already there, trudging through clutter.

"So, I guess stealth's out the window?" I deadpanned.

"You want to be next out?" Karl turned, his crossbow with him.

"We're on a *ground* floor." I glared down the stairs and into darkness. "Idiot."

Karl rumbled a laugh as he started down.

"Hold—" I laid a hand on Karl's shoulder. "You smell it?"

"Eh?" Sir Alaric frowned. "What?"

Karl didn't turn; he was focused on the down. "You fart?"

"Well, yeah, but there's something else, too. Something dead." If anyone was still down there, they knew we were here, so I carried on full-bore. *"Oy, Rudiger, you blackguard!"* I called into the void. "You come on up quiet, hands to the fore and empty as my heart, and it'll go smoother for you." For us, too, but murderers rarely give a damn beyond their own skins. I knew it true of myself. "Cross my heart. Hope to die…"

We waited.

No one answered.

"Fuck it," I said. "Onward. To glory."

"Yar," Karl trekked onward, me at his shoulder, brandishing the lantern in one hand, Yolanda ready for the devil himself in the other.

Karl held up a clenched fist. *Halt.* A wide door stood at the bottom of the stairs.

"Got it." I shouldered past. "Ready?"

"Yar."

"Don't shoot me in the head."

"I'll aim fer your arse."

"Good." A burst of bent bravado to heat the blood and I let loose, a sharp rasp of breath, a hand to the wall, then hurling forth bodily, throwing my weight into my heel and taking the door above the knob. There's just something viscerally satisfying about kicking in a door, something that clicks with the heart. The soul. Some innate tendency of man. Maybe it's just the base pleasure of wrecking something that works.

The door was old and crusty and splintered on impact, folding nigh in half but somehow not collapsing completely. The jamb-half clung persistently to hinge while the latch-side shattered inward.

The stench hit me first, a gale reek, a hammer fist to my senses. "Jesus." I breathed through my mouth. "Smell it now?"

Karl grunted assent.

I ducked the hanging wreckage and shouldered blade-first into darkness.

A glimpse of movement from the corner of my eye *"Wha—!"* and something struck me. Hard. A gush as the air left my lungs, and I was off my feet, weightless, rough arms crushing my midsection and driving me back, back, back smashing against a wall. Yolanda clattered somewhere as my head ricocheted off stone, stars cascading before my eyes.

But I kept my feet, spreading out, remaining upright more through buttressing against the wall than anything else. I twisted, over-hooking one arm. Hucked a blind uppercut. One, two, three, hammering flesh, face, bone. Growling and gnawing at my mail shirt, the bastard clamped down. His arms squeezed, my ribs squealing in failing protest as he folded me in half to the ground.

"Fuck!" I smashed him, kneed him, but had nothing behind it.

Karl roared in the cavern twilight. "Move!"

"Shoot—" I croaked.

The bastard paused a second, distracted maybe, loosening for sure, and shifted, trying to muscle me over. Use me for shield duty. Cowardice chicken-shitting at full bore, I squirmed, bucked and turned, jamming a thumb into his eye, growling obscenities while I finger-fucked hard, scraping nail against slick concave bone.

"Arrrgh!" The bastard recoiled, shadows dancing in the dim lantern light, a hand clutched to his ruined eye as Karl loosed the crossbow.

Thunk!

The bolt impacted, burying into flesh as I kicked out one of his legs.

Flailing, he slammed down within arm's reach, and I was clutched on and dagger stabbing gut-chest-gut fast as a maid churns butter. He grunted at first impact, realized what was happening on third and by fifth was somehow game again, smashing me back, snarling to his feet.

Room reeling, "Grab him!" I dove for his legs, wrapping my arms round his calf, rolling and sucking it up, slitting his Achilles and nearly stabbing myself in the face. I lost the dagger but grabbed his other leg. Wheezing, rasping, slavering, he spun, hopping, ripping free.

"He's loose!" I scrambled to my feet, ripping another dagger free.

Karl growled, sparks ripping a comet trail as his thane-axe glanced off the bastard's head and along the wall.

The bastard scrambled for the stairs, took them four at a time with me scrambling after, shouting, *"Coming your way, old man!"*

The bastard barrel-assed up, moving like a rabid beast, forearm-bashing Sir Alaric aside like a scarecrow on a blustery day. Sir Alaric groaned against the wall, clutching his chest, sliding down, curled crumpled across the floor.

The bastard was up and out the door before I could make the landing, "Sir Alaric!" I rasped, and he flicked his hand, waving me on, *"Go … go on."*

I burst out the chapel and hauled across the way, past the gaol, towards the tent city. The bastard tore through the front of a tent and slashed out the back to the sound of screams, disappearing in the haphazard labyrinth of the squatter camp. The sky had one eye cracked awake with dawn grey, and I followed the sound of footsteps splashing through mud.

"Karl—" Huffing, I stopped behind the tent he'd cut through. "See where he went?"

"What the hell?" A man poked his head out, a rusty carpenter's hammer clutched in his fist.

I ignored him, scouring the ground for prints. "Any idea?" The ground was lousy with them. "He can't get far."

Folk were emerging from tents, looking none too happy, and all too armed.

"This way." Karl trudged off. "The gates. Odin's eye…"

"Oy!" More folk roused, heads poking out like rats from a warren.

"Yeah." I trotted through the tents and lean-tos, looking for fresher prints. "He can't get far." My new mantra. Repeat it enough and it'd come true. I'd sunk steel into him. Six times. At least. "I gouged his eye and slit his bloody Achilles, for God's sake." And Karl'd skewered him then sheared nigh on half his face off.

He couldn't have gotten far. Couldn't have lasted long.

But he had. And he did. And he kept on doing.

Sir Alaric finally caught up to us, gimping along, clutching his chest, lurched over, concave as a question mark.

"Strong work, old man," I deadpanned.

"Apologies, lad. *Errrg…*" Sir Alaric wiped his nose with the back of his hand then hefted his sword in the burgeoning dawn. *"But then, this usually does the trick."* It was dripping crimson from point to hilt.

…over tankards of flat ale came tales of a monstrous folk who dwelt within a valley more remote than any dared travel. They ate the flesh of man, drank of his blood, worshipped a demon god.

There were stories galore, yet then, there were always stories…
—War-Journal of Prince Ulrich of Haeskenburg

Chapter 12.

DEAD END," I called back up.

We were back in the chapel's wine cellar. Or crypt. Or root cellar.

Or whatever the hell it was.

Sir Alaric didn't answer. I was fair sure he was slumped at the top of the stairs, nursing a broken sternum and wheezing like my dead grandma after huffing her Sunday pipe. And I was thinking hard on that pipe-weed, remembering its blue vanilla smoothness, the cool wrapping tendrils contorting in dragon shapes. Cause I was breathing through my mouth.

We'd tracked Rudiger through the Grey-Lark Forest. By prints and by blood. Then lost his trail once the blood stopped and he'd made town. Which was odd. Usually, a bloke's blood stops running, so does he. But the world's an inbred blackguard sometimes. Most times. And it's nigh on impossible to track a mark across cobble unless you're heeling him direct. Eyes on the prize. Or hearing at the very least. But it didn't matter, cause he was curled up in the attic of some derelict villa. Or wedged against a post on the far side of a fence, some mongrel worrying away at his cooling corpse. Wherever he was, he was dead.

He had to be.

"Footprints…" Karl ran a hand along the crypt's wall. "Some old. Some new."

"Some borrowed, some blue."

"Hrrmm?"

"A bloody fucking mess," I said. But no bodies. The footprints were a jumbled scrawl of days or weeks or even months' worth of trekking. Not to mention our recent festivities. "Over there." Something caught my eye. "That." Across the left wall was what looked like a slash of black. "Blood?"

It looked like blood, but *old* blood. Not fresh, at any rate. I sniffed at it, almost gagging from the stifling corpse-stench, but could just make out the sliver of copper tang beneath the brazen beast. "Smells like it."

Karl stalked over, scratched a fingernail through the stain, dabbed it to his tongue. "Yar. It's blood."

"Just what the hell's wrong with you?"

"You gonna swoon?" Karl stalked off.

Wasn't much to the chamber. Maybe twenty by forty. Well-built, except for the collapsed wall section at the far end. Karl stared at it, gripping his beard.

"Hey, old man," I called up. "Why'd they leave here?"

"Didn't want to be squatting in no dank cellar, I'd hazard."

"No. The keep. Set atop this hill? And with that wall? More defensible if shit ever goes sideways. Which is what it inevitably does. Buildings are overgrown as Wenelda's legs, but the bones beneath are strong. Hale. Hell, even down here, the stonework's solid."

"Yar," Karl cocked his head at the rubble, "except fer this."

"Still better than that claptrap Schloss," I countered.

"Hrrrm…" Karl prodded a crevice with the haft of his axe, "I'd wager it so."

"Well?" I asked back up.

"King says jump, lad…" Sir Alaric wheezed.

"Yeah." I stalked through the scrum of collapsed earth and stone that'd washed in like the tide. "This collapsed a while ago. Years maybe." Smooth stones formed the intact walls. I could barely feel the joints between. "When'd they abandon it?"

Sir Alaric let out a gust. "Near some thirty years, give or take."

I ran a hand along one of the collapsed stones. A big bastard. "Hmm…" I stopped, feeling a notch, and peered close. Four parallel lines marked the stone. "What's this look like?"

Karl trudged over.

"Could use a little more light, old man," I called up.

Sir Alaric still didn't answer, he just adjusted his lantern, tin scraping on stone, casting a dim glow down our way.

"Thanks." I pointed at the notched stone. "Here."

"Hrmm…" Karl squatted.

"A tool-mark? Mason's sigil?"

"Don't look it but, yar. Must be. Ain't Ogham." Karl hunkered along through the debris, pointing. "Got some more. Here and here. There, too. Looks to be they match up."

"From the quarry? Construction?"

Karl ran his hand along a set of marks. "Don't know."

"If they're not tool marks, then what?"

"Looks more like…" Karl shook his head. "Nar. Must be tools."

"Think someone brought it down on purpose?"

"Yar…" Karl grunted absently, feeling along the collapsed wall, ducking his head between massive blocks, checking each crevice. "But there's got to be…" He stopped next to a broad slash of black and ducked down. "Here. Hold." He laid his shoulder into a block and grunted as he slid it aside.

"Try not to bring down the rest til I'm gone." I trudged back up the stairs. Sir Alaric sat atop, head down, breathing. Rasping. "Gonna make it, old-timer?"

"Aye, lad," the old man thumped his chest, tepidly at best, "I'm right as rain."

"Well, rain falls and splatters everywhere, making a general nuisance of itself, so…"

"Arrr," Sir Alaric clutched his ribs, forcing himself slowly to his feet, "don't make me laugh."

I helped him up, dusted him off. "Want to tell me what the hell's going on?"

"By the hound, I wish I knew." Sir Alaric rubbed his sternum.

"Bullshit."

"Oy," Karl called up from below, "got something."

"We ain't done," I said and started back down.

Karl was still in the process of using his thane-axe to lever a block aside. I gave him a hand, dropping my shoulder into it. A monster nigh on three and a half feet tall and twice as wide, it inched, growling across the floor. "*Odin's teeth*, it reeks."

"It's… Your… *Rrrg*… Breath," I groaned.

But we manhandled it aside. Eventually. I collapsed against the wall, heart pounding in my ears, vision going fuzzy. I felt the side of my head. My fingers came away sticky. Red. Warm.

Karl hunkered on his knees, peered low, head in a crevice. "Here."

"Here, what?"

"There's a tunnel back there." Karl slapped a palm against the old stone. "Look." A crevice gaped between two fallen stones. Just a sliver of liquid night. "It's tight. But I'm thinking we can fit."

"How deep?"

"Gimme a moment to whip out my cock and measure."

"Not very then?" I asked innocently.

"Heh…" Karl shoved the haft of his thane-axed in with one hand. It kept going, swallowing up to his shoulder. "Goes beyond." He peered in. "Hrrmmm… Don't feel no air moving. But there's space back there."

"Maybe you should crawl in?"

"Maybe you should go fuck your face?"

"If only God had graced me—"

"Would you two stop clucking like inbred hens," Sir Alaric groaned from above. "Want me to crawl down there and do it myself?"

"Yeah. Absolutely." I stepped aside, hand out to guide the way. "You're skinnier than either of us."

"And nearer to dead, too," Karl grumbled.

"Well," the old man considered for a moment before coming to the conclusion we all knew was foregone, "fuck off, then, the two of you."

"A tunnel dug in?" I said. "Or out? Any ideas, old man?"

"Fresh out, lad." Sir Alaric groaned. "Only tunnel I know's from the old gaol down to the execution chamber. And it's still locked. Only King Eckhardt's got the key."

"Execution chamber?"

93.

"Aye. Part of a move toward civility. Out of sight, out of mind."

"That's no fun," I pouted.

"Hrmm," Karl pointed with his axe, "the something-dead's back there."

"No shit." I hissed up the stairs, "We calling it a day?"

Sir Alaric called back, "Sun's still waxing."

"Right." I sheathed Yolanda, drew a long dagger, offered Karl a stilted bow. "After you."

"Nar," Karl crossed his thick arms, "it's your turn."

I laid a hand to my chest. "Yet, t'was I who kicked in the door."

"Kicking in doors ain't crawling headfirst into graves."

I stood with arms akimbo. "Don't tell me you remember?"

"Siege at Jaarheim," Karl rumbled instantly.

"Shit." We'd been point-men on an anti-sapper crew, digging counter-tunnels against toothsome moles. It'd been close quarters for a long stretch. No light. No space. No air. No nothing but darkness, dirt, and iron. And those were the good parts. I knew he was right, knew it before I even asked, but I'm an optimistic shit sometimes but only to my detriment. "You're sure?"

"Yar."

"Fuck." Snatching the lantern from his open hand, I ducked past, bumping my shoulder into his chest and knocking him back a pace. Peering into the crevice, I slapped the dust off a chunk of overhang. "It gonna collapse when I'm halfway through?"

"With any luck."

"Right." The crevice was wide enough but only just so. Tight. Contortingly so. Crushingly so. But I made it work.

Rock scraping against my cheek, my neck, I slithered through, lantern to the fore, undulating onward, as exposed as a snail outside its shell. "*Come on…*" I head-butted a sharp stone, swore, forced on through. "You're right." The crevice widened after a few feet. "There's a tunnel."

Scrabbling free, I stretched out, took a deep breath. "*Jesus—*" Choking, I covered my nose and mouth and lifted the lantern, squinting through the mirk, and froze. "I found him," I gasped. "Ahem. Them. I found them."

It was a dank, earthy tunnel, roots slithering in through the ceiling, and it was littered with corpses. In the wavering lantern-light, the tunnel yawning off into darkness, they sat propped against the wall, splayed out across the floor, folded over in half in ways my eyes fought to conjure sense of. Some'd been here a stretch, bone showing, clothes not more than rotten chaff. Others were more … recent.

"*Odin's teeth—*" Karl scrambled like a badger from the crevice, spitting grit and shaking dust from his beard.

"Watch it, would you?"

Karl barreled onward. "How many'd the old man say?"

"He said '*enough.*'"

Karl cocked his head toward the dead. "And how many's that, you reckon?"

"More than enough."

* * * *

I leaned Yolanda against the wall as Karl, pulling hand over hand on the rope, yanked a corpse from the crevice. It was Brown Cloak, the last bloke seen alive with Rudiger and the freshest of the pack. "Wait—" He got hung up on something, just his cloaked head poking free.

Karl yanked harder.

"Jesus. Easy." I scuttled forth, ducking headfirst back into the crevice. "You're gonna tear his bloody leg off."

"Think he'll squawk?"

"Well, no, but—" I hovered precipitously above Brown Cloak's chest. "Here. Wait. *Wait!* God damn it. Foot's hung up under a rock." I reached in. "Just a moment—" I took a long gander into the darkness beyond. Rubbed my eyes. Blinked.

Had something moved beyond the gloom? Or was it a trick of the eye? Stare long enough at the abyss and your idiot mind'll start concocting phantoms from sheer boredom. Or terror. I sniffed, swallowed, rubbed my eyes and focused on the grim task at hand. "Just a moment. Foot's wedged in good and tight." I pushed the corpse back, tried worrying the foot from beneath the stone, gave up. "Shove him in a little."

Karl did as I bade and Brown Cloak's knee bent up.

"Yeah. Now hold him steady." I stomped on his knee, feeling bone in his kneecap not so much as give as turn aside in a manner not meant to. But his leg straightened and foot rasped free. "Alright. Pull."

Karl tore him free.

Alone in the tunnel, I glanced up, reaching for the lantern and thought something moved beyond the abattoir grounds, thought I heard something. A giggle. Maybe. Dry-mouthed, I swallowed, swore, grasped the lantern and scrambled out arse-first fast as I could, scraping my shoulders, bumping my head, nearly knocking myself senseless.

"Whoa—" Karl grabbed me. "You alright?"

"Yeah." I steadied myself against a block. "More or less."

"Yer bleeding again." He nodded at the side of my head.

"Yeah. That Rudiger packed a wallop."

"Yar. Maybe two."

I raised my hands. "I'm fine."

Karl frowned.

I clambered up, dusted off, took a gander at our hard-earned prize. Brown Cloak lay curled up in a pugilist's position, balled fists and knobby knees to his forehead, a sad, wizened thing that somehow gave the impression of a baby bird fallen from its nest. "Not much to him." I shook my head. "What? Maybe seventy, eighty pounds? Practically just a kid."

"Eh?" Sir Alaric hobbled down the stairs, using his old sword cane-wise, wincing with each step. "Young Parwicke said he was an older bloke. A taller bloke…"

"He seemed the freshest back there," I said. "Only one not showing bone. And he's got the brown cloak."

Sir Alaric frowned. "Fair commonest of colors, lad."

"Yeah. Sure. Must be one of the others." Gripping the corpse by the shoulders, I rolled him over, face-up, pulled back his hood and — *"Whoa"* — staggered back. Brown Cloak had a beard of stubble, grayed in parts, and he was balding. "Caesar's ghost…"

"Yar." Karl scratched fleas from his beard. "Ain't no kid. We draw him out, hazard he'd be taller than you."

"Not as handsome, though."

"Yar," Karl said, "got ya beat there, too."

Sir Alaric watched our proceedings with fists on hips and a grim schoolmarm glare in his eye. Tsk. Tsk. Tsk.

"It's how we do things." I shrugged in elegant explanation.

Karl snorted.

"Well now, that's two accounted for," Sir Alaric said. "You see Young Parwick's Grey-Lady amongst the dead?"

"No."

"Think mayhap you missed her?"

97.

"If she's further down the tunnel? Sure."

Sir Alaric frowned at the crevice.

"Hmmm, look. There's something wedged under him."
I grabbed Brown Cloak's shoulder. "Here. Roll him a bit." I
dug a hand under the small of his back. "A satchel." I tugged
it free then unlooped it from over his head.

"What's in it?" Grimacing, Sir Alaric eased himself down
to one knee by the corpse.

I looked inside, shook my head. "A bottle of wine and
two loaves of bread."

"Would you quit your fooling?" Sir Alaric spat.

"I ain't." I brandished the wine bottle. Sloshed it a bit.
Pulled the stopper. Took a whiff. "Smells alright." I wiped
the mouth of the bottle and took a swig. "Not bad,
considering."

"What?" Karl patted Brown Cloak down. "That it's
corpse wine?"

"I said *considering*." I handed Sir Alaric the bottle. "And
you were just licking blood off the wall."

"Be needing to give him a thorough go-over back on the
slab." Sir Alaric glared with one eye into the bottle then gave
it a sniff. "Which means we'll need to lug him back. The
others, too."

"We?"

"Aye." Frowning, Sir Alaric took a tentative swig.
"Might be we can identify some of 'em. Can't have families
wondering what became of their loved ones. Believe me, lad,
it's worse not knowing."

I couldn't argue with him there, but going back into that
bloody crevice...

"Now let's get to it." Using his knee for support, Sir
Alaric levered himself up, rickety legs shaking, clutching his
chest and groaning all the way, letting loose a torrent of

breath before finally looking expectantly at the two of us.

Karl and I scowled in unison.

A look of wide-eyed innocence blossomed on Sir Alaric's crusty mug. "What?"

"Holding your back *and* groaning?"

"Too much, eh?" Sir Alaric hefted the bottle and took another slug, "Don't you worry, lads, I'll bear my fair share."

...as we approached the farthest valley, this desolate land of monstrous denizens, we thought ourselves well-suited to the task.

We were not...

—*War-Journal of Prince Ulrich of Haeskenburg*

Chapter 13.

BEARING MY END of Brown Cloak's burden, I ducked through the doorway, my head brushing the ceiling, which only intensified the cell's caustic crush of impending doom. Deep breaths. Happy thoughts. A slug of whiskey.

Karl had no such problems. Being a stunted, misshapen troll had its occasional advantages.

The extrication of the corpses had gone about as well as such drudgeries go. We hadn't found another Brown Cloak down there. And we hadn't found the Grey-Lady, either, which was confounding, and figured her for a survivor or accomplice. Either way, Sir Alaric had sworn out a warrant.

We laid Brown Cloak unceremoniously across a stone slab a foot shorter than he was tall. Sir Alaric leaned back and ran a hand over his balding pate, muttering to himself, chewing his dead pipe, one hand gesticulating as he muttered low to a portrait hanging on the wall. It was of a man maybe my age, imperious of eye, with a slash of red hair atop his head and upper lip.

"Talk to me, old man."

"Eh, what?" Sir Alaric massaged his eyes with thumb and forefinger. "Apologies."

"You alright?" I raised an eyebrow toward the portrait.

He waved a hand. "I'm fine, lad, truly and I am." He patted the portrait frame. "My old man. Sometimes I run ideas by him, see what he has to say…" He snatched a large book stuffed with loose papers and opened it to a blank page. "You're eyes still sharp?" He dipped a quill pen into ink.

"As my wit."

"Oh?" Crestfallen, he stepped back, proffering a hand towards the corpse. "Well, even so, go on and tell me what you see."

"A shit-show?" I commented.

Karl chuckled, but Sir Alaric was busy lighting his pipe, so I got to it.

Above the slab and corpse, three lanterns dangled on lanyards, focusing their concerted light on a polished brass mirror. It worked fair grandly but it would've suited me fine to see less. "He's on the far side of middle-aged. Like Parwicke said." I cracked my neck and took a deep breath. "Seems far lighter than he should." I looked to Karl. "Unless I'm a modern-day Herakles?"

"You ain't." Karl leaned back against the wall, arms crossed, watching. Dissecting the dead wasn't his specialty. The living, now…?

I shrugged. "Face is all … Hmm … sunken in." Suffused by the light, the finer aspects of Brown Cloak's desiccated corpse lay bare. He was grey. Contorted. Gaunt. "Got some scratches to his forehead and right cheek." I parted his hair in a few spots. "Abrasions and lacerations along his scalp. Hmm. Right side again." I worked my way down. "Bits of stone in his beard. Crushed into his flesh. Right side again. Like he had his face cheese-grated across a wall. The floor. Something."

I grasped the bloke's skull, squeezed it gently, then firmly, feeling for the telltale sign of bone scraping on bone. But there was none. "Skull ain't broken." Whatever he'd endured hadn't been pleasant. Or quick. "Skin looks, hmmm…" I prodded Brown Cloak's cheek, working at it with my fingernail. "Feels like hard-tack. Or dried beef. Or—"

"You hungry?" Karl sneered.

"Starving." I pulled Brown Cloak's eyelids up. The orbs were sunken, shriveled, opaque, the way a fish's gets after it's been dead a stretch.

Sir Alaric's eyes glimmered, ropes of blue smoke wending out as he scribbled.

Wincing, I dug under Brown Cloak's ratty beard, ran my thumbs along the ridges of his throat, down to where it softened, then round to the back of his neck. "Neck's intact. Nothing but sloughing skin and disappointed lice." I chewed my lip. "Hazard we're gonna need to get more personal."

Sir Alaric patted along his belt. "Got a blade?"

One magically appeared in my hand. "Maybe."

"Mind stripping him?"

"Handsome devil like him?" I slit the bloke's jerkin from neck to sternum and peeled back the worn fabric, exposing splotchy skin and wizzled chest hair. His sternum and ribs stood stark on his pigeon chest. The heraldic device of the common man. "Fella lead a rough life. Or a rough death, anyway. Starved, looks like."

Sir Alaric fixed me with one eye. "You been there?"

I looked at Karl. We'd had our more-than-fair share. "Yeah. Sure. Who hasn't?"

I felt along his rib cage. Despite standing out clear as day and looking fair intact, I palpated them, anyway, sliding from sternum round back to spine, working a finger along each, the interstices between, starting at the collar bones, hoping to feel something maybe I couldn't see. "Siege at Jaarheim. Lasted near a year. Well-past scarfing back rats. Nigh on activities the church elders frown upon except during sacraments." I pressed down again on his left side. "They weren't bad roasted, truth be bare. The rats, I mean. Hmm…" Was that a creak? I pressed again. Yeah. Like stepping on a loose floorboard. "Got a broken rib here." I massaged deeper, feeling another creak round the back. "Ribs, plural, actually. Two, uh, no three."

"Where?" Sir Alaric set his pen aside and untied Brown Cloak's shoes.

"Here. Lower left ones. Floating one, too. Almost at the spine." I feigned a left hook to an imaginary body. "Fella took some lumps. Or one good one, at least. By some canny diplomat versed well in the politics of the fist."

"Huh?" Karl raised an eyebrow.

"A good-punching guy."

"Oh. Aye. Yar."

I fought off rolling my eyes. Barely.

"Think mayhap it was you yanking him from that crevice?" Sir Alaric pulled a shoe off.

"Fair sure we didn't break anything." I paused, reconsidered. "His left knee, maybe. Foot, too. Got hung up under a rock." I cut the rest of his shirt open down to navel.

Sir Alaric huffed as he pulled off the second shoe. A mismatched pair. Both worn through in more than one spot.

"Got his money's worth," I deadpanned.

"And then some," Karl said.

"Huh…" I pulled open the rest of Brown Cloak's shirt, cocked my head, trying to take it in, figure out what I was seeing.

"What?" Karl and Sir Alaric both looked up.

"His abdomen's," I gave it a tepid prod, "mushy."

"No bone there," Karl said.

"Yeah, no shit, Aristotle." I frowned. "I mean, it's his skin. It's fairly hanging off him." The way his flesh oozed out to either side of him, it looked fair like he'd melted. Or deflated. I grabbed a fistful of it, pulled it up, stretching. Could have grabbed two. Three. More. "*Jesus.*" I let go. "Feels like a flaccid foot-ball."

"Eh?" Sir Alaric took up his pen again. "What do you think?"

"What do I think…?" I think I wanted to get the hell out of this shrinking coffin. Away from this dead prick. Out of this ramshackle keep, this backwater burg, this cancerous land. But it wasn't going to happen. Not soon enough to suit me, anyways, so I took a deep breath. Settled. "I think we ain't done looking. Hang on." Brown Cloak's arm was torqued funny. I felt along the shoulder. "Arm's … rrrrg … yeah. Out of socket. Didn't notice it with the rigor." I nodded toward his left arm. "One of you tear his sleeve?" It was torn from the wrist up past his elbow.

"No. Get caught on something?" Karl shook his head. "The rocks?"

"Looks torn from the cuff up."

"What do you think, lad?"

"Don't know. Nothing, maybe." I examined the arm. "Here. He's got a puncture wound at the elbow. Hmm. A couple, actually." I felt along. "Skin's puckered. Withered. Like when you're too long in water. More light."

Karl adjusted the mirror.

"Good." Using my thumbs, I eased a puncture open. "Not much blood. None really. But it's wet. Slick. Cool."

"Eh?"

I rubbed my thumb and forefinger together, "It's … gooey."

"Not blood?"

"No, it's clear. Kinda like…" I held them up to the light. "Snot from a sick kid's nose."

"You've a keen edge with words."

"It's a gift." I wiped my hand on the dead guy's shirt.

"Eh?" Sir Alaric scribbled.

"Mmm… Holes. Yeah. Puncture marks." I stuck the tip of my blade in, gently, probing. "Deep. Scoring the bone."

"A blade?"

"Dago, if anything, but it doesn't seem right."

Sir Alaric swallowed. "Think he offed himself?"

"Eh? I'd hazard not." I shook my head. "Imagine trying to end it all by poking around the inside of your elbow."

"Contortionist?" Sir Alaric ventured.

"Why not just slit your wrist? And where's the blood? He should be covered in it. There's a fair-large vessel running through here." I traced a finger along the inside of his arm. "A gusher. And most who go the way of Socrates choose the quick knick."

"Way o' who?" Karl rumbled.

"Old dead guy who knocked back a concoction to allay his woes. But this wasn't that."

"Aye," Sir Alaric said. "So was there blood down there? The tunnel?"

"Yeah. But not enough where we found him. No fresh blood in the chapel, either."

"So he wasn't killed there." Sir Alaric lifted Brown Cloak's arm and squinted at the wounds. "He was killed somewhere else and lugged there."

"Except that the kid saw him walk in. Saw both of them, all three of them, walk in. Altogether."

"Shit. Right."

"Yeah, I know. Damn witnesses. They screw everything up."

"Known more than a few weren't worth their salt."

"Yeah. Me, too. Hell, most of them. But the kid lead us right there. And his descriptions were sound." I took a long breath. "So then, Rudiger, our killer, and the Grey-Lady, lead the poor bastard into the chapel. Down into the tunnel. Through that bloody crevice. I don't know how. Or why. Maybe they promised him something? Lured him with the bread? The wine? Whatever. So they lead him downstairs, set upon him, stripped him down—"

"Huh?" Sir Alaric cocked his head.

"No blood on his clothes." I held a hand out. "Stands to reason they stripped him down before they killed him."

"But again, where's the blood?"

"The tunnel." I let out a long breath. "Must've done the deed further down, I suppose."

"So after they stripped and killed him, then what?" Sir Alaric shrugged. "Dressed him back up again?"

"Shit." He had me there.

Starting at Brown Cloak's right cuff, I slit up his sleeve, exposing a wizened arm little more than bone. Should have belonged on some palsied geezer and not some fella just past his prime. But I saw nothing.

"Didn't," I screwed my eyes shut, "didn't the kid say something about a ... a big belly? Something like that?"

"Hmm..." Sir Alaric considered. "Aye, I suppose he did, now you mention it."

"Folk that are starving sometimes get big bellies. Strange, yeah? While the rest of you's wasting away, your belly keeps growing in defiance. Gravid with rage. Indignation. Hate. Whatever you got left keeping you to your feet." I threw up my hands. "I don't know. The arm seems more along the lines of some animal bite. A dog? Wolf?"

"Tunnel wolfs?" Karl laughed.

"It's *wolves*," I corrected.

"Blow me."

"Thanks, I'll pass," I said. "But if it were wolves, they were dainty wolves. Only nibbling his arm. Nary making a mess. Leaving behind all this … well, *some* meat."

"The Grey-Lady helped," Karl said. "They held ole Brown-Cloak down, let the wolf do the work."

I shook my head. "That's a pretty stupid theory."

Karl grunted in assent.

We stood in morbid silence listening to nothing but our inner fears, Sir Alaric chewing his pipe.

"Something's gnawing at your craw, old man. That's plain as day." I could see my breath mist with each syllable. "You tell us what it is, maybe we can do something more than sit here jerking off."

Sir Alaric splayed his hands out over the corpse, lamenting, "It's just this business with this fella and the," he swallowed, "the others."

"You knew him?" I scoffed. "*Them?*"

"Well, no, but—"

"Then don't bullshit me." I chopped a hand. "You've been around the block. There and back. Ain't no way some stranger's gonna go tugging your heartstrings." I shrugged. "And I've seen worse. You've seen worse. Hell. We've all seen worse." It was true. As strange as this was, it wasn't some massive bloodbath. It wasn't Sluys. Wasn't Crecy. It wasn't Asylum.

"Aye, lad, a sad truth." Sir Alaric ran a hand over his pate and muttered, "I told you to keep on moving."

"And I agreed. Heartily." My thoughts went to Avar and Chadwicke, refitting the *Ulysses*. "But what I want and what I deserve are ever at cross purposes."

"You and me both, lad," Sir Alaric shook his head, "you and me both…"

The nameless clan-holt sat deep within the bowels of the monstrous
Carpathians, a hard land, a joyless land, a dark land.
    Yet we would labor to bring it to light.
—*War-Journal of Prince Ulrich of Haeskenburg*

Chapter 14.

MY MIND WAS REELING as I trudged through the mud, toward the keep, skirting the tent city strewn like cobwebs across the corners of the yard. I didn't see Stephan, dwelling amongst his flock, but I could see lips pursed, heads turning, eyes watching, judging, as I made my way along.

It was a bite mark. It had to be. But from *what?* Jesus. A bloody animal? A beast?

I glanced up at the hoary old breaking-wheel, a charred skeleton standing like in homage to some fallen god.

Corpses... Tunnels... Teeth marks...

I couldn't help running with it through all the myths, all the fables, all the legends I'd ever heard. The ones everyone'd heard. Everywhere. I'd traveled, more than most, in the service of my old Uncle Charles — God rest his cantankerous soul — dispensing justice from the Ice-Lands to the north, the ancient lay of the dragon-men, beyond Outre-mer in the east, south to the land of Afrika and far west, beyond the pillars of Herakles to distant shores. So I'd heard it all. Or enough at least. Tales of the revenants of old Angland. The cold draugar of the north. Vyrkolakas of the Athenians. Skade-gamutk of the Skraelings. What have you.

At heart? Nigh on all the same. Corpse-men awakened from dead slumber by a terrible lust, scrabbling up from their tombs like worms through the earth, visiting terror in the dead of night. Long fingers soiled black with grave-earth. Stinking breath. Obscene hunger. Preying first on those they held dearest in life. Family. Friends. Lovers. Devouring the soul. The flesh. And, of course, drinking blood.

And it was bullshit.

All of it.

It was a rash of consumption. Of plague. It was sweating-sickness or the grips. A bad well or the horse-fever jumping ship-to-ship, person-to-person, clan-to-clan. Some indiscriminate killer preying on his own folk. A rabid wolf loose amongst sheep. But for some reason, it's easier for folk to believe some thrall of the Devil's been set loose. Easier to believe in black magic and necromancy rather than face the fact that God had just stopped giving a shit. Stopped watching over us. Stopped caring.

If he ever had.

A constant smash and crash of blunted weapons from beyond the breaking-wheel marred my ragged solace. Within a few steps, the training grounds slid into view, the cause of the disturbance plain.

Sir Gustav was thrashing someone. And thoroughly. One of the princes, by the look of his fine armor and slender build, both depreciating rapidly. I figured it for Prince Eventine, the non-crippled one, though by his stance and current state, it wasn't a given. He was down on one knee, weapon and shield wilting like willow branches.

To be fair, Sir Gustav had the advantage.

You stroll into a proving ground with blunted weapons against a hammer-head like him, and you'd best go down quick or beg for mercy. Or both. Blunted weapons won't even scratch a fella like that.

No, for a bloke like him, you'd have more of a chance with honed weapons and ill intent.

Find the chink. Dig it in. End it quick.

A few others stood on tiptoe on the stockade rails, peering over the top, watching on and wincing. The twins, Harwin and Sir Roderick, smirks plastered across their chinless toad faces. Rotund Sir Aravand pointing out one of the many faults in the Prince's strategy, if you could call it such, to his mean little prick of a squire, Morley.

Sir Gustav walloped the princeling in the flank, *"Uuullg!"* folding him in half and toppling him headfirst into the mud.

"Tiiiimber!" von Madbury called through two hands, sitting astride the stockade fence.

Sir Gustav let loose a booming laugh from within his great helm.

The others followed suit.

I kept on moving.

"Got to keep that guard up, Your Highness." Von Madbury hopped off the fence. He waved a hand, his attention elsewhere. "Or down, as it were." He adjusted the Mongul tulwar strapped to his hip, all the while eyeballing a peasant girl hustling across the way, an armload of laundry smothered in her white-knuckled grasp. "Oy, lass!" Von Madbury waved a gauntleted hand. "Come over here." He patted his thigh and sneered. "Got something to show you!"

As soon as the princeling had scrabbled up to one knee, Sir Gustav swatted him across the top of the helm, sending him sprawling lifeless into the muck. Sir Gustav stared down a moment like the big lummox he was then turned his vacant glare on me, the black slit of his helm emotionless.

"Oy, lass!" Von Madbury pointed. "You there!"

The girl froze, eyes wide, whiskers twitching, a rabbit mid-field catching a whiff of fox.

"Keep walking." I marched on past.

Clutching her laundry, lips pressed together, she hustled on.

"*OY!*" Von Madbury pushed himself upright, indignant. "You hear me?"

"My Prince?" Brother Miles, a war-priest with a fair bit of mileage by the look of him, knelt by the princeling's side and shook his shoulder. "Eventine? Please. Squeeze my hand if you can hear me."

"He dead?" I stopped by the fence, made a show of leaning over it, eyeballing the felled Prince. "Sure looks dead."

Sir Gustav shifted, his bucket head angling down as he toed the Prince a couple times to little effect. "Uh…"

"Eh?" Von Madbury stared after the fleeing girl. "What?"

"Him." I pointed down. "Your *liege-lord's* first-born son and rightful heir."

The good Prince Eventine still hadn't moved.

"Easy now, my Prince…" Brother Miles gingerly opened the face of the Prince's helm.

"Son of a—" Von Madbury clambered over the fence, shoved Brother Miles aside, and was on his knees in the mud a moment later. "What the hell'd you do?"

Sir Gustav shrugged. "T'was a glancing blow," he sniffed, and though his face lay hidden behind a tooled masque of steel, I felt as though somehow he were smirking.

"You fellas sure like beating the snot out of helpless folk." I laid a hand to my chest. "Now don't get me wrong, I get it. Hell of a lot easier than beating folk who can defend themselves."

Seven pairs of eyes turned my way automaton-smooth.

"But not smart, crowning the progeny of the hand that feeds you," I said. "Your bloody meal ticket. Son of the man

112.

you swore to protect. Man you'll swear to protect someday. *Should* he live that long."

"Man wants to be king, he needs to know how to fight," Sir Gustav countered.

"A fair point, but I prefer my kings to suffer as few head injuries as possible."

"Fuck off."

"Your highness…" Von Madbury pawed the Prince, rolling him over with Brother Miles's aid. *"Highness!"*

The Prince's arm flopped limp as cooked spinach.

"He breathing?" Harwin stroked his nonexistent chin.

I shielded my eyes against the sun. "That blood oozing out his ear?"

"My Prince—!" Von Madbury slapped him across the face. Hard.

Sir Gustav, on the other hand, only had eyes for me.

Von Madbury hunkered back as the Prince suddenly rolled. He gurgled something that might've been, *"I — I'm alright…"* then puked up a fair amount of something brown, countermanding his point something fierce.

Brother Miles crossed himself and murmured a prayer skyward.

"Ah. Good." I hocked a wad of spittle. "Some advice, fellas. I'd see fit only to wallop the crippled one. Not as much sport, maybe, but you can't break something already broke." I turned and started back on my way. The girl had disappeared into the relative safety of the tents, and von Madbury's face burned a glorious red, matching his eye-patch.

"Want a go-round with the steels?" von Madbury tapped a finger on the pommel of his tulwar.

Squire Morley snickered.

"Naw," I patted my belly, "just ate."

"Dinner's in an hour."

"Then I'm too hungry."

"Hey, Gustav," von Madbury stood, "this coward and his brother were calling for your head on a platter the other night. Ain't that so, my Prince?"

Prince Eventine muttered something lost to helm and dysphoria and the churn of broken turf.

"I did." Sir Gustav still had not broken his glare. "I did, indeed."

I had to give it to him, the man could glare.

"Why not step in?" von Madbury beckoned. "Sir Gustav'll go easy on you. Won't you?"

"Aye, Dietrick. Right ho. Easy…" Sir Gustav rumbled.

Those still clinging to the fence chattered like inbred apes.

The Prince was up now, lurching in circles through a fugue, Brother Miles giving chase.

"We need to know how skilled you are in case we need use you," von Madbury sneered.

"Use?" I turned. "Only thing I see you two using is your hands to stroke each other off."

The apes laughed at that, too.

I offered a flourish.

"What'd you say?" Sir Gustav marched straight for the stockade fence as though to smash right through it. "What'd he say?" He tore his helmet off and cast it aside, nearly braining the Prince anew. "Say it again to my face."

"Why? It getting you all worked up?" I thumbed at von Madbury. "Talk of hand-jobbing old one-eye?"

Von Madbury was at the fence, too now, seething. The Prince fell back to a knee, puking, the war-priest by his side, stroking his greying mustache in concern.

"You yellow?" Sir Gustav's voice boomed.

"As the sun," I answered, walking off.

Chapter 15.

"IT IS TOLD, Sir Luther, you saved the Black Prince's life at Crecy," King Eckhardt said over his trencher of split-pea soup. Steam rose swirling before him as he dabbed at his chin with a frayed napkin, his face pale, a near sickly green by shimmering lantern light. "They say you cut down five men reach to him. Five, then stood over him whilst the maelstrom swirled."

I felt the blood drain from my face. I didn't talk about Crecy. Crecy'd been bad. Watching the damned French stalking forward, the Oriflamme unfurled, knowing there'd be no quarter given. None taken. Crawling from corpse to corpse in the aftermath, shoving my dagger through visor slits on order of King Edward, making sure the bastards were truly dead, hoping they were, knowing some weren't. It's something killing a man in combat. But what we were doing... "Truth be bare, Your Majesty, I don't recollect much. I consider it a blessing."

"Yes, well... Mmm," the King pursed his lips, "I trust the accommodations for you and your compatriots are sufficient?"

"Yeah, Your Majesty, absolutely, and then some." I paused, my spoon halfway home. "Truly, we're all in your debt."

"Oh, I'm sure we can think of some means of recompense," drawled a voice from beyond the great hall doors, the Queen gliding smoothly through, her vermilion dress flowing behind. Von Madbury stalked along in her wake, his one eye glowering, that curved blade still at his side. "Eckhardt, darling." She paused before the King, offering a bow, smirking all the while beneath lowered lashes.

"Oh? My queen chooses to grace us all with her presence?" King Eckhardt set his napkin aside and stood, as did everyone else. "How … auspicious." He pulled her chair out. "I take it your chronic melancholy has abated, my dear?"

"Don't be such an arse, darling." The Queen's eyes glittered as she took in the table, pausing for a decidedly long and unsettling moment upon me. Not that I could blame her. The corner of her lip twitched in a wry smile before she broke her glance and sat, the King woodenly pushing her chair in behind. "I'm merely trying to be a gracious host by offering thanks to our new sworn sword … and guests."

"To be sure," the King took up his spoon and sipped, "it is good to have you once again gracing our banquet table."

"*Banquet…*" The Queen smiled pertly to herself as she unfolded her napkin and tidily spread it across her lap. "Hmm…"

"Times are lean, the winter harsh." King Eckhardt's look could have curdled glacier water. "My wife is ever the treasure to remind me." He punched back a huge gulp of wine. "Seemingly at every turn."

The Queen stifled another smirk, half-hidden behind a glass of wine, her glance dancing back across the table, settling on me. "My husband thinks to chide me," she whispered loudly behind a raised hand.

She seemed somehow familiar, though I couldn't quite place her.

"He thinks only to allay any further embarrassment." King Eckhardt gripped his flagon.

I hid behind my raised flagon, knocking it back like the coward I am. Though to be fair, I started a trend.

"And he has yet to meet with failure," the Queen sang.

"Enough." King Eckhardt stood.

"Ahem," Stephan cleared his throat and rose. I froze. Stephan had deigned to leave his flock of refugees to sup at the King's table with the specific intent of holding his royal feet to the fire over Sir Gustav's lack of punishment. We'd argued at length over it. I'd lost. So I figured we'd be strung up about halfway through the second course. "We appreciate the fare and hospitality, Your Majesty. It is most excellent."

"You'll tongue-lash him later, I trust?" I coughed under my breath.

Stephan cleared his throat and smiled. Garishly. And so there it was, my brother, attending specifically to be a righteous prick, and ending up trying to smooth the King's ruffled feathers. My brother. He could do right, but only the wrong way.

Father Gregorius stood, raising his flagon. "A toast! To King Eckhardt, and his endless generosity."

"Here! Here!" I smote the table, raised my flagon, and launched to my feet along with the others, glad for a distraction. Any distraction.

"Please. Please. Sit. I beg of you." King Eckhardt quelled, dimming to a simmer, waving us all down. "'*Excellent*' is a stretch and '*endless*' an outright sin, especially for a priest, but I suppose that's why I keep you around, Father." He took a drink, casting his wife a grim eye. "Though I suppose in this clime any fare might be deemed *excellent*, and a full belly is as close as any dare believe *endless*."

The King's great hall was anything but. To call it a coffin might've been more apropos. The long table consumed the lion's share of the room, with only a small walkway around the edges for the servants who must've trained by walking sideways on tightropes. "I only wish there were enough room at my table for all of your compatriots."

"One is ill, Your Majesty, and his wife and children wish not to leave his side," I said. "But they, too, wished me express their fervent gratitude."

"They are welcome. Most welcome." King Eckhardt bowed his head. "I've had fare sent to them."

"Many thanks," I said.

"I'm sure they could have sniffed out the kitchens," von Madbury dabbed his napkin to the corner of his mouth, "given ample chance."

King Eckhardt stiffened.

"What…?" von Madbury glanced up as innocently as a one-eyed chimera.

The Queen gripped his arm and whispered something in his ear.

"Your Majesty," Lady Mary cleared her throat, "your collection of paintings is unlike any I've ever seen." She was sporting a new hand carved by Stephan which was head and shoulders above and beyond Karl's gnarled monstrosity. From across the table and covered by a glove, it was difficult to discern from the real thing. "Why, the *Galahad and Grail* hanging in the foyer is simply stunning. And all the portraits. So lifelike. Might I inquire as to who the artist is?"

The Queen glanced up.

"Yes, well," King Eckhardt turned, "we have Sir Alaric to thank for all." King Eckhardt held out a hand. "A man of many talents. Warrior. Justiciar. Portraitist."

"Many thanks for the kind words, my lady." Sir Alaric shrugged uncomfortably, seeking solace in his cup. "You as well, Your Majesty."

The King waved a hand.

"And the many portraits capture a likeness…" Lady Mary droned on gushing at length about portraits and painting and realistic shadowing while I took in the hall.

A few others were gathered. The King's twin sons, Prince Eventine and Palatine, both seated to King Eckhardt's right. Prince Eventine, despite sporting a fresh black eye and swollen lip, seemed a hale young lad.

Prince Palatine, on the sinister hand, was Prince Eventine's warped reflection. He'd either been born a cripple or had it thrust upon him by some fell accident of youth. Thoughts of Sir Gustav hammering Prince Eventine into the mud sprang to mind. Prince Palatine's chair bore high armrests and a leather strap to hold him somewhat upright while he used his one functional arm to sup. A servant stood poised behind, eyes to the fore, hands clasped behind his back.

"Yes, indeed, my lady, t'was my father taught me." Sir Alaric leaned toward Lady Mary. "I find it soothes me. I've pioneered some techniques…"

Sir Dietrick von Madbury sat to the Queen's left, his one-eyed gaze continuously scanning the room, often meeting my own, but settling more often than not on Lady Mary.

"…and so Sir Alaric was able to restore the vibrancy of color through use of a combination of…" King Eckhardt explained, pointing up at one particularly gruesome painting depicting four knights standing about a monstrous, crowned demon crucified upon a breaking-wheel. Poised, they stood ready to pound a stake through its heart.

To von Madbury's left sat the neckless captain of the King's guard, Sir Gustav, who hardly paused to breathe between fistfuls of torn bread and slurps of drooling soup. He never cast a glance my way, his attention fixed solely on the meal before him. He seemed that type of chap, one thing at a time else lest his mind fissure.

Across from the two blackguards sat a pair of ladies in waiting, the Ladies Tourmaline and Ludmilla. Next to them sat the chinless twins, Harwin and Sir Roderick. The quartet epitomized the pervasive sense of the Haeskenburg nobility, the sense that the noble folks' high-born ancestors, on the whole, and with rare exception, had fucked one too many cousins.

Queen Haesken raised an eyebrow my way, laying a finger upon her lower lip, her eyes glimmering. I immediately found my flagon's contents extremely interesting.

"…most fascinating, Your Majesty." Lady Mary dabbed her lip. "A grim depiction, to be sure. What story does it relate?"

"The tale of King Gaston, my lady," King Eckhardt said. "One of my ancestors."

"I should be more than happy to relate it to you, my lady." Prince Eventine unconsciously smoothed down his hair as though to cover his bruised eye. "We could tour the Schloss? We have tapestries as well. Indeed, t'would be an honor. An honor most grand."

Lady Mary bowed. "I should be forever grateful, my Prince."

"An old family legend, my lady." King Eckhardt watched on intently, his gaze unreadable. "Fell times long past. Eh… Forgive me. Best take young Eventine up on his offer for I'd prefer not to spoil everyone's appetite."

"Too late, my darling, for the meal already has." The Queen cut into a hunk of meat. Some type of meat.

The room fell silent until von Madbury snickered like a shit, which he most certainly was.

"Aye, well…" King Eckhardt shifted as though sitting on a tack. "It pleases me to see someone take an interest in the history and culture of Haeskenburg."

"Oh, do go on, darling." Squinting in appraisal, the Queen settled her gaze upon Lady Mary. "She's striking, is she not? The hair, though? So short. A new style from Paris, perhaps?"

Lady Mary shook her head. "It was shorn against my will, Your Highness."

"A gripping tale for the telling, no doubt." The Queen leaned forward. "You could do with some care, surely, but a vessel well-crafted, indeed. As I'm sure all of the *noble*men at this table are wondering, are you married, my dear?"

"Nay, Your Highness," Lady Mary answered. "Widowed. And recently."

"To have no master gripping the far end of your leash?" The Queen laid a hand to her chest. "Telling you when to stop. When to go. What to do and how to do it? However must you manage? I read a book by a woman — do you believe it? A church-woman. Catherine of Sienna, and she claimed a mystical marriage to Jesus. We should all be so lucky." The Queen's fingers curled into a fist, gripping her napkin. "Forgive me, my dear."

"There is no need, Your Highness," Lady Mary said.

Von Madbury surreptitiously tipped her an imaginary cap.

Lady Mary nodded back, woodenly.

"Ahem…" King Eckhardt's glare was a flock of daggers cast the Queen's way and not a one seemed to hit its mark.

"Perhaps one of my sons might ... er ... gift us with a song?" King Eckhardt held out a hand. "Prince Eventine?"

"Eh?" Prince Eventine blinked out of a wistful fog. "Pardon father, what?"

"A song, son, if you would be so bold?"

"Father," Prince Eventine touched the side of his swollen lip, "I'm afraid my jaw has suffered much today and so should my attempt." Indeed, he spoke suddenly with a pronounced lisp. "And Palatine is the one truly gifted with song."

King Haesken pursed his lips. "Both of my sons are fine singers," he explained. "Palatine, if you would be so good?"

"Father, I—" Prince Palatine reddened, but in the end, nodded at his father's desperate gaze. "Certainly." He cleared his throat then began, his voice a clarion call, even and strong and at cardinal opposition to his ruined physique.

"Amidst the wild November snows,
I strolled amongst a murder of crows.
From skeletal boughs on high they watched,
And judged me false for wicked I thought.
Descending in droves they pecked out my eye,
For all of my words I uttered were lie.
I screamed like the maids whom abed I forced,
Then buried beneath the ground I—"

Von Madbury blasted up from his chair, knocking it over backward. For a protracted moment, he stood quivering, poised, dinner knife clutched in his fist, his cyclopean glare simmering Prince Palatine's way. "If you were but a man..."

I thought things were about to get interesting. Or *more* interesting. Then the Queen placed her hand upon his, easing the knife down. "Dietrick..." she said softly, and he released it before shouldering through a servant then stomping out.

"Dietrick, please—" The Queen set aside her napkin and rushed after.

Someone coughed midst the reigning silence.

"A catchy dirge for all its bleakness and veiled accusations of rape and murder," I said and, despite the fact he'd tried rhyming *thought* and *watched,* began clapping. Others added some half-hearted measure to the lauds. "Another, perchance?"

Lady Ludmilla beamed my way. She had a fair smile and seemed quite taken by me. Unfortunately, she seemed quite taken by a virulent case of pink-eye, as well.

Prince Palatine stifled a crook-necked yawn. "You'll have to forgive me, Father. I hate to be rude, but might I beg leave to retire?" He discreetly shouldered free from his support strap. "I fear I may have overexerted myself."

"Of course, my son." King Eckhardt forced a wan smile. "Go. Rest."

"Thank you, father." Palatine braced himself on the table with his good arm and levered himself to his feet. One was clubbed inward, and for a moment I feared he'd topple. So did the servant and his brother, but Prince Palatine cast them both a venomous glare, freezing them mid-step. "Thank you for the empty sentiment," he lurched along, "but I've managed this far alone."

...spoke in a harsh guttural pidgin halfway between the gruntings of swine and the wails of wild dogs. Low-browed hulking brutes, the men. Teeth jutting upward like tusks...
—*War-Journal of Prince Ulrich of Haeskenburg*

Chapter 16.

KING ECKHARDT stood waiting upon the battlements of the Schloss, crenels rising left and right, the wood craggy, worm-ridden, raw. Beyond, homes and cottages, their roofs manged bare to the rafter, huddled like ticks on the humped backs of a pair of skeletal hounds. Below, an immense bale-fire blared in the town's square, flickering, rippling, hurling shadow waves slashing across the night.

"Good evening, Sir Luther. Thank you for coming." King Eckhardt paused at my approach, his tattered mantle bowing out, onerous, in the misted wind. He held a hand out to a wine bottle and flagon set on the parapet. "Are you thirsty?"

I thumped my chest. "I'm steadfast in that regard."

Frowning, he sipped from his flagon, turning back to the lay of his paltry domain.

The night air was thick, weighing heavy on my chest, a labor just to draw breath. The King wanted to ask me something but didn't know how. *Prevarication*, a word that came to mind. Not a desirable trait in a king. "Thank you once again for your hospitality," I said just to break our communal fugue.

"It ... It is nothing." Sucking on his teeth, King Eckhardt shook his head slowly, to and fro. "I would pay a small fortune to know what you think of me after … after that debacle."

"Dinner, you mean?" I poured myself a measure of wine.

"Sadly, yes. What else?"

"Well, the fare was—"

"Nay." King Eckhardt chopped a hand furiously. "The fare was shit despite your brother's attempted pleasantries. And Father Gregorius's pronounced sycophancy. I speak of what transpired. How poor a shadow me and mine cast. By the book. Or perhaps it was solely me."

"It was refreshing." I shrugged. "Most couples are more concerned with looking like they have a happy marriage than actually having one. You two, though…?"

The King massaged his brow.

I shrugged. "My father once stabbed one of his vassals in the eye during dessert."

"It wasn't von Madbury, perchance?"

"Sadly, no." Upon the misted wind came screaming, far off, contorted, muted by distance, degree. "Could be arranged, though."

"Hmmph." His smirk was wry, grim, bare. "Don't tempt me."

"I was only half-joking." Or quarter. Maybe eighth. I grimaced. "Man like that's a cancer. To the bone. Even if he doesn't kill you, he'll cripple you. Everything around you."

"The long walk…" the King murmured.

"He got something on you?"

"What? Hmm… Nay." He rubbed his throat. "Still, I must apologize for my family. For my wife. For myself."

"Kings need never apologize." I stared off, half-listening to him, half to the screams.

"Aye, to be sure, but even so." His fingers wandered through his wispy beard, gripping it, nearly tearing it out. "I was not raised to be king, you see? I was to be a wandering hedge knight. Bereft of claim. Of duty. The yoke of responsibility. The freedom of the open road, adventure, the whole world lain bare before me. All for the taking."

"Cold nights. Empty belly. Lonely beds," I countered. "And it's usually *from* you that the taking goes. The world's a set of shackles, Your Majesty, with a fit for wrists of every shape and size."

"And is there a key?"

"Yeah, sure. Wine, women and—"

"Song?"

"No." I squinted him up and down. "Was gonna say a pine box about six foot by two."

"Aye. Truth." The King took a sip, gesticulating with a splayed hand. "You toil your whole life trying to hold something together that begs so desperately to be torn apart."

"At least you give a damn," I offered. "I've known a few who didn't." More than a few, but I was in a politic mood.

The screams came again from below.

"I was the fourth-born son." King Eckhardt took a drink. "My brothers died young. And so responsibility was thrust upon me. My shoulders. It required some time to '*take*' as they say, and I don't know for certain that it ever truly has. I waver between times where I am either far too lenient," he shook his head, "or abominably cruel."

"Where lies your current mind?"

He scowled sidelong.

I shrugged. "Just getting the lay of the land."

The screams drowned away, deposed by another sound that started at a sharp staccato dissonance, slowly morphing into something regular. Rhythmic. Recognizable. Leaning out over the wall, I scanned the wretched town.

Someone was pounding nails. A lot of someones. A lot of nails.

"Alas, Sir Luther, I fear it's too soon to tell."

"A devil's balancing act." Down in the town square, surrounding the bale-fire, stood some half-dozen crucifixes. "Not that I'd know. I have elder brothers as well, though none of us were to be kings. And all still draw breath, as far as I know." Unfortunately.

"You hail from Asylum, I'm told." His breath steamed in the cold.

"No. Just my last stop."

"And what was it you were doing in Asylum?"

"Same thing I do everywhere." I side-armed an old roofing tile into oblivion. "Trying to not get killed."

"Was it that bad?"

"No," I said, "it was worse."

The moon had risen and a chill taken the air. Frost would cover the ground come morn.

"King… T'is but merely a word." King Eckhardt crushed the remnants of tears from his eyes. "Y-Your father is a knight? A lord?"

"Yeah."

"A man of power." King Eckhardt sniffed. "And how much land does he possess?"

"A breadth of land some ten leagues by twenty, give or take."

"Hmm. Look at my land, Sir Luther." He held a splayed hand out to the great beyond. "The whole of my domain encompasses as far as you can see on a clear day. Perhaps a quarter of your father's lands. And mine are not bountiful. Mostly wood and swamp. Few arable fields. Trees are our only solace. My people and I? We live upon the trade up and down the river. And with the plague…"

"Trade's dead."

"Yes. The Schloss has stores, but they run thin." King Eckhardt gazed out toward the campfires burning within the Grey-Lark Forest to the north. "How my people survive I know not. Sir Alaric and you toured the camps in the old keep today."

"*Toured?*" I said. "We were stalking a murderer."

"Even so," the King waved a hand, "what did you see?"

"They're surviving on dregs, Your Majesty." I held up a hand. "Wait. Did I say survive? I meant subsist. They're starving. Sick. Squatting in a derelict keep. A hardy folk, but they're being ground to dust. Day by day. Inch by inch. Piece by bloody piece."

"Sir Alaric says you performed admirably." King Eckhardt pursed his lips.

"Technically, the blackguard got away."

"Yet, I'm told he suffered grievous wounds. Killing wounds."

I nodded with certainty. "He's somewhere wearing dirt."

"Because of you."

"Yeah. I suppose." Karl and Sir Alaric had done their fair share, more than, but screw them.

Below, scourgers filed into the town square, one after another, gathering about the bale-fire, hurling in lengths of wood within until the tops of the dancing flames outstripped the roofs of surrounding buildings.

"Just when we are laid so low." King Eckhardt bowed his head. "Those fiends. It started with my Jews. Those brave enough to remain faced a pogrom. And when they were gone, the fiends began stalking the streets at night, burning good Christian homes, shops, everything. They held trials in the very streets."

"I heard."

"Meting out justice. My justice. Usurping my divine right—" King Eckhardt hurled his flagon into the night then wiped his chin with the back of his hand. "There are worse things, to be sure." He ground his teeth. "You understand what I want?"

"No. Not even a little."

"I want these devils gone. Punished. I want order restored. I want…"

"Blood-simple slaughter?"

"It pains me that this has come to pass, you see? That these abominations have infested my lands. My people. I feel as though…" King Eckhardt paused a moment, considering, a rarity for a king, even a hedge one. "Ceding control to such madmen. Aye, and yet still here I stand. A King. Impotent as a gelded horse."

"What happened to your fighting men?" I asked. "Greener pastures?"

"If such exist in these fell times."

"And why me? You don't even know me."

"Yet I remember you. And Sir Alaric vouches for you." King Eckhardt took a breath. "He is a loyal fellow, you see? But aged and slow, his soul shackled nowadays to drink and melancholy. And those that remain…?" He rubbed his throat. "Gustav represents the flower of the Haesken court."

"Sometimes all a job calls for is a heavy hammer."

"Tell me that after you've spoken with him at any length."

"I'll pass."

"Aye. A wise choice. And von Madbury? The man's a blackguard. At best. He and my—" His hand shivered into a fist. "Did you catch the passion play at dinner?"

"Palatine's song seemed to vex him."

"Aye," King Eckhardt said. "Rumor, you see? It trails that man like a fume."

"Yet you keep him around?"

"He has … ingratiated himself to the Queen. Her *queensguard,* she calls him." He stared down at his hands. "It … It matters not."

"Your son's brave." I wisely changed tacks. "You're proud of him."

"I'm proud of *both* of my sons," King Eckhardt said curtly, "though Palatine did indeed make me proud this night. It's your children's strengths that make you proud. And their weaknesses that cause your heart to ache fit to crumble." He shook his head. "Forgive my candor, I sound like a woman."

"Yeah, I was thinking the same thing."

King Eckhardt cocked his head, lips twisting in a sour smile.

Below, the chanting rose, punctuated by screams.

"I want them gone." King Eckhardt's grimaced. "I want Haeskenburg mine once more."

"How many are there?"

"Fifty or so when they came. But … with the madness? The despair? It's nearer one hundred now."

"A hundred…" I whistled low. "That ain't nothing."

"No. Indeed. It is not."

I did the math. It didn't take long. "It'll get ugly."

"You said blood-simple slaughter…" King Eckhardt ran a hand through his thin hair. "I would wish it not so. I would wish you spare my small-folk. They are good folk. Staunch folk. Merely led astray in time of strife by a wayward charlatan bearing hollow promises. This man," King

Eckhardt licked his lips, "this Nazarene, I would have you…"

"Cut the head off the snake?"

King Eckhardt rubbed his hands. "In my youth, I fought alongside the Teutonics and Sword Brethren. Outside the town of Wolmar. And Ragit. My father sent me north for 'seasoning,' as he called it. An old familial tradition. It was the butchery of old men, women, children, and little more."

"What war's all about."

"Ragit was bad. Very bad. Like your Crecy, perhaps." King Eckhardt stood ramrod straight for a time. "I cannot claim any vast expertise in the art of warfare, but I understand such matters can rarely be so simple as merely 'cutting off the head of the snake,' as you say. Yet, if it ever were possible, I should wish it so."

"And he's the one killing your folk? You're certain?"

"Look, Sir Luther." King Eckhardt stepped aside, pointing toward the square. "Yet not to the flames. Let the light wash from your eyes. Do you not see? The crosses lining the square? A dozen now, perhaps."

And there was one poor bastard crucified to each.

"Have you proof against such poison, Sir Luther?"

The scourgers erected another burdened crucifix.

"Proof, your Majesty? No," I said, "but I have an idea."

...their wanton females. They alone were in some instances pleasing to the eye, with their long arms and fecund forms, their fierce gazes alluding to some other, baser quality beneath. Thoughts of my nubile, young bride so far away fettered my mind with an unnerving and pervasive constancy.

Once again, I was forced to find succor where succor there was to...
—*War-Journal of Prince Ulrich of Haeskenburg*

Chapter 17.

THE AFTERIMAGE mirage of loaded crosses supplanted the darkness before my eyes, the beat of hammer on nail pounding through my heart as I opened my bed-chamber door. It was little more than a broom closet at the end of the hall. No window. Room enough for a bed and dented piss pot. Barely. *Cell* would've been more appropriate. Still, my gob was salivating in anticipation of the promise of impending sleep despite my designs for the morrow.

The door struck the bedpost, and I slid around it.

"You don't remember me, do you?" a voice whispered from the deeper dark.

"*Jesus*—" A fistful of dagger sprouted in my fist and at the speaker's throat. Poised there, pressing cold steel against warm flesh, I froze. The scent of perfume and wine struck me as I yanked a woman into the tepid glow of light trickling from an old tin lantern dangling in the hall. "Lady Mary, what the—?"

But it wasn't Lady Mary.

"Jesus Christ..."

It was the Queen.

"I, err, ahem..." I glanced out into the hall. A ghost

town. Thank Christ. I could see weeds tumbling in the yawning wind. A gallows rope twitching in the breeze. I swallowed, sheathed my dagger. Mentally composed my will and last testament. "Apologies, Your Highness. For … ah … nearly knifing you."

"Apology accepted." Her eyes glowed.

"Your Highness, if we—" I glanced at the open door.

"Close it," she said. "I won't bite."

"Ain't *your* teeth that worry me, Your Highness."

"Your Highness? Oh, no. Please. That's my husband." The Queen wrinkled her nose. "And fear not, he's toothless as an old hound."

"Toothless hounds can still howl. And you watch the ones come running. They'll have teeth and then some."

"Very well." She leaned in, reaching past, and pushed the door closed. The wine on her breath was strong. "We'd best keep quiet, no?" She pressed a finger to her lips.

I winced, swore beneath my breath, swallowed, trying to fill the empty void yawning wide in the pit of my gut. "How … ah … can I be of service?"

The Queen laid a bejeweled hand upon a bedpost. "Is Lady Mary your lover?"

I froze. "Huh—?"

"You thought I was she when first you opened the door, yes?"

"Oh. Yeah. That." I winced. "No. Not even close. I just assumed…"

"Does she harbor carnal feelings toward you?"

"I…? *No.*"

"And you're certain?"

"She's commented on multiple occasions that I disgust her." I stiffened as voices echoed down the hall. "Physically. Emotionally. Spiritually, whatever the hell that means…"

"Even so, I hesitate to wonder if you hold such feelings towards her." The Queen cleared her throat. "Excuse me. It's only she's so beautiful and that she need not try to be so. Whilst we others flounder and fight and prim and preen all to garner a lesser result. Perhaps it is merely age. Hers. Mine. The disparity between?"

"You do alright," I almost bit back but didn't because I'm stupid and make bad choices, particularly with regards to the realm of women. "Now, my Queen, how is it I can serve you?"

"Very well." The Queen brushed a stray lock of hair from her eyes. "I'm merely trying to ascertain whether Lady Mary might be a suitable match for Young Eventine. A mother's duty. He seems enamored. And finding a match who shares no branches of one's family tree can be quite a challenge here. What is her character?"

"She's suitable, and then some," I said. "Tough as nails. Smart. Honest. She did say she'd join the first convent we came across, though."

"Hyperbole?"

"I don't know what that means." I reached for the doorknob.

"I thank you, Sir Luther. I … I must confess my visit concerned not only Lady Mary." She smiled shyly. "I also wished to reacquaint myself with you."

"Your Highness," I let out a deep breath, "I'm afraid—"

"Sir Luther, please, relax." The Queen laid a warm hand to my rough cheek and leaned in close, her eyes gleaming, and something struck a chord. "Breathe."

A memory, decades-old, of a girl nigh on unrecognizable except for those eyes. Those clear blue eyes. Where they'd been ablaze with scorn at dinner, leveled at her husband, they now shown with a soft somber glow.

"Blue as an autumn sky," I smiled.

She was Elona, Sir Alaric's eldest daughter. I studied her face, her azure eyes, seeing past the years, a young girl of fifteen who'd always been around, always watching, always waiting, always praying. I remembered her perched on a warped bench in Sir Alaric's painting chamber, hands on her lap, head down, clutching a kerchief, tears rolling as she wept, surrounded by a stoic, silent, two-dimensional audience. "I remember now."

"That brings me no small measure of joy." The Queen clasped her hands on her lap. "How long has it been? Lord above, I hesitate to count."

"You were little more than a girl."

"And you were naught more than a boy."

"A newly minted squire." I thumped my chest. "Ready to take on the world."

"You were kind to me."

"Yeah...?" I chuffed a laugh. "You met me before my downward spiral, Your High—"

"Elona." She grimaced, digging her nails *scritching* into the bedpost. "Call me by my name. *Please.*"

"Elona." I bowed. "Apologies. It's been a long day. A long decade. I'm sorry, I don't—"

The Queen cleared her throat. "You're working as a sell-sword?"

"A *lowly* sell-sword. For your father. And your *husband.*"

"And how is my *dear* father?"

"You saw him tonight."

"We ... forgive me." Queen Elona looked away, "We've not spoken for some time. He finds my lack of—" she worried the fabric of her dress, "it is a private matter, festering, from a long while past."

A pregnant pause to the sound of me sweating buckets.

Then it hit me, all the pieces, all the parts, all came flooding back. Jesus. Lady Catherine, Sir Alaric's wife. Elona's mother. Her disappearance was the reason we'd trekked here so long ago. Twenty years? Twenty-five? Sir Alaric had begged, cajoled, practically bribed my Uncle Charles to come, to hunt down her supposed murderer. And so we had. *Come,* anyways. Nigh on three seasons in the hunt we killed, but nothing else. "I'm sorry we never found anything," I said. "Did you ever learn aught of her? Did your father…?"

"Nay, and there lies the crux." She leaned forward, hands clasped, fingers interwoven, and for a moment, that sad little girl had returned. "My mother had been a great beauty. With wit and charm and a grace … unsurpassed. Did you know? She was to have married the King of Bohemia had she not fallen in love with my father."

"Well," I admitted, "he is dreamy."

"Imagine," her eyes shined, "she turned down a chance to be queen of a significant kingdom. A kingdom of weight. Of consequence. Substance. A kingdom that could change the world. So unlike here. So unlike…" She shook her head. "And she? She was everything that I am not. When she—"

"Your Highness. Lady. Elona. Don't."

She looked up. "Don't what?"

"Don't relive it."

"Relive what? Her death? I don't even know that she died. She was sick for a long while which was difficult enough. And then she simply…" her voice cracked, "she simply disappeared. Vanished. The very line of demarcation in my existence. There was *before* that day, and there was every day after. My every waking moment a nightmare consumed by it. I relive it constantly. The hurt. The loss. The … everything. Have you ever lost anyone close, Sir Luther?

Anyone dear?"

"One or two," I said.

"You garnered some form of closure then, despite the pain."

"Yeah, I suppose, sure."

"But us?" Her chin quivered. "Me? Never knowing? Questions ever baying at the back of my mind. Was she murdered? Was she another who disappeared? Or perhaps she thought to mitigate our anguish at her slow demise. I pray every day still. Pray that perhaps she came to her senses. That she retrieved her health. That she … that she simply abandoned us." She glanced up, grim, sad, beautiful, as tears cut a swath down her face. "Perhaps she's the Queen of Bohemia even now? Attending balls with lords and kings…"

"I've met the King of Bohemia, and he has no balls," I said.

She smiled at that. Almost.

"And she loved your father," I said. "Stayed with him. For him. That ain't nothing. And that kind of love can maybe make even a shit-hole like Haeskenburg seem like Elysium."

"Elysium…? Have you stood downwind of him as of late?" The Queen shook her head. "They ignored me, did you know?" Her eyes glazed over again, threatening to spill free. "Set me aside. Told me to do my duty. Comfort my father, drowning in his grief. His cups. How? How does a child bear that burden? That responsibility. And my sister, Jane?"

"I remember her, too." Elona had always been in the company of her younger sister, invariably holding her hand, whispering words of encouragement, wiping tears, fighting through her own sorrow to make the young girl smile, even if for the briefest of moments. "And I remember you doing what you could."

"What I could? Yes. And still, it fell woefully shy." The Queen shook her head slowly. "Jane took after my mother. A true beauty. She would have married into some great house. Could have…" She sniffed. "She'd not have been stuck here."

I swallowed. Said nothing.

"Jane's soul died the day my mother disappeared," the Queen said. "An empty, hollow thing from that day forth. I tried to fill her with … something. Something of worth. Of value. Of purpose. To be her strong, older, wiser sister, but…" I could feel her breath on my face. "It was only later when she took her own life that the ledger was finally balanced. My family lost, gone, washed away." She swallowed. "I was suffering the same loss as they but could find no succor. Anywhere. My father, a broken man, yes, but at least, grown. But me? Still but a child? Who did I have? What did I have?" She wiped her cheek. "How can they expect you to be a whole person when so much of you is lost?

"And then you came. And at my wedding reception, you made me laugh. Japing. Joking with the hounds. I think it the only time…" The Queen reached forth and squeezed my hand. "The only time I laughed. I thank you for that. Thank you for taking the time to make a useless, insipid girl laugh on a cold autumn night so many decades ago."

"What's *insipid* mean?" I asked.

She smiled finally, at that one. "Thank you for showing me that there is still some good in this world, something beyond duty and sorrow. And if you would forgive my behavior at dinner. I had been drinking to excess—"

"Is there another way?"

"As of late?" She shook her head. "No. And I've found that the ill will I harbor toward my husband is a vessel which often overflows. I'd not—"

Outside my door, the sound of feet padded by along with furtive whispers.

"Shhh—" I touched a finger to her lips. They were warm. Soft.

Servants, most likely, but a servant's word could spark flame quick as tinder. And if that flame spread…

I swallowed after they passed, retracting my hand. She wasn't breathing. Neither was I. Her eyes shone by the light through cracks in the door. They were blue, they were broken, they were beautiful.

"It brings me pleasure to know I offered you some small measure of comfort in your hour of darkness." I peeled her fingers, one by one, gently, from mine. Her hands trembling. Or was it mine? "But you must go, Elona. If you were found here—"

She kissed me then, on tiptoe, gripping my shirt, drawing in tight, and purveyor of sane choices that I am, I didn't stop her.

Chapter 18.

A SLIVER OF GREY SUN peeked over the horizon, casting shards of light across Father Demtry's corpse, dangling, twirling ever so gently from a frayed rope looped over a long horizontal branch grown seemingly for the specific purpose of hanging poor, bloody bastards. And Father Demtry was the poorest. The bloodiest. His head crooked horribly, plastered to one side, neck obviously broken and then some, tongue lolling out, desiccated and cracked like some fat black slug, stifled halfway through its crawl to freedom.

"Good hanging tree." Karl spat aside in keen appreciation.

"Yeah." I took a step back, shielding my eyes, looking up, taking it all in. "Like the Good Lord himself crafted it just so." The tor overlooked the bay and the town. "Daresay a lovely spot, even."

"Perhaps you two can build a cottage here and retire?" Stephan squinted up.

Karl split a grin, "You do make me proud now and again, lad."

"Something bothering you, brother?" I asked. "Like maybe sleeping outside on the cold hard ground?"

With a look like he'd swallowed a gallon of bile, Stephan muttered something and crossed himself.

"Jesus..." I'd thought it the priest's vestments dangling

til I realized it was his skin. From the waist up, it'd been flayed off, flensed down in ragged strips, his front, his back, his everything. "Sure gave it to him good."

"Crows've got at him," Karl grunted.

"Can always count on crows." I spread a horse blanket on the ground beneath the dangling horror.

Stephan covered his mouth with a handkerchief. "Let's get him down."

Karl was already on it. With his thane-axe, he chopped the rope, and the carcass crashed down in a muddled heap.

Stephan shook his head.

Karl shrugged, "Dunna think he'll mind."

I glanced over at Sir Alaric, seated in the front of the wagon. "You *could* help."

"*Could's* a loaded word, and for sure," Sir Alaric chewed his pipe, "but being an old geezer's got to be good somewhere. I'm picking here."

"Awesome." Karl and I each took corners of the horse blanket and hefted Father Demtry, "One… Two… *Three—*" and hurled him into the bed of the wagon.

"Are you two serious?" Stephan hissed.

I looked at Karl and he at me. "Occasionally."

Sir Alaric slid aside and Stephan, hunched and muttering, snatched the reins. Karl and I lounged in the back with the clearly departed. I craned my neck, avoiding Sir Alaric's keen gaze, fearing he'd somehow sense what happened the night before between me and his daughter. I ran a finger along the collar of my coat-of-plate shirt, digging into my neck. "See anyone yet?"

"Been watching us since we left the Schloss." Sir Alaric pointed with the stem of his pipe. "And whilst you were pruning the Good Lord's own rotten fruit, a hand-full of 'em slithered out the town's walls."

"Fat Jesus one of them?"

"Wha—" Sir Alaric coughed.

"The Nazarene," I clarified.

"Eh? Oh." Sir Alaric scratched his nose. "Nay. Saw a tall fella, though, rail-thin."

We started down the hill. First thing this morning, King Eckhardt had announced by crier at the camps and decrees nailed to town gates that Father Demtry's corpse was to be cut down and buried properly. This morning. On hallowed ground as befitted his priestly station. Between the lines, what the decree stated was King Eckhardt was growing some sack and reasserting his kingly authority.

We figured on a response.

And we figured on responding to that response.

"Aye, yar, I see 'em." Karl adjusted his thane-axe. "And they us."

"Where?"

"Beyond that great willow."

I squinted, trying to suss shadow from shape, "Yeah. Alright."

Sir Alaric took a long pull on that pipe, gathered up his crossbow, stuck a foot in the stirrup, bent his back and groaned, muscling the string back.

"Need a hand, old man?" I asked.

"I'll manage." Sir Alaric winced, locking the string back in place.

The wagon trundled down the hill, creaking and moaning and shuddering almost as much as Sir Alaric.

"We shouldn't have come." Stephan shook his head.

"No. *You* shouldn't have come," I growled. "Jesus. Always aiming to save the damned world."

"As opposed to what you're set to do?"

"And what's that?"

"Take the easy route."

"Yeah, well, I'm like water in that regard."

"First, he reneges on punishing Sir Gustav, now this." Teeth bared, Stephan snapped the reigns.

"Sir Gustav's down there waiting to spring the trap," Sir Alaric said. "Wouldn't do to punish one of your best fighting men, lad. Not in this clime. Not afore a fight."

"He promised." Stephan glared at me. "And you promised you'd talk to him."

"Ain't the time for squabbling," I said. "And holding his feet to the fire didn't seem prudent."

"Granted. But they say this Nazarene can heal the sick." Stephan chopped with an emphatic hand. "They say he can *raise* the dead. Miracles, Lou. Just imagine. If he's able to perform them, we can't kill him. We can't." He looked to Karl and Sir Alaric for agreement. Sympathy. Humanity. He found none. "Am I the only one who sees that?"

"You're in the wrong wagon, brother," I said. Cause he was. Sir Alaric was under orders to end this religious prick. As was I. Head of the snake, and all. And Karl was Karl. Killing was the only thing he was good for.

"But if the light of the Lord shines within him—"

"We're to arrest him, lad." Sir Alaric patted the warrant in his coat pocket.

"And when he doesn't cede to your demand?"

Sir Alaric said nothing; he just smoked his pipe and cradled his crossbow, humming softly.

"We'll see if he can raise himself?" I offered.

"The Lord's gifts would not be bestowed upon a man of evil intent."

I pointedly ignored him. "How many down there, old man?"

"Five."

Karl methodically sharpened the edge of his thane-axe. *Shunk… Shunk… Shunk…* It was a noise that over the years had come to bolster me through troubled times. And these were those.

"They'll be on us soon as we hit the gate." Stephan worked the reins, cooing to soothe the skittish horse. "Easy, girl. Easy."

"That's the plan."

Saint Wenceslaus' Church sat at the foot of Gallow's Tor, a stone-throw outside the confines of Husk's wall, looming through the trees. It was a small church, little more than a shrine set amidst a graveyard. We got there in short shrift.

"Here they come," Karl said.

As we rounded a bend, five scourgers barred our passage. They looked beat and frayed and worn to hell, all effigies of our crucified Lord in differing stages of molt and malnourishment, but a lunatic shine glowed with an unnerving verve in their collective eye.

A tall, thin blackguard lurched haphazard to the fore. "Halt, you heathen dogs!" It was Skeleton, from the other night, the one inciting riot in the courtyard. "Turn back!"

Stephan tugged on the reins, "Whoa!"

"By order of the Lord, our God," Skeleton spat, "you're to turn back and return the blasted pederast where you found him."

I leaned over to Sir Alaric. *"I think he's talking about you."*

Sir Alaric knocked out his pipe and said nothing.

Skeleton rose to his full height and fury, his head big, awful, ungainly. "Be gone!" A stiff wind might've bowled him over. "Now!"

"Jesus, I can see your nipples." I squinted. "Mister, I

don't know your name, but it's tough taking a bloke serious as such."

"By order of His Majesty, King Eckhardt Haesken the Third of his name," Sir Alaric barked, "you're to disperse immediately and discontinue these seditious actions. Refusal will result in swift and exacting punishment."

"We have the authority of the Lord Almighty." Skeleton gripped the handle of his scourge.

"Please, good sirs," Stephan raised a hand, "our sole desire is to perform our Christian duty and lay this godly man to rest."

"Godly?" Skeleton's sneer revealed teeth as brown as his robes. "Did you not hear? The man was a sinner."

"Please, sir, if I may—?" Stephan pleaded, warned, cajoled, cause he knew what was coming.

Skeleton ripped his scourge from across his neck and let it dangle from his fist.

"Stand down." Sir Alaric set a foot on the buckboard and took aim. "Take a walk, friend. Don't look back."

"Ain't your friend," Skeleton growled and he and his comrades started forth. "By the Lord God I christen thee—" Skeleton cocked his arm back to flay Stephan, and in that instant, Sir Alaric calmly squeezed the trigger and the crossbow staves jumped — *thunk!*

Point blank, his bolt buried to the birds in Skeleton's chest. Staggering back, he grunted, a look of astonishment bulging his mad eyes as he gasped, mouth working, no words forthcoming, only an empty hollow 'O' as he tripped over the low wall and toppled backward.

The four left made to charge when Karl leaped out, landing in the muck, feet spread, his thane-axe hungry. I was by his side in an instant, Yolanda gleaming bare. We said nothing.

But they got the gist.

Pipe clenched between gritted teeth, Sir Alaric deftly reloaded. No groaning this time. No moaning. Just staid, practiced movement, done a thousand times.

Stephan gathered his aid-bag and vaulted from the wagon. "Let me have a look—"

"Get back!" I collared him, yanking him nearly off his feet.

"He's dying." Stephan tried to shrug free.

I bore down. "So bloody well let him."

"Let. Me. Go."

I hurled him back against the wagon.

"No, he's — *Lord … no.*" Stephan slumped in defeat when he looked. Really looked.

The four scourgers glanced at one another.

I stepped to the fore, Yolanda at my shoulder. "My brother's trying to save you," I explained. "I'm not. So you can go, or we can see how this shakes out, yeah?" Not much argument against a loaded crossbow and bared bastard blade, not to mention Karl the homicidal dwarf. Begging maybe? Or they could hang their hopes on superior numbers. But if they'd the stones to stand tall someone'd be eating iron, and these blokes were sporting burlap wraps rather than mail. "Shove off. Take a stroll back to somewhere that ain't here. Start a farm. Fuck some sheep. *Live.*"

Skeleton moaned softly, fingers plucking at the bolt-feathers dead center in his chest. A fine shot. His fingers stopped moving after a tense moment, then so too did the rest of him. The other four lowered their scourges, seeming uncertain, teetering on the edge. All's they needed was a little nudge.

"Shit." I glared past them.

Here came that nudge.

Through the trees, down the path, from the town, came chanting.

A moment later, devil-smirks slithered across cracked lips. "Our brothers come to cast judgment upon thee!" One of the four bellowed to the sky, dropping to his knees, his brethren following suit.

"Through the trees," Stephan pointed, "more coming. A lot more."

"Shit. Yeah. I see them."

"Let 'em," Karl planted his feet.

The scourger horde came stomping down the road, through the trees and around the church, a long foul procession of brown and grey and ragged madness. Crucifix and banner were hefted haphazard on pike and rod and bent tree limb. The Tome-Bearer stumbled along, leading the raucous march, the withered old geezer's hair frizzed out like a lightning-struck bird's nest, a wild gleam in his eye as he toiled, grunting under the massive burden chained to his neck.

"Lad," Sir Alaric warned, "might want to signal Sir Gustav."

I glanced over at the church. "Best keep them under wraps til there's a clean shot."

"Rabble," Karl spat.

"*Mad* rabble," Sir Alaric countered.

"Fair enough." I swallowed. "How many?"

"Judas priest," Stephan's lips moved, counting beneath his breath, "a lot."

Shit. "About what I counted, too."

Sir Alaric knelt, taking careful aim. I could hear him breathing slow, smooth. Beside me, Karl was grinning mad. He loved this shit. Which was reassuring. Sort of.

Three scraggly Jesus-urchins clambered from the pack and collapsed, heads down to their raw hands and knobby knees, penitent in the cold muck. The Tome-Bearer staggered forth behind and flopped his tome across their backs, slapping like a dead fish, knocking one unconscious. Leering like an inbred pedophile, he tore open the cover, yawning like the mouth of some fell beast, the spine squealing, creaking, crackling in protest.

"Love poems?" I wondered aloud.

"Lad…" Sir Alaric warned.

"Relax, old man," I glanced toward the church, "tell Father Demtry some jokes."

A hush swept over the mob.

Clomping down the lane came the Nazarene, a massive crucifix borne across his shoulders. Skeleton's four comrades, penitent in the graveyard dirt, rose salivating, their hands clenching and unclenching on scourge handles.

"By order of his majesty," Sir Alaric rose, pipe in his mouth, crossbow aimed at the Nazarene, "King Eckhardt Haesken, the Third of his name, you, sir, are under arrest! Lay down the cross and surrender yourself. Smartly now!"

The wagon sat on our right flank, the stone wall to our left. Beyond, it was gravestone and cross for thirty yards to the small stone church. Inside were King Eckhardt's men, Sir Gustav in charge, waiting on my signal. Von Madbury peeked out the front door.

"Surrender yourself!" Sir Alaric repeated. "NOW!"

Lord, I wiggled a finger in my ear, the old man could yell.

The Nazarene halted in front of the impromptu altar, the massive tome perched atop, scowling as he studied the scene before him. The Tome-Bearer latched onto him, whispering in his ear. The Nazarene's gaze fell upon us. Sir Alaric's crossbow was still aimed his way.

The Nazarene didn't seem much to notice. "Brothers," he raised a massive paw, "drop your tools of warfare. Shrive yourselves of thine iron skeins. Then come. Join us. Join us in the true religion of Christ. Ken his path through self-mortification. The ultimate faith of spoken word upon caustic road."

The Tome Bearer barked out a chant, slow and rhythmic and wrong.

"Lad," Sir Alaric said without looking over, "do it."

"Done." I raised a hand toward the church and made a fist, signaling Sir Gustav.

The Nazarene lowered his paws. "What say you?"

We waited.

Nothing happened.

Sir Gustav did not spring forth. He didn't attack. He didn't *anything*.

I caught a fleeting notion of von Madbury, his visage slithering grim back and into shadow, his hooded eye the last image before the door snicked shut, reverberating in my mind like a coffin lid dropped.

"Go brothers!" The Nazarene pointed toward the church.

An arm of scourgers split off, enveloping it, a stout Jesus-bastard wailing away at the front door.

"Lad?" Sir Alaric hissed.

"We're screwed," I breathed as they shattered the front door and streamed inside.

Sir Alaric cursed under breath and down the length of his crossbow as the scourgers emerged from round the back of the church. *"They're gone!"*

"Fuck it." All or nothing now. I pointed Yolanda at the Nazarene. "Kneel down and grab some mud."

"You took the life of a believer in exchange for passage of the damned?" The Nazarene ignored me as he strode toward Skeleton's corpse. "They have eyes but are blind."

"Should teach your folk some manners," I said just for something to say.

"Manners…?" The Nazarene's eyes blazed. "Your hanged man was a fiend."

The Tome-Bearer's chant redoubled, was taken up by the horde as it began to deform, spreading out, encircling us in a palisade of filth and madness.

"Get in the wagon," Sir Alaric hissed.

"No—" Stephan stepped in my way. "Wait!"

"You daft, bloody…" I shoved him aside.

"You…" The Nazarene's eyes narrowed and set upon Stephan. "The Lord's light doth blaze within though you walk in shadow. True believer, aye, though you partner yourself with familiars to the devil." His gaze flitted to me. "Oh, how it will be to burn."

"Down on your bloody knees." I swallowed. "You're under arrest."

The scourgers jostled around us, pressing close, jockeying for position, jackals waiting their turn at the kill.

"You think me a liar?" The Nazarene shrugged the massive crucifix off his shoulders, thudding on the ground. "Or perhaps you think me mad?" He looked down at Skeleton and shook his head. "You shall witness the truth. Your faith shall well up inside like a geyser fit to burst." He knelt and clamped a paw on Skeleton's forehead. "You have no right to leave me yet, brother."

The Tome-Bearer hunkered forth, slathering aside page after page, a rictus of glee crippled across his face as he took up a new chant, the horde following suit.

"*Fear not,* BROTHER!" The Nazarene stretched a quivering hand high to the dawn's light, gripping the sun in effigy. "Restoration be at hand! A struggle though it be, come back to us! Come back! Follow our voice. Follow our faith. Do your good work." Glowing in the nascent dawn, his fist whisked down, plunging to the wrist inside Skeleton's chest as easily as though it were water. "Hallelujah!"

"Holy—" I swallowed.

"*Aaaaeeee!*" Skeleton thrashed instantly alive.

"Come back, brother." The Nazarene clutched Skeleton's throat. "We as yet have need of thee."

Even Karl gave pause.

"*Rise!*" The Nazarene clambered to his feet, hand buried in flesh, and heaved Skeleton on high, screaming all the while.

"*RISE!*" As one, the horde fell to its knees, chanting still, fast now, faster. "*RISE BROTHER! RISE!*"

"Fear not, brother!" The Nazarene bore him aloft like a babe. "*'What is life?'* be the question." Skeleton's eyes bulged, his body shivering, quivering, limbs writhing, flailing, as he screamed, as steam hissed from the fist gouged into his chest. "Duty and pain be the answer!"

"Mother of God," Stephan whispered.

"Agony, the divine serum!" The Nazarene lowered Skeleton to the ground, setting him upon his feet, steadying him tall, "Easy now," and tore his fist free, crimson slick with dripping viscera. Clutched in his fist, steaming, was Sir Alaric's crossbow bolt. "Did Christ not suffer at the hand of his father? Did he not suffer for our sins?" He snapped the bolt in twain then cast it aside. "Did he not sacrifice himself so we might revel in eternal glory?"

Skeleton wilted like a daisy, clutching his chest, his heart, his vitals. Swirls of steam rose twisting in serpent coils.

"*Now or never,*" Karl growled low, "while they're down."

"No—" I hissed back.

If we attacked, we'd take some down, more than some even, yeah, but we'd all die.

The Nazarene stood triumphant. "Rise now, brother."

The chanting devolved into a slurry of animal grunts and yowls.

Mouth agape, Skeleton lowered his hands, revealing a massive puckered, star-shaped scar etched across his chest. "By the lord…" He wobbled like a newborn fawn, but the Nazarene steadied him, holding him close in his thick-fingered grip. "Steady your heart, brother, your legs, and walk with me a while.

"Like Lazarus, you have risen reborn," the Nazarene bellowed, "and Lazarus shall I name you. And you shall spread the word of the Lord. By word and by deed and, yea, by presence alone." His eyes fell to us. "Indeed, all present this day shall speak the word and by such action shall our numbers blossom. Apostles all, I name thee."

The horde roared, glares locked on us as they rose from their knees, starting forth from all sides, closing in, murder etched plain in grim visage.

"Hold!" The Nazarene raised both hands and the horde stilled. "Our work here is done, brothers. For the now. Let them be. Let them inter their damned. Let them expend their sweat and toil in an act of empty desecration." He caught Stephan's gaze. "Come now, brothers," a trench yawned open through the horde as the Nazarene strode through, a slithering mass of grubby paws reaching to out grope him as he passed, "there are worse evils that plague this land."

…my hand trembles as I write to Mother that Father fell amid the most dire of circumstances.

By the Lord, how shall I ever again look her in the…
—*War-Journal of Prince Ulrich of Haeskenburg*

Chapter 19.

FATHER DEMTRY'S excoriated corpse slid into the grave, thudding headfirst into the soggy bottom, all tangled and bothered in an arrested somersault of flaccid limb and contorted spine. His denuded skull leered up, back, over his shoulder, nigh on a hundred and eighty degrees the wrong way.

"Voilà." I wiped dirt and crusted blood from my hands.

"Excuse me." Head down, muttering, Stephan shouldered me aside, climbed into the grave and started rearranging the corpse to a more suitable position. As though it somehow mattered. "Jesus please," I heard him plead softly, "lend me strength…"

"So what the hell just happened?" I turned.

"Which is it you mean?" Sir Alaric sat in the wagon, his beard frazzled, eyes bloodshot, smoking like a chimney. "The standoff? The betrayal? Or the God-damned bloody-fucking miracle?"

"Business first. Always." I fixed him an eye. "The betrayal. You said Gustav's a staunch bloke. But seems like he was able to both turtle-up *and* rabbit at the same time. So, again, what the hell happened?"

"Eh…?" Sir Alaric tapped his pipe on the side of the wagon. "Known him since he was but a lad. Lord. My squire for a time, even. Strong arm. Sense of honor. Tireless. Fond of combat. Over-fond, truth be told. Admittedly, not overmuch to speak of between the ears, if you catch my meaning."

"He's a bleeding idiot."

"Aye, lad, hit the nail on the head." Sir Alaric lifted his pipe. "But even so, I can't ken how—"

"I can." I cut him off. "Someone was yanking his chain. Question is, 'who?'"

"I'd not want to disparage another's sense of—"

"Von Madbury," I said without hesitation.

"Not sure…"

"Jesus Christ. Are you blind?" I spat. "Maybe it was Squire Morley, then? Yeah. Must've been him that had the power and guile to precipitously call off the dogs of war." I rubbed my chin. "Think the little shit even shaves yet?"

Sir Alaric looked like nothing so much as a doleful old hound that wanted only to go back to bed.

"Why's King Eckhardt keep him around?" Stephan asked, neck-deep in the grave.

"Because he's weak," I said. "Because it's always easier to sit back and do nothing. Hope everything works out. Somehow. Somewhere. Someway. Which is piss-poor policy for a beet farmer let alone king. Or…" I itched some flea bites at my neck, "maybe the bugger's got something on him?"

Sir Alaric intently studied the stem of his pipe.

"Now me? If I were king?" I shrugged. "I'd gaff him through the ball-sack and hang him upside down from my gatehouse."

Sir Alaric ceded a despondent nod. "Aye, lad."

"C'mon!" I smote the side of the wagon. "We should be dead. Only reason we ain't is the Nazarene's off his rocker. That," I fixed Stephan an eye, "and he's got a crush on you, apparently."

Stephan shrugged and set back to making the three-day-old corpse presentable for the wagon load of dirt we'd be shoveling on his mug.

"Gonna make for one hell of a homecoming," I said. "Madbury's a fair sword arm, yeah?"

"Better than fair." Sir Alaric licked his wizened lips.

"Better than fair, huh?" I sheathed Yolanda. "I'll have Karl kill him, then."

"Let it lie." Stephan tossed the shovel up. "We've bigger fish to fry."

Sir Alaric scratched his beard. "Have to see where the King's thoughts lie with the matter."

"The bastards abandoned us," I said. "I'd say we have the moral high-ground. Which is a first for me."

"Not a first, brother." Stephan felt for purchase about the grave's edge. "Decades shorn of practice, perhaps, but not a first."

"Need a hand?" I stood over him.

Stephan scowled up as he slammed his hook right where my foot'd been before I snatched it back.

"Too soon?" I asked.

He half-smirked then jumped, hauling himself up onto the earth by his elbows and knees, and scrambled out gracelessly.

"Gonna say some words?" I glared down into the pit. Father Demtry did look more comfortable now. It'd been a low bar set, true, but it was fair undeniable.

"I said them when I was down there." Stephan donned his cloak, tying it off with one hand.

I brandished a hungry shovel. "Expeditious."

"Sure." Stephan craned his neck toward the town walls, looming beyond the trees. "Any sign of Karl?"

"Nay, lad," Sir Alaric said.

"We can't kill the Nazarene."

"I'd beg to differ." I started shoveling dirt. "Once Karl finds where he's holing up, that's exactly what we're going to do." Karl'd taken off, lagging along behind the horde, tailing, watching, waiting.

"You saw what I saw, brother." Stephan took up a shovel.

"And what the hell'd I see?"

"A miracle from God."

"And you?" I glared at Sir Alaric.

"Reluctantly," he swallowed, "I got to agree."

"This fella seem like the type the Almighty wants leading the charge?" I asked. Stephan opened his mouth to reply but I cut him off. "And if you say that the Lord works in mysterious ways, I'll knock you on your arse alongside Demtry. Then bloody-well bury you, too. The church has summarily excommunicated those lunatics for heresy. The *infallible* pope himself."

Stephan tapped his chest. "I'm a heretic, too, remember?"

"Right. What the hell'd we just finish doing?" I stabbed a finger down toward Demtry's corpse. "And the Nazarene didn't just kill him. Didn't just hang him. He *flayed* him first. That seem like something our Messiah'd condone? Jesus, are you blind?" I turned. "Is everyone fucking blind?"

Stephan leaned on his shovel and wiped his brow.

"Then what was it *you* saw, lad?" Sir Alaric asked.

"Me?" I stabbed my shovel into the pile and dumped it in. There was something satisfying about it. Maybe it was just that shoveling dirt on a dead fucker's mug was one of those menial tasks where hard work yielded immediate results. "I don't know. Black magic, sorcery, necromancy, and shit, maybe, *possibly,* a miracle."

"Maybe?" Stephan scoffed. "How do you explain it?"

I straightened up. "Slight of hand?"

"Slight of what?!" Stephan's eyes blazed. "You think he was pulling coins from kids' ears? Rabbits out of hats or cards from up his sleeve?"

"No," I thrust in another shovelful, "but I do think the bastard was dealing from the bottom of the deck."

...initial penetrations beyond the boundaries of the clan-holt were executed with a diplomatic hand. But Hochmeister Gaunt lead the initial sortie, as it was his venture. A man more obviously suited to warfare I have never met...

—War-Journal of Prince Ulrich of Haeskenburg

Chapter 20.

WE SMELLED IT long before we saw it. Heard it, too. Or the exact opposite. The stillness, the quiet, the dead silence. A void in the body of life around the town square. A stifling quality. No crows. No wind. No scourgers.

Which was good.

Or bad.

Depending.

Between the wattle and daub cottages, a forest stood upright and bitter as the cold morning raw. A dozen crosses, the ones I'd seen from the Schloss's acropolis. Upon them, the dead watched.

"What did the Nazarene mean by '*we have eyes but are blind?*'" Stephan snapped the reins and we lurched on through.

"Don't know." I stifled a shiver. From the cold. Obviously.

A cold breeze took up, fluttering scraps of tattered garment, breathing licks of life back into the damned. Leering faces. Ragged teeth. Skin stretched drum-tight over bone. Crows had gotten at their eyes, their lips, their noses, all the places crows ever got.

"He mean them, you think?" Sir Alaric glared up at the dead.

"Think he's dropping hints in the form of poetic metaphor?" I scowled.

Sir Alaric shut his trap and grumbled.

In the center of the square lay the smoking remnants of the great bale-fire.

"Burn here most nights," Sir Alaric said.

"Are we certain the Nazarene committed this atrocity?" Stephan asked.

"Fair certain, lad."

"I saw him and his brethren here last night." I pointed northeast up the hill to the Schloss's acropolis, visible through a break in the huddled row of buildings. "Saw them digging. Hauling. Hammering away. It was like something from the bible. One of the shitty parts." In my mind's eye, I saw the scourgers toiling, dragging cross and corpse across cobble, digging, hammering, raising them up, one by bloody one.

The nearest had been a woman. Once. Her skin was the dull brown of fresh-churned clay. Her iron-grey hair'd been done up in a failing braid, strands of frayed wire crazing out from stem to stern. A ghost sheen of frost glistened where the sun hadn't yet hit.

Stephan scratched his chin. "Look like they've been dead a while."

"I heard screaming," I said.

"Could have been the scourgers."

"Yeah. Sure," I conceded. "Can you pull up alongside?"

"Aye." Stephan snapped the reins, driving the wagon alongside the old crone.

Like the rest, she was trussed round the upper arms and chest. Thick iron nails protruded from her wrists and tops of feet. The timber crosses looked to be old rafters or lintels. Posts and joists. Whatever lumber the bastard scourgers could lay their stigmataed palms on. A child had been crucified across a door and left leaning against an old baker's busted-up shopfront.

"Did you actually see the Nazarene kill them?" Stephan asked.

"No." I shook my head.

Sir Alaric cleared his throat, offering a, "Nay, lad, but—"

"Then it's possible it wasn't him." Stephan craned his neck, steering the wagon alongside the old crone's crucifix. "That good?"

I drew a dagger. "A touch further."

"Lad…" Sir Alaric looked my way for support.

"Just a little bit…"

Stephan drove the wagon forth a foot or so. "Now?"

"Yeah." Standing in the back of the wagon, I slit the ropes binding the crone's arms to the cross. They stayed in place, still held by the rusted nails. "Timber…" I slit the ropes binding her torso. Her weight was too much for the nails alone, and she tumbled forth like a rotten log. I stepped aside, tried easing her fall but gave up when she slithered from my grip, crashing into the wagon-bed.

"Judas priest, Lou." Stephan and Sir Alaric both glared.

"What?" I wiped grime on my pant legs.

"Here, take these." Eyeballing the cross, Stephan handed off the reins to Sir Alaric and clambered into the wagon-bed. He stood by the bare crucifix, peering in the same direction the corpse had. "They're all facing the same direction."

"Yeah, so?" I looked up, around, shrugged. "What of it?"

"It's a message." Stephan's eyes narrowed.

"Yeah. It says, *'Go away.'"*

"When we sailed in we couldn't have seen this from the Abraxas, right?" Stephan pointed west toward the river.

"Because of the buildings."

"Yeah…" I conceded. "We could see the bale-fire's glow."

"And we couldn't see it from up on Gallow's Tor." Stephan pointed southwest.

I followed his arm, half hoping to see Karl trudging back. But no such luck. Still off on his errand. I glanced at Sir Alaric. In concert, we both said, "No."

"I don't mean to tread on your theory, Sir Alaric."

"Call me Red, lad." Sir Alaric winced a smile. "Both o' you. What my friends called me, back when I had 'em."

"Red. Alright." Stephan patted him on the shoulder. "Could you see them when you went to the old keep? That's even higher than as Gallow's Tor."

I thought for a moment. "No. Probably not." I looked to Sir Alaric. "Red?"

"Nay, lad." Sir Alaric pointed to the northeast. "That line of buildings shields it."

"But you said you saw it last night." Stephan hopped out of the wagon. "Where were you?"

"The acropolis of the Schloss," I said, "with the King."

Stephan stomped to another crucifix, took a bearing, his hook arm aimed out straight. "With these buildings and this angle," he stomped to another cross, "the only place you can see all of these dead on is from the roof of the Schloss."

"Dead on, huh?" I smirked. "How about if you're walking through the square?"

"True. Hmm…" Stephan fingered his lip. "But every one of these corpses is looking, no aimed, directly at the Schloss. If you wanted to send a message to folk in the square—"

"Scare the shit out of them, you mean?"

"Aye. Then would you not face them outward? To ensure that no matter which street were taken in — there's six, mind you — you'd be confronted by the dead?" Stephan stomped across the way. "Look. If you come in from the south or east as we did, you see only their backs. The only direction you're truly confronted by the full brunt is Nail Street. There." He took another bearing. "In line with the Schloss's sight-line."

"More or less," I admitted.

Sir Alaric clambered from the wagon and trudged over, following Stephan's outstretched arm then whistled. "You've a keen eye, lad, mark my words."

"So what?" I crossed my arms. "So, it's a message. To the King? A warning?"

"Perhaps…" Stephan glared up at another corpse.

"*Perhaps?* Are you bloody serious? We've a dozen crucified corpses all pointing one way. What the hell else could it mean? *Keep up the good work?*"

"I think we need to keep looking."

"Alright. Sure. Yeah." I gave the horse a quick glance to make sure it didn't look like bolting, then stood up and examined the cross.

"See anything?" Stephan called over.

"Not through the stink." I waved a hand. The nails that had been driven through the corpses' wrists and feet had pulled through when she fell. "Let's just get this done with, yeah?"

We droned on in corpse-borne misery, pulling down the dead until we'd finally reached the last one.

"Almost…" I gritted my teeth as I sawed away at the rope holding up the last poor bastard. "Hmm… What the—?" I leaned in, squinting. "They pulled this poor bastard's teeth out." He was a well-dressed fella, his high-collared frock of quality make though death and despair and weather had robbed the wind from its sails. His gaunt face stared impassively as I cut away the last of his bonds. *"Timber—"* I stepped aside.

But the corpse didn't fall.

"Huh…? Must've been a carpenter hammered this bastard in." I checked his hands, prying them clean off the nails. "What the…?" Still, he didn't fall. "Only thing holding him up's, what?" I checked him head to toe. "Another bloody miracle?"

"Nay, lad," Sir Alaric pointed with the stem of his pipe, "you missed one."

"Huh?" I stepped back, rolling an ankle on the corpse pile. "Where—?"

"Rose of Sharon…" Stephan crossed himself.

"A big one," Sir Alaric said. "Dead center."

Just protruding from the corpse's chest, and what I had initially taken for a frock button, was the beaten head of an iron stake driven clean through the corpse.

…with gifts of masterwork leather goods and tools of steel and iron, items that were beyond their ken to make. Indeed, they wondered at their construct as well the construct of our arms and…
—*War-Journal of Prince Ulrich of Haeskenburg*

Chapter 21.

SHHH—" Lady Mary pressed a finger to her lips as I closed the door, my arms overflowing with fresh linen and blankets. Ruth lay abed next to Abraham, clutching his hand, staring at the ceiling, unblinking, numb, her soft hummed mumbling interspersed between Abraham's staccato snores.

Lady Mary stormed silently across the room and took the linen. *"Thank you,"* she mouthed.

Joshua sat at a table, still reading from the worn old copy of the Talmud. Sarah leaned draping against his back, swaying, squinting over his shoulder, her lips moving as she sounded out words.

I winked at Lady Mary, cocked my head towards the doorway.

Lady Mary set the linen down then followed me into the hall. "How did your *meeting* go?"

"Meeting?" I raised an eyebrow.

The hallway was empty. Dinner was nigh upon us and most of the servants off hustling.

"With the Nazarene?" Lady Mary said.

"Oh that. Yeah." I chuffed a cold laugh. "About as well as everything else."

"That bad?"

"Worse. But we're all still here. Still alive."

I hoped.

Cause Karl should've been back by now. He'd been gone all day. *Deep breath*… The shit I'd give him if those fuckers crucified him. "Ruth's finally trying to knock off? Good. I was worried."

"I still am." Lady Mary pulled the door almost closed. "She won't sleep. She never does. She merely lies there humming, staring, mumbling."

"Maybe I can find an apothecary?" I offered.

"No. It's not that." Lady Mary rubbed the back of her neck. "Well, it is but — you heard that jibe from von Madbury at dinner last night?"

"My new best friend?" I said. "Yeah. I heard it."

"He's trouble, mark my words. I don't trust him. I don't trust any of them."

"I'm right there with you," I said.

Lady Mary appraised me like a woman poised to buy a horse and just noticing a cracked hoof. "And the Queen…" She glanced down the hallway. "Is there something between you two? Some history?"

"Huh?" My face felt suddenly hot.

She crossed her arms and glared.

"Yeah. Alright." I cracked my fingers, feeling red. The past night flashed through my mind, the Queen on tiptoe, leaning in, her scent enveloping me. "It was barely anything. Just kid stuff. From a long while back. I was kind to her is all."

"You?"

"Jesus Christ," I scowled. "Yeah me."

"It isn't safe here."

"Yeah. No shit. Where is it safe?"

"I think I'll remain here during dinner." Lady Mary glanced one way down the hall then the other. "I … I don't think I could bring myself to eat."

"Oh?" I raised an eyebrow. "Figured you'd be itching to get free. Kick off your work shoes, doff your maid's apron, sup with the betters." What I didn't say was that she was gonna miss one hell of a dinner-show.

"I don't know. I can't place it. But there's … something wrong with this place."

With visions of loaded crosses skirting through my mind, I didn't argue the point.

Lady Mary fingered her wooden hand. "How fares the *Ulysses?*"

"Finally hauled up in dry-dock. Chadwicke's checking her over. Avar's probably getting in his way." I sighed. "She needs to be refitted. At the very least. Good news is the one thing Haeskenburg has in abundance, besides crippling mediocrity, is lumber. Gonna be a while, though. A month at the least. Probably more."

"I can scarcely believe it."

"Yeah. I know. *Mediocrity's* a vast overstatement."

She shook her head, almost cracking a smirk, though it could have been my imagination. "If there's anything I can do—"

"No. You're doing it." I nodded toward the room. "They need someone strong looking out for them."

Lady Mary bit her lip. "Ruth is having some difficulties—"

"She's nuts on the way to bat-shit crazy," I finished for her.

"No, it's that she's—"

"Under an unreasonable amount of strain." I held my hands up. "It's no dig. Believe me. I'd have cut and run long before if I were wearing her shoes. But she's fixed on standing there, Atlas to the world on her shoulders. Crushing her by degrees." And *degrees* was generous. And by *generous*, I meant total bullshit.

Watching Ruth was like watching a sapped wall start to give. You can't see it initially, but you feel it. The ground shivering beneath your feet. Next, you hear it. The rumble as the supports yawn, bend, cave, hidden stones shifting, mortar drizzling rivulets of crumble. The ground's trembling hard now, bucking beneath your feet in anticipation of the big show.

"I've seen von Madbury skulking about." Lady Mary frowned.

"I'll have Karl here as much as possible. Do what we can. But we're in it now." I glanced at her wooden hand. "Might want to keep the hook one on."

She looked away. "It's monstrous."

"Yeah. Exactly. We need more of that on our side."

"Is there anything else?"

"Yeah, one thing." I unslung a satchel and dug a trio of books out. "Here. It's a copy of *Sir Gawain and the Green Knight* and *The Canterbury Tales*. And an Old Testament."

She raised an eyebrow.

"I borrowed them from the library. And by *borrow* I mean *stole.*"

"I thank you but," she looked annoyed, "I have no time to read—"

"For them. The kids. They've been reading the damned *Talmud* for nigh on over a month." I laid a hand to my chest. "I mean, I've never read it myself, but I imagine it's boring as shit the first time around. And having to read it five hundred times? Day in and day out...?"

Lady Mary raised a hand. "I gather your meaning." She accepted the books and fanned pages of *The Canterbury Tales*. "Hmm... I've never read it."

"Well, there's some parts in it they maybe shouldn't read. *The Wife of Bath. The Shipman's Tale*, too." I tapped a finger against my lips. "Maybe a few others? Maybe you should just read it to them." I glanced inside the door. Ruth was still mumbling. Was it prayer? "Best ask Ruth first, though, at any rate."

"Certainly."

"And tell her Stephan brought it, yeah?"

"Yes. Of course." Lady Mary made to close the door. "Now if that is all?" She tucked the books underarm as Joshua poked his head out.

"Hi, Mister Luther," he beamed.

"Hey, kid." My stomach rumbled. Dinner. Part of me was looking forward to it. The other part was smart. "Maybe I can snatch you some paint from Sir Alaric." I straightened and slid my hand over my heart. "You could paint my portrait."

"Back inside, children." With a look of consternation, Lady Mary laid a hand on Joshua's shoulder and drew him back in the room. "I thank you for the kindness, Sir Luther."

"See? It's possible."

Lady Mary bowed her head. "I apologize."

Sarah peered from behind Lady Mary's legs. Wide-eyed, she offered a tepid wave of only her fingertips.

"Greetings, milady." I winked.

Sarah giggled.

"Inside, children. Please."

Sarah disappeared and Joshua materialized almost immediately.

Lady Mary rolled her eyes. "*Judas Priest.*"

"Relax," I said. "I'd have been crawling up the walls or setting fires if I were them."

Sarah reappeared by her brother.

I smirked. "You want to hear a joke?"

Lady Mary stepped in, "I don't think your jokes would be—"

"Relax. Jesus. Am I a cretin?" I held up a hand. "Don't answer that."

Lady Mary crossed her arms and stood back.

"So, these two muffins were sitting in an oven." I held up two fingers. "The first muffin says, *Dear me, it's certainly getting hot in here.*" I dug a finger into my collar, panted, fanned my face.

"Huh?" Joshua glanced up.

"It's a joke, Joshie." Sarah elbowed him.

"And the second muffin points at the first and yells, *Jesus Christ, a talking muffin!*"

Sarah's face lit up like the sun. She covered her mouth and giggled. Joshua, stunned at first, finally got it, snickering after a moment. "Muffins can't talk."

Lady Mary, offering a sardonic smirk of her own, herded the children back into the room. "Go sit down. Please. Joshua— Put that down. I'll be back in a moment." Lady Mary glanced over at Ruth. "Best you be back on your way. Wouldn't want to be late for dinner."

"Prince Eventine's gonna be sore about you not showing up." I shook my head. "Queen's sniffing around for a match, too."

"A match for the Prince?" Lady Mary raised an eyebrow. "Or a match for her?"

...*effort it had been, between the King of Hungary and the Grandmaster of the Teutonics. This was before the Great Schism, before the lies, the sundered trust, before the bloodshed. In those days, it was the pagan savages whose blood alone we spilled.*

T'was a far simpler time.
—War-Journal of Prince Ulrich of Haeskenburg

Chapter 22.

YOU ABSOLUTELY CERTAIN you ain't French?" I snarled. "Cause that was some of the timeliest cowardice I've ever seen. And could you please pass the bloody salt?"

Sir Gustav sat across from me, his fingertips digging into the table, glowering beneath that one huge caterpillar eyebrow stretched across his awesome forehead.

"And you," I ground my teeth von Madbury's way, "is it the eye-patch that makes you a shit? Cause I've never known a bastard wearing one who wasn't."

Von Madbury wiped his beard down with one hand, a sneer contorting his mug. "You insufferable—"

"Dietrick. Sir Luther. Please—" The Queen raised a hand.

"You're a pair of yellow bastards." I scowled down the table at Brother Miles, Harwin, Sir Roderick, and the rest of them. "And that goes for you, too."

Lady Ludmilla fanned the Lady Tourmaline, who had swooned precipitously.

"*Gentlemen!*" Prince Palatine lurched onerously to his feet.

No one listened. No one cared. Prince Eventine raised a hand, murmuring something lost in the wash.

Von Madbury took a gulp of wine, biding his time. Letting it build.

Sir Gustav was not. He stuttered in wild mania, unable to vomit word or meaning out of the great big empty hole situated in the middle of his stupid face. He was seconds from launching himself across the table. Von Madbury laid a hand gripping into Sir Gustav's shoulder, muttering a jawfull of something awful.

Sir Gustav froze at the touch, eyes blazing, a sneer creasing slow and malign across his thick lips. "Aye." He nodded to himself, no doubt untangling the miasma of convoluted thought cobwebbing the jagged innards of his hollow ogre skull. "I challenge you to a duel, you … you *filthy* skunk."

"*Skunk?*" I slapped the table. "Jesus Christ. Are you serious?" I turned to Lady Ludmilla. "Is he bloody serious?"

"I-I—" Lady Ludmilla gasped, still fanning her friend.

"I believe he is, brother." Stephan frowned. He wasn't enjoying this. But then, I didn't expect him to be. Truth be told, neither was I, but I was faking it as best I could. Sir Gustav might've been a great-big oaf, but that didn't mean he wasn't adept at killing. Great-big oafs made some of the very best killers the world had to offer. But I knew now, for sure, that it'd been Von Madbury who'd sealed the deal. Von Madbury who'd pulled the strings. Von Madbury who'd left us high and dry at the Nazarene's tender mercy. Sir Gustav was just his oafish pawn.

"Could you take it down a rung?" Stephan said sidelong. *"Please."*

There were seven of the King's men on the far side of the table. On mine? Me and Karl and Stephan and the ladies-in-waiting whom I was fair sure were looking to trade sides. Not that I blamed them. Stephan was near-worthless in a fight and while Karl was worth any three of the others, that left four to me unless Lady Ludmilla proved aces at fisticuffs. It seemed unlikely.

"There'll be no dueling." Sir Alaric limped into the hall, looking like a scarecrow with the stuffing kicked out. "How many fighting men are we? And how many are they *outside* the bleedin' walls?" As Sir Gustav started counting on his sausage fingers, Sir Alaric snarled, "Not enough to be losing any of us, you fool. We've murderers and maniacs loose and you're fixed on killing each other. Lord grant me strength." He leaned his cane against his chair. "Now, grab some pine and shut yer gob unless you're stuffing it with grub."

"Of course, *master* justiciar." Von Madbury continued leering while Sir Gustav took his seat, somehow looking both incensed and wounded.

Sir Alaric's gaze fell on me. A hard glare but with a softening need. Begging. He was begging me to stop. To reign it in. And not wanting to fight the big oaf in a square duel, I twitched a nod, remaining standing as King Eckhardt entered the hall. Stephan rose by my side.

"On yer feet." Sir Alaric growled.

"Gentlemen…" Settling into his chair, King Eckhardt rubbed his furrowed brow. "Sir Alaric has apprised me of the … events that transpired at the church. Or, did *not* transpire, should I say?" His gaze fell to von Madbury then slid over to Sir Gustav who fairly writhed under his frigid appraisal. "Sir Gustav," King Eckhardt maintained the pressure for some time before offering a lifeline, "it was a miscommunication, no doubt?"

"They were rabble, Your Highness." Sir Gustav gripped the tablecloth. "Filthy. Stinking. Rabble. Unarmed for the main. Unarmored all. What good's a fighting man who can't stomach that?"

"A fair point," von Madbury announced.

King Eckhardt's eyes simmered cold. "A *miscommunication*, I said?"

Karl clutched his dagger beneath the table. So did I. So did everyone.

"Eh…?" It took a moment for the idea to crawl its way through Sir Gustav's ears, burrow down the tunnel, skitter along the narrow confines, lodge itself like a mouse prick in his tiny brain. "A-aye, Your Highness." Sir Gustav's glare fell. He forced a nod. "T'was one of those. A-A miscommunication."

"For the plan had been set," King Eckhardt said, "and was rather straightforward, was it not?"

"Y-Your Majesty, I apologize. Aye." Sir Gustav inflated his chest. "T'was my command. I … I was concerned that with the fighting men gone from the keep for so long, trouble might strike here, and this — this *stranger,*" he pointed at me with a sausage finger, "was taking his blessed time. Gabbing like a magpie with that loathsome scourger." He stifled a sideways glance to von Madbury. "But, aye, it was on my order. So," he offered a shit-bow, "my apologies. Again."

King Eckhardt's gaze set upon me next. "Is that sufficient, Sir Luther?"

"I believe we're still owed a flogging." I took a pull of brandy, swallowed, wiped my chin.

Sir Gustav's eyes bulged bloodshot wide.

"You speak of debts?" King Eckhardt studied me, lips pressed together, eyes hangdog weary. "Is it not also truth that you owe me a head?"

I glanced at Karl. He'd returned before dinner with the sad-sack news that the Nazarene had given him the slip somewhere on the south-side.

"It'll get done," I said.

"Then I shall expect it. And soon."

"Yeah. Sure. Soon."

"Your Majesty," Stephan set his napkin down and stood, "might we not address the miracle we all bore witness to?"

Lady Ludmilla whispered behind her hand to Lady Tourmaline, just awakened. The men remained silent, their glares iron barbs aimed Stephan's way.

King Eckhardt took a slow measured sip. "Sir Alaric spoke to me of it at length. I wish I had been present to bear witness for, indeed, it seems beyond the realm of man. Into the realm of biblical legend. I would hear from someone better versed in such matters." He glanced down the table. "Father Gregorius, if you would be so kind?"

"Yes, Your Majesty, certainly. Ahem." Father Gregorius dabbed his chin with his napkin, pushed back his seat and rose, straightening his vestment. "Gentlemen, I am no inquisitor to be wholly expert in such matters. But," he raised a finger, "I am a man of God, and the event described so lucidly by Sir Alaric can fall into but one of two categories. It was either a miracle of the Lord God himself or magic of the blackest sort. Are we all in agreement?"

A scattered draggle of unsure heads bobbed up and down, nodding stupidly. At best. A bunch of idiots in class, looking down, away, hoping the professor wouldn't call on them. Down the table, someone burped, Harwin, possibly.

"I would agree," Stephan said.

"I'd place it firmly in the realm of black magic, Your Majesty," von Madbury announced with all the confidence born of ironclad ignorance.

"And heresy!" Brother Miles smote the table.

"You two must have eyes in the back of your heads," I commented.

"I've borne enough of your jibes, Sir Luther." Brother Miles stroked his greying mustache.

"Your Majesty, this Nazarene brought a man back from death." Stephan glanced down the table. "With the exception of the ladies present, we all bore witness. Every single one. The Nazarene reached into the man's breast and withdrew a crossbow bolt from within. He breathed new life into him." He looked to me, eyes begging for agreement. "Was that not what you saw?"

"Yeah." I cleared my throat. "It was a kill-shot, Your Majesty. Without a doubt."

"But was this fellow indeed dead?" Father Gregorius's eyes narrowed.

"Truly? I don't know," I admitted. "Didn't get a shot at examining him up close. But he was down. The bolt buried in his heart. And I've seen men not die *immediately* from such a wound. But the bastard's bags were packed, and he'd set foot on Charon's skiff, that's for damn sure."

"Be that as it may," Father Gregorius lifted his bible in emphasis, "I would err on the side of *black* magic. I have difficulty believing the Lord our God blessed a derelict such as this Nazarene with one of the many powers of Christ."

"Your Majesty, please, let me parley with him." Stephan rose. "If this Nazarene can indeed raise the dead, or heal the wounded, would that not be worth something? What if in truth he is the reason you've remained untouched by plague as many have claimed? Would that not be worth saving? Understanding? And, yea, indeed, harnessing? Has there not been enough death and drek in these fell times?"

"I'll not argue you on that score, young Stephan," King Eckhardt admitted, "but this fellow represents a threat to me and my kingdom. I believe you had a hand in clearing the town square?"

"I did, Your Majesty."

"So you saw. And I thank you for the service. As well for the other services you've provided with regards to Father Demtry and my people."

"He crucified all those folk." Father Gregorius dabbed his chin with a napkin.

"Not to mention the Jews he drove out or murdered," I added.

"Yes, Sir Luther, though," Father Gregorius raised a finger, "there is some precedence in the canon for such deeds. Why, during the First Crusade, Pope Urban II sanctioned the murder of—"

"Barbarity," Stephan scoffed.

"Nay, *boy*. Pontiffs throughout the ages have Christened them *infidels*, have they not?" Father Gregorius locked gazes with Stephan. "And indeed, Urban II went so far as to state that he would grant absolution to any party committing such acts of filial religiosity. Why, I believe—"

"Filial … religiosity?" I muttered, but Stephan was on it.

"Whole cities were burned for that absolution." Stephan was ready to launch across the table and bury his hook hand in Father Gregorius's eye. It would've been something to see under other circumstances.

"Surely you question not the doctrine of papal infallibility?" It was Father Gregorius's turn to be offended.

"Which pope?" Stephan asked coolly. "The one in Rome or the one in Avignon? The Great Schism has muddied the waters."

"Remember Paris—" I kicked Stephan's foot under the table, hoping to jog memories of that fine city. He'd had a similar exchange there, where a mob incited by some bastard priest had nearly burned him at the stake over a similar

misunderstanding. Or heresy. Or witchcraft. Depending on your point of view.

"The Lord our father is the Alpha and Omega," Father Gregorius bulled onward, "the beginning and the end and thus encompasses all in his vast cosmic embrace."

"Or perhaps he's simply the beginning and the end?" Stephan countered. "And perhaps everything in between is us. Only us. Our lives. Our choices. Our triumphs. Our failures."

"Blasphemy." Father Gregorius cast his napkin aside. "Heresy!"

"Barbarism!" Stephan spat. "You advocate the killing of—"

"Hey, *fucking cool it,* would you?" I hissed out the corner of my mouth.

Stephan opened his mouth to retort when I dropped a hand on his shoulder. A heavy hand. A crushing hand. I dug my fingers in and pulled him around til we were eye to eye. "Have a drink, brother." I shoved my flagon in his face and tilted it back, forcing him to drink lest he stain his best shirt. His only shirt. "Relax. They're already dead."

"Not *all* of them," Stephan hissed low, snatching the flagon away, taking a sip, and only *maybe* the hint. "And there's still more dying. Daily. In the wood camp. Up at the old keep. Judas Priest, in this very yard. That blackguard you hunted is still alive, still stalking folk, still killing them."

"Baseless gossip garnered, no doubt, from the riff-raff in the yard." Father Gregorius locked glares with Stephan. "The small-folk are meant to live and to toil and to die, for that is their lot in life. Sometimes they have difficulty discerning fact from fable."

Stephan held his ground. "A boy went missing from the Grey-Lark camp last night."

"Rudiger's dead," I said. "He ain't killing anyone, brother."

"Well, Lou," Stephan took a gulp of wine, "someone is."

Chapter 23.

NORTH THROUGH THE GREY-LARK FOREST, we commenced a new hunt. For a new killer. Three days shot to shit, and still nothing but more folk going dark. More sleepless nights tracking rumor and gossip with all but shit to show. I was haggard, spent, dreaming of sleep on my last two legs when I knocked on their door. "You rang?"

In the corner, Lady Mary sat cross-legged by the hearth, playing some hand-clap game with Sarah and Joshua. It looked like a shoddy affair, but the children were smiling, giggling, carrying on. A fine thing to see for once. Juxtaposed against that was Ruth's look of consternation at my arrival, confirming that she, in fact, had not rung for me, would never ring for me, would deign only to allow me in because Abraham had in fact rung for me. "Sir *Luther...*" She said it the way most people say *crabs,* and not the ocean kind.

"What is it, my lady?" I glanced past her to the figure lying motionless abed. He looked roughly the same but diminished somehow. By degrees, perhaps, but that's why they called it consumption. "Is he...?"

"Oy vey." Ruth trembled. "No, not..."

I let loose a bated breath. Good. Having the children and Lady Mary carousing through children's games in view of a cooling corpse would've paled even my stunted sense of decorum.

"It…" Ruth rose, unconsciously smoothing her hair, frizzed out in uneven jags. "It was I who wished to speak with you. Sir Luther. Might we?" She hesitated a moment, her hand on Abraham's shoulder, frozen, unable to move. "In the hall, perhaps?"

Lady Mary glanced up, lips pursed, mid-clap with Sarah. "Go on, Ruth." Lady Mary stood and smoothed out her skirts. "I'll sit by him."

"Thank you, my lady." Ruth's eyes were blood-shot like she hadn't slept in days. Like maybe since we'd got here. Like maybe since ever.

I glanced down the hall. It was early, desolate, dawn. I'd had trouble sleeping even when the chance presented itself, the thought of Rudiger's arms gripping, his crushing embrace, me unable to breathe, hovering just beyond the veil. Cold sweats and hot panic. That's what awaited me whenever I closed my eyes. New nightmares ever in supply to supplant the old. "It's cold out here."

"I shall survive." Ruth gathered her shawl then shouldered through the doorway, easing it shut with a protracted squeak.

"I'll have that greased for you."

"No, no. It has to be…" Ruth knelt by the door, laying her open palm against its smooth surface, running it down to the floor, from hinge to knob, inspecting it close, studying the grain. "It has to…"

"Uh," I paused, "what, '*has to,*' my lady?"

Ruth glanced over her shoulder, exasperated. "They *changed* the door." She gripped her lower lip, muttering to herself. "They must have. It looks the same, but…"

"Who … ah … *changed* the door?"

"I heard them last night. Scratching." Ruth shook her head and scoured the surface again. "Deep. Long. And I heard them creeping down the hall. So soft. So quiet." She tapped her ear. "But I heard."

"Who?"

"I ... I don't know." A facial tic distorted her face. "And I heard his voice again." She licked her cracked lips. "Last night. He was talking. Saying. I don't know what he was saying."

"You're not really narrowing it down."

"You don't believe me?"

"Was it von Madbury? Lady Mary said—"

"Von-*who?*" She grimaced, waving a hand, "I ... I don't know."

"Been getting any shut-eye, Ruth?"

"Admittedly, I ... I've had my difficulties." She bit her lip, nodding to herself, offering one last glare at the door. A glare full of venom. Of disgust. Betrayal. "Forget the door. Forget it. The door's not important." She reached beneath her shawl. "Here. It's for you."

"It...?" I half-expected a shank to the gut.

Clutched in Ruth's harpy claw was a letter. "It's addressed to you."

"From?" I took it.

"Someone placed it in our laundry." Ruth chewed her nails. "I don't know who. But your name's on it." She pointed, "There," and retracted her hand like I was a bear-trap set to make her Lady Mary's twin. "See?"

I flipped it over, waved it, half-bowed. "Many thanks."

As I turned to leave, her hand lit upon my elbow. "Sir Luther…"

I paused. "What is it?"

"They say there's a man in Haeskenburg who can heal the wounded." Ruth was wasted, shivering, looking worse than I felt. And I felt like hammered shit. "A man who can c-cure the sick. The afflicted. A man who might…" Her lips pursed hard, strangling her last words.

Shit. "You've been talking to Stephan, yeah?" The bastard had gone blabbing behind my back, hamstringing me with my debt to Abraham. Maybe I wouldn't kill the bastard Nazarene if he could cure Abe. That was the play, anyways.

"It matters not with whom I speak." Ruth rose up straight, trembling. "What matters is whether it is possible. Whether this story holds truth? Please, Sir Luther, I beg of you, tell me. Is there such a man?"

"Truth's not always cut and dry."

"I don't know what that means. It sounds like waffling. Like obfuscation. It sounds like prevarication."

"I don't know what any of those words mean, though I am partial to waffles."

Her eyes blazed. "Is there a man in this town with a gift for healing?"

I took a breath. Bloody fucking Stephan. "At the old church, I saw something I can't explain. We all saw it." I laid a hand on the door. "A miracle? Black magic? Trickery? I don't know."

"Tell me what you saw."

So I told her.

Tears welled up in her eyes. "A man who can draw back the caul of death."

"Even if that's what I saw, he's *allegedly* a Christian, and you—"

"Are merely a Jew. Yes. Thank you for clearing that up. Be that as it may, do you think — is it possible he could cast away Abraham's sickness?" Ruth snatched at my arm with raptor talons. "Is it possible?"

"I don't know." I raised my hands. "Honestly." I peeled her fingers off my arm, firmly, gently. They felt like dried twigs. "I think it unlikely."

"Unlikely, yes. But, do you believe," she foundered on a jagged shoal of hope, "it might be possible?"

"I don't know, my lady." Not after I bash in his skull. "He's gone to ground." Slit his throat. "He's a scourger." Cut off his bloody head. "A *Christian* scourger." I let that sink in, fester, spread.

"And you're a Christian, yes?" Ruth sneered. "A Christian who owes me. Owes Abraham. Owes us everything, might I remind you?"

"No need."

"Then do what you can. Do it soon. Do it now."

"Sure." I nodded curtly. "What I can…"

Her eyes narrowed. "And bring us a bible."

"I brought one."

"No. A New Testament. A Christian Bible."

"Shh…" I finger to my lips as glanced down the hallway. "Loose lips, my lady."

"Such a comfort. Knowing only the aegis of ignorance lies between our survival and utter demise."

"They won't know," I lied.

"And if they do?"

"I'll handle it."

She eyed me balefully then offered a nod. "If a Christian could perform miracles on behalf of a Jew, would he?"

"I suppose there's a first for everything." I turned the letter over as Ruth closed the door.

There was no imprint in the wax seal other than an indent from someone's thumb. The poor man's seal. I waited til Ruth'd gone back to her personal Purgatory, if that was a

Jewish thing, before I cracked it open. It was short. Sweet. Written in a hand that was either a child's or someone just learning to write. It specified a place and a time. No wasted effort: *Courtyard. Tent City. Noon. Alone.*

"What does it say?" Lady Mary closed the door behind.

"It's from the King," I whispered behind a raised hand. "He thinks I'm *very* handsome." I fanned myself. "Oh lord, whatever shall I do?"

"Sure it's not from the Queen?" Lady Mary sneered.

"Jesus," I sniffed, "you snuff the fun out of everything."

"Fun?" she deadpanned. "Here? Seriously?"

"And what about you?"

"What about me?" Lady Mary crossed her arms daring me to speak.

"You and the handsome, young, eligible Prince Eventine," I said. "Play your cards right and you could be queen someday. This," I raised my hand and slathered it across an imaginary horizon, "could all be yours."

"You heard me." Lady Mary frowned. "The first convent. The *very* first."

"Right," I said. "Just go easy on Stephan when the time comes, eh?"

Lady Mary bit something back.

"Apologies." I folded the note, tucked it away. "I'll be on my—"

"Wait — Sir Luther. Please." She leaned in, voice low, "What does it say?"

"It's a meeting. Soon. Why?"

"Fine." Through pursed lips, she carried on. "It's Ruth, she—"

"Looks like shit? Worse than her husband? Her *dying* husband."

"She gives her share of food to her children and Abraham."

"Want me to force-feed her? I'm sure that'd win her over."

"Unlikely." Lady Mary shook her head. "That ship has sailed, I think."

"Yeah. Right to the bottom of the river." I turned to leave. "She asked me for a bible. I'll get her one. And whatever extra food I can. If there's any."

"Alright."

"If there's nothing else…?" I asked. "I've a pressing engagement."

"For what?" She glanced down again at the letter.

"Probably to get murdered, why?"

"I thought if anything might jog Ruth from her stupor, it would be the children. Perhaps if something could bolster their spirits, she might be bolstered, as well. Your idea with the books. It was thoughtful. If you could gather more?"

"Why not ask yourself? Pull some strings with Eventine? I'm sure he'd help."

"I'm afraid to leave Ruth, is all." Lady Mary glanced over her shoulder. "She … she's so far away right now. Please…"

"Alright," I said. "I'll think of something."

"Wait." She laid a hand on my shoulder. "And watch yourself."

I paused. "Are you in love with me, my lady?"

"What?" She retracted her hand. "*Judas Priest*, no. I'm concerned."

"Concerned about your burgeoning feelings for me?"

"No." She scowled, wiping her hand on her skirt. "I'm concerned you might get murdered and leave us all in the lurch."

"Well, I guess that's a start. Here." I handed her the letter. "Burn it after you read it. And if I do turn up murdered or missing or worse, tell Karl. He'll probably throw a party."

Chapter 24.

I SWALLOWED as I slid alone through the labyrinth of cool shadow of the Schloss's refugee camp. Canvas walls rose all around, filtering the sounds but not stink of humanity. Stephan was nowhere to be found. Would've been a boon to have him jawing at my side, the word of the Lord and all, but then again, with his altered promises on Sir Gustav's lashing, I wasn't sure how solid his footing was with the locals. And the note had said to come alone.

So I looked around.

A fine place for an ambush. Couple fellas scheming in concert? Standing behind cloth walls? Brandishing daggers? Even in broad daylight, it'd be a simple thing surprising a bloke, knifing him, muscling him gagging back into oblivion. Might only take a second. They had the forethought to bring a shovel and they wouldn't need even to lug him. Do some digging out of the sun and shine, a little sweating, a little swearing. Have a nice patch of green come mid-summer and none the wiser.

Nonetheless, I slid further into its midst, gripping my dagger, watching, waiting, wary. The Schloss loomed above, crooked as an old miner's spine. Dozens of black windows glared down, any one of which might hold unfriendly eyes. The ever-present clack and clatter of war-training in the yard staccatoed the air. Von Madbury and Gustav, training up some press-ganged recruits.

Muffled behind the stretch of canvas, voices muttered low all around, occult, oblique, unintelligible.

I slid further in, stepping carefully over a guy line, ducking another, moving behind one of the taller tents, a sodden affair, masking me from the Schloss but leaving me fair exposed to anyone atop the walls. I glared up. The fella manning the gate tower, Taran, had his feet propped up and head down and was earning his keep the old-fashioned way, hoping no one noticed him shirking duty.

Someone behind cleared their throat.

I stiffened, waiting on a knife thrust. A quick punch to the kidney. The spine. A rip across the neck. When none came, I turned, forced a breath, then another, could still feel Rudiger's arms constricting my chest, crushing me down, helpless, weak, small.

"Anyone see you come?" a man, not more than a shadow, asked from inside the slit-door of a tent.

"No," I lied. The whole bloody castle might've seen me, but it's always best to start off with your best foot forward and mine was lying rotten through my teeth. "Took the long way." I pointed off. Somewhere. "Round the stables, kept to the wall, the shadows under the walk." I raised an eyebrow up at Taran. "Sleeping Beauty's sawing wood."

Shadow shifted, hovering just out of sight. "Can hear him from here."

"Can hardly blame him." I mindfully released the grip of my dagger, finger by finger squealing in rusty protest, let my arm hang loose, natural, ready. "Exhausting work. Obviously." I glanced around. Nothing but tents as far as the eye could see. "You coming out? Want me to come in?"

Shadow sniffed, shifted, considered. "Naw. Best we both stay put."

"You don't trust me."

"No."

"You ain't stupid. Good." Someone inside the tent at my back shifted, the zip of something dragging lightly across fabric. It could have been a blackguard aiming a crossbow at my spine. Could've been some poniard-wielding bugger looking to add some murder-holes to my kidneys. Or it could've been some young maid suckling her young. "What is it you want?"

"You seem a good chap," Shadow said, "for a knight."

"And you seem quite the handsome fellow," I said, "for a shadow."

"Huh?"

"Forget it," I breathed. "So why is it you think I'm so good?"

"Saw you last week with your brother, at the scourging. Standing up to them. And then helping out Lianna the other day."

"Lianna…?" I drew a blank.

"Young girl. Blondish. Pretty. Was hoofing it across the yard when that one-eyed son of a bitch took notice. Could tell he was set on taking more."

I shrugged. "Anything to blacken his eye."

"The man's filth. Or worse…"

"They say you can *always* judge a book by its cover."

"That what they say?"

"No. But screw them, it's true. Mostly. What is it you want?"

"To help you."

"Truly? Got a ship I can borrow? A horse that can hoof it through the swamps? Over the pass?"

"Huh? What?"

"Whiskey, then?"

"No." Shadow paused, shifted, gathering himself. "You know about Husk?"

"I'm learning," I said.

"They say you're one of them fellas what went hunting for the murderer up the old keep."

"Yeah. Sure." My hand had found my dagger again, all of its own accord. "Rudiger."

"Rudiger, eh?" Shadow said. "That what he's calling his self nowadays?"

"Was."

"Huh?"

"He's dead."

"Oh, aye? How?"

"Running with scissors," I explained. "Should've listened to his mother."

"You sure?"

"Sir Alaric gutted him," I said. "So, yeah, fairly sure."

Shadow considered. "He been disappearing folk up there some time." The man chuffed a cold laugh.

"What's funny?"

"*Up there* sounds like it's only up at the old keep."

"Yeah?" I sniffed. "So what's that mean? So what?"

"Been folk disappeared all around."

"The Grey-Lark Forest camp. Yeah. I heard. We're looking into it."

"Was one last night, too. Here."

"Here?" I looked around at the riot of tents. "You sure?"

"Aye. Happened a couple tents away. Young fella. Name of Crispin."

"Crispin?" Jesus. "Anyone know?"

"You do."

"Anyone with teeth?"

"You're a knight. You've teeth."

"I'm naught but a trumped-up hedge knight wallowing on sabbatical. Sir Alaric's leading the glorious charge. Why not bark up his tree?"

"Twenty years ago? Well, mayhap. Aye." Shadow drew in a long breath. "Nowadays? Man's a drunken old sot."

"Easy. That's what I'm aiming to be someday."

"How about my brother?" I glanced around. "He's living here. Somewhere."

"After what happened with Sir Gustav?" He snorted. "Or *didn't*, I should say. Anyways. You know about this … this Rudiger?"

"Sure. See him nowadays, he's leaking like sieve."

"Mayhap not so much as you think."

"Oh?"

"I see'd him yesterday, glooming down round his old haunt, the big lumber mill off Archer. On the Tooth."

"What were you doing down there?"

"Taking shit that wasn't mine. Anything useful I could lay hands on. Stealing. Surviving. Starving. Like everyone else round here."

"Couldn't have been him."

"Except it were."

I licked my lips. "Convince me."

"I see'd him up at the old keep a few weeks past, too. Why me and mine left it. Came here. And I recognized him, only … only Rudiger weren't his name back when I knew him. From afore. Last summer. Name when I knew him was Crennick. And aye, I'll never forget his cursed face."

"Yeah? Why's that?"

"He was murdering back then, too. Year back, come summer. It were my niece he done killed. Elouise. A winsome lass. It were … a bloody thing. A bloody, awful thing." His voice cracked, and he took a moment to regroup. "T-T'was your man hunted Rudiger down and brought him in."

"My man?" I started. "Red, you mean? Sir Alaric?"

"Aye. Him."

I straightened as though from a blow. "You absolutely sure?"

"Aye. Sure. For certain. He and Brother Miles frog-marched him in. Half the folk down on the Tooth seen it happen. I was one." But a stone's throw from where hanging priests was suddenly all the rage. "Days later, manacled and busted to shit, King and company walk-o'-shamed him on past half the town. Up the road to the old keep. Folks cheering the whole way. I was one."

"So what happened?" I asked. "Slap on the wrist? King Eckhardt's a mite soft for a king maybe," I looked around, "but even he'd drop the hammer on a child-killer."

A breeze kicked the tent door almost open. "Word was ole' King Eckhardt had him done in." He made the noise people make when they draw an imaginary knife across their throat.

"Public execution?"

"Execution, aye, but not public. No one seen it happen."

"Seems like a complete waste of gory spectacle."

"Way it's done round here now. Didn't used to be. No sir. Used to be they breaked 'em on the wheel. Left 'em to the crows and rot."

"Ah, the good old days."

Shadow said nothing.

I could hear him breathing. "Any idea what they do to them now?"

"King beheads 'em up at the old keep. The old gaol.

Him and that one-eyed prick. Gustav, too, sometimes. Down in a tunnel."

"Really…?" I frowned. "Alright. Well, factoring in the obvious, if what you say's true, he didn't execute Rudiger. Or Crennick. Or whoever he is." I scratched my beard. "So he must've escaped."

"Sure. Must've."

"And you saw him stalking around down the Tooth. The big lumber mill, yeah? Yesterday?" I squinted into the dark. "You weren't all fucked-up drinking?" I asked cause I wasn't sold. Well, it was cause I was an asshole, *and* I wasn't sold, but it was also cause eye-witnesses were about as useful as tits on a windmill.

"No, sir." Shadow put his fist to his chest. "Ain't had nothing to drink."

"You'd stake your life on it?"

"I'd stake my life, my body, my soul."

"Then show me your face," I said.

For a moment, I thought we were done. Thought maybe he'd bolt out the tent's arse end. But he drew the flap back. "Lianna's father," I said. It was a guess, but a fair-good one. He had her hair color, her eyes, her features. Though they looked a fair sight better on her.

"Aye."

"What's your name?"

"Giles."

"I told you, Giles, Sir Alaric punched him in to the hilt." I patted Yolanda. "Through and through. Think anyone could shake that off?"

In my mind's eye, the Nazarene grimaced as he slipped his hand inside Lazarus's dead flesh, groping around in the warm wet red til his fat fingers found the bolt-head skewered through layers of skin and fat, through cage-bars of bone, lodged solid in dense heart muscle. And when he yanked it out, Lazarus opened his eyes and hollered to God.

"Don't seem he knows how to die," Giles said.

"He's an ignorant bastard, I'll grant you," I nodded, "but sometimes all it takes is a second lesson."

...Kragen's corpse was found buried within brush on the outskirts of the clan-holt. He'd been emasculated with one of the many tools we'd brought to win over their hearts and...
—War-Journal of Prince Ulrich of Haeskenburg

Chapter 25.

IT WAS A BIG BASTARD, there was no denying it.

"That's the one, yeah?" I glared at the mill laid out along the river like a dead giant.

"Whew…" Sir Alaric stopped, gripping his side, wincing. "By the hound." He didn't look so good. He was pale. Sweaty. Old. "Aye lad, that it is." He lifted an arm as though it were made of lead and pointed. "Down along yonder, the near side, might be best."

The mill itself was a beast. A rectangle-shaped footprint, walls of brick and mortar that went on for ages of eons.

"Shit," I commented, looking up at the wall, its sagging roof just visible in the dying twilight.

"Yar…" Karl unshouldered his axe.

"Hey Red," I fixed him the eye, "how about me and Karl do the heavy lifting on this one?"

"Truly lad," Sir Alaric chewed his pipe, "I ought go in with you."

"Fair enough. I'd just rather your dead-eye was out here." I patted Karl on the top of the head. "Have me and the troll play the hounds to your hunter." I pointed toward a row of derelict houses down the way, commanding a view of the mill's far side. "Flush the bastard out and right to you." I dusted off my hands. "Voilà."

Sir Alaric laid a hand on my shoulder, and mumbled,

"Thanks, lads." It was his turn to fix us both the eye, "You damn well watch yourselves," and ambled off into the dark.

"Well," I breathed away a sudden tightening in my chest, "no time like the present."

"Tomorrow'd work, too," Karl rumbled.

"Yeah. Hell. Next day might be even better."

But we both trudged forth.

The Abraxas flowed by, south to north, rippling along, its current unseen but still turning the enormous wheel set in the mill's side. Unseen gears rumbled the ground beneath our feet, massive drive-shafts of squared timber rotating, working reciprocating saws up and down and up. Mundane most days, but here, alone, amid a ghost town with naught but that occult rumble? Unsettling. Like God grumbling down from on high. Or something equally ungracious up from below.

But it'd cover our approach, so there was that.

The door looked to be of the fair-stout variety.

"You smell it?" Karl asked.

"Dribs. Drabs. But yeah." He was talking on the death-reek emanating from inside. I'd smelled it before Sir Alaric'd split. "You ready?"

"Yeah." I drew Yolanda. "Locked?"

Karl laid a paw on the doorknob, gave it a surreptitious twist, shook his head, *No*. Karl shouldered his axe.

"Wait." Deep breath. "Let me."

"You feelin' alright?"

"Blow me." I adjusted my shield. Having a half-inch of oak embossed with iron between me and this bastard seemed the height of sound reasoning. But I'd been wrong before. "I'm good."

Karl twisted the knob, and I shouldered through, shield leading, gut wrenching, Yolanda waiting in the wings.

The air was alive with the swirl of millstone dust and reciprocating saws. But that was all that was alive. The stench hit like a hammer. An abattoir stink. Fresh death. Blood and piss and shit. Lances of moonlight shone in through the high thin windows, knifing down, illuminating things best left unseen.

"Bloody hell…" I slid forth.

It was like the tunnel but worse. No old bones. Just … all fresh.

"Watch it." Karl kicked something aside that once was human.

"Yeah." I breathed through my mouth.

The mill was mostly empty space except for structural posts and the squared-timber machine shafts intruding from the riverside.

"Bloody beast is loud." Karl wriggled a finger in his ear.

"Yeah," I said but was fair sure he couldn't hear me.

A pair of crimson-stained millstones churned together in the center of the room, grinding along endlessly, rumbling, tumbling, rolling nowhere. Along the left side were the pounders. One after another they rose and fell, thud, thud, thud, slamming into a wood-slab. The right half of the mill was amassed with stacked barrels and crates. A fair few were busted open. I figured the rest for empty given the current economic climate. But you never know.

I lead on, my back to the left wall, ducking machinery, shield angled always toward the far gloom. Karl switched grips, stalking along behind.

I paused halfway down along the wall. "You hear it?"

"What?" Karl said.

"From outside." Something jarred against the regularity of the machinery.

I raised an eyebrow at the disengage lever along the wall.

Karl shook his head, *No.*

I nodded. Best not tip our hand. Any more than we already had.

Beyond the grind of millstone and river burble were voices. Many. Concerted. Chanting. *The scourgers,* I mouthed. A look to Karl's eyes and he kenned it, too.

"Let's get the hell out of here."

Ripping at his beard, scowling, Karl turned—

From beyond the churning millstones, a shadow broke, knocking over a barrel, bolting pell-mell for the far door.

"Oy!" Karl was on it instantly, me playing second hound, barking at his heels but gaining, my long shanks loping me onward, drawing even, passing him as the figure reached the far door. It was Rudiger. I could make out the empty socket, the gleam of skull where Karl'd shorn off half his face. How the hell—?

The chanting jogged something.

The Nazarene. He must've healed him. It had to be. They were in this together.

Whatever *this* was.

Nightmare teeth bared, Rudiger tore open the door and turned, ducking my cut by degrees and coiling to spring. Off-kilter, I righted, back-swung as his fist cracked my shield. The impact knocked me whirling back, but I spun, whipping out blindly, praying to Thor and Tyr and Jesus Christ, catching Rudiger below the shoulder. His grasping hand somersaulted high, a sordid sight, his eyes bulging incredulous wide.

Staggering back, Rudiger lurched for the open door, froze, and I caught him full bore in the chest with my shield, ramming him stumbling out into early dawn. His gore-stained claw scrabbled at the rim of my shield as I forced him back, driving him into the open, hooking one of his feet with my own, tripping him, sending him crashing to the mud.

But damn, was he fast.

On his arse in the mud, one limb missing, he sprang up almost before he'd touched. Yolanda poised from the roof to strike, he smashed into me, splitting my shield to kindling as I piled back, head smacking off the mill's titan-wall. Stars exploded. Gasping from my knees I jabbed, hoping for another blind miracle when the bastard rose up and swatted Yolanda flipping from my grip.

Disaster. Imminent.

I dove aside as a crossbow bolt zipped from somewhere, burying itself in Rudiger's back. He didn't even blink. His red eyes blazed as he grasped Yolanda. "Did you kill her?" His voice was a rasp.

"Huh—?" I scrabbled crab-wise back. "Who?"

Another bolt buried in his side.

"You…" Rudiger winced, stalking after me. "You should have."

Then he swung.

I flinched, raising my hands. Not much else to do with your arse in the mud, back against the wall, sword blaring for your head. Maybe lean into it, turn perpendicular, make it quick. Clean. Easy on the undertaker.

I'd have been dead but for Karl, charging through the door, catching Rudiger across the gut with a cut that would've given a seasoned oak a run for its money. Rudiger folded in half, a weird shrieking growl erupting as he twisted, tearing the thane-axe from Karl's fists and flinging him aside.

As Rudiger's corpse-blackened fingertips scrabbled at the axe, I staggered up and bashed him across the head with the remnants of my shield, dropping him to his knees. He turned, teeth gnashing as he dug at the embedded axe.

Fixated. I raised the shield again, overhead, two-handed and brought it down. *Smash!* Again. *Smash!* Again. *Smash!*

Rudiger gurgled something, a lone hand raised to ward off encroaching inevitability.

Staggering, I swatted his hand aside and slammed the shield down again across his skull.

Rudiger collapsed into the mud, forehead shattered inward, teeth missing, mewling like a half-drowned kitten.

My shield had shattered under the onslaught, only the central boss still intact, playing the knuckleduster, the rest either gone or hanging on by twisted splinter. Broken, beaten, dazed, I dropped to a knee in the mud, reaching for Yolanda.

Only then did I realize we were surrounded.

Chapter 26.

ACROSS THE ROAD, they waited. Between old mills, they watched, huddled shoulder to shoulder, a silent jury of a hundred, maybe more, some naked, some stripped to the waist, scrawls of scribbled scripture written in crusted blood, crowns of twisted thorn wrapped around skulls. Torches rippled in their mist. A denuded forest of crucifixes stood at their shoulders.

Central amongst them stood the Nazarene, his distended belly brown with grime and wiry hair. Over his shoulders, he bore a scourge, twisted leather thongs braided with jags of ragged glass and rusted iron.

Rudiger withdrew his hand, Yolanda in his fist, and aimed her point at the hollow of my throat.

I gripped the remnants of my shield.

"Here..." Rudiger's voice a sibilant slur of spit-shattered tooth. "Please..." He flipped Yolanda, catching her by the blade, proffering her hilt. "Take it."

"Come to me, brother!" The Nazarene bellowed.

I blinked.

He wasn't talking to me.

He was talking to Rudiger.

The Nazarene strode onward, Lazarus leering by his side, hunched like some under-stuffed puppet. Others followed, the whole lot of them, emerging from alleyways, down the street, coming out of the woodwork, clambering over walls, converging from on all quarters. And from somewhere unseen, the high-pitched ever-present squeal of the Tome-Bearer, the chants following his lead.

"End it." Karl drew a pair of hand axes.

"P-please…" Rudiger inched across the mud, prodding me with Yolanda's hilt, his breathing ragged, desperate, raw. The haft of Karl's thane-axe, its head still lodged in Rudiger's guts, cut a furrow through the muck.

Fear blazed in his eyes. An odd sight in this horrid thing once a man and now something more, something less, something different, something wrong. Hair drangled down, plastered across the denuded bone of his face, his lidless eye bloodshot, nestled in its socket. "Please," he grimaced, "*you* do it."

Casting the last of my shield aside, I snatched Yolanda and stepped back, raising her overhead, the executioner's stroke. I'd had enough practice, too much experience, and Yolanda's edge was so sharp.

"Stay your hand, brother!" the Nazarene bellowed.

"What are you?" I hissed.

What teeth Rudiger still had grated. "Do it!"

"Tell me," I said.

"I'm a dead man."

"No shit." My mind raced. "Who's the *she* you meant?"

"The Grey-Lady."

I adjusted my grip, licked my lips, swallowed. "And what'd she do?"

"Everything." His head fell as he wept, shoulders bobbing.

"Where is she?"

"Hiding. Somewhere." Rudiger sobbed. "Until the hunger takes her again. Now please—"

"Back off," Karl snarled, stepping between me and the horde. "Do it, lad."

Rudiger drooled pink foam. *"Please…"*

"Brother!"

I exhaled and swung, my arms lead and dropping, precise as an automaton's, no thought, no emotion, no wasted movement — s*chluck!* Rudiger's head plopped in the mud then so too did the rest of him.

The Nazarene halted shy of Rudiger's corpse, the cant of his jaw set in firm disapproval. "You need not have done that. I would have spared you the pain."

"Didn't feel a thing," I lied.

"The killing of a man burdens the soul of even the basest churl, brother."

"I ain't your brother. And I'm fair sure he wasn't a man."

The Nazarene studied me. "If not a man, then what?"

"How the hell should I know?"

"A rabid wolf to be put down?" The Nazarene's eyes narrowed. "Aye."

"You going to raise him like you did that leering pumpkin-headed fuck?" I sized up Lazarus. Getting killed hadn't improved his looks. Or health. Or demeanor.

"You cut off his head," the Nazarene explained.

"Yeah, well, sure…" I shrugged.

"He told the truth, though, it would seem." The Nazarene scratched his prominent belly. It was only now, up close, that I saw the constellation of star-shaped scars peppering his chest and abdomen, as though someone'd gutted him with a spear. Over and over. "A child of Cain. Of Lilith. Marked. Know you the book of Lilith?"

"Sure, my grandma used to read me bedtime stories from it."

"You jest of things best left unknown. Unsaid. Forgotten. Even so. She yet stalks this land." The Nazarene tugged on the handle and head of his flail, draped across his shoulders. "This was his lair?" He glanced at the mill building.

"Yeah. There were … I don't know." I rubbed my chest. "A lot inside."

"Bring out the dead, brothers!" the Nazarene bellowed. "Bring them all!"

Like a swarm of ants the horde streamed into the mill, piling in, body after body, fighting for purchase at the door. Others set about digging holes, scrabbling at the earth with bare hands, ripping at it with torn nails and bent, gnarly fingers.

"What are you going to do?" I gripped Yolanda.

"Shrive them. Consecrate them. Crucify them."

The brethren began emerging, fighting out the door as they had to get in. One bore an arm. Another a leg. A pair struggled with a torso.

The Nazarene turned. "Grant them absolution!"

I watched as those bearing crosses laid them in the street and pounded nails into the disparate parts. Tying off a leg here, an arm there, forming a man-shaped monstrosity. A man's head with another's torso, one arm a woman's, the other a child's. It might've been funny if it weren't so abominably fucking horrid.

"Yes! Yes!" The Nazarene's arms rose toward the sky. "Now raise them on high! Raise them up to the Lord!"

The brethren levered the crosses upright, setting the butt ends into holes.

"And now, he!" The Nazarene stepped back and the brethren swarmed over Rudiger's corpse, dragging it atop a hoary old crucifix. They set to pounding nails through his palms and feet, binding his hands with rope. One Jesus, a small wiry bloke with the forearms of a stonemason set to prying out Rudiger's teeth with a claw-hammer.

"Might be our best shot." Karl nodded at the Nazarene's exposed back.

I blinked, watching them hammer a stake through Rudiger's chest, pinning him to the cross. Karl wasn't wrong. It could be done. But with Lazarus and a horde of the others watching the Nazarene's back, watching us, closing in, salivating?

"We'd be next," I said, turning tail and hoofing it the hell out of there.

...convened before the entire contingent, the clan-holt elder accused Sir Kragen of taking liberties with the clan-holt slattern, bereft of her consent.
—*War-Journal of Prince Ulrich of Haeskenburg*

Chapter 27.

BY BOTH CUSTOM and law, the wine cellar was dark and dank and cold, my breath visible in the dim trickle of lantern light. Five long racks ran parallel, two along the walls, three down the middle. All bare. A few boxes of cheese and barrels marked 'poppy oil' stood stacked crooked in the corner. The cellar was larger than the keep warranted, but who was I to complain? About the emptiness, maybe, but there was a grand scheme I could only appreciate.

I knew someone was there before I turned. That feeling, that prickle of awareness dancing down my spine, tingling out to all quarters. Someone, standing there in the darkness, watching, waiting. But I needed a drink and so I bloody well took one.

Then I turned.

"Thirsty?" I offered the wine bottle. One of the last. Still young, untutored and raw, but it knew the trick. Slaying the nerves. Dulling the mind. Quashing the images, the visions. Visions of Rudiger, penitent in the muck, his teeth gleaming a jagged pink, rivulets of grey flesh dangling off.

A shadow stepped from between the racks. Von Madbury. I could tell by the way he was standing with that stick jammed so longitudinally up his arse. He stutter-stepped to a halt, stiffened, fixed his coat, if not his manners. "Krait."

"In the flesh." I could see him only in silhouette but knew he'd said my name with a sneer. Sometimes you can just hear it. Beyond, past the wine racks and crates, on the far wall, a stout, iron-banded door stood ajar. After a heartbeat, it slid shut surreptitiously as though by magic.

"Have you seen Sir Alaric?" I asked. In my mind's eye, I saw him off in the dark, wreathed in the fume of smoke and impotence and death, attempting his own liquid trick.

I took another swig, still trying to drown back those bloody teeth.

"Thieving from the stores?" von Madbury harrumphed at the bottle firmly entrenched in my fist. "Theft from here costs you a hand."

"Well, there goes my love-life." It wasn't true, I was near ambidextrous, but why sully a good jest with onerous facts?

"You're disgusting."

"Oh. Apologies." I laid a hand to my chest. "Didn't take you for the delicate type. Especially when your friend was scourging in that kid."

"It can always be arranged."

"Huh?" I straightened. "For me, you mean? Cause you weren't clear. Or I'm drunk. Or maybe both." I hefted the wine in salute. "Either way, I'll pass. Besides, it's all part of my contract with the King. *Imbibeture in perpetuity.* I believe that's the language devised and agreed upon."

"You're a liar."

"You got me." I waggled a finger. "But it sounds good if you aren't really listening, yeah?" I pointed towards the far door. "What's back there?"

Von Madbury puffed up his chest. "Nothing concerns you."

"Nothing?" I made a show of scratching my head. "Why

go through all the trouble of putting a big bloody door there for nothing?"

"The dungeon," von Madbury flexed his hands open and closed, "and oubliettes."

"Oh?" I rubbed my belly and took a step. "I could do with a piss."

"Piss upstairs." Von Madbury shifted, blocking in my path.

"Keep a fastidious dungeon, eh?"

"Go piss somewhere else."

"Where?"

"Anywhere not here."

I pointed toward the door. "But I want to piss *there.*"

Von Madbury reached surreptitiously behind his back. Just not *surreptitiously* enough. Tough doing anything on the sly with a word that big.

"Whoa." I stepped back, hands raised. A funny thing it is, being a prick. Sometimes you don't want trouble, aren't fit for it, like me, like then, with Rudiger's teeth burning foremost in my mind, but you get into rhythms in life and do things by rote, like poking the bear, cause it's just what you do. "Who's back there?"

His lips pursed. "No one."

"Your trousers are undone." I pointed with the arse-end of the bottle. "Can see your ties dangling from here."

Von Madbury stiffened, wanting to look, to check, but knew he'd already tipped his hand.

"So…?" I cocked my head. "You marched down in the mid of night just to rub one out?"

His teeth ground together, muscles in his jaw working double-time.

"I admire your dedication." I made a show of glancing around. "Clomping all the way down here. Some privacy, I suppose." I rubbed my arms, bouncing on the balls of my feet. "A little cold, though, yeah?"

He tensed to lunge, draw his dagger, murder me in the dark.

"And the larder?" I waggled a finger. "I thought that soup tasted off. But to each his own. I knew a fella one time, an archer out of York, short fella, no front teeth, couldn't consummate the act unless he had his pet dog, name was Rufus — or was that the archer…?"

Von Madbury let his dagger hang behind him where I couldn't see. But I knew he'd drawn it cause so had I. And he'd seen it, too.

Question was, did either of us want to die down here?

Cause it was fair likely. A dagger duel? Down here? Drunk? Jesus. Everyone's growing holes. And then some. "Mayhap it's that whore you brought along with you?" Von Madbury puffed up, scowling, liking the sound of his own voice.

"Karl, you mean?"

But von Madbury hadn't heard me, and if he had, he kept right on at it. "Your sweet lady. Mayhap she's in there now, begging for it. Aching for it."

"You ain't her type."

"Oh, I'm a fit for all types."

"Yeah. You've a real way with women." I gripped my dagger. "And I hear you sniffing around again and the only thing you'll be a fit for's a hole in the ground."

"Tough talk." Von Madbury took a step forward.

And so did I.

"Dietrick, please…" came a muffled voice from the darkness beyond the dungeon-door.

Von Madbury paused.

I squinted past.

The door stood ajar.

"You in there," I called. "You want to walk out of there and not have to do anything you've no mind doing, come on out. I'll stand by you."

Von Madbury drew a sharp breath, stiffening, but didn't turn.

"No. I … I'm alright." The door didn't open.

I stood there, dagger point aimed at von Madbury's lone eye. "You heard what I said."

Von Madbury stood there seething as I backed out.

Near the top of the stairs, I found a sliver of dark to hunker in and waited, watching mute and motionless as one of Sir Alaric's portraits. Not long later, von Madbury emerged from the stairwell. And, not surprisingly, so too did the maid, though she looked an awful lot like the Queen.

...the accusation doubtless was true, indeed, for I had witnessed the deed.

Yet Sir Kragen was a knight, and she but a God-less savage, so I amended my testimony accordingly...

—*War-Journal of Prince Ulrich of Haeskenburg*

Chapter 28.

SIR LUTHER?" Prince Palatine glanced up as I poked my head into the library. "Oh, hello." It was a long thin room, practically a hallway, with barely enough space for the bookshelf let alone table. A book lay in the Prince's lap, his deformed hand steadying it, the other poised carefully, mid-turn of a page.

"My Prince." I offered a brusque bow. "Have you seen Sir Alaric?"

"No, I've not." Prince Palatine marked his page and closed the book, wincing as he readjusted himself in his high-backed chair. "Is everything alright? I ... I had heard there were more killings." He crossed himself.

"Yeah. The Carvers. Family of squatters down on Pine Street. We're heading out as soon as we get our shit together." It'd been days since we'd heeled Rudiger. Seven days of hoping there'd be no more disappearances. No more killings.

A forlorn hope, it turned out. A vagabond had been found strewn across an old abandoned wood-shop. Two more on top of those searching derelict buildings across Husk. Two days of following and in turn dodging the Nazarene and his madmen. Two days of fumbling. Two days of failure. But then, I was an old hand at failure and could pull a week's worth of it standing on my head. "Sorry to bother you." I turned.

"Wait. Please. Sir Luther—" Prince Palatine struggled to stand, his useless chicken-wing arm folded awkwardly across his midsection. I caught myself staring as he unconsciously worked down his sleeve. "I-Is there anything I could do to help?"

"Sorry, kid." I shook my head. "I don't think so."

"Oh…" Prince Palatine settled back, crestfallen, and gazed out the window. "Alright."

I paused at the door. "Well, actually, if there's any books you've got that the kids might like that you could part with for a stretch…? I, uh, borrowed *Sir Gawain* and *The Canterbury Tales* for them. A few others, too." I ran a hand through my hair. "Hope you don't mind. I can get them back to you if—"

"Oh no, it's my pleasure." Prince Palatine straightened. "I'm glad to share my meager store. And *Sir Gawain* is a wonderful tale. One of my — wait. *The Canterbury Tales?*"

"Uh … yeah."

"Sir Luther," Prince Palatine pursed his lips, "I'm afraid *The Canterbury Tales* are not wholly appropriate fare for young and impressionable—"

"Yeah… Yeah, I know." I'd groveled like a swatted dog when Lady Mary'd blasted me over *The Miller's Tale.* She'd had to do some crude quick-stitch tailoring to patch the tears she'd made over the truly prurient parts. Which were also the best. "Got anything that doesn't involve fornicating in trees? Or bare-arsed Frenching? Something with pictures?" I scanned the bookshelves. "Hmm…?"

Prince Palatine wrestled himself out of the chair. *"Piers Plowman* is measured, staid. Fertile soil for young minds."

"With all due respect," I waved a hand, *"Piers Plowman* sucks balls."

The Prince stifled a smirk. "Hah… Yes, well, quite right. I suppose I can but only agree. My mother made me read it when I was young. I suppose I equated it to some form of torture at the time. Now … what would I have wanted to read?" Prince Palatine rubbed his chin. "Hmmm? Something with action, perhaps? Adventure? Dashing heroics?"

"Now you're talking."

"Here." Prince Palatine angled awkwardly up on tiptoe, reaching, wincing, and wiggled out a book, inch by inch, til it fell and he caught it in the crook of his bad arm. "How about this?" He held it up, waggling it. *"The Song of Roland."*

"A personal favorite." I took it, patted the cover, cracked it open, taking in the glorious illuminations of armored knights going toe-to-toe with the Saracen menace. "Thanks."

"You're most welcome." The Prince grimaced as he settled back into his chair, willing his body to bend.

"What are you reading?"

"Oh." Prince Palatine lifted his book, exposing the spine. "Ockham. William."

"Ockham?" I rolled my eyes. "Jesus."

"You've read him?" Prince Palatine smirked.

"Talk about torture," I scowled. "I'd rather slit my wrists than suffer through his razor. It'd be more humane. Quicker, too."

"I don't know…" Prince Palatine shrugged awkwardly. "He speaks to me. Less is more. A crystalized simplicity lying unimpeachable at the heart of all things." He smoothed his hair and glanced out over the breaking-wheel. "Besides, it's quiet at night. Quiet and peaceful."

"No jackasses in the lists smashing the bag out of each other?"

"Yes," Prince Palatine smiled, shaking his head, "something to that effect."

I nodded up to the stacks. "You've a fair collection for a small town."

"Merchants know I'll pay good coin for any books traveling up and down the river." Palatine laid a hand on the book's cover. "Books about anything. Adventures. Stories. Histories. Anything and everything."

"No clear preference?"

"Preference? Escape is my preference." Palatine held out a hand. "Escape from all this. All … them."

"You should try whiskey," I said. "It's less effort. Less time-consuming. And Ockham'll tie your brain in knots."

"And whiskey shall untie them?"

"No," my fingers flitted off toward the stars, "it'll just melt them away."

"Sir Luther, forgive me but…" Prince Palatine pressed his lips together, "I … I think you should stride with care. I mean with von Madbury. Sir Gustav. Along with the whole cohort. There's been talk."

"They've done more than talk, kid," I said.

"Ah, the church incident, yes. Forgive me. I meant simply that I've heard recent rumblings."

"They scheming out in broad daylight now?"

"Nay." Prince Palatine shook his head. "But we cripples along with children and the mentally bereft share the ignominious trait that men will divulge their darkest plots in their company and believe them blind. Or deaf. Or dumb. Please, watch you back."

"I appreciate the advice," I said. "And I might offer you the same? That song you concocted at dinner? Like to get a man's throat cut."

"Song? Nay." Prince Palatine winced. "But a few rough-hewn stanzas. Von Madbury doesn't warrant the time and effort a full piece would require. Half-arsed jibes, though? Certainly."

"Fair enough."

"Besides, I can handle von Madbury in my own *crippled* way."

"Apologies." I raised both hands. "Sure you can."

"My infirmity is my aegis, you understand? A strange dichotomy. Not one to be admired or sung dirges of, but proof against poison, as it were." Prince Palatine grimaced. "And in any case, I don't fear death, Sir Luther." He patted his bad arm. "How can I fear death when life is so cruel? So abominably unfair. Did you know," he laughed, "there are rumors that I was the firstborn?"

"Yeah. Sure. I've heard it."

Palatine frowned. "I queried Mother about it once."

"And what'd she say?"

"Nothing. But her silence was deafening," Palatine sighed. "I suppose it was correct. The image of a crippled king having a fit? Soiling himself in front of his entire court? Too low a bar set even for Haeskenburg." He adjusted his crippled arm. "Lord. The small places of the world."

"Not much difference anywhere, kid, truth be told."

"Well, I wouldn't know." Prince Palatine frowned.

"Most places are small at heart. Shitty. Self-serving. Like most of the people. You find someone who thinks otherwise, some idealistic prick believes in the inherent goodness of man, run the other way."

Palatine squinted up. "You mean someone like your brother?"

"Yeah. Exactly like my brother."

"He's brave, though, is he not?"

"Stupid would be my word."

"He, too, is crippled and yet fears no retribution." Prince Palatine sighed. "He stood up to Sir Gustav that first night. I saw him from this very window. I admire him for that. For dwelling amongst them. I admire him for trying."

"Everyone does."

"But not you?"

"No. I do, too. But I'm close enough to see the cracks in the foundation holding up the ivory statue."

"Sir Luther," Prince Palatine's eyes narrowed, "I wonder what it is precisely that you're doing here?"

I scratched my head. "I'm working for Sir Alaric and your—"

"That's not what I mean. You're a stranger, an interloper some would say, from a far land yet poised to strike out again, tonight, risking your life on account of what? Honor? Justice? The good folk of Haeskenburg?"

"Jesus, no." I picked a book up from off the table, *The Ecclesiastical History of the English People.* "Coin. This is straight up mercenary work. Anyways, you asked before if there was anything you could do to help."

Prince Palatine's eyes grew wide. "Yes?"

"Any other histories?" I patted the book. "Something local? Something that might … I don't know, offer some insight. Anything into what's going on?"

"You mean the deaths? The disappearances?"

"Yeah."

"Hmm…" Prince Palatine squinted up at the stacks, his lips moving as he read through titles. "I know every book here, Sir Luther. And there's nothing that comes to mind. Haeskenburg seems never to have warranted any in-depth study. Unsurprisingly. But I shall endeavor to ask around.

217.

Perhaps Father Gregorius has some occult tome buried away in a dank cellar."

"Thanks, kid." I turned to leave.

"Sir Luther, I … I heard you were the one that killed that Rudiger fellow?"

"Yeah, well, he needed a little killing."

"And … what does that feel like?" Palatine massaged his neck. "Killing someone?"

"Hmm." I shook my head. "Can be the best damn feeling in the world. Or it can be like a long, protracted kick to the gut. Like you've been hit so hard everything inside's just … hammered up all broken into your throat. All coarse and jagged and off-kilter. Like you're always on the verge of puking it up. Shards of bone and warm wet red. Can't breathe for holding it back. Holding it down. Holding it in." I rubbed my throat. "It's usually the latter."

"That sounds awful."

"Yeah."

"But, what if they don't warrant it?"

"Who we talking about?" I fixed him through one eye.

"Whoever it is you're hunting." Prince Palatine shrugged unevenly.

"It's an *execution* when the King sanctions it. And once he sanctions it?" I shrugged. "They warrant it."

"I always imagined laws were to protect people."

"Sure. They protect the folk who make them. And the threat of violence lies stark and naked behind every law, every edict, every writ ever conceived and brought to fruition by the will of man. To suspect otherwise? Folly."

"And you think that's enough? That's sufficient cause to act as judge, jury, executioner?"

"As long as I don't think on it too hard."

"Forgive me, but that smacks of shoddy reasoning."

"That's generous, calling it *reasoning*."

"But you're a justiciar."

"A while back I was. Sure. But now?" I shrugged. What the hell was I? An attack dog. At best. And at worst…?

"Well, surely you must hold some opinion in matters of—"

"Rudiger was a murderer. He had to die. That's my opinion. The Nazarene's the same. End of story."

"And this Grey-Lady?"

"Myth, local legend, folk tale," I said. "And I'll find her or I won't."

"How do you know the Nazarene deserves to die?"

"Your father says he does."

"And one man's opinion is enough?" Prince Palatine stared at me a moment, focusing hard as though my edges were getting fuzzy.

"I'm just a hedge knight, kid. I do what I'm told."

...Hochmeister Gaunt and a clan-holt elder, a monstrous stoop-shouldered brute named Arboleth, argued the impromptu trial's verdict. The Hochmeister demanded the bitch's head on a pike while the elder demanded the Teutonic contingent depart in short shrift...
—*War-Journal of Prince Ulrich of Haeskenburg*

Chapter 29.

WE'D COME at the bitch sideways. The slow way. The smart way. Sneaking like rats up the back alley, skittering in through the shattered back door. Was a fair-good thing, too. For us. The front door slammed open and a horde of footsteps pounded out and away. Company. Just leaving. And not the kind you sip tea with.

I stepped through the kitchen carefully, gingerly, tiptoeing over the corpses. The scourgers had descended like locusts en masse on the joint. The floor was spattered with a collage of bare footprints coming in from every which way. Every door, every crevice, every window. Handprints slathered across the walls like some pagan temple.

Bloody. Muddy. Bad.

I paused by a window, Yolanda in hand, balanced, poised, reassuring against all the clandestine fuckery the world has to offer. Above, wood planks creaked under Karl's delicate tread. The troll could be fair quiet when it suited him. The front door hung open, nigh on off its hinges, twitching back and forth, creaking in the breeze.

Out on Pine Street, a woman's screams devolved from slurred gurgle to hideous giggling laughter.

A cold sweat seized me along with that iron band bound across my chest, contracting, squeezing, crushing. I stood in the cold, wreathed in darkness, watching, part of me incensed, the other part — the smarter part, the honest part — grateful. Grateful I was in here and she out there.

Torch flames and chants led by the ragged Tome-Bearer all played to the overarching beat of scourge castigating flesh. The Nazarene's scourgers holding court under the sable arch of night.

I took a knee by the window.

Stephan and Sir Alaric crept in. They'd seen the corpses in the kitchen. The Carver family. How could you miss them? A father, a mother, the little girl. All ruined. Ravaged. Raw.

"Shhh…" I laid a finger to my lips, cocked my head toward the window. "We missed the party." And by *party*, I meant the complete opposite. "Watch your step." I glared down at a young scourger, peach fuzz spotted across his cheeks, leveled outside the kitchen door, his eyes gone, throat ripped out, mouth gaping frozen mid-scream, silent echoes ripping through my mind. *Deep breath…* His lash lay in a coagulated tangle matted across his smooth chest, steam still rising from his blood.

"Rose of Sharon…" Crossing himself, Stephan gaped outside. "Good Lord."

"*Two* half-assed curses?" I scowled.

Sir Alaric steadied himself against the wall, huffing. "What's the word?"

"Word is we're too late."

He pointed toward the window. "Meant out there."

"Yeah. There, too."

The woman screamed again.

"It her?" Sir Alaric pushed upright off the wall and brandishing his sword, swearing through his teeth.

"Fair sure." I watched on.

By torchlight, the horde chanted, more pouring down the road, a serpent of flame and fury, rounding up like a vortex in the square, forming a human redoubt. Bodies jostling, flesh red-raw from lesion and lash and who-the-hell-knew-what-else? Bare feet splashed through slush and puddle. In their midst crouched a woman. Maybe. Teeth bared, hissing like a cornered plague rat, she turned, the side of her face yet untouched illuminated by caustic moonlight. She'd been beautiful once.

A lull in the chanting left the unsettling sound of the woman's broken laughter echoing across the street.

Sir Alaric snatched a peek out the window. *"By the hound—"* He gripped the sill and made to clamber out.

Grunting, I caught him, stiff-arming him off-balance against the wall, hissing, "Stand. The fuck. Down."

"Brothe—" Stephan gripped my shoulder.

"Rrrrg... He's gonna ... get us killed." I shrugged Stephan's hand off, still throttling Sir Alaric. "Take a bloody look. Close. Hard."

A faint hiss, Stephan's intake, as he focused, as he saw.

The woman should've been dead. Dead, and then some. Her back'd been scourged asunder, lash marks crisscrossing from neck to legs. But that was nothing. One of her arms was bone from shoulder to elbow, flesh rolled down like loose hose. The left side of her head was stove in like a broken eggshell. The scourger limp in her grasp should've been dead, too. He at least had the good grace to have his bags packed and one foot up on the wagon. Limp as a drowned kitten, he lay sprawled across the road, twitching, head twisted nigh on full around, neck wrung like a Beltane goose.

"Back, you godless fiend!" a scourger jabbed with a lowered pike.

Hissing, the woman, the thing, the Grey-Lady, ripped the fallen scourger's head up, exposing his throat, her nightmare teeth bared black with blood. As she bit down, Lazarus stepped in, ripping his lash across her face.

"Lou, ease up," Stephan hissed, "you're killing him."

I froze, barely, willfully, incrementally. Sir Alaric's face was purple.

I shoved him back.

Rubbing his neck, rasping breaths, eyes bulging and teeth bared anew, Sir Alaric tottered for his fallen sword.

I laid a hand to his shoulder, *"Quiet*—" and he swatted my hand and belted me. His hooking fist crashed off my temple, and I should've dropped but didn't, so I struck back, a quick right cross to the chin, dropping him solid.

"What in the Lord's name—" Stephan hissed, catching the old man, cradling him comatose to the floor.

"Shit…" I rubbed my knuckles.

The Grey-Lady cast the carcass aside and sprang like a hell-cat at Lazarus. Pike lowered, another scourger stepped in, catching her through the midsection, skewering her through and through. It barely slowed her. Up the pike, she clambered, hand over hand, nails biting into wood, pulling it through her, scrabbling toward the beleaguered scourger, still holding on, too scared, too shocked, too frozen to let go as the Grey-Lady's clawed hand buried into his mouth, grabbing his chin, rip-twisting it to shard.

"Fiend!" Lazarus lashed out.

Others barrel-assed in, jabbing with pikes. Lazarus raised his lash and brought it down across the she-demon's back. Her neck. Her head. Grimacing pink, she dodged a lash and lunged forth quick as an asp, wood splintering, pike-heads snapping off, taking Lazarus in the chest and off his feet, pinning him to the mud by his throat.

"Easy, Red." Stephan covered Sir Alaric's gibbering mouth. "Shh… Easy. Relax—"

"Please—" Sir Alaric gurgled.

"Quiet." I pinned him down.

"Brother," Stephan reached out reflexively, "ease up."

"Then keep him bloody quiet." I let go and Sir Alaric gasped.

Stephan spoke low in his ear, Sir Alaric's eyes welling, wide, far-seeing.

"Sister!" boomed a voice from beyond the torchlight. From the serpent of torch-fire winding up the road, the Nazarene strode forth, a massive crucifix borne across his broad shoulders. "Release him!"

The Grey-Lady froze, poised like a hunted lioness, glaring back. Viscera dangled from a wound in her abdomen, fouling what was left of the tattered rags that once upon a time had been a noble woman's finery.

"Jesus Christ—" I sheathed Yolanda, unslung my crossbow.

Stephan glared up. "What?"

I shoved a foot in the crossbow's stirrup and drew the string back. "Show's on."

"Her end is foregone." Stephan stared off in horror. "There'll be no final acts of mercy."

"Ain't jawing about *her*." I set a bolt in the crossbow's groove. It was a flesh arrow, wide and barbed and merciless sharp. There'd be no digging the fucker free.

"A pyre, my brothers!" the Nazarene bellowed into the night. "Raise it high!"

The scourgers set about bashing in the windows and doors of the cottage across the street, flinging in torch after torch after torch. Black smoke began boiling from its guts.

"Lad?" Karl crept down the staircase, his eyes narrowing on Sir Alaric.

"Having a fit or something. Don't know." I nodded toward the kitchen. "Watch the back. Keep it clear."

Karl gripped his thane-axe. "Aye."

"Release him!" the Nazarene boomed, the flame behind him mounting. "Release him, and I shall release you!"

The chant changed, morphing to something lower, harsher, darker.

The Grey-Lady half-stood, poised as though in confusion, eyes glimmering the color of a waning moon, a line of liquid crimson wobbling from her ragged maw. Lazarus scurried free from her distracted grasp.

"Good! Come now, sister!" The Nazarene shrugged the cross off his shoulders, thudding to the ground, and beckoned with arms wide-open as the world. "And I shall shrive thee."

The scourger horde deformed, parting in schism, fissuring open like a gangrenous wound all the way to the Nazarene. Taking a tentative half-step, as though drawn by unseen shackles, she twitched a giggle, letting loose a sad lonely peal that silenced the night all but for the crackle of flame.

I swiped detritus off the sill, laid my crossbow across it, steadying her, waiting for the open shot.

"Red?" Stephan whispered behind. "Can you hear me? Can you move?"

Sir Alaric groaned.

"Drag his arse out." I was close enough for a clean shot, but far enough that the ensuing foot race might not be a foregone conclusion.

Sir Alaric rolled over to his knees at the wall, the

window, shaking, sobbing. "Please…" He laid a hand to my shoulder.

"Get him out of here." I shrugged free, took aim.

He pawed at me again, and I shoved him back.

"Please," he moaned, "l-let her be."

"Ain't her I'm aiming for, Red."

"Brother—" Stephan turned.

"You didn't have to come." I scowled. Turned. Aimed. Forced my breathing slow. "I *told* you not to come."

A screech, a scream, and the Grey-Lady tore on as though compelled, staggering along through the gauntlet, pounding barefoot across dirt and grit, down its gullet, each scourger taking a rip at her, slashing across her back, her head, her legs. She stumbled, splashing into the muck, black fingers clawing furrows.

"Rise!" The Nazarene stood silhouetted against the mounting blaze, smoking like some hellfire devil. *"Shrive thyself of sins, sister!"*

The Grey-Lady moaned and wailed, her voice changing somehow. "Please," she cried, "I beg of you, no—"

"Absolution is at hand!"

My fingertips touched the trigger. I took a deep breath and lined up the fat bastard, feeling my heartbeat through palm and fingertip, pulsing, bobbing the weapon ever so gently to the rhythm of my empty heart.

"You don't have to do this," Stephan said.

"Pain shall be your succor!" Arms outstretched like Christ on the cross. A perfect target. 'X' marks the spot. "Your salvation!"

I squeezed the trigger, *"Shit—!"* then released it, stopping shy as sky-scraping Lazarus lurched from the line, blocking my shot.

Skeletal death himself, Lazarus snatched the Grey-Lady by a fistful of hair and yanked her squealing to her feet, casting her stumbling down the line, scourges cracking, flaying, spraying blood and flesh in her wake as the Nazarene engulfed her in his vast embrace. Skin split upon his broad shoulders, scorched black with lightning crackles of raw pink as he hoisted her high.

Feet kicking, she struggled and wailed and sobbed.

"Come with me, sister!" The Nazarene stepped back towards the flames. "Walk with me a while. Let me show you the light!"

"No—!" Sir Alaric clambered for the front door, but Stephan collared him, clamping a hand across his mouth, wrestling him back.

I lowered the crossbow. "What in the hells…?"

Flames licked over the Nazarene's shoulders, scorching black tendrils licking blistered skin, grasping, caressing, blackening, burning. Her legs kicked and kicked, but the Nazarene's vast girth held her fast and bore them both step by step back towards Hell. Whatever'd happened, to make her do what she'd done, be what she'd been, in that last moment, with the moon-glow caul over her eyes shorn lucid-clear, she was human once more. I knew it for truth because it was so awful. So unthinkable. And something so awful and unthinkable couldn't help but be true.

As the flames poured out like wyrm's breath, the Nazarene hurled her forth into blazing hell, and she screamed black bloody-murder.

I didn't blame her.

...that a melee broke out in the midst of the gathering. Hochmeister Gaunt, a giant of a man versus Arboleth, no less keen a weapon for his gray hame, came to blows before a great bale-fire. It seemed some sort of biblical battle of Jacob versus Esau, Gilgamesh versus Enkidu, the Archangel Michael versus...
—*War-Journal of Prince Ulrich of Haeskenburg*

Chapter 30.

SIR ALARIC WAS THREE SHEETS to the wind and dragging anchor across rocky shoals. At best. It was plain even in the gloom of the *Half-King*. Scrunched up against his table, his head rose, rheumy eyes squinting. "Huh?" He reached for his sword, found only empty scabbard, settled back when he saw it was me. "How'd you find me?"

"Wasn't hard." I eased the door shut. "Just followed the scent of impotence, desperation, and bitter disappointment." I held two fingers up to Sweet Billie, toiling away behind the bar.

"An alluring scent." Sir Alaric rubbed one eye. "Familiar with it?"

"Intimately." I shook the wet from my cloak, folded it aside, took a seat. "Ask me about my wedding night sometime I'm drunker than you."

"Hrrm... Unlikely to be anytime soon." He chuffed a laugh, muttered to himself, took a swig of wine.

"How's the jaw?" It was swollen a purplish-red.

He worked his jaw back and forth. "Clicks a bit."

"Sorry about that." I nodded thanks to Louisa as she set a couple of flagons down. "You look like shit."

"Thanks." He grimaced. "You don't look much better."

"Don't want to outshine the boss."

"Aye and for sure." Sir Alaric held his bottle out to me. "Here."

"Straight from the bottle?" I raised an eyebrow.

"The one great relief. Take a few pulls, I'll look grand as Saint Peter."

"Total bullshit, I'd imagine," I wiped the mouth of the bottle, "but just to be safe," I took a swig, swished, sloshed, swallowed, "cause I heard Saint Peter's an easy ten."

Sir Alaric grinned, his beard scraggly, nose purple-dark, eyes fighting for focus. "Better?"

I laid a hand to my heart, "Marry me."

"Already spoken for." Sir Alaric snatched back the bottle. "Besides … heard yer wedding night tactics need some work."

"A bloody lie." I puffed up my chest then deflated. "Ain't *just* wedding nights."

"Not overly," he burped, "excuse me, reassuring."

"Consistency should count for something."

Sir Alaric looked set to keel over. "What'd I tell you the first day I saw you?"

"Well," I screwed my eyes shut, "that was quite a while back."

"Oooo…" Sir Alaric stretched out a leg. "Getting old."

"You were reminiscing about my Uncle Charles. The good old days."

"Nay. Piss on the *good* old days." He wiped a hand down his face. "I damned-well told you to ship back out." He sneered down, shaking his head, a palsied dog. "But you didn't listen. She didn't listen. No one ever listens…" He shook his head to himself. "But then, I'm an old geezer now and ain't that the truth? By the hound, I still feel like a lad of eighteen summers in here." He tapped his temple. "Just every time I wake in the morning, try to move, take a piss, a shit … I remember it then. Remember it hard." His hand balled into a fist. "Did ya think I was jesting?"

"Wasn't sure, I suppose." I shrugged. "Didn't have much choice either way."

"How about now?"

"Soon. *Ulysses* is near done."

"Aye," was all he said.

I took a pull on my ale. "How's the stock at the Schloss?"

"Near gone."

I took a breath. "Gonna get rough."

"Ain't rough already?"

"Long as you're drawing breath, can always get rougher."

"Aye, and for sure, words to live by." Sir Alaric slumped. "Words to die by…"

"Amen." I stared off into the hearth. "Red, what the hell's going on?"

"Can you hand me my pipe?"

I slid it across. "Mixing poisons?"

"I'll get lucky one of these days." His veiny hands trembled as he tamped pipe-weed in. "Choose the right combination."

"What happened last night?"

Sir Alaric lit his pipe. "What do you mean?"

"Are you fucking kidding me?" I hissed. "I mean the woman. The Grey-Lady, for God's sake."

Sir Alaric's closed his eyes. "Don't want to talk about her."

I throttled my hand into a fist. "What about you, then? Losing your shit?"

He shook his head, took a drink.

"Rudiger then," I said. "He was fair spry for a fella stabbed clean through the gut."

"Well, we're a sturdy folk, these parts."

"And his teeth? Her teeth. They look normal to you?" I slapped the table. "Jesus! The bite marks on Brown Cloak? You putting any of this together?"

Sir Alaric flinched at the slap.

"They say you caught him before."

He straightened at that. "Err … who?"

"Rudiger."

"Wha—?" Sir Alaric scowled. "Who says?"

"Fella insistent on secrecy. Said it was last summer. Said he went by Crennick then. A child-murderer. Little girl from the mills. Shit. What was her name? Louise? No. Elouise. Yeah. Ring any bells?"

"We're a sturdy folk, aye, but all a bunch of liars, don't you ken that?"

"Sure. And then some, but why lie about this?"

"Who the hell knows?"

"Well…?" I asked. "Is it true?"

"How can it be?"

"The King going soft on crime? Maybe he branded this Crennick or Rudiger instead of execution? I don't know. Or maybe banished him and he returned?"

"Banished? Heh. Wish he'd banished me."

"You didn't recognize him?"

"It was dark down there." Sir Alaric took a drink, wiped his mouth. "At the mill, too. And both times it happened so fast I didn't get a square look. Coulda been my own father and I'd not have known him."

"If you're done?" I snatched back the wine.

"Go on." He shrugged. "I hate wine."

231.

"Yeah, me, too." I bent the bottle back. There was naught but a trickle. "More folk disappearing all the time. Some last night. Back up at the old keep. You hear that?"

"Aye, and for sure." Sir Alaric waved a lazy hand. "Can't do nothing about it, but I heard."

"What do you mean?"

"I mean, how's anyone to know where folk are going? Disappearing each day? Could be leaving of their own accord. Hop the wall. Sally forth out the gates. Head off to the other camps. Or going back to their homes. Squatting. Or what have you."

"Dangerous here, too."

"You got me." Sir Alaric shook an imaginary pair of dice, blew smoke across them, and rolled. "Why they call the game of dicing *hazard,* lad. There's hazards everywhere. And if there is some heavenly spot shorn all free of danger, I bet you it's still cold and wet. And there ain't no food. And somewhere, out there, plague's waiting on fuming in."

"You forgetting some of the disappeared folk, your folk, *reappeared?"* I asked. "Parts of them, anyways? Cause even if you forgot, I keep getting keen reminders in the form of abattoirs in unexpected places."

"Well, I am old."

"But not fucking blind."

"All the same." Sir Alaric reached into his shirt and withdrew a paper. "Here."

I took it, glanced it over. King Eckhardt's seal held it shut. "What is it?"

"You're a real educated bastard, ain't ya? Can read and write and all? You tell me."

"I'd rather hear it from you."

"King wants you taking over lead as justiciar."

"Me…?"

"You're a mite slow for an educated son of a bitch, ain't ya?"

I straightened. "I don't want it."

"He's the King," Sir Alaric drained the last of the bottle, "he don't give two shits about what you want."

...did not take long for war-madness to infect the rest of the two parties.

Monstrous fiends against the flower of Haeskenburg's nobility and the Teutonic Knighthood's most able...

—*War-Journal of Prince Ulrich of Haeskenburg*

Chapter 31.

KING ECKHARDT'S WARDROOM was a dank hole on the third floor of the Schloss. The rafters sagged and water dripped even though it'd stopped raining hours past. The smell of mold and decay hung thick, cloying in the air. We stood huddled around a small table, King Eckhardt at its head. Sir Alaric was in attendance, physically at least, as were Prince Eventine, Sir Gustav, Father Gregorius, and von Madbury.

"And so yet again, you failed to bring my father the head you promised," Prince Eventine sniffed, fighting off a glance to the man sitting to his left. But I caught it. Von Madbury, naturally.

"It ain't baking a cake, kid," I said.

"I'm no *child.*" Prince Eventine drew up. "I am a prince of the blood, heir apparent, and you shall refer to me as such."

"Don't make me throw you over my knee," I deadpanned, meaning every single word.

"Why I—" Prince Eventine gawped. "You could never—"

"Gentlemen!" King Eckhardt barked. "Please. Eventine. Enough. Sit. Everyone, by the book, sit." He lowered his hands. "This news is troubling, to be sure. This Grey-Lady, you say? And Rudiger? Or Crennick, rather?"

"Take your pick." I'd broached the Crennick conundrum in private with His Highest Majesty. And His Highest Majesty had admitted to recalling Crennick. His crime. His capture. His execution. He'd waved off the rest.

"You claim that he, that *they* were," King Haesken struggled, "something more than human?"

"Something *less*, but yeah, that's the gist." I glanced Sir Alaric's way for support.

Sir Alaric took a bored swig of something, glowered, grumbled into his cup.

I smacked the table, "Think you could maybe—"

King Eckhardt cut me off, "It seems likely to me that these two aberrants, for lack of a better term, must be some form of progeny of this blasted Nazarene. How else could they have survived such egregious wounds?" He turned to Father Gregorius. "Would it not seem so to you, Father?"

"The Nazarene…" Father Gregorius bobbed his head like a dog having his haunches scratched. "Absolutely, Your Majesty."

"Now, wait—"

"Nay, Sir Luther, listen." Father Gregorius brandished his ever-present bible. "Why, you yourself witnessed a similar act with the blackguard Sir Alaric felled by crossbow. Obviously, this Nazarene has the ability to … to confer life upon those who should otherwise embrace death. And, undeath is a term oft used with regards to the state these creatures dwell within."

"And Father, you believe this Nazarene to be in a state of undeath?" King Eckhardt took a sip of wine.

"Most fervently, Your Majesty."

"The Nazarene?" I straightened. It'd been something that crossed my mind. And it made sense on some level. King Eckhardt had a point. How else had Rudiger survived those wounds? But on another level, one I couldn't fathom, something in my gut just felt wrong. "I ... I don't know."

"You don't have to know. You aren't expected to know," Father Gregorius explained. "You've no expertise in such matters. I propose that none at this table can claim such expertise. But King Eckhardt is correct. It is plain as day."

Prince Eventine, Sir Gustav, and von Madbury bobbed their heads wholeheartedly.

I took a sip of sour wine. Made a sour face.

"You remain unconvinced, I see." The King rubbed his beard. "Sir Luther, you claimed the Nazarene raised a man from the dead, yes? Did he not? By the book, is that not a commonality amongst such tales of grave-walkers, spawn of Cain, things of such twisted misery?"

"Your heretic brother's opinion, notwithstanding," Father Gregorius added, "earlier, with regards to the incident at the church, you thought it as likely to be necromancy as miracle."

"I ... well, yeah, I suppose." I couldn't help shaking the feeling that the teeth of a hidden trap had sprung, biting into my leg, sticking me fast.

"Indeed, this risen man may well be in a state of undeath, rather than resurrected life. Indeed, they all may be."

I frowned.

"Your shit-heel brother," von Madbury leered from across the table, "and where might he be? Strange, he's not here serving his king? Seems I recall he was preaching leniency with regards to that fat fuck." He cast a look Father Gregorius's way. "Think he's harboring a soft spot for another of his heretical brethren? And is he still calling for my head?" He laid a hand on Gustav's shoulder. "Or is it mayhap his?"

"Both," I confided. "Wants matching bookends."

"Well, I—" von Madbury straightened.

"This is neither the time nor the place." The King cut him off with a chop of his hand. "Sir Luther, proceed. This man risen from certain death if not death itself, this man, this abomination, this Lazarus, still stalks the land under the thrall of the Nazarene, yes?"

"Yeah," I conceded, giving von Madbury a look that translated correctly meant *'suck my balls.'* "But if Rudiger and the Grey-Lady were his, too, why'd he want them dead? I mean, *truly* dead?"

"It lies beyond my ken," King Eckhardt took a drink from his cup, "yet perhaps such creatures, such devils and demons and the like are akin to men, vying ceaselessly amongst themselves for supremacy?"

"Yeah. I don't know," I grumbled. "Maybe."

"They were at odds, that appears obvious," Father Gregorius barreled in. "Would you not agree?"

"Sure, but—"

"Hold." King Eckhardt glanced toward the door. "Your man has returned presently from his sortie. I would that we all hear what tale he has to tell. He seems a man of no small competence."

"He's a moron," I corrected.

King Eckhardt blinked, then squinted, studying me as though for flaws in a fine sculpture. He'd find a spidered-web of cracks and in force if he knew where to look.

King Eckhardt raised a hand toward the door. "Enter, sir." He turned as Karl entered, flanked by Brother Miles and Squire Morley. "Sit. Please. Have a drink—" The King's eyes went wide. *"By the book…"*

"Yer majesty." A swath of blood stretched across Karl's face, down his armored torso, ending at his right thigh. He

237.

looked as though he'd slaughtered a cow. With his teeth.

"Are you injured?" King Eckhardt inquired.

Karl a waved blood-crusted paw. "Naw." He ripped off a hunk of bread, chomped a piece, and plopped himself down by Sir Alaric's side.

"Sir Alaric, could you—" the King said.

"Eh…?" Sir Alaric offered his numb gaze Karl's way. "Oh, aye. Here." Sir Alaric offered a tattered scrap of napkin.

"Thanks." Karl patted his forehead with the scrap then tucked it into the collar of his bloodied mail shirt for I had schooled him vehemently in the art of courtly manners. Sir Gustav snorted which for once summed up more or less what I was thinking.

Karl poured himself a measure of wine then promptly killed it as swiftly as he killed everything else.

"Goodman Karl. Ahem," King Eckhardt started, though where he got the *Goodman* from was a mystery to me, "how went your foray?"

"Ahurm…" Karl glanced down the table, taking a deep breath. He wasn't much for talking in front of a crowd, even one as anemic as this. It amazed me how a bastard as fierce and mad as he, without a care for his own personal safety, could shy from speaking in front of a roundtable of such mediocrity. "I … err … skulked after them scourgers again. Ferreted the fuckers through the Tooth and Old Jewtown. Watched 'em burn a couple empty cottages til they got bored. Then I tailed 'em up to the top of yon neighboring tor. Took up station within that largish building atop it. A squatters' haven. Fortified with a nuisance wall." He scowled at Father Gregorius. "Looks like a monk's asylum or some of yer other Godly nonsense."

"The leper-house—" Prince Eventine smote the table.

"Yes," King Eckhardt said. "Saint Marculf's."

"Aye. Well. Didn't see no lepers. Only scourgers." Karl picked at clotted blood flecking his beard. "Infesting the place like rats. Main building and cells. Few outhouses. All gone to misery."

"Not full of its usual blissful ardor?" I commented.

"Fuck off," Karl rebutted.

"You entered the grounds?" King Eckhardt asked.

"Nar." Karl shook his head. "Couldn't get no shot with him dallying amongst them lunatics. So I clomb the roof of a neighboring building. Watched 'em trudge in. The Nazarene's set himself up inside the main building. They're all there, bunked down fer the time being."

"I want him dead." King Eckhardt said it quietly. He said it firmly. He said it without any shred of prevarication. It was the first thing he'd said that sounded as though it came from a king.

Karl crossed his thick arms.

"We have him." King Eckhardt's hand clenched into a fist. "And how would you go about it?"

"Your Majesty," Sir Gustav stood, "I'd be most honored to—"

"*Quiet.* Sit. Be still," King Eckhardt snapped. "I asked Goodman Karl."

Sir Gustav stood with his dumb jaw hanging.

A lovely sight.

"How many men you got?" Karl asked.

The King eyed von Madbury. He'd been training up some of the small-folk. It'd been slow going, near as I could tell, but with a teacher like him…

"Twenty-five," von Madbury said. "Half of that little more than rabble."

"Hrmm…" Karl grumbled. "Easiest way? Catch him holed-up. Today. Now. Send in some bastards with oil. Start a few quick burns and stave the doors shut. Windows are high. Narrow. Tough to climb through. A right proper fire'd solve yer problem, I'd hazard."

I glanced the King's way. "You said you didn't want blood-simple slaughter."

"Aye. Yes. Well… It still holds true, and though I rue the situation, Sir Luther," King Eckhardt took a tentative sip of wine, "this Nazarene must be ended. He challenges my divine right. And a kingdom divided is destined to fall. It has been struck such blows already. And if he should indeed be a servant of the Lord, divine providence shall no doubt shield him." The King fingered his jaw. "Yet, if I wished to spare the masses?"

"Spare the masses?" Karl ran a blood-crusted hand through his greasy beard. "Hrrm… Well then, yer talking daggers in the dark, yer Majesty."

...glory there was to be had by all, and the slaughter was prodigious if not wholly complete.
—War-Journal of Prince Ulrich of Haeskenburg

Chapter 32.

ON THE EVE OF BATTLE a mad bastard once told me, "The heights of elation in the immediate aftermath of an act of violence are matched only by the depths inevitably to follow." Tucking another dagger into my belt, already jangling with steel, I couldn't help but agree. My heart was pounding, palms slick with anticipation. Highs and lows. The during and the after. I'd take a tenfold portion of both over a slice of the *before*. That queasy quagmire of uncertainty, feet shifting, sinking, wondering, waiting.

I glared up as Queen Elona slid into my room, closing the door behind.

"Jesus..." I hissed.

"No one saw me."

"You're the bloody *Queen*," I said through gritted teeth. We'd met twice since that first time and not since the night with von Madbury.

"You've been avoiding me," she said.

"No," I lied.

"Please. It doesn't matter." The Queen shook her head. "Shall my father accompany you?"

"Why not ask him yourself?"

"I would, but..."

"He'd talk to you," I said. "He wants to. I don't know what's between you two, but he would. He worries the hell about you."

"He," the Queen licked her lips, "he's spoken of me?"

"No. But I see it in his eyes. Whenever you're around. Jesus. Whenever you're not…"

"Please." She laid a hand on my cheek. "Beg him off. He's in no shape to attend to your designs."

I swiped her hand off. "And what are my designs?"

"Murder."

"Good," I said. "At least you've no illusions."

"And…?"

"And your father's a grown man."

"What does that mean?"

"It means he makes his own decisions."

"And that means he's going with you?"

"Yeah," I said. "He insisted. Adamantly."

"But you're the justiciar now."

I straightened.

"And if you're the justiciar, you can order him off."

"He'd kill me if I did."

"He'll die if you don't."

"You don't know that." What I didn't say was maybe that would've been better for him. For her. For everyone all around.

"Have you looked at him?" The Queen turned to the shadows. "Have you seen? He's spiraling downward. He's frail. Weak. The drink has him worse than I've ever seen. And I have seen." She pressed a fist to her lips. "Please. Order him to stay. To remain. To guard the gates or … or something. Anything. Please." She reached for my hand. "Do it for me. Please."

I retracted my hand reflexively. "Don't do that."

"Do … what?"

"I saw you and von Madbury," I said. "So this, me and you, whatever it is…"

"What?" The Queen straightened. "How dare you insinuate—"

"*Insinuate?* No. It's plain as dawn. And please. I don't care. That's how you keep him in line, yeah? Fine." I dismissed her with a wave of my hand. "But it was fair obvious from the start. You three are like King Arthur, Guinevere, and Sir Lancelot, the shitty version." I bit my lip. "Apologies, but only a blind man could miss it. And the King for all his legion of faults is not blind."

The Queen straightened, the straight line of her lip trembling.

"Oh?" I said. "You thought maybe you were slick enough that no one knew? That it was a secret? That's life in a castle. I knew the moment you sauntered in. So your husband knew. Everyone knew. Everyone knows."

She slapped me across the face. "You are—"

"Your sons *know.*"

Cocked back for another go, her hand trembled, faltered, fell, "I—"

"Listen, I don't care," I spat. "It's none of my business. You don't owe me anything. Nor I you. Except my sword-arm. But don't go plucking at my heartstrings, yeah? They were slit a long while back."

"Sir Luther, I don't—"

"In the wine cellar."

She pursed her lips, swallowed. "You don't know what you saw."

"And I don't care. Like I said. But this is over. Whatever this is."

Her teeth bared in a split grimace, "You're like all the rest."

"That means I'm moving up."

"No, in point of fact, I was mistaken." She raised her chin. "You're worse."

"Than von Madbury? Elona, please—"

"Don't call me that. Not now." The Queen rounded on me, finger in my face. "Do you know why you're worse? Why you're worse than Eckhardt? Worse than that shit, von Madbury? Yes. Worse than all the rest of them?"

"No, Your Highness," I crossed my arms, "why?"

"Because you didn't use to be."

…they possess a small cadre of warriors seemingly inoculated against any normal means of modern warfare…
—*War-Journal of Prince Ulrich of Haeskenburg*

Chapter 33.

SAINT MARCULF'S leper-house stood south of the Schloss von Haesken, at a major — for Haeskenburg — crossroads a couple blocks west of the southeastern gates. We'd done our due diligence, strolled round the nuisance wall. Taken its measure. The building was shaped roughly like an ant, head pointed north. Two main buildings, hospital and church, the head and body, respectively, with six smaller wings, or legs, in keeping with my shitty metaphor, made up the living quarters.

"See anything?" Karl grunted up to Stephan.

"Yeah, your mother," I grinned, *"Goodman* Karl."

Karl shoved me against the chimney.

The house we were in was a wreck. It looked like it'd been hit by a firestorm. Char-smeared walls. Naked floor joists spanning above. Floor spongy beneath. All the blessed amenities.

"Would you two knock it off?" Stephan hissed down through the hole in the ceiling. We'd chosen him, despite the fact he'd only the one hand, for the second-story job of keeping watch. He stood balanced on one of the joists, peering out a ragged hole.

"Fuck off," Karl's stout finger nearly lit into my eye, "with the shit about my mother."

"Fine." I rubbed my shoulder, glared up at Stephan. "Well? You see anything?"

It was apparent from his scowl that he saw two assholes beneath him, both figuratively and literally, fucking around, but he bit it back, sour taste and all, and swallowed. He was fair adroit at that. But then, he'd had years of practice. "A couple of scourgers and women just stumbled in." Stephan glared down. "I'm guessing they're all bunked down for the day. But it's clear now — hold." He raised a hand. "Got another one taking a stroll. Wait til it's safe."

"Safe...?" Karl growled.

"Hang on."

The wall surrounding the leper-house was only five-feet and change. It'd been raised more to stifle the eyesore of the afflicted living than any security measure. Not much call for anyone storming a leper-house. Anyone sane, that is.

"Lou," Stephan hissed down, "the Nazarene may be the only means to save Abraham."

"Yeah." I glared up. "Heard you the first time. Fifteenth, too."

"You heard, but you don't *listen*. The Nazarene's no creature of the night, whatever the King and Father Gregorius claim. You know that."

"So you're the expert now?"

"More expert than you."

"That's like saying Karl's the tallest bloke in a room full of double amputees." I tested the edge of my dagger. "King wants the fat bastard dead."

"And what's he done?" Stephan glared down. "Truly? What crimes do we know he's committed?"

"Jesus. There's the priest," I started counting on my fingers, "then there's all those poor bastards he crucified in the town square." I glared over at Karl. "How many, you hazard?"

"Are we sure—"

"And how about the Jews?" I asked. "He scourged or burned half of them and ran off the other half."

"So says the King and his sycophants," Stephan countered. "Brother, at least make some attempt at ascertaining—"

"The King agreed to forgo wholesale slaughter in lieu of one lone assassination. You want a hundred souls on your conscience? Jesus, you should've heard Plan A."

"After all you've cost Abe, you won't even try?" Stephan pressed.

Karl scowled.

"That old chestnut." I punched the wall, which was always the smart play. Break your hand. Beg off what needs doing for four to six weeks. "This why you came? To save that piece of shit? To falter our resolve while we stand on the brink? Jesus, you don't think I've enough shit on my plate?" I closed my eyes, thought back to Sir Alaric seething when I ordered him not to come. To stand down. His lower lip trembling. Him fighting to hide it. Seeing the last vestiges of his broken spirit crumble.

"No," Stephan said, "I came to perhaps save Abe. That's all."

"Yeah, well that's one thing. But, Jesus, giving Ruth false hope with your bullshit theories."

"It's not false hope," Stephan spat. "I came here for Abe, but also for you and Karl." Stephan crossed his arms. "Well, mostly Karl."

Karl grinned.

"We clear yet?" I hissed up.

"Judas Priest." Stephan rolled his eyes. "Yes. Get ready."

"Bring a stepladder?" I sneered at Karl. "Or are you gonna need ten fingers?"

"Yar. You can start with this one." Karl offered me one.

"Now—" Stephan hissed.

Karl piled out the door, thick legs pumping, ripping ragged across the street. He leapt and grabbed the top of the wall, pulling himself up and over, disappearing an instant before I jumped and pressed myself up. Over. Down.

We landed on the far side, in damp shade, behind one of the cells. There was still snow here, wedged against the wall, tucked out of the sun. For a piece, we hunkered and listened, waiting to see if anyone had noticed. A hawk soared past overhead, two crows squawking after. "Gonna be us before we know it."

"We the hawk?" Karl rumbled. "Or the crows?"

"Only time'll tell." I rose from my crouch. "C'mon. No rest for the wicked."

The leper-house loomed atop Savior's Tor, comprising the bulk of the southern half of Husk. Smoke trickled up from the chimneys. Smaller, single cells lined the inner yard. A small cemetery lay in the northwest corner.

I followed Karl as he loped clockwise along the compound's wall, keeping it on our left, the line of monk cells screening our right. He paused at each break, peering out. Refuse littered the yard.

Karl dropped to a knee. "Hold."

A haphazard gaggle of scourgers and women staggered up the rise, laughing, glugging back, tossing bottles, tricking in one by one.

That tightness in my chest cramped suddenly down, crushing slow, squealing like a rusted vice. Rudiger's teeth gleaming. The Grey-Lady screaming. Burning.

Karl fixed me an eye. "You alright?"

"Yeah," I lied.

The door opened again, and a scourger lurched out, staggering to one of the crosses upright in the mud, swigging back a bottle of something before collapsing piecemeal to the ground. Splayed beneath the cross, he rolled onto his back, onerously, his tumescent, belly engorged, pale, straining, naked to the sky.

"Sorta reminds me of you," I forced out.

"I ain't the one with the history of '*can't hold his drink.*'"

"Always been an avid student of history." I squinted toward the open door beyond Drunk Jesus. "Think that's God telling us something?"

"I don't listen to pissants."

"Don't let Stephan hear." Rubbing my chest, I strolled out into the open.

Karl followed.

Our gear was back with Stephan. We'd both donned plain-spun robes. I had a ring of thorns wrapped round my forehead — I'd clipped all the prickers on the inside cause, unsurprisingly, they hurt like hell. For about the hundredth time, I patted the daggers sheathed on a belt inside my robes. Karl had a pair of hatchets and daggers and his maniac strength. We each had a scourge wrapped over our shoulders, too, the only weapons we could carry out in the open. I was missing Yolanda something fierce, but there was no way I could fit her under the robes. Same with Karl's thane-axe. Commit to assassination and you go to the last full measure. Halves get the wrong bloke killed.

As we passed Drunk Jesus, laid out across the lawn, at the foot of a lilted cross, his head palsied up. "The glory of God be with you, brother…" He burped, winced, forced a swallow. "P-Pardon." He blinked, squinted, fighting for focus. "Eh?" He fought to elbow himself up. "Do…" he swallowed, "do I know you?"

"Sure," I forced a grin, "we're the very best of chums."

"I…" he glared back toward the leper-house, gears lubricated with gut-rot turning, "I think not." He opened his mouth to holler.

"Go back to sleep." I knelt on his arm, pinning it, the dagger I'd drawn sliding between his ribs in a gush of blood and bubble before he knew what was happening, forcing him down, back, into the mud, my hand muffling his gob. "In the name of the Father, the Son, and the Holy Ghost." I stifled his cry, pinning him til his thrashing quelled, til I couldn't feel the pulse of his heart hammering through the hilt of my blade.

It didn't take long.

I closed his eyes, leaving my hand atop his forehead as I offered some gilded prayer in case unseen eyes were prying. "We good?"

The cross loomed overhead.

"Aye, good…" Karl grunted, kneeling on Drunk Jesus's other arm, shielding us from the leper-house, his head on a swivel, wolf eyes all agleam. "Definitely. Maybe."

"Not overly reassuring." I unsheathed my dagger from Drunk Jesus's chest, wiping it surreptitiously on the inside of my robe.

"Weren't meant to be. Roll him over on his side. Fella's just sleeping one off."

"At the very least." I did as Karl bade then was up and strolling for the door.

It was dark inside, the air thick and humid with the stench of unwashed body, the blue smoke of smoldering fire. Of soiled linen. Of corruption from both body and form. A struggle just to inhale. But exhaling? A May Day parade.

The wing was, indeed, living quarters. Or had been. Subsistence quarters, more like. Rickety cots lined the walls end to end, some overturned, some broken, some barely hale. Scourgers lay atop them, splayed out haphazard, limbs lolling over the side like cataracts of flesh, a few snoring, some dead as Drunk Jesus. Well, nearly.

A caterwaul of black laughter boomed in the confined night, reverberating of stone walls, shivering the fume hanging thick and acrid in the air. I kicked a bottle skittering across the floor —*shit*— and froze.

Karl glowered.

The bottle rotated there in the world's least sexy game of spin-the-bottle, coming finally to rest, pointing at some lucky fella lain out across a bent bed, his hairy feet poking from the ends of his ragged robe.

"Oy," someone barked, "close the bleeding door! Yer letting all the heat out."

"And the air in," I muttered, breathing through my mouth.

Karl wisely ceded to the unnamed voice's demand, yanking the door shut and trapping us in the fetid swamp of stifling twilight. Random torches sputtered here and there, casting dim ripples across staid slivers of rationed daylight. Shadow demons slid along the ceiling. Rats skittered underneath from cot to cot. I canted my head toward the far end of the room and started toward the church-proper, the garrulous laughter booming in the gloom. The air vibrating. The floor shivering. Or was that just me?

I knew that voice. That laughter.

Karl stiffened. So did he.

Moving through the room was traversing an obstacle course, stepping over bottle and limb, maneuvering around overturned bed and broken chair.

"Oy…" A pumpkin-sized face leered in through the door. Shit. Lazarus. By one long loping arm, he hung there, a bottle of wine raised to his lips as he lurched past, laying a hand on my shoulder, *"Bless you, brother,"* before stumbling onward, long-legged as a drunken stork.

"You as well, brother," I grunted back, sliding through the doorway.

Twin rows of pews filled the massive space. The ceiling vaulted up some fifty feet, disappearing into the hazy gloom. A stained-glass portrait of Saint Marculf, patron saint of lepers, decked out in festering boils blooming rose-like across his face, illuminated the room along with a bonfire crackling smoky and low. A haphazard mishmash of entwined, engorged, entangled flesh lay strewn amongst the remaining pews.

"Yes…" the Nazarene's voice hissed from afar.

Bent down, practically on our knees, we crept towards a dark mound looming beyond. The sound of glass cracking, crunching, tinkling in a scintillating cascade, and wood bending, yawning, creaking, all accompanied a chorus of sharp animal grunts.

I raised a hand and crouched, Karl at my back.

"Yes…" the Nazarene's voice reverberated.

Ahead stood the mound. Broken pews'd been axed and split and piled high, sharp edges and nails jabbing up. Atop the pile sat a makeshift throne, all crooked and jagged, hewn together by bent nail and twisted will.

Squinting, I crept onward, masked by the pews, trying to suss out who sat atop. I had a fair guess.

"YES!" The Nazarene gripped the throne.

The grunting. The heaving. A beast. Two-backed. The Nazarene and some wench.

"Maybe yer religion *ain't* so bloody dumb," Karl hissed.

I couldn't argue. It was the most moving Mass I'd ever witnessed.

"Yes…" the Nazarene lounged back, one leg up on the

makeshift armrest as he licked the neck of the wench straddled across him. Her legs splayed wide, entwining round him like vines as she moaned. His fingers entangled in her long hair.

"This normal?" Karl rumbled.

"No," I whispered, "it's usually a priest and altar boy."

"Uhhg…" she moaned, her hips working, sliding up, sliding down, sliding long, sliding slow. "*More…*"

"The Body…" The Nazarene took a slurp from a chalice then raised it high, dousing them both in dribbling crimson, "and the Blood…"

The wench arched back, mouth open, tongue lolling, lapping in the sacrament. When the cascade ended, the Nazarene cast aside the chalice and stood, bearing her still astride him, turned and wrestled her down, flopping atop, arching his back as he thrust. Blood oozed down his frame from the blistered road-map of lash and scorch marring his flabby back. Puckered old star-shaped puncture wounds stood out, matching those from his chest and abdomen.

I couldn't watch, and yet, I couldn't *not.*

Karl on the other hand was already moving, a dagger back-swept in his fist. He tapped me on the arm.

I snapped out of it and followed, moving at a crouch along the ends of the pews, each one holding another in a long treasure trove of shit I didn't ever want to see. Glazed eyes goggled back as I passed. Bodies lay strewn. Hairy backs heaved. At the front row, Karl paused, looking back.

I held up a hand, signaling, *Wait,* as I forced myself to breathe, long and slow, willing the vise gripping my heart to loosen.

The Nazarene lay flopped still atop the wench, fairly near to closing the deal. If we took him now, we'd have to deal with the wench and that meant shutting her up. And there was only one sure-fire method.

"*YES!*" The Nazarene grunted, clutching the creaking throne, arching, shivering, collapsing. "A benediction from the lord." A moment later, he struggled up to his knees, shards of wood clattering. Catching his breath. Drool coursed in a long tendril dangling from his lip.

He wiped himself off with his half-shorn robe, cast it aside, and clambered down the wreck toward the back. A vanity partition, engraved with intricate bas-reliefs of Saint Marculf blessing a legion of lepers, cordoned off the far end of the church sanctuary. The Nazarene snatched a bottle off a comatose scourger, ripped a swig, then pulled open the door and trudged through.

I signaled to Karl, *Go.*

He scurried toward the door.

Blade in hand, I followed him, moved past, slid through.

Karl closed the door behind.

The Nazarene stood in the corner, leaning tripod-wise against the wall as his piss splashed, steaming up from the cold floor. "You aiming to fix me in the most holiest of holies?"

I froze.

All he had to do was raise his voice and hell'd come calling.

"Nothing to say?" The Nazarene shook himself off. "Had plenty to jaw on about the day you thought you had the drop on us. Yer cocks all faltering when that blackguard in the church turned yellow, though, eh?

"And here you come stealing in for more murder." The Nazarene smirked, his teeth all crooked and brown. "You hazard yer the one on the side of the Good Lord?"

"Hazard I ain't," I said, "but, then, I ain't the one pissing on his floor."

"Well." The Nazarene took a swig of wine and wiped his chin. "A right honest feller, eh? Then why keep doing it?"

"Same reason you crucified all those people."

"Well now, sure enough, I crucified them all, Father, I do confess," the Nazarene cocked his head, studying me, "but I didn't kill none. Not a one." He swiped a hand across his balding pate. "Merely planted 'em up where yer King'd be like to see them. See what he done. See what he hadn't."

"Hadn't done what?"

"'Hadn't done what?' he says." Wine trickled from the corner of his lip. "Lord, forgive him. The ignorance. He knows not what he does. Says. Dribbling excrement all the while." The Nazarene winced as he straightened, "Ah…" his back popping in succession. "Failed in his mandate from the Lord. In his duty to protect the small-folk. *His* small-folk. King's supposed to, aye? First rule, ain't it? Most important? His manifest-fucking duty. Supposed to dub knights like you to shield them from wrong. From dark. What a head-scratcher it is when it turns out you all *are* the dark."

"And what's that make you?"

"Me? Heh. Oh, I ain't nothing, truly. Just a vessel. A conduit. A nexus." The Nazarene tossed the bottle. "Look at me. Journeyman work at best." He scratched absently at one of the scars puckering his chest. "Heh. Don't suspect I'll amount to nothing in the end. Nothing but bones and marrow and worm."

I gripped my dagger. "Karl…?"

"Door's shit," Karl rumbled. "Wall's shittier."

The Nazarene squared up. "That time already?" Those brown teeth again, his thick arms open, wide, inviting. "Well, come to me then, brother. Word of advice, though—" He gripped a fistful of flabby abdomen. "Might need more pig-sticker than that."

Balanced on the balls of my feet, licking my lips, I froze. "What happened at the church? At the mill? The fire?"

"Have to be more specific." The Nazarene's eyes squeezed in suspicion. "Was a lot happened."

"You pulled a crossbow bolt from a dead man's chest. Then raised him up. And the Grey-Lady, the woman—"

"Woman?" The Nazarene leered. "That weren't no woman, brother. Not no more." He settled back a moment, smiling something broad, something horrid, fingernails picking at another scar. "Yer eyes don't see. And yer ears don't hear. So how can you trust them? How can you know what you think you know?"

"Tell me about the man with the bolt."

"You must mean old Lazarus."

"Didn't look so old to me."

"Man was dead." The Nazarene shrugged. "Can't get no older than that. Methuselah old. Now he's beyond old."

"Beyond death, you mean?" Words of the King and Father Gregorius echoed through my mind. "You mean he's *undead?"*

"Undead? Him? *Lord above."* The Nazarene scowled. "You're twisted round and round and inside out. Should read the Good Book. Miracles of the Lord inside, brother, miracles of the lord. It'll untie yer knots. Stretch yer eyes. Widen yer senses. Listen to yer brother. Can see him gleaming inside and out. The powers of Jesus? Privy to us all when we possess the faith. The will. The gumption."

"Why should I believe you?"

"Why should I care if you do or don't?" The Nazarene straightened, rising to his full height. "You ask me about *undeath?* About death? About murder?" He pointed a thick arm. "Go ask yer King. He's the expert. And ask him about *strigoi,* too, while yer at it. See what fork-tongued lies the bastard spews."

"*Strigoi…*" I swallowed. My thoughts ranged to Abraham, laid up in bed, dying, maybe dead. "Can you heal the sick?"

"Heh… You come to kill me?" A greasy smirk stretched across his broad mug. "Or beg me for help?"

"Ain't sure yet," I answered truthfully.

"Well then, let me share with you a little secret—" the Nazarene raised a hand aside his maw. *"It ain't mine to offer."*

"Lad—" Karl warned.

I turned.

From beyond the sanctuary partition, scourgers started screaming.

...we had learned the name of our foe. It was an ancient name full of fell purpose...
—*War-Journal of Prince Ulrich of Haeskenburg*

Chapter 34.

SALLOW SMOKE SLITHERED from underneath the partition door, breathing in through the wall joints, forcing inside the sanctuary in grasping tendrils of hell-spume. Muffled screams erupted from beyond, the sound of bare feet flapping, of choking, gasping, wheezing. A window shattered, glass shard raining across stone.

"Do you hear it, brother!" The Nazarene's eyes bulged razorback red as he charged at me, growling like some pit-bear shorn of its chains.

A bank of smoke rolled over, consuming me as I met the Nazarene's charge, hooking over and under his arms, trying to pivot in place, let his force flow over me, past me, but he hooked my leg with his and we both went tumbling as one.

A moment's panic. Pant-shitting terror.

But I caught my footing, jerked him right and threw him over my left hip, feet arcing, him hanging on, both of us crashing into the partition.

"*Shit—!*"

The whole partition ripped free, toppled down, wood shards raining as we landed at the foot of the mad throne. The acrid choke of thick smoke as I landed atop. Him flailing, smashing, bashing with blunt arms. Shadows cavorting through the fume. Visions of Hell. But even from his back weren't the fucker strong? He arched to roll me, but

I braced with an outstretched arm then ripped up with the dagger I'd somehow stuck in his flank.

"Yes!" he cried, the bloody-fucking weirdo.

The altar-throne loomed above, catching fire, detritus avalanching around us.

"*Brothers!*" The Nazarene's paws worked up my neck, taking a grip on my ear, my hair, jaundiced thumbnails digging into my cheeks, gaining purchase, inching up like maggots for my eyes.

"Fuck … *you!*" I ripped the dagger free and shoved it to the hilt in his chest, forcing him back down at arm's length. Then I did it again.

"Absolution!" He cried, blood bubbling, as he muscled me down. Crooked brown teeth bit into my cheek, and I screamed murder. He gnashed and spit and bit again.

"Bastard—" Twisting my dagger and hammer-fisting his arm, I wrenched my face free, yanked the dagger and stabbed again and again and again.

He roared as I pried his head back, slashing an elbow for his face, missing, overbalancing. Instantly, a body tore past in the smoke, knocking me sideways and the Nazarene rolled atop me, grinning crimson as he wiped his chin. Bale-fire burned up the rafters of the church. "The body and blood!" He tore my dagger from his chest and raised it above. "A benediction!"

A shadow-flash of dull grey steel whisked from behind and into the back of the Nazarene's skull.

Thud!

The Nazarene pitched forward, catching himself on all fours over me. I tucked one leg up and squirmed as Karl bashed him again. *Thud!* Axe flashing. *Thud!* Blood drooled from the Nazarene's maw, his face a ruin of red.

I shrimped free from under the monstrosity as he dropped prone to the floor, felled like a great oak.

Hacking, coughing, Karl stood above him, feet set, two-handing that hand-axe overhead like splitting logs. Again. *Thud!* Bone broke in the Nazarene's skull, shattering eggshell inward, and he went limp. I collapsed back, trying to catch my breath. It couldn't. Smoke poured from all six of the wards, the heat rising hard, rising fast. Scourgers and dames bawling mad havoc from inside, outside, all around, feet pounding, fists hammering on doors, on walls, on windows.

"Jesus…" I rolled over. Coughed. Hacked. Grabbed my head.

"C'mon." Karl grabbed me by the collar.

"Which way?"

"Not that way." Karl slid by at a crouch, trying to keep below the smoke, dragging me onto my belly and letting go. "Over here." He crawled badger-fast back toward the sanctuary. "Was a door back here somewhere."

Beside, the Nazarene shifted, moaned, the broken slur of air hissing past swollen tongue and broken teeth, a soft whistling vibrato through crushed air passage. His hand slithered for my ankle.

"Are you fucking serious?" I kicked free and scrambled over the partition ruin, a broken bas-relief of Saint John the Baptist's head glaring up at me from Herod's divine dinnerware.

Blood pounded in my ears to the chanting from … from somewhere. *Jesus.* Everywhere.

Ahead, Karl struck wall. "Look for a door." He shoved me off right.

I followed the wall, pounding along, slapping, prodding, feeling for jamb or passage or door. It was all stonework til I struck wood. *Door!* Hand splayed, groping blind, I felt along it, feeling the coarse grain, the individual planks. "Karl!" I choked, gasped, hammered the door. "Over here! Door!"

Behind, in the abyssal churn, planks shifted as something slithered across the felled partition. Wood shards fell. A dark shade materialized, limb flopping out wet on stone, reaching, pulling, dragging a massive shapeless carcass behind.

I shoved open the door.

"Karl!" My cry was little more than a gurgle, but Karl was through the door and at my side a moment later, huddling past as I slammed the heavy door shut. There, in the dark of a close passage, leaning against the coarse wood grain, I heard it again. Felt it. The chanting. The screaming. The horrid thing coming. "Did you see it?"

"What?" Karl hacked up a lung.

"Gimme your axe." He thrust it toward me, and I wedged it under the door, kicking it in sound.

"What the hell you doing?"

"He's still alive." I staggered back.

"Who?"

"Him." I spat.

"I caved in his fucking squash."

Something splatted against the other side of the door. Something heavy. Something wet. We both froze. Then the sound of fingernails digging into wood, dragging down, finding metal. The doorknob turning, someone pressing in. But the axe held.

"Open it." Karl drew his dagger.

The door bowed inward, flexing in the middle slowly, inexorably, groaning like an old ship, bound in shifting ice, devastated by degree.

Smash! The door shuddered as thunder struck.

Cowardice being my life's work, "No fucking way," I came to quicker and bolted past Karl, grabbing him by the collar, dragging him from his stupor, hauling him from the smoke and fire and misery, tripping past chair and table, kicking our way through til we hit the far wall and found another door. Smoke oozed from underneath it.

"Shit."

The door behind cracked under another blow.

I turned the knob, shouldered it open, a bank of heat dropping me gasping to my knees. Crawling blind then, through glowing smoke, til I hit wall. Karl banked left and I right. "Door!" I found it again, lurched for the knob, twisted it, dropped my shoulder, but the door didn't budge.

"Staved shut…" Karl spat, casting about for something. Anything. But there was nothing.

Again, I dropped my shoulder into it. It still didn't move. "Shit." I glared at Karl. "Where's the other axe?"

"In the blackguard's head," Karl rasped.

"Well shit," I said, and I meant it.

…first light of dawn, armed to the teeth, fifty knights sojourned deep into the vast chasm that was their lair, hoping to catch them amid their daylight slumber.

It became apparent the strigoi *were not alone…*
—War-Journal of Prince Ulrich of Haeskenburg

Chapter 35.

STEPHAN GRIMACED as he wound a swathe of slit homespun cloth round the head of a fallen scourger laid out across the ground, soot blackening his mouth, his nostrils, his teeth. Muttering to himself. Gibbering. Drooling. His face was flayed in burnt curls, blisters raised tumescent, scattered across his charred neck, his chest, his everything.

I looked away.

He was but one of many. And whether he was lucky to have gotten free of the charnel house or not, I wasn't willing to say. I was only willing to say that he'd be dead soon and even with his gift for treating wounds, it wouldn't matter one whit what my brother did.

"*Judas Priest,* Lou, what happened to your face?" Stephan squinted up.

"Fat Jesus, trying to get fatter." I winced, touched one of the bite marks.

The leper-house grounds were littered with scourgers, most still alive. I didn't figure it for long term. "What the hell happened?"

"I was at my perch." Stephan continued wrapping. "Watching. Waiting. I watched you and Karl go in. Saw what you—" He paused a moment, frowning. He was thinking on what I'd done to that scourger, Drunk Jesus. Maybe I hadn't needed to do it. Maybe I had. Stephan worked past it, though, saw now wasn't the time for preaching. "You were in for a while when I saw them skulking past."

"Who?"

"Gustav and von Madbury. For certain. They were wearing cloaks. Sir Aravand, too, I think. And some of the others. Some of the new ones."

I nodded.

"It wasn't long after you entered. And it went as Karl suggested. They hurled in burning oil vials, staved the doors shut, then turned rabbit."

"Well, I do hate seeing a good plan go to rot." I ran a hand through my hair, let out a breath. Jesus. Bunch of bloody bastards. But what'd it mean? Had King Eckhardt ordered it? If he had, then Lady Mary, Abe and Ruth, the kids, were probably all dead. Or had von Madbury and Gustav gone rogue? Or were they acting under someone else's auspices? The Queen's? Our last conversation flashed through my mind. "Jesus. How'd you know which door?"

"I didn't. I freed all of them." Stephan rubbed his neck. "Yours was last." He was covered in soot, too, blisters risen in droves across his bad arm. They didn't seem to bother him. He moved to another patient, one not breathing, so he kept moving.

"We've got to get the hell out of here," I said.

"I can't leave." Stephan tucked in the loose end of a bandage. "Look around." Stephan made the sign of the cross. "So many. It's cold now, but once the sun sets…"

"They're gonna die. All of them." I kept an eye to the leper-house, seeing in its bowels the monstrous shade of the Nazarene shambling toward me through the smoke. Crawling like a thing. A horrid, broken *thing*. I couldn't blink it away, couldn't shake it off, couldn't force it gone. I stifled a shudder. More nightmare fuel. "So what's the point?"

"Rose of Sharon…" Stephan tied off another bandage. He'd been cutting his own clothes and those of the dead for dressings. Packings. Bandages. Anything. "They need bandages, food, water." He pointed toward the monk cells set along the wall. "There's enough vacant cells that we could set up a makeshift infirmary. Or one of the nearby houses."

The leper-house had collapsed, the lion's share, anyways.

"What you need," I growled low, "is to get the hell out of here before they find out who the fuck you are."

Stephan frowned. "I didn't cause this."

"And you think that'll matter?"

"I'm not afraid."

"Not being afraid won't matter when they're scourging the flesh raw off your spine."

"Be that as it may." Hunkering low, he duck-walked to his next patient, a woman. Her long hair'd been singed off half her skull, and she shivered something awful, eyes blind, lips working, trying to speak. Stephan glared up at me. "Brother, please."

"Fuck." I tore off my scourger robe and laid it across her. Then I started shivering. While she kept right on shivering. "Jesus Christ."

"Here, sister." Stephan gently lifted the woman's head and set a flask to her lips. "Drink. Yes. I know, I know." The woman murmured gibberish but found the cool metal with her lips and sipped a dram of ephemeral solace. "Yes. Good." He dabbed her lips with the corner of my erstwhile robe. "We're missing something, Lou."

"My robe, maybe?" I hugged myself against the raw. Karl was off gathering our things. Probably wearing his cloak *and* mine. Lolling back with his feet up. Watching from afar. Grinning. Sweating. The little troll bastard. "Or our collective sense of urgency?"

"That priest they scourged and hanged?" Stephan said.

"Father Demtry?"

"Him. Yes. Well, I put Red's feet to the fire after you left the other day." Stephan moved on to another scourger whose leg'd been crushed. His breathing was regular, rhythmic, shallow. More of a reflexive fish gasp than anything more. The kind a man does just shy of his final bow. "It was over something the Nazarene said."

"About Demtry being a pillar of the community?"

Stephan leaned forward, whispering in the dead bloke's ear, then looked up. "Seems there were more than a few stories of him taking liberties with some of his younger parish members. And that wasn't all—"

"A man in power taking liberties?" Aghast, I laid a hand to my chest, fanning myself furiously. "Say it ain't so."

"True and unfortunate, yes," Stephan glowered, "but still, it doesn't make it right."

"So maybe he got what was coming to him."

"It's not that simple, but—"

"Jesus Christ, would you just pick a side? You can't walk barefoot across a sword's blade your whole life."

"Better to walk across it than use it." Stephan fixed me with those keen eyes. "Once you do, you think it's the solution to all of life's ills."

"Pick a bloody side," I reiterated, syllable by syllable.

"Whose?"

"Mine for once."

"Yours?" Stephan set his jaw. "Along with the King who ordered this? Your King?"

"Bite your tongue. Ain't my King. He's my meal ticket. And I'm going to sort it out."

"Sort it out?"

"Yeah," I scowled. "Sort. It. Out."

"What are you going to do?"

"What needs doing." I glared back at the smoldering ruin.

Stephan slid over to another scourger. "What is it you're thinking?"

"The Nazarene. I … I talked to him in there." I shivered. "He said the poor bastards he'd crucified were already dead. The ones in the town square. Said he hadn't killed any of them. Claimed he did it as a message to King Eckhardt. To tell him he'd failed his people. Shake him from his stupor."

"You think he was lying?"

"No. Worse." I swallowed. "I think he was telling the truth. Jesus. I think *King Eckhardt* was lying."

"So perhaps the scourgers aren't the villains?" Stephan looked around.

"I don't know." I touched the bite mark on my face. "They ain't the good guys, that's for damn sure. But…" I looked down. Away. Anywhere but at him. "Jesus Christ, I don't know."

The scourger's gibbering death rattle ceased abruptly, his arms crippling back, automaton smooth, nestling in the matted grass.

Stephan closed the bastard's eyes and performed last rites, then rose, turning toward the leper-house. It was burning still, but it was a slow burn, a smolder, blisters of smoke rolling up, blotting out the stars. Across the cold ground, scattered scrums of survivors huddled for warmth by their own makeshift fires. "The Nazarene's dead, isn't he?"

"Could have used him out here, huh?" I took in the entirety of the shit show before me.

"Lou—"

"Yeah, he's dead." I swallowed. "Or, shit, I don't know... He should be."

"Judas Priest," Stephan frowned, "what's that mean?"

"Karl," I lowered my voice, "caved his head in with an axe, but ... forget it."

"Forget what?"

"He..." I closed my eyes, saw the shattered face leering, the crooked brown teeth, my memory so clear now despite the smoke, so intricate, so vile, so precise. "I don't know. It was dark. The smoke thick. I could barely..."

"Brother," Stephan frowned, "just say it."

"Maybe he ain't dead. Somehow. Like with Lazarus. Or Rudiger. Or the Grey-Lady. Or he was, but he was..." I clutched my chest, "still moving. Still crawling. Still coming after me."

Stephan raised an eyebrow. "Karl see it?"

"No. Only me." I ground my teeth. "It was probably the smoke. Jesus. The stink. The terror. The horror." I closed my eyes, shook my head, tried moving past the visage of the dead monstrosity stalking me through the hell-scape only to find Rudiger's teeth gnashing from the other end.

"What are you going to do?"

"Like I said. Sort it out."

"Is that wise?"

"No. Not even a little." I took a breath, hocked up some guttural phlegm, spat it aside. "Not even close." Black as tar. "Never wise talking to kings. Getting involved with kings. Better to be some nameless sod scraping away a pittance in some barren field west of Nod. Thought maybe King Eckhardt was different."

"He's not," Stephan said.

"Yeah. And we're in it now."

"I'm sorry I forced the issue. You were right. We shouldn't have come."

"We'd be at the bottom of the river if we'd have listened to me." I shrugged. "Not saying it wouldn't have been better, but it doesn't matter." Another section of roof collapsed in a shower of embers. "What matters is Lady Mary. Abe and Ruth. The kids. I'm going back."

"And then what?"

"Don't know, brother. Since when do I know anything?"

...fully half of our remaining Teutonic brethren hath fallen to their inhuman might.

Yet we have discovered their lair.

—*War-Journal of Prince Ulrich of Haeskenburg*

Chapter 36.

OY, YOU DIRTY red bastards!" I hollered up through both hands. "Open the fucking gates!"

The Schloss von Haesken's gates loomed above. They did not suddenly, magically, mystically, open. Karl hocked up a lunger and spat. It was black with soot and oozed down the gate, inching like a hesitant slug. Karl's crossbow was loaded for bear and held at the ready. I didn't know what sort of reception awaited us. I was not expecting all roses and song.

"Piss off, now, won't ye?" barked a voice from atop the gatehouse.

"We're here on King Eckhardt's order," I shook my fist, "so open the fucking gates!"

Karl raised an eyebrow at my clenched fist. "You're doin' a fine job."

"Bite me." I didn't even look at him.

"Taran, open the gates!" bellowed a voice from beyond the wall. Sir Alaric. "Let 'em in!"

"I-I can't," Taran's voice whined. "Sir Dietrick ordered—"

"What?" Feet stomped up stairs. "I'll skin your hide, you clay-brained wastrel."

"It were on—" The sound of someone being slapped allayed the conclusion.

Flickering torchlight followed as Sir Alaric's head appeared above the ramparts. "Hold, lad. Hold on—" he called down. "Been … rrrg … a stretch since I pulled guard duty." The sound of a lever being pulled, followed by cascading chain. "By the hound… It's unbarred. Give it … give it a stout push."

I dropped my shoulder into the right-hand gate and pushed. A figure appeared as I stepped through. "Ye ain't allowed inside!" Taran thrust a hand in my face.

"Best listen to your betters, kid." I cocked my head toward Sir Alaric as he pounded down the stairs. "Or elders, at least."

As Taran glanced over, I kneed him in the balls. Hard. He folded like a tin breastplate. On his knees, teetering like a cut tree, waiting on the wind, he fell into the dirt to the sound of a cat mewling. *Satisfaction*, a word that came to mind. But then, I'm a small man.

Taran struggled to rise.

Then he froze.

With fair-good reason.

"Keep moving if you like, lad," Karl set the toe-hook of his thane-axe against Taran's throat, "my axe ain't."

"What the hell happened?" I scowled down at Taran.

"Huh…?" Taran replied very, very carefully.

The courtyard looked as though a hurricane had torn through. Debris lay strewn in the muck. A few tents stood, but most were flattened or, at best, leaning last-call drunks, coat tails flapping in the breeze.

"Mass exodus."

Amongst the carnage, bodies lay scattered.

"Yar, for the most part," Karl rumbled.

Sir Alaric was huffing something fierce when he finally reached us.

271.

"Where's Lady Mary?" I said. "And the ben Aris?"

"Lad…" Sir Alaric looked like shit, haggard, even worse than usual. "King Eckhardt's dead."

"What?"

"Murdered," Sir Alaric swallowed, gasped, clutching his side. "He was murdered. Stabbed."

"Jesus Christ."

"Heard what happened at the leper-house," Sir Alaric huffed. "Best get moving. Ain't safe for you here."

"Ain't safe anywhere, old man."

"But even so," Sir Alaric pointed past me, "best you be heading back on out."

I glanced over my shoulder at the open gate. I won't lie. We could have kept moving, hiding, til the Kriegbad Pass opened. Or the *Ulysses* was hale. It was tempting. Fair tempting. But if I'm famous for one thing, it's always making the worst choice. "Me and mine are still within these walls, yeah?"

"Aye and for sure, lad, but—"

"They still alive?"

"For the now, but—" Sir Alaric turned as the Schloss's front door burst open.

Sir Gustav and Von Madbury marched out, armed to the teeth, clomping strong. Brother Miles and Prince Eventine and the others filed alongside, the whole retinue phalanxed at their back. Von Madbury's mouth was flapping the whole while, spouting hate through rictus and jeer.

"You know about any of this?" I spat.

"Lord." Sir Alaric latched onto my shoulder, his hand quivering. "No. I heard about it just now, I swear. I — I been…"

I could smell the booze hard on his breath, emanating from his body, his pores, his soul. "No worries, old man," I said. "And I'm sorry about before. About leaving you behind. About…"

"Forget it, lad," Sir Alaric groaned. "And I'm sorry for—"

"Forget it." I drew Yolanda singing free and clear as an angel song on summer morn. "There's work to be done."

"Jesus, now ain't the time—"

"I'd beg to differ." I shrugged free from his grasp. "Hold!" I held up a hand to the encroaching phalanx, "or your man here's done." I muttered down to Taran, sprawled in the muck, a point of Karl's steel contention caressing his precious neck. "They fond of you, boy?"

Taran gulped, closed his eyes, started praying.

"That'd be a *no.*"

Prince Eventine and Brother Miles gave pause. The rest? Not even a little. Von Madbury waved them on, and they fell in like automatons while Sir Gustav kept marching at the fore. He wasn't the pausing type. The thinking type. The living type.

"Don't kill him just yet," I hissed at Karl.

"Yar."

Sir Gustav, veins on his bull-neck bulging, was nigh upon me, eyes blazing as he cast his scabbard aside and took up his naked war-blade. "Blackguard!"

"Krait, please," Sir Alaric groaned, "there's too many. Y-You can't afford this."

"Never been much good with money, old man," I deadpanned, the numb whisper of impending doom settling like a leaden shroud across my soul.

"Sir Gustav!" Sir Alaric croaked. "Put up your blade! Men. Dietrick. Prince! *Stop this!* We none of us can afford it!"

Sir Gustav didn't hear, and if he did, he didn't listen.

No one did.

"You challenged me before, yeah?" I strode toward him. "To the death?"

"Aye!" Sir Gustav bellowed.

"Then I bloody-well accept!"

Neither of us stopped.

"Sanction it!" I yelled.

"It's sanctioned," Sir Gustav bellowed.

There were no more words after that.

He wasn't the *words* type.

My throat was raw as fuck. Coated in scales of smoke and char and leper ash. I hacked and spat. Kept on walking.

Thirty feet…

Twenty…

Fifteen…

Clomping through the muck, kicking aside tent poles and clutter, before the breaking-wheel, Sir Gustav drew his war-blade back mid-stride as I entered range. His teeth ground together, lips curling back in an animal snarl as we came together swift as two rams clashing.

Overhead, he swung, a great galloping arc that might've felled an oak.

"Die!" he roared, his blade careening at my face.

Sliding forth and pivoting just so, I caught his blade crashing, biting at an angle into mine, my point riding in, wedging his aside a whisker wide of my face, his power flowing past, over, steel rasping against steel, sparks ripping ragged. My feet were rooted, unmoving. And Yolanda? Steadfast and steady as true north, she caught the blackguard through the eye on point, gliding in and through, soft as a lover's whisper before jagging matter out the back of his skull.

Sir Gustav's war-blade plopped in the muck, his arms dangling limp, and for a moment, we just stood there, linked by flesh and steel, life and death, a visage of idiotic incredulity contorting the oaf's dullard mug. Jaw agape, thick lips working like he was trying to say something, form some last testament worth its weight in goat shit.

Mumbling. Drooling. A hollow groan.

Then he dropped.

"Murder!" someone screamed.

"Fuck your murder." I stepped on Sir Gustav's face and muscled Yolanda scraping free. I pointed it at Prince Eventine. Shock and awe as he stammered. "Now where's your bloody father?"

...strigoi along with their guardians were indescribable.

Through surprise and sheer number, we slaughtered them, but our cost was dear. Of the fifty who penetrated into their lair, only eight escaped, and of those, two are crippled in body while three in both mind and spirit.

Sir Elliot, my boon companion, my childhood friend, my brother in arms, lies amongst the fallen.

—War-Journal of Prince Ulrich of Haeskenburg

Chapter 37.

THE BARE-BLADED TRUTH was I didn't give a shit about King Eckhardt. And I didn't give a shit about the princes. The Queen. Any of them. But that, along with the general disbelief of what'd just happened to Sir Gustav's face and my sword got me in through the Schloss's front door before the big dope finished twitching. A last glance back at all of them standing round, gawping down, muttering in disbelief, before Karl slammed the door.

Abe and his family's room was locked. I didn't have the key, so I made do how I always. Took a couple boots but the door ceded firmly to my vigorous demands.

"Holy Hell..." I gasped.

"Sir Luther—" Lady Mary scrambled forth. "What in heaven's breadth is going on?"

"Nothing good." I glared up. "Pack whatever you can carry."

A halo of ashen faces stared back. Except for Abraham's. His bore a bluish cast, and each breath he took was a labor. A struggle. A nascent defeat. *Imminent,* a word that came to mind.

"Get out!" Tears streamed down Ruth's face as she read my mind. "You have no right — get away from him!"

"Right and wrong's got no purchase here, Ruth."

"Leave. Him. *Alone.*" Her hands balled into fists.

"Ruth…" It came as barely a whisper, the echo of a whisper. "Please…" Abraham's eyes cracked open, those brown orbs, once so clear, so full of thought and weight and wisdom, now clouded by the shroud of impending doom. *"Krait…"* He whispered no word, he merely mouthed it through tremulous lips. *"Take them."* He pointed. *"Go."*

"Ruth won't." I knelt, lowered my voice. "Not without you."

"I know." He swallowed. *"P-Please…"*

Fumbling for something to say, something useful, something meaningful, I failed, prodigiously, only nodding at his drowning silence.

His brow furrowed, lips pursed in frustration, a Herculean task considering, and I felt his hand clutching at my belt, fumbling for my dagger. "Trying to do me in, old-timer?"

"No…" He withdrew his hand, dropping it to his chest, *"Me. For me."*

"I know. Jesus. I know."

"Please," Abraham coughed. It was like a half-drowned kitten choking on a thimbleful of milk. Ruth was back, shoving past, clutching his hand, embracing, murmuring vapid platitudes. Grimacing through her hair, his teeth pink with hacked spume, Abraham mouthed, *"Please…"*

Again, I said nothing, just offered a cool glare, a curt nod, and gripped my blade.

He seemed to settle after that.

"Pack your shit." I turned to the kids. "Apologies. *Stuff.* We need to get the hell out of here. Heck." Jesus.

277.

"No." Ruth glared.

"Time's short."

"Don't presume to tell me what my husband needs. What my family needs. What I need!" Ruth gripped the bedpost with a harpy claw, the shattered pieces of her self stitched together by something tenuous, something taut, something fixed to burst. "And there is hope. You said so yourself. The man who can heal, the Nazarene, he's coming." Lady Mary was at her side, hands to her shoulders, muttering. "He's coming *tonight.*"

"Ruth, please," Lady Mary murmured. "He's trying to help—"

"He ain't coming, Ruth," I said.

"He is!" Ruth shoved Lady Mary off then clutched at my mail shirt. "And … and we'll convert. Tonight. There's a priest. The Father — Father Gregorius. We'll take vows, and the Nazarene—"

"The Nazarene's dead." I peeled her hands off my shirt.

"What—?" Ruth's lips contorted. *"No!* It's a lie."

I hesitated, wondering if the Nazarene was yet drawing breath and knowing sure-as-shit if he were, somehow, through grace of God or his empirical opposite, he'd be in no mood to come curing my boon companions, newly converted or not.

Lady Mary's eyes quivered. "Sir Luther, what has—"

"No." Ruth clawed up to her feet. "No! It's a lie!"

"He's dead." I pointed at the kids. "And they're next. You're next. *We're all next.* Soon as those bastards outside gather their limited wits."

"No!" Ruth sputtered.

"Quiet—" I barked as though it'd make some difference.

"Please, Ruth." Lady Mary raised a hand. "They locked us in here like animals—"

"No! Th-there isn't much time." Ruth clutched Abraham's face, leaned in, kissed his cold blue lips. "Oh, my dear. My dear. My love. Don't fear, don't fret," she smoothed back his sparse hair, "he'll come. I've seen him. He said he'd come! We'll get out of this together—"

"Lady Mary," I rose from my knee, "take the kids down to the great hall."

Ruth's hands balled into fists. "No."

"Lady Mary—"

"Damn you!" Ruth came at me, launching her frail form, clawing for my eyes.

Abraham lifted a hand, purple lips working, voiceless, eyes pleading.

Ruth was frail. Starving. Hadn't slept in days. But she possessed a maniac strength born of desperation and hate.

"Jesus Christ!" I caught her by the wrists, ragged nails straining for my eyes as she poured into me, squealing, wailing, gnashing, driving me backward, tripping over a chair and flat on my back. A snap and a squeal as her left wrist broke. I let go, "Ruth, for God's sake—" but she kept on coming, clawing, busted bones and all, with her good hand, her bad hand, her teeth and knees and whatever else she had. I slipped backward on my arse, her nails raking my face, catching her by the elbow on her back-swing, driving a foot into her hip, upending her and ripping her down, smashing face-first into the floor.

The kids wailing…

Blood pounding…

Lady Mary screaming…

I blinked. "Jesus…" I hadn't meant to slam her, but then, I hadn't meant *not* to, either. "Lord…" I clambered up.

Lady Mary knelt, pawing at her. "Ruth…?"

She might've been dead.

"Her wrist's broken," I growled.

Abraham lay seething, pink foam eking down his chin, his head craned toward Ruth, eyes roiling in desperation, madness, hate. At the very least.

"Alright." I drew my dagger.

"Sir Luther!" Lady Mary stopped me cold. "Sheathe it. Put it away! Rose of Sharon. Now!" She pointed toward the door. "Joshua! Sarah! Out in the hall. Go. Now."

The kids ignored her, pawing at their listless mother.

"You against me, too?" I snarled.

"Judas Priest—" Lady Mary closed her eyes and shook her head. "Look! For the love of God, look." She pointed. "*Look!*"

The kids peered up, first Sarah then Joshua.

"F-Father…?"

Then came the waterworks.

"No, he's…" I stammered, stopped, straightened, lowering the dagger to my side, hiding it behind my back. Then I dropped it, clanging to the floor. Abraham's face was frozen in a rictus of rage and hate and agony, his body contorted over as his last act in life had been watching me beat the shit out of his beloved wife.

"I'm sorry, Abe. Sorry for a lot." I swiped my dagger off the floor and headed out the door. I had bigger fish to fry.

...in celebration, the Hochmeister ordered the remainder of the clan-holt prisoners crucified. We had no proper stock, so we made do with the wheels of our wagons.

We supped that eve to the music of hammers falling, bone shattering, of men, women, and children screaming.

It was a tepid celebration.

—War-Journal of Prince Ulrich of Haeskenburg

Chapter 38.

QUEEN ELONA SPANNED the doorway like some black widow slathered across her web, her slender arms gripping the jamb in some piss-poor attempt at denying me access. Her eyes flashed with an animal panic. "Sir Luther. Please. I beg of you. Leave. This—" she swallowed, "this doesn't concern you." Past her, King Eckhardt lay in his bed. It was fair clear even from the hallway that he was dead. Dead, and then some. "I-I'll not have you disturbing him."

The corpse-king lay abed, staring at the ceiling, his mouth open in silent scream, limbs contorted out, fingernails black. His own sword had been driven through the right side of his chest, jutting out like some extra appendage, pinning him to the bed like a bug in a collection.

"I'll try not to wake him," I deadpanned.

"I didn't do it." I could smell on her breath she'd been drinking. A lot.

"Didn't say you did." I raised my hands. "Now what the hell's going on?"

"But that's what they'll think. What they'll all think." She was starting to make Ruth look calm and reasonable by comparison. "It was Dietrick. It … It had to be." She wiped slaver from the corner of her mouth.

"Is that what you believe? Or what you want to believe?"

"Does it matter? For the love of God, please, go."

"I've gotta take a look."

"You say you're a shit. A scoundrel. Well, prove it."

"Where've you been?"

"I... For the love of God, leave." She pointed past me down the hall. "If you'll offer no help. No hope." She clamped down, nails biting into the jamb. "No anything."

"Elona. Move. Please," I said it softly but kept moving forward.

"You," she sneered. "You'd not lay a hand on a lady."

"Go tell that to Ruth." I pushed past her, gently, firmly, inexorably. "Pardon me. Again."

The Queen recoiled as though to strike me but froze. "You think you're so smart. You all think you're so God-damned smart."

"If I was smart, I wouldn't be here."

A smile slid trembling across her face. Gears turning inside. Ragged. Rusty. Sharp. Then she turned and strode off down the hall.

What the hell was that?

I paused a step inside the King's bedchamber, scanning the floor. Made sure I wasn't going to spoil the portrait painted. Old rushes covered the flagstones, offering a pallid, forest scent. King Eckhardt's chambers were spartan and close, a small shuttered window the lone source of light. Dust hung in the air. Coat-of-plate armor, the King's empty scabbard, a gold-embossed crossbow, and other accouterments of war were slung over a rack set by the window, a dagger glinting on the sill.

I glanced at the King's face then didn't again. A scream of silent anguish was cast onto it. Lips curled back over gums black and shiny as coal. Teeth protruding. A grimace like a cornered rat. The whites of his eyes engorged with blood. Open. Glaring. Accusatory.

Thoughts of Abraham's face, fresh in my mind, supplanted the King's. I shook it off. Or tried to, anyway.

"Odin's eye." Karl appeared at the door. "Don't pay to be dead."

"Not today," I said. "The Queen just left. She's in a state. Make sure she doesn't let our friends in. Hazard the lads might be emboldened to commence our lynching."

"Lynch…?" Karl's brow furrowed.

"Jesus Christ." I looped an imaginary noose round my neck, yanked up, and stuck out my tongue. "Come up here and bloody-well hang us."

"Us…?" Karl grinned toothily before disappearing. "I didn't kill nobody."

"Yeah," I muttered, "not lately, anyway."

From out in the yard came shouting. The Queen. Father Gregorius. Von Madbury. A discussion. Heated. The Queen marched out the front door toward her one-eyed paramour. The Schloss's full retinue of fighters had gathered below, still huddled round the fallen form of Sir Gustav, laid out in the yard, arms crossed over his chest, sword laid out upon him. It was a vast improvement.

The screaming came again. Harsh. Shrill. Jarring. As one, glares rose from the corpse to the Schloss's gaping front door then to me. Von Madbury acted first, walking, then jogging, then hauling.

"Hey, fuck-face!" I hollered.

"Eh—?" Von Madbury skidded to a halt, glaring up. "Krait, you bastard! What the hell do you want?!" he roared as Karl's shaggy head appeared in the front door, slamming shut an instant later.

"Oh, nothing." I pulled back inside, took a deep breath.

I turned back to the corpse-king. Ran a hand through my hair. It was hard to equate that rictus of pain with the insipid countenance of the man I'd spoken with mere hours past. Always an odd thing. A haunting thing. Seeing someone dead who'd only so recently been otherwise.

I'd seen my share.

The night before battle, the two of you drinking and dicing and swearing and praying. Jawing on into the night long past when you should be sleeping. Resting. Staying sharp. Then comes the aftermath, so sudden, so sharp, and you're staring down at a hunk of flesh and metal, wondering what you're going to write the poor bastard's family. What you're gonna tell them to make sense of it all when you were right there and can't make heads or tails. So you start thinking up all the gleaming poetics you can muster to deify the departed when you know in the hellfire pit of your gut it won't matter what you do, what you say, what you write. So you do nothing, say nothing, write nothing cause you don't want to be the last nail in a loaded coffin.

But you can't do that with a king. Not when you're in his service. Entwined in the morass. And until we'd beat feet, I was entwined. My brother was entwined. Lady Mary and Karl. All of us. Entwined round our necks by nooses, wind blowing, toes gripping the rough-hewn planks of the trap door beneath.

Alright. Focus.

I inspected the bed, drawing back the linens and blankets torn asunder when the King died kicking in his throes. Jesus. Dying in a nightshirt? Skinny legs sticking out all pale and hairy? Small dignity in that.

The sword piercing his chest had been very neatly done. It'd come in at an angle through the ribs on his right side. I pulled his nightshirt up to see if I was missing other wounds. I wasn't. One good thrust, nigh on to the hilt. Through the lungs. The great vessels. The heart.

Rigor mortis had set in. His arms were like wood, ramrod straight, stiff. He'd been dead a while. A few hours at least. Using his limbs as levers, I gripped and lifted. "Rrrg…" Jesus. I readjusted. Moving a rigored corpse is a pain in the balls. Took some doing, some awkward fumbling, like trying to flip a table by grasping the bottom of one leg, but I managed. Eventually.

"Hmm…"

The sword stuck out through his back. It'd pinned him to the bed when he'd toppled over backward. Or he'd been lying down when he was stabbed. Blood soaked the sheets, the mattress, pooling in a clotted mess.

Outside, von Madbury pounded on the keep door, demanding it be opened by order of the Queen. Of the King. Of the Lord God Almighty. Seemed Karl was deaf, though, or a piss-poor listener, or just a downright stone-walling prick, which happened to be precisely why I kept him around.

When I was done with the corpse-king, I wrestled him back near to how I'd found him. "Hmmm…"

"*Hmmm*, what?" came a voice from the doorway.

"What the—?" I banged my head on the bedpost and nearly ended up alongside the corpse.

Lady Mary stood at the door, peering in, a look of consternation twisting her lip. "Here. Your face." She dug around a knapsack and withdrew a handful of bandages and a small bottle. "We have to clean it up." She unstopped the bottle then upended it into the bandages.

"Ain't bleeding anymore."

"Bites are renowned for festering." Lady Mary paused when her gaze fell upon the King. "*Sweet mercy…*"

"Wrong on both counts." I pulled the linens up, covering the corpse-king.

"Who…?" she stammered.

"I'm fair certain it was suicide," I deadpanned.

"Where…" She stood there mesmerized for a moment. "Where's your brother? And what the hell's going on?"

"Out ministering to the downtrodden. And you tell me. I've been busy."

"I don't know." Lady Mary dabbed some concoction on my cheek. It stung like hell and I told her so. She didn't seem to care. "We were prisoners."

"Even you?"

"I can't bandage it." Lady Mary grimaced, tucking away the bottle. "Prince Eventine offered to release me. In exchange for my hand."

"The wooden one or real?"

"I'm glad you still have the time to be an arse."

I offered a bow. "I hope you told him to fuck off."

"Not in those words, exactly, but yes, more or less." Lady Mary fingered the tip of her hook hand. "Rose of Sharon. That was hours ago. And we … we heard something from outside. Screaming. A panic. A commotion."

"Yeah. They ran off the camp folk." I thought on the corpses littering the yard. "Those they didn't run *through,* anyways." I glanced past her shoulder. "Ruth…?" I didn't know what question to ask.

"Still out cold. The children are…" Lady Mary ran a hand through her hair. "I have to get back. There's nothing to pack. A few blankets. A jug for water. Nothing else to take. Nothing to…" She glanced toward the window. "Things are falling apart."

"Yeah. And then some."

Lady Mary crossed herself as she took in the corpse-king. "I always thought he wasn't what he appeared to be."

"Despondent? Weak? Indecisive?"

"Aye. Yes. Well… Perhaps he was exactly what he appeared to be." Lady Mary crossed herself again for good measure. "I suppose I merely hoped he wasn't. Or prayed."

From outside came the sound of someone taking an axe to the Schloss's front door.

Thunk…

Thunk…

Thunk…

"Company." I glared out the window. "Have you seen Sir Alaric?"

The hacking continued. But it was a stout door. And it had Karl buttressing it.

"I saw a light in his room." Lady Mary stood at my side gazing out the window. "Something inside him's broken as well."

"Lot of that going around." I shrugged, tapped my chest. "I've a special place in here for overwrought drunks languishing under the thumb of weak kings." I raised an eyebrow toward the King's weapons rack. "You any good with a crossbow?"

Pride was not a thing we clung fast to in our pyrrhic victory.
—*War-Journal of Prince Ulrich of Haeskenburg*

Chapter 39.

WITH HIS HAIRY-TWIG legs splayed out from beneath his moth-eaten nightshirt, a bent-framed portrait tucked under one arm, Sir Alaric lazed across the floor, leaning against the foot of his bed, propping him upright. Sort of. A gleaming knife leaned across one leg, a flaccid skin of whiskey by his side. He was drunk off his arse. At the very least. "You work fast," I said.

"Come to pay yer last respects?" he slurred.

"That'd require me to have had first respects," I deadpanned.

"Heh. Don't surprise me." Sir Alaric cracked an eye. Fire rippled soft in the hearth, a tangy smoke thick in the air. He had a belt looped tourniquet-wise round his bicep.

"Chimney needs cleaning," I coughed, meandering through the stratified smoke, and pushed open the shutters. "Jesus." It'd gone quiet outside. Which could've been a good thing or not. But probably not. "Or the damper's closed." I waved a hand. "Either way, you need a bath."

Sir Alaric frowned over at the meager fire, shrugged, cinched the tourniquet tight with his teeth then set the belt buckle. "One way's as good as another."

"I'd beg to differ." I appraised him solemnly. "But you're doing it right. Mostly. Warm fire. All snug as a bug, sipping liquid sunshine in a soft balmy haze. Could be worse." I sniffed. "You're missing a pretty young lass to sing sad imminent sorrows, though. I could send for Wenelda?"

"Pretty?" He squinted in suspicion. "Young?"

"Sorry," I held out my hands, "short notice, you understand?"

"Hmm? Naw." Sir Alaric wiped his mouth then clutched the knife. "As such, ain't sure I could rise to the occasion. I've had trouble since..." Veins bulged on his forearm. "Well..." he closed his eyes and nodded, fingers working as he opened and closed his hand, "you'll just have to do."

"Well, I am pretty," I admitted.

He chuffed a stunted laugh, dabbed an eye, took a swig.

Stacks of unfinished portraits leaned against the walls. Some outlined. Some half-painted. Others nigh on complete but missing that final sheen of professional polish. The one under his arm was the exception. It was a masterpiece.

"What the hell happened here?" I asked.

"Feel it's fair evident."

"Give me something." I crossed my arms.

"Prefer to not talk on it presently."

"Oh? When?" I asked. "Tomorrow good?"

"I'm sorry for all this, lad." His old hound dog eyes wept clear. "Truly, and I am."

"You should be. You're the only one left who's not a complete asshole." I eyed his knife. "And now you're fixed on taking the easy way out?"

"Easy?" Sir Alaric considered a moment. "I don't know. All's I know is I'm sorry about ditching you with so much unfinished business. Navigating a shit-storm blind through the pitch black of night."

"You are a useless old prick, but you're still kicking. And that ain't nothing."

"My wife's dead, lad." Sir Alaric clutched the portrait to his chest, fingers gripping the frame. A woman I could only describe as majestically beautiful stared out from the canvas with soulful brown eyes. Lady Catherine. She looked … strangely familiar. "Used to hear her some nights. Alone in the dark. Alone. Freezing. Sickness gnawing holes through her. But scratching at the door, begging to be let in. But I can't never find the knob. I scrabble up and down, left and right, but ain't nothing there." He moaned. "And she's right there, by the hound, she's right bloody *there.*"

"It's just a dream, Red," I said.

"Sometimes I wonder."

"And you've still a daughter who needs you."

"The high and mighty Queen? Heh. Naw. She don't need no one," Sir Alaric said. "Made it clear she don't need me. Lass can fend for herself. Always could. Better at all this shite than me. Her sister now…" He dry-swallowed something back. "And I … I'm just an old, beat-down law-dog who can barely lift his prick let alone a sword."

I shrugged. "It is what it is."

"And what it is," Sir Alaric struggled for the word, "is shit. Is horror. Is — *lord in heaven,* failure." He took a drink. "I was supposed to serve. To protect…" He winced as he formed a flaccid fist. "Was supposed to…"

I nodded at his hand. "How's it coming?"

"Nigh on there." He pursed his lips. "Naught but pinpricks."

"Good," I said. "Who ordered them after us at the leper-house?"

"Eh? Oh, I … I don't know," Sir Alaric winced. "I'm cut off, y'see? Sold out. Impotent. A damned eunuch. You were there. Stripped me of my station. Cuckolded me. *Again.*" Sir Alaric scowled at the wineskin then hurled it across the room. "Understand something, lad. If I'd known they was coming your way… If I'd known when or how or … or anything, I'd have done something. Warn you. Stop them. Something. *Anything.* On my life, on my soul, I swear it."

"I know it, Red."

He slumped. "I … I thank you for that, truly and I do." Sir Alaric raised an eyebrow. "Been meaning to ask, what the hell happened to your face?"

"Wenelda. Getting frisky. You should see my cock. What's left of it, anyways."

"Appreciate it, but I'll pass."

Sir Alaric leaned back, losing his balance, knocking over Lady Catherine's portrait.

"Easy, old man."

"It's nothing." He struggled back upright. "Did what ye had to."

"Red," if I could just get within arm's length of his blade, "what's *strigoi* mean?"

"What? Eh? Don't…" Sir Alaric rubbed his belly. "Where'd you hear it?"

"The Nazarene," I grimaced. "He told me to ask the King. See what he says. And I did, but the King wasn't in any shape to answer."

"And that's a fact."

"Those poor buggers crucified?" I said. "Wasn't the Nazarene killed them, yeah?"

"I…" Sir Alaric's knuckles turned white on the knife hilt, "I don't know, lad."

"What do you know?"

"Not enough. Not … not nearly enough."

The stacks of unfinished portraits leered, a silent jury watching with consternation, mute accusation, awaiting final judgment.

Sir Alaric hefted his knife, tottering almost ass-over-tea kettle again. "Fair travels."

"Put the blade down."

"Decision's made, lad." Sir Alaric set the blade against his forearm, biting into a risen vein. Just a quick nick and the world'd run red. "Foregone. That's the word…"

"Fuck your foregone. You're telling me you're sorry for stranding me in a shit-storm? Then don't. Suck it up. Stay. Help make it right."

"Right?" Sir Alaric sucked his teeth. "Ain't no such thing. Not now. Not ever. We both ken it."

"No shit. Then help get me and mine out of here. Jesus. Be a knight."

"I told you what I was. What I am. And what I ain't."

"I know where you're at. And I know where you want to be. But I need you here."

"How fares the *Ulysses?*" Sir Alaric muttered.

"Dry dock still." I slid a little closer.

"That's close enough," Sir Alaric warned. "Wouldn't want to stick you by accident in a tussle. Won't do no one no good." He grimaced at the knife, trembling in hand. *"Come on, lad—"*

"All those poor bastards you swore to protect." I poured it on. "All those poor pricks turned out into the streets. Into the hills. All of them starving and wasting and dying one by bloody one. Gonna cut and run on them, too?"

I could see him staggering beneath my blows but withstanding, numb as he was.

"I…" Sir Alaric swallowed slowly, precisely, his Adam's apple jumping. "You made your point, lad. Now, for the love of God, make your peace."

I held out a hand. "Give me the damned knife."

"I'm steeled to it now," Sir Alaric snarled. "Ain't you seen? Ain't you listened?"

"I'm thick as shit."

"Honor demands—"

"Honor demands you get me and mine out of here. Honor demands you find who killed your King. And honor demands you find your wife's killer."

"Two out of three…" Sir Alaric's voice cracked. "You don't ken it. I just want to see her so bad—"

"And you will. We're all piloting that skiff white-knuckled downriver, a full gale howling at our stern. And there's no stopping. No coming about," I said. "She'll be there waiting when you arrive. So do something. One last thing. Do what *Catherine* would want you to."

"I…" Sir Alaric crumbled beneath my final blow.

It was a low one, using his wife, but life and death? You throw whatever combination'll land. Whatever'll do damage. I held Lady Catherine's portrait out at arm's length and whistled. "She was a real looker, yeah?" I set it down across from him, leaning it against one of the stacks. "What was she doing with an old hound like you?"

"Lad…"

"What was she like?"

Sir Alaric's frigid rictus trembled to a halt, a germ of warmth taking root as the grim shroud of determination melted. "Aw, lad," he choked out, his knife clattering to the floor, "but weren't she grand…"

...departed to the croak of a desiccated crone, cawing like a raven after our departure.

That she was still able to draw breath after her ordeal was the last testament to the hardiness of her slaughtered folk.

—War-Journal of Prince Ulrich of Haeskenburg

Chapter 40.

SIR ALARIC GROANED, drooling as I dragged him up, limp as a dead fish, onto his bed, rolling him over. I rubbed my back. My neck. He was a pint-sized old geezer but seemed of the variety whose bones were made of lead. Or I was just getting old. Weak. Pathetic. Leaning over, back creaking, I grabbed the one boot Sir Alaric still wore and yanked it off. "Jesus."

Sir Alaric didn't answer, but a voice from behind said, "You're a man of dichotomies in stark opposition, if you don't mind my saying."

I stiffened. Recovered awkwardly. But it was only Prince Palatine. "What the hell's a dichotomy?" I turned.

"I think you know more than you let on." Prince Palatine leaned against the doorjamb, his crippled arm clutched to his chest as though by some unseen sling, a thick book pressed into its crook. "Earlier in the yard, with Sir Gustav." He dabbed a tear from his eye. "Forgive me. And now," he nodded toward Sir Alaric, "with grandfather. How do you explain that? A man who plays the part of death-dealer in one breath yet savior in the next?"

"Savior's a bit strong." I yanked a blanket up over Sir Alaric. "But to each his own. Besides, Sir Alaric's a good man. Or at least tries to be. Gustav? Well, not so much."

"Is it all that simple?"

"Yeah. Sure. Unless you don't like sleeping nights." I did a half-arsed job of tucking Sir Alaric in. "You want to be up til dawn, mind racing, untangling endless knots, that's as good a subject as any. Your failing marriage is another." I started counting on my fingers. "Being a horrible father. Or human being, in general. Wondering if God truly exists, and if he does, why's he hate us so much. Then taking a hard look at us, and knowing exactly why." I straightened, brushing my hair aside. It was gritty with dried blood. "You saw your old man?"

"Yes," Prince Palatine twitched a spaced nod, "it was…"

"Yeah kid," I said, "it sure as hell was."

From outside the window, someone shouted epithets into the night. A blade was unsheathed and clanged against a shield.

"Are…" Prince Palatine crushed away tears, "are you going to let them in?"

"Doesn't seem prudent." I looked out the window. The Schloss's front door was still intact. "Maybe once they simmer down."

"Unlikely to be anytime soon."

"I had that same thought," I said. "Another thought I had was maybe you might try and let them in."

"Might I assume it would cause a problem?"

"Yeah," I said slowly, carefully, "it would."

Prince Palatine pursed his lips.

"And not to put too fine a point on it, my Prince, but I'm not so gallant a knight that I wouldn't hurl a cripple headfirst out a window." I held up a hand. *"Defenestration* is the word."

"Well, I… I thank you for your candor."

"You're most welcome." I bowed. "And I'll ask you to remain in your room. Or the library, I suppose."

"Yes. Of course."

"I could knock you around a bit so your people know you didn't give in too easily?"

"A grand gesture, Sir Luther, and I thank you again, but I'll pass." Prince Palatine gripped his book tight. "Benefits of being a cripple. No one expects anything of you and so you can never disappoint them."

"Sounds wonderful. Might try it sometime." I glanced at his book. "More trouble sleeping?"

"I fear I shan't. Not tonight. Maybe not ever."

"Not Ockham?"

"No. My family treatise. I found it in the vault. Under lock and key. It is perhaps, what you were looking for earlier."

"Any hints as to the maelstrom churning?"

"I…I've only just started." Prince Palatine adjusted the large tome. "I need something to occupy my mind. Something to make me forget, even if only for a short while."

"Let me know if you find anything useful. Anything about *strigoi.*"

"*Strigoi?*" He frowned.

"Yeah."

In the courtyard below, the same someone screamed bloody murder. Or its near approximation.

"You saw what my father did?" Prince Palatine shuffled to the window. "To the tent city? The refugees? His people? His own people?" Prince Palatine shook his head. "His last order to those … those…" He swallowed. *"Clear them out. Forthwith.* My father's final act. The exodus and murder of his own folk.

"No wonder everyone hated him," Prince Palatine spat. "Patron saint of half-measures. Blotted ink. Of clipped oaths. What kind of man takes in those he's sworn to protect, only to turn them out? And at the end of a spear?"

"The kind of man who's like most," I said. "A little good. A fair cut bad. And a lot of nothing in between."

"He was the keeper of the law."

"Maybe he was thinking of you and your brother when he drove them out?" I shrugged. Jesus. Why the hell was I defending him? "Maybe he did it to protect you? Shit. I don't know."

"And does that make it right?"

"You got something you want to say to me, kid?"

"My father's last thoughts… Mother of Mary." Prince Palatine fumbled his tome, almost dropping it. "What you said before. I can't not think of them. His last moments. The look of horror. Sheer terror. Oh, Lord…"

"Here." I offered up a flask of something from Sir Alaric's nightstand. At the grimace on the kid's face, I heard the blade scrape past bone as it sank into King Eckhardt's chest. *Schlunk*. Could hear him screaming. Thrashing around. Kicking. Then not. "Might take the edge off." Just to be sure, though, I took a pull.

It passed.

Prince Palatine limped over, cane in hand, grasping onto the foot of the bed. He took the flask, a furtive sip, and plopped down at Sir Alaric's feet. Sir Alaric rolled over, his arm flopping. He licked his chops, farted prodigiously, then settled into snoring.

"Don't think on it too hard," I said.

"But you just said—"

"Using me as a model for successful living's not liable to help you achieve it." I stared at the flask in his hand. "Take another pull, and when you're done, kill the rest. Doctor's orders."

"A-Alright." Prince Palatine took another sip.

"My brother likens it to walking barefoot along a rusted razor." Mouth watering, I stared at the flask. "The more you keep balance, try not to fall, the deeper the cut."

"Being a king?"

"King? No." I waved a hand. "An afternoon stroll. I'm talking about being a good man."

He glanced up at me. "You've had some experience?"

"A while back, I had some notions about what a good man was supposed to be, what he was supposed to do, how he was supposed to do it."

"And what happened to those notions?"

"More often than not, they got all those around him killed."

We skulked in silence through the night. Bone-weary and broken, we escaped the Carpathians with little more than our lives and the rusted armor clinging to our bowed backs.

—War-Journal of Prince Ulrich of Haeskenburg

Chapter 41.

SOME BLACKGUARD out in the courtyard was wailing something awful. And with fair-good reason.

In the midst of the great hall, Karl sat at the dinner table, littered with weapons of various types, sipping from a mug, cradling his crossbow like a babe as he stroked a hunk of wax along its string. *Shunk... Shunk... Shunk...*

I glanced at the weapon of war. "Gonna play me a tune?"

"Sure." Karl snatched an apple off the table and tossed it my way. "Balance it on yer head."

"They stopped chopping down the door." I caught the apple. Deftly. Dashingly.

"Yar well, we had a good talk." Karl continued waxing the string. "They agreed to stop chopping, and I agreed to stop shooting." He thumbed over his shoulder at one of the murder holes flanking the front door.

"Ah," I took a bite of the forbidden fruit and snatched a peek, "ever the master of the high art of compromise." One of the Prince's retinue sat in the mud, a crossbow bolt through his thigh. It was Taran. I sighed. "Poor bastard can't catch a break."

"Catches crossbow bolts just aces."

"Well, we all play to our strengths." I snatched a crossbow off the table, ran my fingers along its stock, the string, inspecting it stirrup to tiller. It was a gnarly old bastard. Big. Powerful. Weathered. Suffused with a grim sense of purpose.

"I shuttered all the windows. Latched them." Lady Mary marched into the great hall, the King's majestic crossbow cradled in her arms. "But there's too many. With but a ladder and axe it's but a matter of time"

"Yeah," I said. "How're Ruth and the kids?"

"Distraught. Disheveled. Shattered." Lady Mary pursed her lips. "Glued to her beloved's side. On the verge of insanity."

"So about the same?"

"Yes," Lady Mary conceded. "What was it you saw in the King's chamber?"

"Same as you." I stuck my foot in the crossbow stirrup and pulled the string back, locking it in place with a satisfying click. Only sound more satisfying? Pulling the trigger. "Nothing to speak of."

"Nothing to speak…?"

"Yeah." I scanned the table, the deadfall of weapons inter-stitched haphazardly across it. "See any bolts?"

"Here." Karl tossed me one.

"Thanks." I caught it, loaded it, took a breath.

"And what did you make of *the nothing?*"

I opened my mouth to reply—

"Sir Krait!" someone bellowed from outside. "Is that you? C-Can you hear me?" It was Prince Eventine. "Please, sir, my mother … she is freezing out here. And Taran, he is dying, I think. I beg of you, open the door for their admittance, if not the rest of us. And please, do no harm to my brother."

"He's coming down," I said.

Karl scowled. *"Who?"*

"Jesus. The bloody cripple."

Karl shrugged. "Who cares?"

Exasperated by my trollish cohort, I hollered through the murder-hole, "No harm'll come to your brother. You have my word." For whatever my word was worth.

"M-My thanks. Is he there?"

I could see a crown sitting loose and uneven on his brow.

"He'll be here soon," I called. "They coronated you out there?"

"Aye."

"Congratulations."

"I … well … thank you." King Eventine looked down, away, his crown slipping. "An impromptu ceremony in the chapel. It was quite … brusque." His first act as King? To come begging at his own front door. *Auspicious,* a word that did not come to mine. He crept forward at a half-crouch, his arms up, hands empty, open, up. "Please, I beg of you, don't shoot. I'm coming to the door. I understand things got … heated."

"Heated?" I caught a glimpse of Sir Gustav lying like a log out in the dark. He was still dead. "Yeah. I suppose so."

"Tell him to open the door!" the Queen screamed from beyond the dark.

"Mother. Enough!" King Eventine turned. "Please!"

"Your mother can scream." I blocked the murder-hole and turned to Lady Mary, whispering, "Mind going up to Her Majesty's rooms? Take a quick look through them."

"Anything in particular?"

I fixed her a deadpan glare. "Make sure her wardrobe's still in fashion."

"Right." Lady Mary swallowed, nodded, bolted.

"Open the cursed door, you blackguard!" the Queen screamed.

"Apologies, Sir Krait," King Eventine confided through the murder hole. "My mother's ... upset."

"I noticed." I muttered behind to Karl, "How long you hazard til they fetch a ladder?"

"Idiots. But still," Karl scowled, "not long."

"Krait, you bloody bastard!" The Queen raged against the blowing gale, her cloak clutched about her, ends rippling, whipping, cracking like whips. What the hell was she doing? Was it acting? Or had it been with me? I could see von Madbury leering as he whispered in her ear. "I'll have you skinned alive! Br-Broken on the wheel! Hanged by your throat like a c-common thief!"

I figured the three mutually exclusive at most and overkill at the least, but I withheld comment.

"Will you g-grant us entrance?" King Eventine stuttered through the murder-hole.

"Got to be honest," I said, "your mother's making me nervous."

"Hey *Stupid,*" Karl growled.

I turned reflexively. "Yeah?"

Karl thumbed over his shoulder.

"Took your time," I said.

"Sir Luther, forgive me…" Prince Palatine stood clutching the door-jamb, breathing heavy. "The stairs are rather ... steep. By your leave?"

"Kid, you're right on time."

"What aid might I provide?" Prince Palatine straightened, found his balance, started forth.

Raising his crossbow, Karl subtly tipped his distrust by aiming at the Prince's head.

"Easy." I raised a hand.

Karl deigned not to shoot but didn't lower the weapon.

Prince Palatine didn't seem to notice, and if he did, his blood was ice-water.

"Krait, you traitorous blackguard!" the Queen-Mother railed.

Prince Palatine glanced at me in question.

"She's having a rough night," I said. "You looking to get your feet cut?"

"To the bone," he answered.

"Go ahead then, kid."

"Mother!" Prince Palatine called. "Mother, please! Calm yourself." He gimped forward, using the table and chairs to aid him until his face was pressed to the murder hole. "Brother, I'm here. Unharmed. All is well."

Which might've been a slight overestimation.

"Alright." King Eventine, blue-lipped and shivering, reached a hand through the murder-hole and gripped Prince Palatine's hand. "Good. B-Brother. Excellent. You … you saw what was done to father?"

"Aye."

"P-Please, Sir Luther," King Eventine pleaded, "n-name your terms and they shall b-be met."

"I'm fair certain your mother's gonna order my head off the instant you're all back inside," I said. "I'd like proof against that."

"On the contrary," King Eventine drew himself up, "I think with a little civility and a can-do attitude—"

"Krait, you soulless reptile!" the Queen-Mother screeched.

I cocked my head. "Is that a *'can-do'* attitude?"

Karl snorted like a wild-boar, which helped the proceedings, tremendously.

"I'd say rather not," Lady Mary scowled as she entered the hall. Offering a curt shake of her head, she mouthed, *"I found nothing,"* and plopped in a seat across from Karl, the King's crossbow gripped in her lap. I felt as though a portion of her wanted the bastards pouring in through that door. I'd hazard it for a fair-sized portion, too.

"I-I…" King Eventine stuttered.

"Brother. Krait. Please." Prince Palatine licked his lips. "An accord can be met. *Must* be met. Tell mother to take a stroll down to the gates and back. To keep warm. Or better yet, seek shelter in the chapel. It's cold but she'll be out of the wind, at the least."

"I told her. Sh-She won't listen. She refuses to cower, she says."

"By the blood! You're King now. Act like it. Demand it." Prince Palatine thrust his arm through the hole and pointed. "Go!"

"But, I…"

"Go!"

King Eventine let his flaccid argument hang limp as his head, marinating in despondence a moment before he broke fully and marched off. "Mother!"

For the gale wind, I couldn't hear what oratory masterwork King Eventine was weaving, but I could read it in his every move. He was pleading for the Queen-Mother to listen. To accede to his demands. And I could read her acid-tongued counter. She was caught between a rock and a hard place. Ignore her newly crowned son's inaugural decree and emasculate him before all of his men? Or acquiesce, ceding the last vestiges of her own waning power? She stood there in the cold gale, a visage of impotent rage frozen across her face before finally storming off toward the chapel.

"What is it you want?" Prince Palatine swallowed.

"Like I said before, to get me and mine out of here alive. And I want safe passage down to the *Ulysses.*"

"It was my understanding she's not yet seaworthy."

"You were misinformed," I lied. While the *Ulysses* was still more of a water-born sieve than ship, there was enough lumber to clap something together that might ferry us across the river. Certainly, there was enough to get to the bottom.

Prince Palatine's eyes glimmered. "And I wish my father's murderer hunted. Captured. Executed."

"So go find him."

Prince Palatine grimaced.

"You heard what I said."

"So say something else," Prince Palatine said. "Say you'll stay. Say you'll do it, and I'll grant you the safety you desire. You have my word."

"Last I checked, you ain't king."

"My brother—"

"How about von Madbury?" I poured it on. "What assurances can you give against him? And Brother Miles? Sir Roderick and all the others? They've tried clipping my wings twice already."

"Allow my mother inside along with Taran." Prince Palatine glanced at his brother. "The others shall remain outside."

"Raw deal for them."

"Indeed, yet they shall endure." Prince Palatine gripped the edge of the murder-hole. "They must."

I glared outside.

"Sir Luther, say you'll do it. Say you'll stay. Say you'll find my father's killer."

"Von Madbury."

Prince Palatine winced as he adjusted awkwardly. "We … we'll figure something out. I swear it."

Outside, the men huddled in a scrum, shivering under the greying light of early dawn.

"Fine," I said, "I'll do it."

"I have your oath, then?" Prince Palatine asked.

"Just said the words, didn't I?"

"Alright." Prince Palatine extended his good hand.

I shook it.

"K-Krait, I…" King Eventine returned, dancing on his toes, rubbing his arms, his misted breath obscuring his face. "Eh? What?"

Prince Palatine apprised him of our deal, and King Eventine looked relieved if somewhat ashamed when a voice from beyond cried, *"Oy, there's a blackguard scourger come calling."*

Von Madbury rose as a figure, a scarecrow of a man, stumbled from the yard, past the breaking-wheel, and up toward the Schloss.

Shit.

I could read it in his form, his gait, his every move.

It was Stephan.

"Why the hell—?" I gagged back.

"What is it?" Karl was on his feet, crossbow in hand, making for the murder holes, looking to reinforce their name and primary function.

Von Madbury drew his sword. The rest followed suit.

It careened downhill from there.

Stephan saw the gathered retinue, a stuttered hesitation in his every step, yet kept trudging onward.

"Run!" I yelled, my voice was lost to the gale.

Von Madbury was up and lurching off, the others loping along like a pack of clockwork jackals, each one stumbling on despite stiff joints, cold bones, frozen blood.

"Run, you bloody fool!" I hollered.

"Is it Stephan?" Lady Mary breathed by my side, crossbow cradled, nestled, ready.

Cursing beneath my breath, I drew Yolanda and laid a hand on the door-latch.

"Lad…" Karl turned for his thane-axe.

"No. You stay. Hold the door." I slammed it with a fist.

"Odin's eye." Scowling, Karl stomped back for the murder hole, waving me on. "Fuck it. Go. *Fuck!*"

"Yeah. Exactly."

"Sir Luther…" Lady Mary swallowed.

"I'll do my best." I cocked my head toward her murder hole. "See its purpose fulfilled, if it comes to it, though, yeah?"

I caught a glimpse of her, pale and wild-eyed, an instant before the door shut and I was left standing in the blaring cold.

By the time I trudged over to the huddled scrum, my brother stood restrained among them. Harwin and Brother Miles had him by the arms while Squire Morley giggled like an imp as he hammered him in the gut. Stephan retched and made to wilt over but was forced upright. Squire Morley belted him again.

"Hold!" I roared.

The scrum as a whole turned at my approach. Twenty-five-some-odd men.

Grinning slick through shiver, Von Madbury drew a dagger from behind his back. "Willing to bargain now, eh?"

"No, I just came out to cool off." I tugged open my collar and fanned myself. "Too damned hot in there."

The look on their collective faces? Almost worth it. Squire Morley hammered Stephan again and Brother Miles and Harwin let go of him, crumpling forward to the frozen ground.

I tensed but didn't move. "You ever get sick of playing the damsel in distress?"

Stephan muttered something but the puke and loose teeth made it tough to discern.

Von Madbury came up behind him, yanked his head back by a fistful of hair and pressed a dagger to his throat. "Don't you fucking say nothing."

"That's a double negative," I said.

"What?"

Bile ran down Stephan's neck as von Madbury's dagger shivered raw at his naked throat. But Stephan blinked. Once.

"L-let us i-in," von Madbury spat, drool coursing down his blue lips.

I ignored him. "Did you see the bloody tent city?" I pointed off toward its ruins. "What these blackguards did?"

Another blink. *Yes.*

"I'm talking at you!" von Madbury screamed. Brother Miles and Sir Roderick and the others started forward, spanning out like the horns of a bull. I took a step back. Then another. What time and space it bought me was fair on nil.

"And you still fucking came?" I screamed.

Another blink. *Yes.*

"Shut your bloody mouth!" von Madbury screamed.

King Eventine raised his voice but the Queen drowned him out, "Seize him!" as she scrabbled like a madwoman from the chapel.

"Are you bloody daft?" I yelled above the gale, taking another step back, raising Yolanda to the high guard. Poised whistling in the wind, I felt it gripping her edge, tugging, pulling, turning her blade ever just so. Brandished on high, gleaming in the storm, Yolanda halted them all a pace. They'd seen me down Gustav. Were calculating their blackguard-math. Twenty-five to one was a massacre five times out of four. But here? Now? Them wooden-stiff with cold and me still spry? Holding the high ground? And two crossbows covering my flanks?

Stephan blinked twice. *No.*

"Shit." Stephan *wasn't* being a bloody idiot. He was doing what he always did, which was worse. He was being a bloody martyr.

"Shut your yap!" von Madbury screamed.

"Is he dead?" I fixed Stephan an eye.

A reluctant pause, followed by two more blinks. *No.*

"Shit."

"I'll do it!" von Madbury foamed at the mouth.

"Let him go." Turning on heel, I headed back toward the Schloss. "He said what he needed."

"I said *I'll slit his throat!*" von Madbury stamped his foot.

"I heard you," I snarled over my shoulder. "So get to it. Cause he ain't worth shit in a fight. And I'm hoping you and yours might be."

Von Madbury straightened, his arms going slack, dagger hanging.

"We'll call an accord until the siege is through," I said. "Your King'll need you manning the walls."

"*Siege…?* Huh? What?" von Madbury said. "Us?"

"You?" I spat. "Jesus Christ. No." I pointed south toward the leper-house. "The *bloody* Nazarene. He's coming, and his lunatic horde's coming with him."

…along with any unnecessary weight we had cast aside weeks past, we bore on through the endless forest, bellies rumbling, belts tightened by degree, daily, hourly…
—War-Journal of Prince Ulrich of Haeskenburg

Chapter 42.

OUTSIDE THE GATES of the Schloss von Haesken, the mob chanted. Like they did. Pounding the walls. The gates. The ground. Hurling curses. Rocks. Fistfuls of garbage. As mobs do. Whether they lug the garbage specifically for said purpose or scrounge for it along the way's always been a mystery to me.

Stephan and I stood atop the ramparts at the gates.

"Watch it," Stephan grabbed my collar and yanked me aside.

"Whoa—"

A nail-ridden board flipped end over end past my head. It landed in the yard, sticking upright in the mud, crooked as a pauper's tombstone.

Across the yard, beyond the breaking-wheel, the once and future king and procession in tow entered the chapel. It was a small procession, the casket leading, borne by King Eventine, Father Gregorius, and Sir Alaric, each one staggering along under its noble load. Queen Elona came next, looking austere and regal as she strode through the churned mud, clutching her skirts up, past a skewered corpse propped against a fence. Prince Palatine labored alongside, using his cane to lever his clubbed foot sucking through the muck.

Stephan crossed himself, muttered a prayer, staring off after the procession. "May God rest his soul."

"How long you think it'll take? Assuming the mob doesn't storm in and slaughter everyone during intermission." I drew the string back on my crossbow. "They have intermissions at funerals?"

"Only for kings," Stephan said.

Across the yard, Saint Gummarus's dullard expression, patron saint of hoary old woodcutters, stared back, frozen in stained glass. "Jesus."

"What?" Stephan asked.

"Even their saints are second rate." Scowling, I slid a bolt into the groove. "He looks like a cross between a shitty hermit and inbred groundhog. Have you ever even *heard* of Saint Gummarus?"

"Well, no, but," Stephan glanced askance as I finished loading, "is that necessary?"

"Mocking made-up saints?" I turned. "Absolutely."

Stephan winced as something heavy struck the wall, shivering its timbers. "I meant the crossbow."

I shrugged. "Better safe than sorry." I thumped the parapet with a fist. "These walls are shit."

"And the crossbow makes you feel safe?"

"No," I patted the stock, seeing in my mind's eye a dark shape lumber through yellow smoke, "I just ain't going alone."

Before the chapel's door shut, I made out Father Gregorius's voice droning on from within, unintelligible gibberish distorted by wind and distance.

I glanced back out as a rock sailed past. "*Fucker.*" Teeth gritted, I gripped my crossbow and brought it to bear, drawing a bead on the blackguard who threw it. A skinny, wasted bastard, with more space than teeth in his scowl, but he had an arm.

"Good thing they haven't brought anything more robust," Stephan breathed.

"Yeah." My heart beat through my hands, pumping my crossbow up and down, point bouncing, ever so slightly. "Like ladders."

Thing about mobs. They're generally unprepared at first. Get worked up and move and grow like some raucous beast in snorting heat. All balls and no brain. Like these fellas. I recognized a few faces amongst the press, a tall lumber-jack, a woman from the old keep, the girl von Madbury had been leering after. Lianna. Figured her father was down there, too, somewhere, if he wasn't behind, lying face down, sucking in the muck.

"Let them blow off some steam," Stephan said. "Then they'll leave."

"Yeah," I said. "Sure. Maybe…"

Stephan said nothing. He just nodded.

I followed suit, kept my yap shut and crossbow leashed.

Dealing with mobs is tricky business. If they're set on violence, the only thing you can do is get the hell out of the way. Or join them. But if they're teetering, unsure, on the fence, just throwing rocks and jibes, let them. Let them do whatever the hell they want shy of clambering over the walls.

I glanced down the eastern section of wall. Harwin and Brother Miles manned it along with a small contingent of new troops. Von Madbury and the rest of his ilk, both new and old, held the west and north. Thankfully — for them — the mob only had eyes for the gates.

The funerary dirge trickling out from the chapel was half-assed at best, but musicians were probably fair scarce at present. Someone was scratching at a lyre with what sounded like a rusted fork. Palatine's voice sounded strong, though. Eventine's? Not so much.

"*Open the gates!*" someone bellowed below.

"Go home!" I hollered back.

"We ain't got no homes!"

"There's plenty of vacant ones!" I barked. "So pick one!"

"Please, good folk!" Hand and hook raised, Stephan stepped out from behind the crenel. "I beg of you, disperse, for your own good."

"Watch it—"

A rock thudded into Stephan's side, folding him in half.

"Jesus." I dragged him back behind the blessed crenel where he crumpled, tongue lolling as he puked into the courtyard.

"Anything broken?" I patted his back. "Besides your dignity?"

Stephan gasped, eyes bulging, drooling, and croaked, *"Don't... Think... So..."*

"Good." I turned back then froze.

The mob'd gone silent.

I peeked round the crenel.

A slit unraveled through the mob. Just a nick at first, it slopped open til the mob fissured in twain. A hooded bloke stood at the far end. A big bloke.

My legs wobbled. I grasped the wall and nearly joined Stephan in feeding the grass.

Towering over the crowd, the Nazarene shambled forth, ambling onerously, like every inch of him was raw nerve.

"Krait..." The Nazarene's voice was a scratched rasp from a hollow cask.

I clutched the wall. Swallowed. Speechless. Legless. Useless.

"What is it?" Stephan pawed at my leg.

Down the wall, Brother Miles and Harwin gawked over, frozen.

"Open the gates, brother!" The Nazarene's voice cut through me. "We bear corpses of the fallen. Those consumed by the conflagration. The assassination. All on the word of your King."

Behind him, a procession of scourgers wormed their way through the parted halves of mob, bearing corpses slung between them. The pallbearers strode to the gates pair-by-pair and laid them down, one-by-one, side-by-side. There were men. There were women. There were children.

"I wish to speak to the King," the Nazarene bellowed.

"King's busy," I bellowed back.

"And what is more important to a king than learning the heart and will of his people?"

"He's dead."

The Nazarene halted at that. "The new King, then."

"He's burying his father." I glanced over my shoulder. "Hoping to keep it to one funeral today."

The Nazarene waved an ostentatious paw over the dead. "These souls weigh upon his."

I lifted my crossbow, aiming it dead-center at the Nazarene's chest. He didn't flinch. He didn't shy. I didn't expect him to. What's a stick to the chest to the man whose skull's been bashed by an axe?

"There shall be more, brother," the Nazarene bellowed. "An ancient evil festers within this land."

"And I'm looking right at it," I said down the length of the crossbow.

"An evil with a hunger for flesh, for blood, for soul. You asked a question before. Would you not hear my answer?"

I fought dry-mouth to swallow. "Get the hell out of here, whatever you are."

"Aye, brother, that we shall, as a show of faith to your new king." The Nazarene offered an awkward nod. For a second, I thought his head might fall off. Plop in the mud. But I wasn't so lucky. "That he might take a stance more germane to the survival of his folk. But we shall send a message to remind him." He glared up, and my bowels lurched. "A message slathered in ash and flame through the night. To remind him. To remind them all. And then shall we return. Tell him he had best get his house in order ere we do."

...write what might be these last pages of this journal, these last pages of my story, of my life, in my own life's blood.
—*War-Journal of Prince Ulrich of Haeskenburg*

Chapter 43.

THE CHAPEL of Saint Gummarus lay barren, empty, cold. The Queen-Mother Elona sniffed and dabbed her nose with a handkerchief as she glanced up from prayer. Darkness encroached from on all quarters, held at bay by the dying light of a single candle set atop King Eckhardt's casket, its flame upright and still as a corpse soldier at attention. The Queen-Mother took a surreptitious nip from a flask. "Shouldn't you be guarding the gate?"

"They're gone," I said, "for now."

"And what is it you want?" She shifted her rosary a bead.

"To pay my respects." I raised my hands. "Won't take long." It wasn't a lie.

"And what do you care?"

"I could ask you the same." I laid a hand on the casket, bowed my head, mumbled some hollow verse. "But the truth?" I looked up. "I don't. Not even a little. I just want to get out of this God-forsaken town in one piece."

"I could say the same."

"Then why not leave?"

"Everything I have. Everything I know is here. My sons. My..." She still didn't turn from her penitent prayers. "Why is it you insist on insinuating yourself in our troubles? First, you barge in with your problems and dump them upon our very doorstep. Then you incite a war with those … those savages."

"Yeah. Sure." I rapped my knuckles on the pew. "I'm the source of all your troubles."

"You murdered Sir Gustav. The very cream of our knighthood."

"That's one hell of an indictment against the rest."

"They listened to him. They followed him. He acted as some counterbalance against…" The Queen-Mother turned and rose, dressed in mourning-black. "And now you're here for what? And don't tell me again it's to pay last respects."

"I promised your sons I'd take a look into the matter." I stared into her eyes. "I'm looking now."

"I…" the Queen-Mother rose, "I've never swung a sword in my life."

"Didn't think you did. And it wasn't a swing. It was a stab. And that's not what I'm talking about."

"Then…" The color drained from her face. "I don't know what you mean."

I shook my head. "Please."

"And what conclusions have you drawn?"

"Just one. And you know what it is."

The Queen-Mother drew herself up. "Just who do you think you are?"

"No one special, I'll grant you, but I'm all you've got."

"You? No, I think not. And on the contrary, von Madbury—"

"Is only proficient at sowing discord to his own advantage," I finished for her. "And Brother Miles can only do what others order him to. And your sons? The one that should be ruling's been crippled by fate. And the one that is? Crippled by something else. And all the others?" I shook my head. "Axes, spears, and swords. Little else."

"My father—"

"Is a good man, but like you said, he's broken," I said. "You could do something to mend it, yeah? Go talk to him about whatever it is split a void between you two. But then, I suppose he could get off his arse, too. Well, not currently, but like I said, I'm standing here cause I promised your sons I'd help. And I'm offering my help to you, too."

"Well, how very *gallant* of you," she sneered.

"Even a stopped clock, Elona…"

"Don't call me that."

"Was a time not long ago you wanted me to."

"Oh?" She adjusted her dress. "You bought that? You believed me?" She shook her head slowly. "Your trouble is you all think you're something more. And you're not." Prim and proper, she rose from her cushion, brushing the lace veil from her face, and strode toward me down the aisle. I enjoyed her walk. Her lips pursed, hips swaying, murder blazing plain and naked her eyes. "And just who do you think holds power here?"

"You're not queen anymore."

"And you're but a bloody hedge knight." She drew herself up. "And a crown is a piece of metal. It's the person beneath who holds sway. And do you think I hold no sway over my son?"

"I'd hazard you do, but he seems bent on finding the killer." I offered my best haughty smirk. Truth was, though, she was right. King Eventine was nigh on as spineless as his father, and I could easily see her sticking her hand slick with crimson, puppet-wise up through his back, pulling sinew like strings, forcing his every motion. "At any cost. His words, not mine. Can you guess where all eyes are pointed?"

"You're a bastard."

"And then some," I laughed. "But please, don't high-horse me. If I'm wallowing in shit, you're knee-deep right alongside me."

Her eyes quivered.

"You hated your husband," I said. "That scene at dinner? Bear-baiting him? In front of his entire court?"

"*Bear*-baiting?" she scoffed. "No. I think not."

"Squirrel then," I conceded, "but he wouldn't take the bait."

"Once again," she bared her teeth, "you don't know what you saw."

"Then tell me."

"You should leave."

"Maybe he finally grew the stones to confront you about von Madbury?" I shook my head. "Gave you an ultimatum? Told you to stop or ... I don't know. You tell me."

"What is it you want?" She swallowed.

"I want to know what happened. I want information. Specifics. Coin of the realm to lord over your son's head til I get me and mine free and clear."

"You want me to confess? Well, I confess. I didn't love him. How could I? How could anyone? And yes, I loathed him. But that hardly set me apart. My father is the only one who held him in any esteem, and then only because he thinks duty, and honor and oaths still mean something."

"The fool," I quipped.

"Precisely." She spat back. "Any man living by such archaic standards can only be considered such. Anywhere else and he'd have been a hedge knight. A nothing. A nobody. Just like you."

"That might've hurt if I had any feelings."

"But here? Because of me? Because of my sacrifices? My travails? My father was elevated."

"So you think he owes you?"

"Yes! Yes, he owes me. Of course. For all that I've done? All I've endured? All that I've sacrificed? They all owe me. All of them." Her chest heaved. "Every. Single. One."

"You're the keystone holding your whole family together."

"Family? Nay. The whole kingdom. But such is the duty that falls to women." She sneered. "And what do we get for our hidden efforts? You men, always trying to tear things down. Apart. Always trying to lord over one another. While we women knit it all back together in dying silence. Bending. Stretching. But never breaking. We'd all be better off without you."

I shrugged. "Can't say you're wrong."

The Queen-Mother paused, studying me as though noticing me for the first time. "I saw what you did to Sir Gustav." She slid up next to me, the scent of rose petals enveloping me as she laid her hand upon her dead husband's casket. "It was ... impressive."

"Two men fight, one's gotta lose."

"And here you are," the Queen-Mother laid a hand on my thigh, "the formidable stranger come to our little-known kingdom, offering succor in time of greatest need."

"Eh...?" I swallowed. "That wouldn't be a dagger behind your back?"

"Sir Luther, please." She craned her neck to look me in the eyes. "Forgive my outburst. Please. Let us be reasonable. Let us be friends once more. We had a falling out, plain and simple." Her hand slid northward. "Yet, I'm certain that some sort of accord can once again be met."

...God-forsaken mountains are endless. Like the titan Kronos, they rise about, devouring the sun, the moon, the stars, along with any semblance of hope, salvation, sanity, and one by one...
—*War-Journal of Prince Ulrich of Haeskenburg*

Chapter 44.

YOU ... DID ... *WHAT?!"* Lady Mary stifled a scream. Nearly. "King Eckhardt's barely in the ground, and here you are—" Lady Mary stuttered in fury, "*porking* the dowager like a swine in heat."

Karl guffawed and slapped me on the back. The fact that, for once, Karl was proud filled me with a cold sense of dread.

"Are you insane?" Lady Mary said. "Or just monumentally stupid?"

I shrugged. "Why not both?"

The Schloss was still ours. *How long?* was another question. King Eventine had the walls and the gate. Guarding it against the scourgers outside and us in. Like Caesar at Alesia. Which in this obscure metaphor meant we were screwed. I set Yolanda down on the table and took a seat by Karl, a ghoulish smirk ripping pink through his rat's nest of a beard. Stephan was more sedate.

"This mean you're king, now?" Karl grunted.

"Yeah. Sure." I pounded the table. "You there! Boy! Bring me my scepter!"

Lady Mary buried her hook-hand an inch deep into the table. "What in heaven's breadth were you thinking?"

I fingered my lip. "Uh…"

"Brother, I—" Stephan started.

"Rose of Sharon, were you blind to her designs?" Lady Mary strangled out.

"Perhaps it was *she* overcome by *my* charms?"

"You have two *bite-holes* festering in the middle of your imbecilic face."

"Well, uh … yeah." I had no witty retort, so I merely did my best to look wounded. It wasn't hard as she'd so clearly pointed out.

"She's ensnared you then." Lady Mary tossed up her hands.

"I don't recall any oaths." I stroked my chin. "So no. And what better way to ingratiate myself? Get her guard down? Buy us some time. Get on the inside."

Karl slapped the table.

"I did this for you," I told him.

"Brother," Stephan rubbed the bridge of his nose, "while I don't approve of your methods, and I'm certain the same could be said of her *father and sons,* perhaps you're not wrong. In this, only." He held a hand up to Lady Mary. "Perhaps it might buy us some time."

"Or our caskets." Lady Mary crossed her arms.

"I'm fair sure those were bought the moment we set foot in Haeskenburg," I said. Which, admittedly, was little to no comfort. "But fair enough. We keep our guard high. Stay in the new king's good graces."

"And the Queen's…" Karl smirked.

"The Queen-*Mother's,"* I clarified. "The question is, when do we allow them back in?"

"Never," Lady Mary said.

Karl grunted, "I'm with her."

"But we must if this ruse is to work," Stephan said. "If they're to take you at your word, that you'll find this killer, then we must allow them in. How can we not without tipping our hand?"

"Rose of Sharon." Lady Mary rolled her eyes.

"We get Ruth and the kids out," I said. "Then they can come in."

"And where are they going to go?" Stephan asked. "Out in the streets? With the Lord-only-knows what set to stalk them? Not to mention the Nazarene and his scourgers? And besides—"

"Ruth can't take care of herself let alone the children," Lady Mary said. "She … she's broken. Gone. I don't know that she'll leave even after Abraham's buried."

"Yeah. Shit. Look." I rubbed my jaw. "We burn that bridge when we get to it. And leave her if you have to. But you're right. We need a show of good faith, yeah? Prove we're in it for the long haul. So we let them back inside. Just the King and Queen-Mother. The priest, too, if they insist."

Karl grumbled like thunder on the far horizon.

"No, listen," I said. "Soon as it's dark, I'll slip the wall, make for the *Ulysses*. Fill in Chadwicke and Avar, then hoof it back." I dead-eyed Karl. "I'll need a distraction. And some rope."

"She's not seaworthy yet, brother."

"We'll make do," I said. "We have to. We'll lash together whatever'll float, make a raft, get across the river. That'll buy us some space. Time. Then we regroup. Figure something out. Build a better raft. Float downriver. Hell, we'll swim if we have to. Bottom line? We're getting the hell out of Husk, and we're getting out tonight."

...a last resort, we reenacted the sacraments of Christ, sacraments we had received hundreds, if not thousands of times back in our towns, our villages, our priories.

But these were sacraments of the wild, sacraments of the broken, sacraments of the fallen, sacraments of the damned...
—*War-Journal of Prince Ulrich of Haeskenburg*

Chapter 45.

THE ULYSSES was a charred husk, still smoking, when I reached her. She sat in dry dock, upon the bank of the Abraxas, timbers lodged against her hull, sticking out like the dead legs of some monstrous insect. I strode slowly up the canal, peering in through the hull, what planking was left all knurled and bent and cracked like the skin of a dragon.

Inside the charred skeleton, someone was sobbing.

I gripped a plank and yanked it clattering free.

The sobbing stopped.

"Chadwicke?" I called into the dead space. "Avar...?"

A sniffled. Then clatter as something toppled.

"S-Sir Luther?" Droned a voice. "It ... It's Avar. Over here."

Ducking the rudder, I saw him sprawled atop a mound of shattered mast and warped decking. Smoke drizzled up from embers still glowing red. I could taste the char in the air. Avar was covered in it, except round his eyes where tears had washed him clean.

"Who did it?" I asked.

Avar laid a hand against the mast, leaned over and puked. "Oh my good gracious Lord..."

"*Good? Gracious?* No. Not even close." The rest seemed

in line with the institution of lordship, though. I ducked through a hole in the hull and scrambled up a pile of detritus. "Who did it?"

Avar wiped his nose. "I…I don't know. A lot of them, though."

"A lot of them…" I echoed. "We're fucked then, yeah?" I sneered. "You get that?"

Avar bobbed his head, blubbering, wiping his tears, smearing them black.

"Then bloody-well start talking."

"I'm sorry…"

"Fuck your sorry. Who? Was it the Nazarene?"

Avar sobbed into his hands. "I don't know…"

"From the Schloss?" I asked.

"I-I…"

"Jesus."

"I…" Avar pointed off somewhere, "was off robbing stock when I smelled the smoke. Didn't think nothing of it. Not with all the town burning. But it got stronger. Then I heard the screaming so I come running back. Hard. See'd them here, setting fire to her. Hacking with axes." He bared his white teeth, stark in his char-smeared face, and hurled a shard of wood clattering into the darkness. "And…"

"And what?"

Avar stood, aiming an accusatory finger my way. "I don't give a hang about your damned ship."

"Ain't much of a ship any—" I straightened. "Where's your brother?"

Avar laid his face in his hands. "You blind, Sir Luther?"

I froze. Looked up.

"Ah, shit…" I sighed. "I'm sorry, kid."

Halfway up the pile of ship-innards, bound to the mast like a figurehead stood a charred corpse, its head geared back, mouth tooled open, black teeth bared, howling endless at the silent night.

Avar's shoulders trembled beneath my hand.

"I left him," Avar sobbed.

"You were getting stock."

"Aye. I was, but…"

"But what?"

"But I lied." Avar was sobbing hard. "B-But I came back when they had him." He looked up at me, babbling sins to his priest, looking to confess, to receive absolution. I had none to offer. "Had him trussed to the mast. And they were fixing to burn him. Fixing to burn it all. And I … I did nothing." He dry heaved. "Just stood there. Just stood there watching. I … I couldn't move. Couldn't think. Couldn't do nothing. Just watched as they beat the life out of him. Cutting on him. Laughing like … like jackals. I coulda done something. Coulda took that axe and, coulda…" He glared at the axe as though it were the source of all his troubles. "But I didn't."

"Kid…"

He shrugged off my hand. "Then the screaming, oh Lord, when he burned. And I just watched from that copse of trees back yonder. Just watched the whole damned time. Just watched…"

Char scaled the back of my throat. "If you'd done something, you'd be right here alongside him."

"I wish I had."

"No, you don't."

"I do. I'm a coward. A miserable bleeding coward."

"There's worse things to be, kid."

"And what's that?"

I glared up at Chadwicke, shining coal-black in the night, screaming silent, and said nothing.

Lamb of God, who takes away the sins of the world, have mercy upon us.

> *The Body and the Blood…*
> *Do this in memory of me…*
—*War-Journal of Prince Ulrich of Haeskenburg*

Chapter 46.

THE SUN BLARED overhead, staving off dawn shivers as we stood upon the acropolis of the Schloss and watched Haeskenburg burn. The Nazarene'd been busy. Chants carried on fell winds reached our ears as tumors of black smoke blistered skyward from all points of the compass.

King Eventine stood hunched in his father's tattered old mantle, a mite too big on him, drawn around him like the flaccid wings of a long-dead bat. "It's all rather a bit … complicated." He licked his pallid lips. "It seems hard to get a handle on let alone explain. I…"

"Go slow," I said. "Use small words."

"I-I fear I'm at a loss." King Eventine turned. "Father Gregorius, w-would you be so good as to…?"

"You are King, Eventine." Father Gregorius clutched his bible to his heart. "The burden lies now upon your brow."

"Please. I-I'm not well. I cannot find succor. Warmth." The King worried at a loose thread dangling from the hem of his mantle. "Brother, please," with eyes pleading he turned, "you possess the greater understanding."

"I'm uncertain that's true," Prince Palatine sighed.

"Please…"

Sir Alaric scowled from the corner, crumpled against the

parapet like a pile of sodden laundry, his eyes glazed, twitching, a bottle of something red and sour clutched to his sunken torso.

"Very ... very well." Prince Palatine grimaced as he adjusted his useless chicken-wing arm against his bent torso. "I shall do my best." He struggled to lift a tome and place it on the parapet, "Oof... The treatise of our family history, Sir Luther. I completed it."

"Dull?" I eyeballed the thick, gnarly old tome.

"Unfortunately, no." Prince Palatine ran a hand through his hair. "Quite the opposite. I fear it has left me with more questions than when I began."

"My family's a bloody mess, too," I said.

"Ours bears a centuries-old blood-sworn curse."

"Well ... I guess you win."

"Do you believe in curses, Sir Luther?" Prince Palatine's eyes narrowed.

"Once upon a time, I'd have said no. But lately? My world-view's broadening."

"I once believed a man made his own way," Prince Palatine said, "an amalgam between the sweat on his brow, the thoughts in his mind, and the beliefs in his heart. And I believed God was either on his side or not."

"And we're all a bunch of Jobs praying for God's thumb tipping our side of the scales?"

"Yes, or something akin to that," Prince Palatine said. "A childish idea perhaps, I know. But now..." He rubbed his forehead with a trembling hand. "I think we have each one of us suspected some modicum of the tale I am about to tell, but..."

"Easier to let sleeping dogs die," I said.

King Eventine wouldn't meet my eye.

Sir Alaric winced, took a swig, offered a look more sour than his wine.

"The story starts long centuries past," Prince Palatine began, "two hundred seventeen years, according to my forefather's journals. Some nine generations.

"Its initial author was Prince Ulrich, our great grandfather to the *Nth* degree. As a young knight, he traveled south for seasoning." He grimaced. "To the *Terra Borza*. The old country. Older than Nod. '*The land beyond the forests.*' It's said to be all vast craggy mountains rising so high and perilous you feel they're poised to crash over you like waves amid a channel storm. The Carpathians, they're called. Have you seen them in your far travels?"

I shook my head. "Heard enough to steer clear."

"Well, it's a wild land, as they say, full of beasts and bandits and barbarians and other things, worse thing, things that slink and shun the light of the day. The King of Hungary had tasked the Teutonic Knighthood with taming this country. Granting it a measure of civility. Shedding a Godly light into the dark crevices where paganism and darker practices festered."

"Like asking a bear to teach a wolf civility," I muttered.

"As the treatise tells, Prince Ulrich joined an arm of the Teutonic army that campaigned deeper than any others before had dared. One hundred holy knights of no small repute. Some stately elder knight commanded the retinue. A lodge hochmeister he was, and he took it upon himself to educate these wayward folk. To drive them to their knees before God.

"And in so doing, he took young Prince Ulrich under his wing. Like a spear, they drove into the heart of the mountains, placating backward folk, educating, eradicating, cauterizing paganistic dogma. All for the glory of God. It was what these men were born to do, lived to do, and they did it well. But within the heart of those far mountains, in some dark distant valley, these knights encountered a clan-holt that was different."

"A place bereft of the blessings and ministrations of our Lord and Savior." Father Gregorius, crossed himself. "Worshipers of things unclean. Things that slunk beneath the earth before even Cain had committed his original sin."

"They worshiped a god who dwelt in the cracks beneath the mountains," Prince Palatine said. "What it was is not written. Lost to the passage of time. What was written was only that this underworld god was a blight upon this world and that it could be sated only through sacrifices of blood.

"It seems these mountain folk were baffled by this retinue of Godly warriors marching into their midst, so taciturn and staid, proclaiming what they deemed nonsense, forcing them to adhere to tenets they little could fathom."

"And the clan-holt folk all changed their minds, yeah?" I said. "Bent the knee? Kissed the cross? Accepted the Lord God Almighty?" I wiped my hands together. "End of story?"

"No, Sir Luther." Prince Palatine fixed me an eye. "It seems, rather … the opposite. Do you know how they educated backward folk in days of yore?"

"Sure. Same way they do now," I deadpanned Father Gregorius's way. "Fire and brimstone. Hammer and axe. The new way's the old. What you can't break, you bend, you batter, you burn."

"Or all three." Sir Alaric tipped back his bottle.

"Yeah."

"Now, see here—" Father Gregorius puffed himself up.

"Fuck off." I turned back to Prince Palatine. "So the story has no happy ending? No shit. Tell me one that does and I'll call it a lie. What of it?"

"That's just it, Sir Luther. I fear this tale lies bereft of an ending for we stand yet in the midst of its telling."

"Jesus." We had to get the hell out of here. "And what act are we in?"

"The final, perhaps," Prince Palatine said quietly, turning to all present, "but only if we, as one, possess the will, the fortitude, the clarity of purpose to do what needs be done."

"The *prologue,* then?" I deadpanned.

King Eventine turned green.

I thought he was going to puke over the parapet, but he mastered it, manfully, cheeks bulging, wincing, and swallowed. *Gulp.* A true leader cut from the very cloth of Arthur himself. "Go on then, kid, let's start the damned finale."

"As I said, these backward folk took not to the ministration. They believed their fell idol superior to the one true God. And they challenged our own Christian God for primacy. It turned to war. War on a small scale, perhaps, but war, nonetheless. Personal. Ugly. Wasteful."

"What war's all about," I said.

"Yes, yes," Father Gregorius fingered the cross around his neck, "now tell them what happened next."

"Settle down," I scowled.

"The Teutonic Master accepted the challenge. And so he and the good Prince led a sortie deep into the caverns of this Blood-God. For a day and a night, they crawled and struggled, lost in darkness, breathing putrid fumes, clambering through filth, feeling their way blind. On the morning of the second day, in a deep cavern, atop a hill of bones, they found the lair of the Blood-God and did battle.

"The Grandmaster sustained a mortal wound, as did so many others, and it fell to Prince Ulrich to slay the clan-holt's blood god. And he did. Somehow. He alone bore the head of the demon back, to burn it for all to see."

"How'd that go over?" I asked.

"Not well. Not well, indeed. Prince Ulrich and the army laid siege to the clan-holt. Invaded it. Burning. Slaughtering. Driving the clan-folk out into the desolate wilds. Those who didn't flee? They died in droves. Being slaughtered, tortured," Prince Palatine glared down into the yard, "broken on the wheel. A tradition carried back." He swallowed. "All suffered. Man, woman, child."

"Just like Jesus taught." How the church'd taken Jesus Christ's message of *'love thy neighbor'* and warped it into bureaucratic genocide had always impressed the hell out of me. It was all about knowing limits. Like a carpenter bending a piece of wood, doing so by degree, patiently, incrementally, tightening clamps just enough, a little here, a little there, that the wood bows just shy of breaking. "Was that from the sermon on the mount? Or the one with all the fish?"

Father Gregorius said nothing. What the hell was there to say?

"Yet these folk, these survivors from beyond the forest, regrouped, and they retaliated," Prince Palatine said. "They used whatever means lay at their disposal. Striking in the night. Slitting throats. Poisoning their own wells. Burning the food-shares and what livestock was left. Slaying the Teutonics but also themselves in the process. They were a hard folk. A proud folk. A folk suited to those vast wilds. But they stood no chance, bereft of their Blood-God. Not against the engines of modern war.

"And yet, still the war lasted longer than by any right it should have, but it ended the way it was ordained to. And when it did, the last person alive was a crone. A bitty, tattered old thing. All bird bones and cackles and rags."

Sir Alaric took another swig and fixed me a dead eye. There was no warmth left in him. No candor. No nothing.

"But still they broke her across that wheel. An old lady," Prince Palatine whispered. "Can you imagine?"

"Yeah," I said, "and ain't it a sight."

"They left her like that. Alive. Crucified. Mangled. My God. And as they marched on out of the clan-holt, with her dying breath, the old crone cursed them. Cursed them all to hell."

"You blame her?" I asked.

"No." Prince Palatine pursed his lips. "That first night the army spent out in the wilderness, marching back to civilization, Hell it was that came calling. A month later and not a single man marched out alive, except Prince Ulrich. And it was written that when he finally returned, he had ... changed."

"How?"

Prince Palatine paused, considering his next words carefully. "The history is nebulous. It changes authors to Prince Ulrich's brother, Gaston. But he writes that Prince Ulrich, now King Ulrich, retreated deep beneath the old keep, the crypts, and was wont never to set foot again in the light of day."

"War can do strange things to a man's mind," I said.

"Aye. If only that were solely it." Prince Palatine looked to his brother, gripping a massive key on a chain around his neck. "Some claimed to have seen him stalking the streets at night. Tall. Gaunt. Twisted. It ... it was then that folk started disappearing. Initially, it was only around the anniversary of King Ulrich's return. Later, the disappearances became ... more frequent."

"How frequent?"

The four men gathered made it a point to look down, away, skyward, wayward. Anywhere but at me.

"Fairly frequent then," I answered my own question.

"It was mostly folk on the fringes," Prince Palatine frowned. "Those who'd not be missed. Their bodies found out in the bog, or stuffed up the trunk of some hollow. Fished up from the bank of the Abraxas, withered as though sucked dry of all humors. In time, folk connected Ulrich's midnight ramblings with the disappearances. The murders. Ulrich's brother, Prince Gaston, writes that men had a name for the creature that stalked the night. A name that came back from the Carpathians. From the old country." Prince Palatine ran a hand through his hair. "They called it *strigoi.*"

"Ken now why folk call it Husk, lad?" Sir Alaric's voice was so soft I could scarcely hear it.

"I'm slow, but I'm getting there." I turned to Prince Palatine. "Finish it."

"Gaston, King Gaston at this point, sought to stop this monstrosity by whatever means necessary." Prince Palatine's clenched fist struck the cover of his family treatise. "King Gaston writes of a quest. A journey deep into darkness, bringing with him the greatest warriors of the realm to fell his own brother, the *strigoi* king."

"And when that failed?" I asked.

"But it didn't fail," King Eventine blurted. "They felled the nightmare king. King Gaston brought back Ulrich's head and burned it upon a pyre for all to see."

"Then why're folk still disappearing?" I asked. "And Rudiger? The Grey-Lady? They were *strigoi,* yeah? Where the hell'd they come from?"

With a grimace, Sir Alaric killed his dregs then hurled the bottle over the parapet.

Prince Palatine looked me in the eye. "I don't know."

"Well, I do." The old keep's chapel flashed before my eyes. The crypt. The tunnel veering off into the distance, the darkness, toward the old gaol, the execution chamber. "Your ancestors lied. Your father lied. They all lied. They came from the old keep. The execution chamber. Whatever the hell was down there still is."

Prince Palatine paled. "Regrettably, Sir Luther, I fear you speak truth…"

"Nay, Palatine," Father Gregorius raised a hand, "your King—"

"Shut your trap." I stomped past him, nearly shoving him off the roof, and looked King Eventine in the eye. "All those poor bastards crucified?" I held up a hand. "It was these bloody creatures. These *strigoi*. Whatever they are that killed them."

In my mind's eye, the Nazarene hurled the Grey-Lady back and into the burning building. I could see his scourgers gathering in a congealed mob of justified hatred, closing like a noose round Rudiger. Could see them pounding nails, staking him to a crucifix, hoisting him up for all the world to see. "Stephan was right. The Nazarene was the only one doing what needed be done, wasn't he? He was hunting the *strigoi*. Killing them. Jesus Christ. Shriving the bodies so they'd not rise, too."

King Eventine's lip quivered. "My father lied b-because he had to."

"Had to *what?*"

King Eventine looked again to his brother, eyes yearning for escape.

"Day one, and you're already one chicken-shit of a king," I snarled.

"Only he was to bear this terrible burden," King Eventine spat.

"Burden?" I scoffed. "He wasn't the one getting *husked.*"

"Sir Luther," Prince Palatine hobbled between us, "my father sought to shield us from his … transgressions." Prince Palatine laid a hand upon his family's tome. "My father was its most recent custodian. I shared its contents with my brother and Father Gregorius and Sir Alaric. And now I share it with you. And now we all know it must be stopped. Now. Forever."

"Strigoi," I grimaced.

"Yes." Prince Palatine nodded. "A plague upon this town. A scourge. And at its heart, as you said, it festers still down in the bowels of the old keep."

I turned, looked out over the dying town, the intersticed docks, the river beyond. I stifled a gasp. A small cog was moored on the far bank, nearly hidden behind the mill buildings lining the Tooth.

"We need someone to delve into the old keep. As King Gaston had done." Prince Palatine hadn't seen the cog. None of them had. "Someone to put an end to this story, this misery, this abomination."

"You mean me." It wasn't a question.

"Who else is there?" King Eventine demanded. "And we'll — I'll send others, too, whoever is able. Whoever we can spare."

"Spare, huh? Might not want to sell it to them that way," I said.

"I… I…" King Eventine fiddled with the massive key.

"Able, huh?" I strolled to the opposite side, all eyes on me, away from the river, the town, the cog bearing all my nascent hopes. "Well, maybe I'd rather be Cain in this scenario? Take a walk." Or a boat ride. "Wander the land of Nod. Hear Nod's nice this time of year."

King Eventine stomped forward, pressing a skinny finger toward my face. "You will do this, Sir Luther. You must."

Crossing my arms, I leaned against the parapet and fixed him a glare. "Look who's growing some stones?"

King Eventine met my glare. "You. Will. Go."

"Fine, you Highness. Alright. You win. I'll go," I spat. "But you're coming down with me."

...such choices made in those days of yore plague me still. Hence it is, I awaken in a cold sweat beside my wife and love and rue that I did not willfully cauterize the festering wound, the disease, the curse that I had become.

But I was selfish then. I was ignorant. I was human.
—Journal of King Ulrich of Haeskenburg

Chapter 47.

RUTH KNELT, broken wrist wrapped up, mechanically dipping a washcloth in water then wringing it out. Clenching it white-knuckled, hand trembling, she dabbed it across her dead husband's forehead. Tears streaming, humming shards of shattered prayer, she broke down piecemeal with each whispered word. Sarah and Joshua huddled by her side, watching, waiting, weeping, she clutching a water bucket, he, her skirts.

"This gonna take long?" I asked.

"She doesn't want to see you." Lady Mary shoved the door closed, forcing me back into the hall. "She was quite plain. And they're saying goodbye. It'll take as long as it takes."

"Yeah, well, make sure it doesn't take too long," I breathed.

"Rose of Sharon, they're saying goodbye."

I pursed my lips, took a deep breath, relented. "Apologies."

"This crypt-venture is a fool's errand," Lady Mary spat. "You know that, yes?"

"Yeah. Sure. But fool's errands are the only work that suits me."

Lady Mary shook her head, "You can't go down there after—"

"Look, I don't want to. Jesus." I lowered my voice. "Believe me. Tunnels are bad enough on their own without throwing blood-sucking demons in them."

"I'm more concerned with von Madbury and the rest of them."

Lady Mary had a point and not just the one on the end of her hook.

"Better he's down there with me than up here with you."

She had no retort to that. Just a grimace. A shake of the head. A muttered expletive. "You're set on abandoning us."

I nodded toward Ruth. She was carefully drying Abraham's face.

"You think she'll leave if it's with me?" I asked. "Truthfully?"

"Rose of Sharon, I don't—"

"She hates me. You said so yourself. And with fair-good reason." I glanced down the hallway. "No. It'll be easier to convince her to get rolling without me in the equation."

"I'm not sure it shall be possible under any circumstances."

"Tell her it's the only way to save her kids. Cause it is. And if that doesn't work, tell her I'm dead. You catch more flies with honey, yeah?"

"Even so—"

"Look. The King wants me to go."

"Then tell him *no.*"

"Already said *yes.*"

"Why? What in Heaven's breadth do you have to gain?"

"Look—" I thrust an arm through the cracked door, past her pretty face, toward the window. "Von Madbury has the gates. And along the northern wall? Brother Miles. East stand Sir Roderick and Harwin, the toad twins. The poxy fella with the crossbow's guarding south.

"Felmarsh," Lady Mary said. "Gideon Felmarsh. And I don't see your point."

"My point? My point is when we go marching toward oblivion, and the King and von Madbury go down along with us, at least half of those bastards standing watch out there'll come along for the ride. Means less eyes on the wall. Less eyes on you." I looked to Ruth, to the children. "And soon as we head down, you slip the wall and beat feet for that ship. You up for that?"

Lady Mary fingered her hook. "And how do you know we can gain passage?"

"Because you're such a fine, smart lady that you'll work it out." I pulled my coin purse from my belt. It was damn-near full. I slapped it into her hand. "And if this doesn't work? Negotiate. Demand. Kick and scream. Whatever it takes. Horrify them with that damned hook if it comes to it."

Nodding, she felt the heft of the purse, squeezing it, tendons stark on her slender wrist. "How'd you come upon this?"

"Been pulling double shifts alongside Wenelda." I pumped my hands up and down.

"Just what is wrong with you?"

"A lot. Yeah. Anyways." I ran a hand through my hair. "Look. Town's got no food. No goods. No nothing. All's it's got is coin. Coin you can't buy anything with."

"Except mercenaries."

"Shitty mercenaries. I demanded hazard pay upfront and the good King Eventine was willing. It'll sweeten the pot if chivalry falls short. Which it inevitably does."

Lady Mary peered out the window. "Where's Stephan?"

"The leper-house still, I think. The King wants someone keeping an eye on the scourgers. He'll send word when he thinks they're coming. Hopefully, you're long gone before then."

"Alright."

"Once me and Karl leave, you find a way over the wall. Under it. Through it. I stashed some rope in my room. A grappling hook. Some daggers. Just do whatever it takes." I dug under my belt. "Anyways. Here's the key. Avar has one, too."

"Avar?" Lady Mary took the key. "How is he?"

"An empty husk of his former self."

"So he fits right in with the rest of us?"

"Yeah. Something like that." I smirked. "Look. Meet Stephan in the cellar of the house behind the *Half-King Tavern*. He'll help convince Ruth. Of course," I leaned in, lowering my voice, "things go sideways, you get on that ship and screw."

"Excuse me?"

"Don't wait for us. Or him. Or her. Or anyone."

"I know what you meant."

"Alright…"

Lady Mary slashed a hiss, "Why is it you assume I have no honor?"

"Because … uh … you don't."

"On the contrary, you simply fail to recognize it because it's not an infantile, excuse-based decision-making process based on pride, ignorance and — excuse me, but — the size disparity between the true length of your manhood versus what you imagine."

"Huh?"

"Lord above—" Lady Mary grimaced. "But if—"

"*But if* nothing." My finger was in her face. "You beg, borrow, steal your way on that ship and you go. And don't look back. And if the captain wants to ship out immediately, which if he's sane he'll do, you go, too. All of you. Any of you. Or just you if it comes to it. Any way. Karl and I are big and ugly enough to take care of ourselves."

"And what about this ancient abomination festering practically underneath our noses?"

Blood draining from my face, I forced a fallow grin, "Better off killing old, decrepit things, my lady. Less running involved."

…see it in my every move, my every word, my every instinct.

Even my young wife and child shun me, and so I retreat deeper and deeper, for longer and longer, arising on occasion only to…
—*Journal of King Ulrich of Haeskenburg*

Chapter 48.

FINALITY IN THE FORM of a boar-spear weighed heavy in my grip, the wooden haft smooth, its head an ugly jag of steel, angular black, suffused by a patina of old rust red. Lead by von Madbury, one by one, mail shirts rustling in the dark, King Eventine's guard filtered into the Execution Tunnel, their glares invariably drifting my way.

I kept my eyes alive, my back to the wall, my expectations low.

"See anything?" I squinted into the gloom. The Execution Tunnel. The Long Walk.

"Nay, Sir Luther." King Eventine cast a sidewise glare as the last of his blackguards filled the chamber. He lowered his voice. "This venture shan't raise their opinion of me."

"Can only go one way, Your Highness," I said. Truthfully.

Like the maw of some subterranean beast, the Execution Tunnel lay bare before us, teeth of a portcullis jagging down as though waiting to snap shut on some jackass fool enough to dare set foot beyond. I glanced around. We weren't short on jackasses. Fools, either. The tunnel traveled onward and downward and out of sight, seeming in its journey to fairly devour the light of our feeble lanterns.

King Eventine adjusted his crowned helm. "Father Gregorius gave me a tongue lashing for agreeing to accompany you."

"But look at you," I loosened Yolanda in her scabbard, "alive and well."

"Aye," the King gripped the key hanging around his neck, "but for how long?"

He had a point. I ceded it fair swiftly.

As von Madbury skirted along the wall I pivoted, keeping him my peripheral.

"Sir Luther?" The King held out a hand. "If you would … guide us?"

"Guide…?" I raised an eyebrow. "Yeah. Sure." I took point beside Karl.

It was our show now. And what a shit-show it was.

Karl grunted as he knelt at the tunnel maw, his boar-spear leveled at the darkness. Air seemed periodically to ooze out from within, a gentle waft as if the tunnel were a living thing breathing. Slow. Heavy. Coarse.

I couldn't wait to get in there.

The rest of the guards circled round their nervous King. He stood hunched and pale in the dim. Probably the first time he'd led anyone anywhere. And here he was leading fifteen men into an open grave. He cleared his throat, licked his lips, "Onward … men," he said, pointing with a flaccid throw of his arm.

Rousing stuff. Reminiscent of Charles the Hammer. Charlemagne. Roland the Fartier.

I offered Karl a stilted bow. "After you."

"How's it you walk with balls so big?"

I shrugged. "Strains the lower back, truth be bare."

Karl chuffed a trollish sort of laugh, his voice echoing as he ducked the overhanging row of iron teeth, stepping inside the devil's maw. I gave a final glance round at the chamber then trudged in after.

The rest'd either follow or they wouldn't. But they were a thick lot on the whole, and after a moment's hesitation, communal pride and fear of ridicule overcame fear of death, goading them onward, inward, downward. Always amazed by that. Men. Warriors. Fools. More afraid of what others think than of death.

Now me? Not so much. But I've never been considered much of a man. I stepped over a large block of stone, the light we bore carrying us onward in a dim globe that felt somehow protective against the encroaching black.

Behind, someone cursed as he cracked his head on something.

Grit crunched underfoot as the tunnel continued down, wending onward til it forked.

Karl shifted his spear. "Which way?"

"Left," I said without any hesitation or reason for doing so. But sometimes it pays to look decisive. Feel decisive. Maybe you don't fool them, but you just might fool yourself.

Karl said nothing, just game me that *"Bullshit"* look then trudged onward.

"Sir Roderick, keep watch to the rear," I hissed over my shoulder. Didn't want something creeping up on us from behind. Old sapper's trick. Split your waiting force in twain at a break and surround the buggers when they make their play. No fun being the buggers. The waiters, either.

"By what right do you order me?" Sir Roderick hefted his boar-spear, his scowl plainly adding *'fuck you'* to the discourse.

I turned on him, Karl at my back. I could feel his devil smirk, the lone source of comfort in all this bloody debacle.

"Get in line, Roddy," Sir Alaric growled.

"Fuck you, old man."

"Do it," King Eventine hissed.

Even still, Sir Roderick stood unmoved.

"Fine." I stepped aside, a magnanimous hand held out, offering all the mysteries of the abyssal beyond. "You can take point, then."

"Eh—" Sir Roderick glanced past me. Swallowed. The color drained from his face. Poured out the seams of his boots. Pooled across the floor. "Apologies. Th-the rear shall suffice."

"Yeah," I turned back to the black, half expecting to sprout steel in my spine, "I thought so."

We continued down, shouldering through bottlenecks and scraping nitre from the walls as feathery roots that had no right being so deep brushed past our faces. Something snapped underfoot. Some sort of bone? A rib. I kicked it aside as I hunkered behind Karl, our spear-points leveled always to the fore.

Von Madbury barked a curse from behind.

"What?" I turned.

"Nothing. Just hit my head for the tenth bleeding time."

"Oy—" Karl dropped to a knee, jamming the butt of his boar-spear into the floor, angling its point forth.

I was at his side, shouldering in, crowding the way, setting my spear angled likewise. "What?"

"Something's coming." Karl gripped his spear. "Coming fast."

Von Madbury and Sir Alaric followed suit behind, and by the glow of lantern light we four waited, crushed together behind a thicket of war-steel and black iron, waiting for a demon to descend upon us in the dark.

"I can hear—" someone started.

"Shut it," Karl grunted.

I heard it then, scrambling toward us. The sound of movement, swift, concerted, powerful. A body sliding past stone. Claws ripping through dirt. The rasp of ragged breath. A stench preceded it, the same tunnel-stench we'd become inured to, but by its efforts suddenly redoubled.

"Hail Mary, full of grace…" someone warbled.

I could hear Squire Morley, teeth chattering, could smell him, or someone else, piss themselves.

"It's a bleedin' hell-hound…" Squire Morley's arm shook as he brandished the lantern, the light wavering like some will o' the-wisp.

"Hold her steady, you damned fool," Sir Alaric hissed.

Squire Morley swallowed and did. Somewhat.

Someone muttered a paternoster.

"Rear-guard," I hissed, "stay sharp!"

The King clutched the wall, eyes wide, panting fast, just short of panic. He wasn't alone.

The thing ahead skidded to a halt just shy of our lantern light, breath hissing as ragged as a punctured lung, a snuffing, slurping, whuffing sound. Two red glints hovered in the darkness beyond our feeble glow. "What in hell's name?" Whatever it was pawed the ground, scraping its claws across stone, snuffling its muzzle like some blind thing catching scent of a kill.

"It isn't coming," von Madbury breathed.

"Sure it is." Karl adjusted his stance. "Just it ain't stupid."

"Not as stupid as us," I said.

"We do take the cake."

"Morley," I whispered without looking back, "it's your show."

Some jostling behind and Squire Morley pressed in.

"It's tight," Squire Morley breathed.

"It's a fucking tunnel." Gritting my teeth, I slid aside as best I could while Squire Morley set his foot in the crossbow's stirrup and cranked the line back, staves groaning under the pull.

"Jesus," I hissed, "next time maybe don't paint its bloody portrait."

"A-Aye." With trembling fingers, Squire Morley set a broad-head in the groove.

"Then throw it."

Squire Morley leveled his crossbow, let loose a pent-up breath, and let fly. *Thwock!* The bolt jumped like lightning from the groove and hissed down the tunnel, thudding into flesh unseen. A squeal ripped through the ether, followed by a warbled growl, somehow rat-like as whatever it was spasmed beyond the light. For the half-beat of a heart, I thought it was dead. Hoped it was. Prayed it was.

But it came at us, scrabbling fast, a glimpse of rancid pale fur and weeping pink eyes, all chittering teeth and black bloody murder. And in that instant, before it struck, so too, did another.

But it came from behind.

"'Ware behind!" Karl yelled.

It was still too late.

The two things attacked in a pincer movement, fore and aft, the sapper's trick I'd feared from the outset. I caught a glimpse of something, the aspect of a monstrous rat. Gargantuan. Albino. Twisted beyond hellish comparison. It's sniveling nose and whiskers whiffing scent, its blind eyes weeping treacle, glaring with idiot malice.

"Holy mother—!" Sir Roderick's cry strangled off behind, swift as a noose snaps neck. His lantern exploded in an orange *whoof* against the ground. Sir Aravand roared in pain, in madness, in death.

The tunnel snuffed black to the sound of chisel-teeth gnashing and flesh tearing, mail rings popping, pinging in quick succession as the thing barreled headlong into our shiltron. Like a wave crashing, it slammed into our thicket of spear. Mine burst into kindling, but the others held, three-fold spears' lugs holding the monstrosity at bay. Claws whisked past my face, knocking my helm flying as I cast my broken spear aside and drew Yolanda, fighting her free in the crush, half-swording her, gripping hilt and blade, stabbing forth and ripping, attacking the darkness.

The thing, the horror, the hell-hound, let loose a squeal of pain and rage as my blade bit, driving deep, a piercing high-pitched stiletto vibrating through my mind. Flesh tendril squirmed like coils of snake, scraping past my face, round my neck, my arms, as I stabbed again and again, ripping into damp rancid fur—

"Forward, you fuckers!" Karl drove forth on stumpy legs, forcing the thing back on the end of his boar-spear. Von Madbury swore beneath his breath as he and Sir Alaric followed.

I stumbled to a knee as the horror lurched back, releasing me. My neck was screaming raw, wet from rasp and slather, but I could breathe. Move. Think.

Stunned, shattered, I clutched the wall for support. Realized everyone behind was dead. Bodies lay contorted, a cadre of tin soldiers smashed across tunnel floor. Some poor simple bastard I hardly knew lay slathered against the wall, neck broken, lantern smashed, oil burning in a small pool the lone source of light.

Sir Roderick lay broken, a tangle of twisted limb and torn mail. Squire Morley's face was … just gone.

Down the tunnel, the shiltron kept moving.

"Your Highness?" I called out through the failing light.

But the King was gone.

So were the rest.

I froze as something shifted in the blackness beyond the charnel ruin, the sound of something licking its dripping chops, teeth scraping across teeth. And that rotten smell… Then a moan, someone begging, pleading, praying. Sir Aravand? King Eventine? *"Oh please, dear God, no—"*

I could have advanced, maybe saved the poor bastard, maybe done something, anything, but I didn't. I turned and I ran.

...the deeper darkness, my ancestors' crypt has become my home, for my kin have seen what I am become and have forsaken me.

They are right to do so.

—Journal of King Ulrich of Haeskenburg

Chapter 49.

I STAGGERED BLINDLY ONWARD, downward, Yolanda gripped blade-back in my left fist, my right out, scrabbling along the tunnel's side, fingertips dancing, palm slathering through dirt and root and stone, feeling along, praying I wouldn't charge headfirst into some hidden horror or bottomless pit. Dirt and grit cascaded. Roots brushed past my head, but in my mind were the long grasping appendages of those ... those things. Plodding on, the rasp of my breath, my whole world. Afraid to pause. Afraid to turn. Afraid that whatever lay behind was drooling down my neck.

Screams pierced the gloom.

I skidded to a halt.

Gasped.

Jesus Christ.

Blood pumping in my ears. Lungs burning. Doubled over. Had I actually heard it? Or were they but echoes in my mind? *No.* It sounded again. Behind. A man screaming. Wailing. The sputter of a smashed lantern, eclipsed suddenly by monstrous shadow.

I swallowed, turned, redoubled my pace, my right hand my lifeline. The ground beneath my feet dipped then turned. Five steps later the tunnel walls disappeared, and I tripped over something, stumbling to the floor.

Daylight blared from above. I blinked. *Mother of Mary.* I could see. Somehow.

Shielding my eyes against the glare, I kicked over, aiming Yolanda back at the passageway. My arms quivered. My curse reverberated. The tunnel glared back like the empty eye socket of some eons-dead cyclops's.

I wiped drool from my mouth. Spat grit. Waited. Watched.

Blood pounded like war-drums in my ears. The rasp of ragged breath. The iron band constricting round my chest. But it meant squat cause that thing was coming. I pushed myself up, focused on the tunnel but offering quick takes of the cavern, the chamber, the hall. Worked stone. Hewn rock. Dungeon-works. A pile of something in the corner. And the far walls, if there were any, lay unseen, limned in liquid shadow. From a crucifix-shaped hole far above, a blade of harsh blue sunlight stabbed down upon a tomb set in the center of the chamber.

Only then did I realize what I'd stumbled over. Sir Alaric. Lying prone in a pool of his own blood. But he was breathing.

I didn't hazard it a chronic condition.

"By the hound," Sir Alaric's eyes cracked open, "thank God."

"A first for me." I knelt by his side. "Where you bleeding?"

"T-That thing…" he clutched at me, slurring, slobbering, blood oozing down his chin. "P-Please. D-Don't leave me."

"I won't, Red." I wrestled free. "Where are you bleeding?"

"I'm … *Heh* … Red all over."

"Jesus." I snatched him by the collar, dragged him back toward the light just as I got that feeling. That feeling of swimming in dark water, deep water, of prey, the instant before the thing slunk free of the passageway.

"Ooof!" Sir Alaric's head clocked off stone as I jump-stepped back, bringing Yolanda up to the long guard.

"What the hell…?"

It cramped my mind just looking at it. What'd they call it? A hell-hound. As good a name as any. Though more rodent than dog, in truth. Shades of a disease-wracked gutter rat but … wrong. Monstrous wrong. Mangy hair sprouted in tufts, pink scaly flesh where it didn't. A tail dragging behind. Two more sprouting crooked and bent. One from its neck, another its side, and more. Its mouth opened and, Lord, *teeth*.

"By the hound…"

"Don't worry," I sniffed, took a step forward, interposing myself. "I've got it."

"The hell you do—"

The hell-hound shifted beneath a cloak of darkness, creeping towards me, its eyes squeezing nigh on closed in anticipation of the pounce. Tumors glistened off its head, red and tumescent. Dripping. Sir Alaric scuttled for purchase, reaching for his boar-spear.

I kicked it back toward him.

"By the hound—" Sir Alaric mumbled.

The hell-hound pounced, jagging past like lightning, snatching Sir Alaric and ripping him back into the passage. *"Lad!"* Only the boar-spear caught on either side of the passage and Sir Alaric's skinny arms, clutching on for dear life, saved him.

Ducking the boar-spear and sliding into the maw past the struggling knight, I lunged, thrusting Yolanda into darkness. Into it.

Then again. And again. And again.

It squealed like something halfway between a baby and skinned rabbit. Awful. So awful I almost stopped. So awful I almost pissed myself. I twisted the hilt, kicked, half-pulled my blade, re-angled and thrust again. A tendril-tail ripped past my face and neck, skin rough, rubbing me raw. I lunged forward, driving Yolanda in to the hilt, the thing squealing.

"Fuck off!" I yelled cause maybe that'd work.

Squealing mad, it caught itself, claws digging in, teeth gnashing at my mail as I tore Yolanda free and swung, but the passage was too tight and I shanked her off the wall, sparks flying as I lost her. I stumbled back, drawing a dagger. My fingers found the passage edge, and I tore myself out into the hall.

"Red!" I hissed and there was Sir Alaric trying to wrap his belt around his thigh. A glimpse of his lower leg just … *gone*. A jagged end of flensed bone. Blood spurting. His hands fumbling. Eyes bulging.

An appendage grasped my leg, tearing me back.

"Yolanda!" My voice cracked.

"Here—" Sir Alaric tossed his blade, sailing past as the thing tripped me, dragging me back.

I rolled, kicked free, scraped across flagstone floor, my hand somehow lighting upon Sir Alaric's boar-spear. As the thing pounced, I snatched up the spear, turned and stabbed. Once. Twice. Three times and it let go, keening raw, its nightmare tails thrashing.

I scrambled back, huffing, gagging, boar-spear aimed forth.

In the open, stalking forth, tails twitching like a stalking cat, the hell-hound paused.

I swallowed. Gasped. Was it the spear? The light?

"What—?" I slid back, got my footing as it exploded forth, tenfold gnashing teeth aimed for my face, and saw only black.

...for years now the strigoi *has preyed upon the populace, overcoming any and all attempts to constrain it. It seems finally that some other avenue must be...*
—*King Gaston's Ledger*

Chapter 50.

IT WAS A HORRIBLE THING," someone muttered, "and I've seen horrible things. Done ... horrible things."

I came to with crushing chest pain. Cracked an eye, rolled over. Barely able to breathe. Gasping. Grunting. My blood-crusted mouth clicking as I stretched it. "Red?" It sounded like him. Jesus. "Red, that ... that you?"

"Sure and it is, lad." Sir Alaric sat leaning against the wall, splayed out, pale and gasping, his belt wound tight round his thigh. And below it? Nothing.

"You look like shit," I said.

He didn't argue the point.

Sir Alaric fumbled his empty pipe trembling to his mouth. "You ever have nightmares, lad?"

"Right now count?"

A pause as he considered, followed by a nod. "I'll allow it."

"Generous."

"We..." Sir Alaric rubbed his eyes with a crimson fist, "we had a talk earlier, you and me. And I ... I wasn't as forthcoming as I might o' been."

"Please." I dragged Yolanda over, scraping across the flagstone floor, over to his side. "Do go on."

"Well now, the rest of the tale's one for the backroom, you ken? Don't want you bringing it up come supper time."

"I'll try to think of something else."

"Listen now, lad." Sir Alaric licked his pallid lips. "I don't know. I … I just wanted to tell you I never got a look at that Rudiger-fella's face."

"It doesn't matter now, Red."

"No," he chopped with a hand, "It does. And I want you to understand that if what they said is true. That I … I arrested him afore. That he was to be executed and wasn't. Just want you to understand…"

"Understand what?"

"That I didn't know. About the whole picture. About this … this thing." Sir Alaric scowled at the carcass, his boar spear lodged in its nightmare maw, its point jutting out the back of its neck. A lucky shot. "Sniffs and snippets, mayhap. Enough puzzle pieces for a smart man to fit to one, but I weren't that. Ain't never been that."

"How could you not know?" I said. "You were the bloody justiciar."

"I'm only justiciar cause my daughter married a king. Otherwise? I'd be lording over some dung heap east of the swamp."

"Even so."

"What? You never turned a blind eye?" Sir Alaric spat. "Never figured it'd be easier *not* asking a question? Mayhap overlooking or forgetting some tiny-little-nothing detail? Something no one would miss? Make your life that much easier?"

"Not when I was good." And it was true. When I was a good knight, a good justiciar, a good man, I'd have stormed through hellfire for the truth. "But that was some time ago."

"Aye," Sir Alaric moaned, "and who the hell was I to question my king?"

A thousand caustic retorts I bit back, choked down, swallowed. Cause he was right. Who was he to question his king? Who was anyone? "What makes them any better?" I asked.

"Us." Sir Alaric pinched some pipe-weed from his pouch, hand trembling, scattering it. "Us letting 'em think they are. And us thinking we ain't. Give us a hand, would you?"

I snatched a pinch of the weed and tamped it in his pipe.

"Many thanks. And what'd you say before, lad?" Sir Alaric said. *"Let sleeping dogs die?"* Well, that's what I did. Just, it's a lesson you gotta learn and relearn that," he swallowed, "once in a while, those hounds come on back, barking, and baying, and biting. Dead or not.

"Him. Her." Sir Alaric whispered. "Them. This — whatever it is — end times? Apocalypse. By the hound, I don't know. I ain't no priest. Ain't no nothing, even when I was something. But folk dying and in droves." He crushed tears from his eyes. "Dead. Lifeless." He swallowed, nodding to himself. "Bloodless."

"Like Brown Cloak?"

"Aye. And him but one of the many." He swallowed. *"Strigoi,* eh? An ugly word. Ugly sound. Just the saying of it. Dark days. Darker nights. Endless. Waiting on the coming of dawn."

"You still jawing about Rudiger? Or the Grey-Lady?" I glared over at the dead thing. "Or that thing?"

"I paid the price. Paid it with interest. Heavy."

"What the hell are you talking about?"

"What's done is done." Sir Alaric gripped my arm tight, fingertips biting in like spikes of iron. "I want you to tell Elona the truth, you ken?"

"Go on, old man, I'm listening." I gripped his cold hand as he spoke.

"I..." He slumped lower down the wall, melting like a warm candle, his grey skin waxy in the half-light "Can't shake thinking on Cat's last moments. Was ... was it over quick? Merciful quick? Or ... was it not?"

"I'd hazard quick, old man."

"Eh?" Sir Alaric blinked as he took a breath, his eyes going final blind, "I ... I'd hazard not."

...and so we, the flower of Haesken's nobility, journey down into the crypts. We know not what to expect other than darkness, drek, despair...
—*King Gaston's Journal.*

Chapter 51.

KARL..." I hissed into the tunnel maw. I didn't want to be near it. The inky blackness had a texture to it. A slick nauseating oiliness. A tingling. Or maybe I just imagined it, chicken-shit prick that I am. But I called out again. Louder. Hoping I'd hear Karl's gruff voice bark back or the clomp of his hobnail boots. So I listened. And I waited. And I heard nothing.

"God damn it..." I said cause I knew I had to go back. Had to check the tunnel. Had to find out what had happened. Had to get the hell out of here.

"Karl!" I shouted.

Then wincing, I waited.

A bead of sweat rolled down the small of my back. There'd been three lanterns with the party. I'd heard glass break. Harwin's. It'd been burning in a pool. So two left back there intact. Maybe.

I turned.

The tomb rose dead center from the chamber floor. An enormous slab of rectangular rock jutting up. As though the chamber'd been excavated out around it. A bas-relief of a crowned king had been carved into the lid. The King stared up at the blazing crucifix of sunlight blaring down. His features were blocky. Unrefined. Journeyman work. Drunk journeyman.

The lid lay askew.

Had it before?

Claw marks scored its empty innards. It reeked of dust and ancient decay.

Beyond the ring of light, across from the tunnel, lay another tunnel, walled up with blocks as high as my waist. Whoever had done it cared not for appearances, only function. Despite it, I pushed on them vainly, hoping for another escape. One that didn't entail the far tunnel.

And the hell-hound within.

Like a man afloat in a sea of despair, I returned to the nimbus of light, reveling in the warmth, the ephemeral safety. Shielding my eyes, I couldn't make out anything but the crucifix-shaped silhouette. There was no way to climb it.

A rasping sounded from behind.

"Red?" I froze.

But it wasn't Red.

Couldn't be.

It came again.

What the—? My heart jumped again at the sound. The long, rough friction, like a cat having a go at a salt lick. I stepped out of the light, eyes adjusting, making some sense, then making none. Thought it was Karl trudging down the tunnel. Or wished, rather. Even to see that bastard von Madbury would've brought me no small modicum of joy. But wishes were like snowflakes, they died as soon as you grasped them.

A pile of bones sat mounded against the far wall. They scattered as something crawled from them, through them, emerging from the darkness. A shape. Slumped. Rough. Human. Ish…

I nearly fumbled the boar-spear as I ducked behind the tomb, holding my breath.

He…

No.

It…

It crawled across the floor, dragging itself along, onerously, with one long skeletal arm. I fancied its joints creaking as It inched toward Sir Alaric. Its hand slopped through clotted crimson, scraping across stone, then retracted to Its withered lips, inserting Its palsied, crippled claw into Its black gash of a maw.

Sucking then. Moaning. Trembling.

I swallowed. Glanced over my shoulder, hoping, begging, praying, for another escape to materialize. But nothing.

The thing shifted again, drawing itself through the pool. Like some palsied beast, It lowered Its head. Its form lay hidden beneath a tattered mantle, bulges writhing sluggish beneath that ermine ruin. Its skin was the color of death.

I don't know if It saw me. If It knew I was there. If It cared.

Its maw split, trembling open, its tongue emerging, the tip of a withered twig sluicing through blood, rasping across stone. A moan of ecstasy crippled forth. Its carcass shuddered as It drank, slurping and sucking and pawing, hunkering, groaning low in greedy black waves.

In fascination, horror, revulsion, I watched, fingers nigh on crushing the spear haft.

The Half-King.

It wore a Haesken crown, but desiccated flesh had metastasized up and around, consuming it all but for the crucifix tips of iron and tarnished gold. It rose up, wiping Its stained maw with the back of Its skeletal claw.

A warbled groan let loose as It loomed over Sir Alaric.

I swallowed. Rose. Stalked forth.

"No fucking way," I said.

It lurched around, stiff, wooden, ungainly.

"Jesus…" I stutter-stepped to a halt, my moment gone. Bravery fled.

Crooked and skeletal and tall, It rose and continued rising, an eldritch wave, Its mantle rippling, bulging, contorting, the impression of naked rat tails writhing beneath.

"Oh holy hell."

Its maw worked, mechanical, wooden, as though trying to speak.

I should have struck, should have skewered It, should have done something, anything, shades of Avar, alone in the *Ulysses's* hull, but words dribbled in crimson spittle, sluicing from that gash of a maw.

"P-Please…" Its mouth worked, constructing word from disparate sounds, its voice echoing in other pitches, other tones, other voices long eons past. It glanced down at Sir Alaric, then at me, recoiling as though somehow ashamed. *"P-Please…"*

I swallowed, tried to anyways, tightening my grip on the boar-spear as I set my heel, digging into the floor.

It raised Its long angular arm, claws ragged and black and chitinous sharp. *"Please—"*

It didn't get to finish.

Boar spears are made specifically to set against a charge, but they work just aces with one, too, and that's what I did, catching It bodily on point, skewering It, driving It back. Rat tail appendages snapped and rasped inches from my face as I drove It slamming against the wall. Pinning It. My feet fighting for purchase as It squealed. As It writhed. As It reached.

Shards of ruined teeth grimaced in frustration, exasperation. *"Please!"* It grasped the boar-spear, scrabbling at the haft.

I set my foot behind the butt of the boar-spear, pinning it, reaching for Yolanda in her scabbard as the boar-spear's tines began to bend back.

"Please—" The Half-King gripped the spear-haft, snapping it in twain.

I lurched forth.

Its nails dug into my shoulder, grasping, and I swung the broken spear haft, slamming It across the face. Knocking It sideways. Almost. The grasping miasma of writhing tail splayed out against the wall, holding it upright.

I smashed It again.

Its eyes shined like shards of coal. *"Please!"* Ripping free and slipping in the blood, I righted myself, drawing Yolanda, the sweet song of her blade ringing free an exalted elixir for my faltering heart.

"Please..." The Half-King took a jagged step. *"No..."*

I swung. An artless, guileless tree-chop stroke, a brute-force action born of fear and terror and desperation. Black-nailed fingers scattered like hail.

The Half-King raised a warding arm. *"No..."*

Another swing and half Its arm was gone.

And still, It trudged forth, all spare and angular, crooked nightmare appendages flaring out from beneath his ruined mantle, eyes burning black as a midnight sun.

It lurched forward and never stopped coming.

And me? I never stopped swinging.

…my husband, my love, my king, Gaston, against all odds returned from his quest, proving victorious.

Yet, something about my love hath…
—*Diary of Queen Anne*

Chapter 52.

I COLLAPSED to a knee on the stone floor, gasping, cursing, steaming in the cold air, Yolanda the only thing holding me upright. The Half-King twitched on the ground, a hacked mass of appendage and horror. Disparate bits wriggling. Parts of man. Parts of beast. Parts of … I don't know. Rat. Vermin. *Thing*. All struggling to make itself whole.

Mother of God…

Dry heaving, stifling it hard, I rose, shouldering Yolanda, forged of lead, my arms jelly, and hefted her on high. Trembling, I brought her down. Again. And again. And again. I kicked slithering limbs away from each other. Screamed. Hacked. Collapsed again.

The cruciform daylight had waned, turning from the white blare of midday to the orange rust red of encroaching dusk. I shuddered. I couldn't to be down here come nightfall.

"Sorry Red." I stepped over Sir Alaric, pale and cold, and leaned out the threshold, a hand to the stone jamb, staring into the abyss. Breathing. Listening. Quivering. Willing myself forward.

And failing.

Karl was still back there.

Somewhere.

The light was fading fast.

That's what finally drove me. And I didn't stride forth like the heroes of old. I was no Lancelot. No Roland. No Beowulf bearding Grendel's mother in her lair. I slunk out like a kicked dog. At best.

"I'll come back," I whispered, sliding into darkness.

Yolanda gripped tight, I held her against the left wall, the one I'd followed down while keeping the broken boar-spear out to my right. The minuscule tingle of tip against stone, *scritch, scritch, scritch,* the sole comfort in my hour of need. I could count on it. Focus on it and not the fact that I was swimming upstream in dark water, surrounded by sharks. After sixty paces, I lost the light. After ninety more, I lost the right wall along with my nerve. Had a moment of rank indecision there in the dark. Of watery guts. A split in the tunnel. Stay to the left and I'd make my way back. Up. Past the massacre. Out.

But Karl'd gone right.

He had to have.

I kept left. Trudged on. Guilt rising in my gorge with each step until I stumbled across someone's corpse. Harwin, I think. I pawed along him. Over him. Found Squire Morley not far beyond. Could tell it was him by that crossbow. I couldn't find his lantern.

Stumbling along, I found Sir Roderick by kicking him in the head. "Sorry…" I lied.

His lantern was broken.

"Come on … come on." I knelt, pawing him like a pauper til I found what I'd hoped.

I turned around, started back down. Kept my left hand to the wall this time. The spear to the right. *Scritch…Scritch…Scritch…* When I lost the right I didn't even pause. I tripped over a stone, screamed, nearly broke my neck, pissed my pants, but I didn't pause.

The floor turned from stone to dirt. As though something had burrowed its way out. Or in. I tripped again and swore, finally figured anything alive down here knew I was coming. Trudging around like some jackass.

"Karl—?" I rasped.

Nothing.

I kept at it. Trudging down, down, down. The tunnel getting tighter and tighter. The air thicker and thicker. Had trouble catching my breath with the walls squeezing in. Compressing my senses. My soul. My sanity. The smell of dirt being overtaken by some mottled stench I couldn't describe. But it wasn't good.

Loose soil cascaded as I brushed past it — and froze. Something up ahead... A moan? Was it human? Jesus. *"Karl—"* I gripped Yolanda and listened. Prayed.

Something shifting? Sliding? Up ahead? Another moan.

It was human.

I hunkered low and made my way til I set my hand into a greasy mass of wet fur.

A corpse. A carcass. It was the other hell-hound. I won't say I squealed like a little girl. If I'd had the presence of mind to, I might've. At best. The hell-hound was laid out across the tunnel floor, blocking it wall to wall. About the size of a lion. Its body covered in damp mangy fur. I gave a cautious prod with the boar-spear.

It didn't move.

Able to breathe again, somewhat, I wiped my hand on my pant leg. Dry heaved. Squeezed past, praying the whole while the thing didn't move, didn't shift, didn't have any babies slithering around inside. *Jesus.*

"Watch it with that thing," growled a voice.

Karl.

My legs went weak. *Oh, thank the Lord.*

Karl shifted, grunting, buried half-beneath the thing. "Gonna lend me a hand?"

I took a breath. A real honest-to-goodness breath despite the caustic fume. "How'd you know it was me?"

"Heard a little girl squeal."

"Wasn't me."

"Right. Musta been the other fella."

"Yeah. A real chicken-shit little bitch, that other fella."

"Just get this damned thing off me, will ya?"

"Alright. Watch it. Can you move at all?"

Karl pulled his torso aside as best he could, and I shoved the broken spear haft underneath the thing, dug it in as deep as I could. "That good?"

"Like a dream," Karl grunted.

"Aces." I squatted and set the haft against my shoulder. "Ready?"

"No."

"Alright," I ignored him, *"watch it—"* and straightened, levering the haft up, shifting the carcass a mite. Karl slithered out kicking and swearing from beneath its fetid bulk. For a moment, he just leaned there against the wall, breathing long, hollow, hoarse.

"You alright?" I pawed along, found his shoulder.

"Just dandy."

"Good." I squeezed. "C'mon."

"You seen Red?"

"Just shut up and come on." He hissed a sharp invective between his teeth as I yanked him to his feet. "Got your axe?"

"Rrrg…" Shifting and scraping, the squelch of something being squished. "Odin's breath."

"Hrmm… Gimme a moment." A wrenching sound, like he was yanking it from the thing's gullet which is what I was fair sure he was doing. After a moment of skin stretching, ripping, came an, "Aye. Yar. Got it."

"Alright," I said. "Can you walk?"

Karl gripped my arm. "Long as it's the hell out of here."

"Was thinking of moving in. Raising a family," I said. "Stay to the left." I kept a hand to his shoulder, Yolanda in the other. We started on. "There'll be a hard turn coming up. After about a hundred paces. Give or take. Watch your step."

"You want to drive this thing?"

"No, but I don't want to be sitting in back, either."

"The left?" Karl grumbled. "Heads us back down."

"Yeah. Red's down there. And besides, I found something you're going to love."

"Yar? And what's that?"

"A king. A dead one."

"Hrrm. My favorite kind."

"Not so much with this one."

We trudged along.

"And what are we gonna do with His Majesty?" Karl asked out of the black.

I patted the skin of lamp oil I'd filched off Sir Roderick's corpse. "Honor him the old way."

...the disappearances and killings have begun once more.
—*Journal of King Gaston II.*

Chapter 53.

I SHOULD'VE KNOWN it the instant our eyes met. Destiny. Kismet. Betrayal. But I was focused on other things.

The sun had set long before Karl and I trudged back through Husk's vaunted gates. And by vaunted, I meant *shitty*. So very, very shitty. It was a ghost town as per usual. No folk slogging about in the claustrophobic alleyways. No lights glowing behind shuttered window. No dogs barking off in the distance. Karl peeled off with a grunt and headed south for the leper-house. I made for the house behind the *Half-King* for our rendezvous with Lady Mary'd and Ruth and the kids.

But they weren't there.

And they weren't at the docks.

So I headed back, waited behind the tavern, closing my eyes and hoping, breathing, shivering, seeing things I didn't want to see and feeling ... *thirsty*. And as luck would have it, a tavern stood just within throwing distance. So I did what I had to. Or didn't, but I did it anyways.

"I'll have a push and a shove," I announced down the bar.

In honor of Sir Alaric. From somewhere up in heaven, he'd smile down beatifically, taking a well-deserved break from boning his gorgeous dead wife. Or someone else's. If that's how heaven works. And it most certainly ain't. But it was a nice thought, and I was short on nice thoughts. Cause every time I closed my eyes I saw that damned thing, that shambling, awful crippled mess of a thing squealing as I hacked it to pieces. And the squealing hadn't stopped as it burned. Then the burning thing morphed into the Nazarene, huffing out yellow fumes as lepers screamed and groped and pawed from all around. And then Rudiger and his teeth, followed by the Grey-Lady, charring to a crisp as she begged for mercy.

"Eh?" Sweet Billie raised her craggy head, offering a dead stare followed by a blink. Like waking from a fog. Or seeing a ghost. "Sure thing … Sir Luther." Her hand buried in a mug. "Coming right up."

"Thanks." I should've seen it. Smelled it. Something'ed it. But like I said, I was focused on quenching my unrequited thirst, quelling my demons, blurring my inner vision.

Sweet Billie forced a lined smile, showing no teeth, and poured. "Heard King Eckhardt's, ah … passed on, they say."

"Yeah. Unfortunate." More or less. *Less* taking the dominant position.

"Well…" she slid the tankard across the bar, "here you go."

"Where's Wenelda?" I asked as something caught my eye.

It was the portrait Sir Alaric had laid a kissed hand upon that first night we'd arrived. Tankard in hand, I meandered over. A painting of Lady Catherine. Absolutely beautiful, much like the one from Sir Alaric's room but painted from a different perspective, from behind, her looking back and over her right shoulder, standing before a field of gold, the trees behind the blaze of autumn flame.

Jesus—

Something in my mind struck, clicking into place like clockwork.

But it didn't matter.

The first blackguard stepped from the kitchen. Gideon Felmarsh. A dumb look plastered across his wart-mangled mug. But he wasn't stupid. Had a loaded Genoese crossbow in those ham-strangler paws. Finely crafted. Aimed at yours truly. Naturally. Brother Miles was the second. Two-fisting that studded mace of his. White knuckled.

I eyeballed it. Funny thing about maces. Men of the cloth can wield them. But not axes or swords. Church gave the say-so cause they're blunt and won't draw blood. Theoretically. It was small comfort.

"Did Jesus use a flanged mace?" I asked.

Brother Miles opened his mouth but fell shy of wowing me with diatribe. He just looked guilty. Not guilty enough to stop what he was doing, but guilty nonetheless.

"Hypocrisy, life's blood of the church," I said.

"Grab some ceiling, you shit-fuck." Felmarsh stepped into the light. He was shorter than me, and even with the flurry of love-bites gracing my mug, I topped him for looks, too.

"Mind if I finish my drink?" I took a sip. "You should try doing something that distracts from your face. Grow out your hair. A mustache. Wear a mask. Might help you with the ladies."

"Ain't got no problem with the ladies."

I backed up. "Bet they have with you."

"Huh?"

Another pair of figures slid from the kitchen. One was King Eventine. The other that shit, von Madbury. King Eventine looked haggard, beat as a dog while von Madbury bore a manic gleam in his one eye.

"Y'know?" I glared at the King, "Your family's curse might just be warranted."

King Eventine paled and said nothing. I hadn't expected him to.

The front door thudded open and another pair of blackguards waded in.

"Fuck your mother." Von Madbury gripped his curved tulwar.

"You talking to me?" I nodded to the King. "Or him?"

King Eventine blinked, stammered, frowned.

"Too bad you weren't born a mime," I said. "You'd've been aces."

"Said to grab some ceiling." Felmarsh trudged forward, shouldering the barkeep aside. "Cunt."

"Apologies." I cocked my head toward von Madbury. "Thought you were talking to him."

The King had the good graces to avert his gaze, "Sir Luther, I don't believe—"

"Shut it," von Madbury shouldered past him, adding after the sad fact, *"Your Majesty."*

"Wenelda available?" I called to Sweet Billie, but she was gone, out the back. Smart. I did my damnedest to ignore Felmarsh. His crossbow, though? Not so easy. I took a long deep breath. There were worse ways to go than a stick to the chest.

"Hands *up.*" Felmarsh jabbed with the crossbow. "And away from the pig-sticker."

"Ah… Apologies. *Grab some ceiling.*" I raised my hands. Slowly. Finally. There were six of them all told. Five if you didn't count the King, which I didn't. "Didn't grasp the reference. But then, I can be obtuse. You wouldn't understand. Not a sharp fella like you." I turned to the King. "Where's Lady Mary?"

"Where she belongs." King Eventine gave von Madbury a sidelong look. "Ahem… She's to be my bride."

"Bet she's through the roof," I deadpanned. "And the others?"

The King stiffened. "I—"

"Shut it," von Madbury growled.

"You have them killed?" I said. "Huh, Your Highness? A madwoman and two kids? Jesus."

Von Madbury hissed something in the King's ear and he stiffened, paled, nodded.

I fixed King Eventine my best glare, even though I knew it was too late, knew he'd lost control, knew he'd never had it to begin with. "You know what you're dealing with, yeah?"

"We know who we're not," von Madbury answered.

"Wasn't talking to you, you sad, limp prick," I said calmly. "This'll end poorly for all involved, Your Highness. Mark my words."

"You were going to take her," King Eventine sniveled.

"No. She was gonna leave with me. There's a difference."

"She's safe. She's where she needs to be." King Eventine drew himself up. "What happened down there? In the tunnel?"

"You ran," I sneered. "I didn't."

"Yes, well…" the King licked his pallid lips, "it seemed the prudent thing to do."

"Can't disagree with you there." And I hucked my tankard sidearm at Felmarsh, cracking off his shoulder in a spider-webbing arc of ale.

"Shoot him!"

Wincing through the spray, Felmarsh shot, *Thwock!* I struck a table, ducked and hurled a chair aside, Brother Miles lurching after.

I slipped a glancing mace blow, booted him in the knee, sweeping his leg out from under him, stalling von Madbury, and turned tail. The two blackguards at the door stayed put, hunters to the hound, ready and waiting while Brother Miles and von Madbury untangled and gave chase, but there was no chase to give. Not in a tavern half the size of an outhouse.

Felmarsh cursed, reloading.

I hurdled through the room and dove, busting through a shuttered window, landing, rolling across the wet ground, coming up to my feet and running like my life depended on it, which is most assuredly did.

"Kill him!"

A bolt zipped past.

Down an alley, I scrambled through trash and matter and darkness, blood pounding in my ears, a hot burn flooding my chest, my lungs, my legs. But I staggered on, collapsing to a knee against a tilted picket fence. My arms … so heavy all of a sudden. Legs, too. Jesus. Waterlogged lead. The fence creaked as I leaned into it. The hot burning was a warmth now, running down my side, my leg, pooling beneath me.

Brother Miles had struck me good. But as I closed my eyes, I realized Brother Miles had missed. Felt the swish of air past my face.

"Odin's eye…" I felt at my side, probing, wincing, gasping, grunting.

And found it.

The sharp end of Felmarsh's crossbow bolt, snapped off in the side of my chest, its sliver-thin end poking free. I picked at it, grimacing, wet fingers slipping on its ephemeral point. *Come on.* Couldn't get a grip. *Come on, you fucker!* And if I could? *What then?* It was deep. I coughed wet red, hacked up a mouthful of pink spume. Wiped my chin. Coughed again, slumping ponderous to the ground. Everything was suddenly so dense. So thick. So slow.

I blinked.

All I could do.

Footsteps crunching through the grit. Somewhere. Somewhere near. Finally laughter. Sharp, nasty laughter. Closer now. But I didn't give a shit, couldn't give a shit cause I was headed beyond...

...at odds finding the requisite bodies and souls to satiate my sire's monstrous appetite...
—*Journal of King Gaston II*

Chapter 54.

ALL WAS DARKNESS. Darkness and chanting, a slow rhythmic hum suffusing the air with an echo of desecration and infinite possibility. But I couldn't breathe. Couldn't move. Could barely think. Something sat on my chest. Crushing me. Inch by inch, ribs yielding to the constant pressure of some torturer's device constricting by increment.

"Fuck him!" A voice snarled. A voice so familiar. "Let him die. Let him die like all the rest. Like all the ones he done killed. Our brothers!"

"JESUS—!" Someone laid the boots into my side and I stiffened, gasped, posturing across the ground like a dying fish.

Dirt and grit bit into the back of my head, my neck, as I tried to cover, tried to flail, tried to anything but failed.

"Beg off, brother," a deep hollow voice sounded. Did it come from beneath the earth? The sky? From the very ether?

Bare feet flapped off to the grumble of curses and fell views of my nature and parentage.

"Brother," the hollow voice sounded closer, louder, deeper, "now is not your time."

Why...? I wanted to ask. Could feel my lips moving, but nothing coming out. I was so tired. So god-damned dense and tired and ready and willing to just lay down and embrace the soft expanse of sweet annihilation.

"Because we say so," the hollow voice said.

Aaaahhh!

I screamed, in my mind at least, as someone grabbed me by the arm and yanked me off the ground, feet dangling, side burning, something wooden lodged unmoving through my chest.

"Come back to me, brother," the voice said.

The hell—?

The pain was nigh on unbearable as a red-hot poker twice the width of my fist slid burning into my side, melting through in a searing hiss, that poker, a hand, probing through, gliding along slick wet ribs, fingers palpating, feeling so wrong, so strange, so awful. Wet and warm. Every inch of my body and soul straining, screaming. The fingers found something awry, and slid between my ribs, wedging them up and down, bowing them, joints bending, creaking, and me?

Trembling. Kicking. Cursing. Screaming. Like a little fucking girl.

Pink burst out from within, a hiss, a torrent, a gush, a waterfall of slop splashing matter across the earth. A quick twist and pull and the thick butcher's hand slipped free. I dropped marionette-limp across the ground, fingers scrabbling at the earth, gasping, hacking, puking.

But I could breathe again.

"There, brother." Something *thunked* into the ground by my face. "The seed of your demise cast into fallow earth."

"What have you done?" came that other voice, that sneering scything sniveling voice.

I opened my eyes and rolled over, feeling at my chest, my sides, my vitals. Hacking up spume, a wobbling trail of it connecting to the ground. The head of Felmarsh's crossbow bolt lay point down in the ground before me, crimson with steaming blood.

"You're alive—" It was a whisper. A hiss. From a grey blob. Grasping hands and hard metal.

I lurched reflexively, pushing away, gasping, groping.

"Lou—" A hand gripped me, arms encircling. "It's me. Your brother. It's Stephan!"

I froze, whimpered, curled. "Stephan…?"

The Blob gripped me, holding me close. "A miracle. Rose of Sharon, Lou, a miracle."

"What the … what happened?" I blinked, working the sight back into my eyes. All was still a blur. The waver of torches burning, tall gaunt mountains looming, no— Figures huddled round, waiting, watching. The stench of blood and iron. Unwashed body and churned earth. The low bass chanting that never stopped.

"It's alright," the Grey Blob morphed into something approximating Stephan's haggard face. He embraced me. "It's alright, brother."

A forest of shorn legs surrounded me, huddled close, shifting from side to side. Pale, sweating, huffing, his eyes bloodshot mad, the Tome-Bearer leered, mounted atop his great burden, its spine cracked, laid out across the ground.

I crushed tears from my eyes. "N-Nothing seems alright."

"You're not dead," Stephan whispered. "And you were close, brother. So very, very close."

"Th-The Nazarene…?" I glared up, blinded anew by the harsh blare of torchlight.

"He's here, too."

I shielded my face. "He gonna kill me?"

"Brother, he *saved* you." Stephan grasped me. "A miracle, Lou, like Lazarus."

"Yeah, but," I rubbed my eyes, "but why?"

The Nazarene knelt before me, slapping a massive paw on my shoulder, nearly shattering my spine. I flinched, trying to shrug free, but his fingers gripped in, just shy of crushing bone.

"Stay." His huge form loomed beneath a hooded cloak. Death incarnate. "I shan't harm you, brother."

"Yeah?" I gasped. "Why the hell not?"

"Because it is what Jesus would do."

I lurched, winced. *"Are you bloody serious?"*

"Aye. That I am." The hooded head nodded sagely.

"Y'know?" I wiped my mouth. "Acting like a true Christian's the surest way of getting crucified."

"Truth be told, I would welcome the release. But there is much work to accomplish and not overmuch time to accomplish it."

"You want something." I rubbed my eyes. "That's it. Isn't it? What the hell is it?"

"What I have always desired, brother." The Nazarene rose, arms wide. "To aid the faithful. Heal the sick. Give succor to the indigent." The Nazarene drew back his cowl, and it was fair evident that back at the leper-house, Karl hadn't missed with that axe. Edges of jagged skull yawned empty as a spent eggshell. Charred bone. Black eyes crackling with mad vitality. "To scourge the earth of horror."

"You could start by pulling the hood back up," I said.

"Keep yer mouth shut!" Lazarus loomed above, behind, as ungainly as a pumpkin on a pike-head.

"Quell your inner demons, brother." The Nazarene raised a huge paw. "For we've greater at hand to combat this night."

"He tried to kill you!"

"Aye." The Nazarene nodded slowly, black ichor dribbling down his neck. "For he believed me the source of the corruption. Yea, and he sought to cleanse this place. And despite his most abject of failures, I recognize the intent of the deed if not the deed itself, for he has seen the light." His eyes narrowed to a stiletto point. "You have seen the light, brother?"

I wiped my mouth with the back of my hand. "Yeah. Sure. *Absolutely!*"

"Aye. So. You believe now?" The Nazarene's eyes bulged wide. *"Nay*... You have seen it in truth, brother. Yes!" He dropped to a knee, pawing me, gripping my shoulders. "I can smell its fell reek upon you. The death. The un-death, brother. The grave earth stink of decade and decay — wait." He squeezed. "You've found its lair?"

"Yeah." I winced up as Karl forced his way through the circle. "Yeah. We found it."

"Tell me what happened," the Nazarene gasped.

"Sure..." Wincing, wobbling, I clambered to my feet, hugging myself against the cold wind freezing my bare flesh. A knot-sized squirm of gnarled scar lay slathered across my right side, weeping pink. "We found the bleeding nightmare, the Half-King, the *strigoi*, and we killed it."

"Nay brother, that you have not." The Nazarene straightened to his full and considerable height, his hollow skull sloshing as he gazed off north across Husk, to the Schloss von Haesken seated upon its sister hill. "You have only made it stronger."

...grates on a man's nerves, continuously, and so I have decreed we abandon Haesken Keep, though it be my ancestral home, for I cannot abide such a fell abomination dwelling below our very...
—*Haesken Family Treatise: King Eckhardt Haesken III*

Chapter 55.

IT WASN'T UNTIL the walls of the Schloss stood before us, all sunken, sad, and sallow, that I heard it. The screaming. As one, we three froze in the lee of the skeleton of a church, halted amidst construction. "But do you believe him?" I asked.

"The Nazarene?" Stephan craned his neck, looking out at the towers built along the Schloss's southern wall. "Yes, brother, I do. I may not know why, but ... he let us go, did he not? When he could have so easily done otherwise."

"Yeah. I don't know." I scratched my chin. "That fucker wants something. And I keep feeling like he's getting it."

As if to punctuate my thought, another screamed ripped out from beyond the wall.

"Thor's hammer—" Karl stuck a finger in his ear and twisted.

"Bugger can scream," I admitted.

"Who is it?" Stephan whispered.

"Don't know," Karl grunted. "Everyone sounds like that, you push 'em far enough."

We ducked beneath the ribs of the church, laid bare for all the world to see. Half-constructed arches of stone, supported by braces of pressure-bent wood loomed above. The screams reverberated distorted and weird through the forest of pillar and stone.

"It's a man." Stephan crossed himself.

I licked my lips. "It's the King. It's Eventine."

They both looked at me. Neither disagreed. Von Madbury had done what I knew he'd do, what I'd warned King Eventine he'd do. And so the King was crying. Reeling. Begging for forgiveness. Contrition. You name it.

And it was awful.

Words the Nazarene had said tolled in my mind like funerary bells. *You've only made it stronger...*

"We have to do something." Stephan grimaced.

Wincing, I clutched my side. "We are." But my feet were sizzling on red embers listening to it.

"We aren't."

"You want us to march up to the gates? Demand they stop torturing the hell out of him? Forthwith? Oh, and throw unconditional surrender in for shits and giggles, too?" I planted my feet. "You're the one said we can trust him, yeah?"

Stephan pursed his lips and nodded. Reluctantly.

"Then trust him."

Another buffet of screams ripped past.

Karl gripped his singed beard. This was even digging at him.

"Fuck him." I drew up, tried acting tough, using my last reserves of bravado, but it fell flat, false, hollow. The scream slid up and down my spine like the tines of a rusted fork. And it wasn't cause it was King Eventine. It was cause if von Madbury were torturing him, he'd probably done the same to everyone.

"Towers this side got only one bastard apiece." Karl squinted up at the wall.

"Yeah..." I followed his gaze. Equations of murder-math streamed through my mind.

Killing a man's easy. Under the right conditions. But these weren't those. And killing one tucked up in a tower? Even a shitty tower like the Schloss laid claim to? No mean feat. And doing it before he alerted his blackguard comrades? We'd need a miracle from the Lord.

Stephan winced at each and every scream. "Brother, please…" was all he said.

"I know. I know." I could feel it, too, the steam kettle whistling. "Shit." We were gonna do it. Whatever *'it'* was. And you could be sure *'it'* was gonna have a fistful of stupid seasoned in.

"Karl," I stared up at the tower, calculating, "take a double-time and gander." Raucous laughter boomed from the far side, and King Eventine's screams hit a trilling crescendo. Von Madbury was taking his time. Having his fun. "See how many are manning the far wall. If those towers are skeleton-crewed, too."

"Already did."

"Then do it again," I barked.

Karl gave me the eye, but ceded.

"Whoa—" I collared Stephan when he tried following. "C'mon, little brother. This is my show. We stay. And we wait."

"But—"

"We. *Bloody*. Wait." I stormed through the church foundation, dragging Stephan past piles of stone and lumber stacked haphazard. Jags of raw-cut lumber rose like ribs from the foundation's midst, arcing over and meeting doppelgangers from the far side. Block and tackle cranes littered the landscape. Then I saw it. A ladder. Stephan was on it in a flash.

I stomped it out of his hands, clattering to the stone.

Stephan turned back. "But—"

I cut him short with a slash of my hand and pointed. "Grab that rope."

Eventine was still screaming. I couldn't call him king anymore. Only authority a man sounding like that had was over his own bowels, and then only a limited while.

"No, we—"

"He knew what road he was walking, brother." I forced out a breath. "Where it lead. One look at that one-eyed bastard and you know his soul." I fixed him a glare, daring him to argue. "Tell me I'm wrong. Tell me I can't judge a book by its cover. Tell me."

Stephan looked away.

"You think that bastard's going to sit all prim and pretty and do Eventine's bidding? When he's the one training up the new men? Whispering all the while in their ears? And the kingdom's in upheaval and ready for plucking? Saw it the first time I laid eyes on him. We all did. Every one of us. Hunger. Ravenous. Rabid."

"He wants to be king," Stephan said.

"Better king over a heap of shit than a turd-lump at the bottom."

Karl stepped over a pile of squared stone, blowing snot out one nostril.

"How many?" I asked.

"Same as before. Two at the gates. One in each tower."

That meant six total, watching the whole of the Schloss von Haesken's vaunted entirety.

"So he's running a skeleton crew while he cuts on the king?" I said.

"Yar." Karl spat.

"And another twenty inside," I said. "Twenty at least."

"What are they all doing inside?"

"I don't like this," Stephan said.

385.

"Who does?"

"We *need* to go, brother."

Karl said nothing, but I could read his warning glare. *We could still just haul arse.*

"Yeah. Shit. I know," I said. "But I can't make you come, either. So if you want out of this cluster-fucked madness, I won't squawk."

Karl snorted. "Piss off."

"Good. So. They're all inside," I said. "Drunk off their asses. Having their fun. We hope."

"A lot," Karl growled.

"Yeah. Jesus." We were all thinking the same thing.

That it was a trap. That von Madbury was cutting on Eventine, baiting us in.

"He must know the King's not the best bait," Stephan said.

"Might be all he has left." I let that sink in, cursing as I shouldered the ladder. "We clear?"

"Yes…"

"'Course we are. Rest of the town's already dead." I frowned. "We come at it midway, it'll give us the longest stretch."

"Brother, we have to—"

"No. We wait. Just a moment longer," I almost said again for maybe the fiftieth time, but the rumble of feet stomping, trudging, marching, emerged from the sadistic delight blaring from beyond.

Karl craned his neck, popping vertebrae.

Up the hill, through the narrow streets, the horde was coming. Men and women and children. Scourger and farmer and fisherman alike. They clomped forth in a mishmash of swagger and song. And gimping along, leading the way, trudged the lumbersome bulk of the Nazarene.

"Thank the Lord." Stephan crossed himself.

"Yeah, sure," I grumbled, "but I still ain't sure the Lord's got much to do with it."

...T'is but a simple matter to remand criminals to the 'oubliette' whence they are quickly forgotten.

Later, under cover of night, the long marched commences at point of blade back up to the old keep...
—*Haesken Family Treatise: King Eckhardt Haesken III*

Chapter 56.

THEY MARCHED UP THE STREET in a riot of masticated glory. Torn banners snapped in the gale wind, followed by chanting. Dancing. General merriment. It wasn't until they were nearly upon us that their menace lay bare. A troupe of broken Jesuses spear-headed the march. Scourges rusting in ribbons of torn flesh dangled over lacerated shoulder.

I hunkered back to the shadows.

I'd said before that riots aren't prepared. Well then, this no riot. This was a company. A brigade. An army. A full-bore bloody cavalcade. They came bearing tools and makeshift weapons of warfare. A scattering of shields and armor. Axes. Plowshares straightened to swords. Sticks and bloody-fucking stones. Amidst the center of the surging serpent, they bore an axe-hacked, torch-blackened tree trunk, roots flared out behind, grasping like kraken arms.

"Good diversion." Karl shouldered his end of the ladder.

"Not many better." I took a breath, clutched my end, but didn't budge. "We stick to the plan."

Stephan stood lookout over the street. "What's the plan?"

"Same as always." I forced him to look me in the eye. "Get in. Get out. No heroics. No bullshit. No suicidal pacts with destiny."

"Ain't this *exactly* that?" Karl rumbled.

"Shut the hell up," I said.

A cold drizzle fell as the mob reached the Schloss's gates, and Jesuses and cobblers and blacksmiths and who-the-hell-knew-what proceeded to spread out along the wall. The guard nearest us scrambled towards the gate. A warning cry belted out from the far towers. A gate-guard fired a crossbow bolt down into the army. *Thunk!* A scourger roared in pain and fell away from the ram, clutching at the bolt sunk deep into his chest. Another stepped in to take his place.

"OPEN THE GATES!" The Nazarene's voice rang.

Lightning fissured the sky and the heavens opened up, rain pouring down.

Another gate-guard ducked back to reload, yelling to his compatriots as the Nazarene emerged like madness incarnate. He ambled tall and ungainly toward the gates. The right side of his head yawned open, cracked jagged, like the maw of some hellish jack o' lantern. Within lay only corruption, sloshing, spilling over his shoulder, down his side, staining half of his body in a black tarry woad.

"TARRY NOT, BROTHER, FOR THE KINGDOM OF HEAVEN IS UPON YOU!"

The gate-guards were up again and aiming. Probably shitting their pants, too, and I was right there with them. Kingdom of heaven notwithstanding, the Nazarene looked more like something from the pit than the on-high aeries of the Almighty.

Shouts sounded from beyond. Feet stomping up stairs, across cobbles, sucking through mud. The guards shot again. A bolt took the Nazarene through the chest. He didn't so much as flinch. Through the black woad staining his body, the Nazarene slathered his hand. Dripping liquid midnight, he pressed it splayed wide against the metal-studded gate. White steam began sizzling.

More guards mounted the gates.

"Shoot him!"

Bolts rained down on the Nazarene, piercing him through the shoulder, the abdomen, the neck.

Teeth grinding, the Nazarene wailed aloud, a cold lonely peal bereft of warmth or life. The ground seemed to pulse, to shiver, puddles rippling, pebbles dancing. A yawning groan as the gates shivered.

"Now?" Stephan swallowed. His hands opened. Closed. Opened again. "Brother—?"

Guards hauled down the ramparts.

I held up a hand.

Karl pawed at an axe at his belt.

"Onward, brothers!" The Nazarene turned toward the horde.

The scourgers lugging the battering ram started forth at a walk, a disjointed jog, evolving into a stumbling gait, synthesizing into quick synchronization, becoming more fluid, more one, as they barreled ahead, lunging forth full bore, the axe-hacked point of the ram ragged and leading them onward.

Scourgers screamed. Roared. Chanted. A murder of bolts flew.

The Nazarene's eyes blazed as he stood in the ram's path, lurching aside only at the final instant. Fire-hardened wood struck the gate, shattering it as though made of glass, sheets of shard and splinter raining down.

"Usurp the usurpers!" the Nazarene bellowed. "Defy the defilers!"

The Nazarene lurched through the gates, over a fallen scourger, the battering ram laid across his chest, one of the ragged branch handles piercing his neck. Others poured through after, streaming around him, past him, a river of ragged madness pouring forth, whooping loud for black bloody murder.

"Now?" Stephan's eyes nigh on bulged from his skull.

Karl and I were both thinking the same thing. *Let's get the hell out of here.*

But we didn't.

"Let's go do this," I said finally, and off we charged into bliss-less oblivion.

...the famine which has lingered far longer than any before.

There is a critical dearth of suitable subjects, and the kingdom, I fear, shall suffer if I cannot find...

—*Haesken Family Treatise: King Eckhardt Haesken III*

Chapter 57.

THE GALE WIND nearly ripped me off the ladder, rain blinding my eyes as I fought for grip on wet rungs. Reaching the top, I ducked back as a shadow pounded past, along the rampart, toward the gates. Mail rustling. Weapons jangling. Jostling. The wooden crenels afforded cover to either side, but I had to poke my head out for a better view. Empty ... for a stretch.

I leapt off the ladder, dagger drawn, and froze.

Below, in the center of the courtyard, a great bale-fire burned. Flames whipped and licked fifty-feet high despite the sheets of cold rain pouring down. Bodies lay strewn across the courtyard.

"Jesus Christ..."

Atop the scaffold and before the conflagration, Eventine lay on high. I couldn't hear him but imagined a slurred mewling slopping liquid from his lips. And with fair-good reason. They'd lashed him cruciform across the breaking-wheel. An under-stuffed scarecrow, his limbs contorted at impossible angles. They'd broken his arms. His legs. Shattered them, bent them, interwoven them through the charred spokes. Above. Below. Above again.

"Down!" Karl barked.

I ducked reflexively, slipping, falling onto my arse as a shadow loomed and blade slashed past.

"Shit!" My dagger skittered off the rampart.

The shadow growled, tugging at his blade entrenched in the crenel. But only for a moment before abandoning it, reaching behind his back.

Splayed out across the rampart, I kicked out. My boot-heel glanced off his thigh as he raised an axe two-handed above his head. I crab-walked praying backward as he stepped forward. Then Karl was hurtling off the ladder, man-handling the blackguard barrel-assing headfirst down into the courtyard.

I groped shakily to a knee, inched forward, glanced over the edge.

Splayed out in the muck, the shadow made a fair imitation of Eventine. Karl levered the blade free of the crenel and tucked it under his belt.

"Don't have enough?" I winced against the rain.

"Never." Karl squinted off toward the gates. "Take the stairs?"

Mercenaries and Jesuses fought amidst a mad scrum on the gate-tower stairs. The Jesuses outnumbered the blackguards two to one, three to one, ten to one, but they had the low ground and the blackguards had actual weapons of warfare, not makeshift implements of self-mutilation and madness. "I'll pass."

Stephan appeared huffing atop the ladder. "Rope." He ducked the coil off his shoulder.

Below, the stables would shield our descent, which was good. The bad? There were blackguards bolting everywhere.

"We can't leave him like that." Stephan grimaced as he made a quick loop and tied it off.

"Who?"

"*Who?*" Stephan shot back.

"Listen—" I grabbed him by the throat. "We're here for

our own. Eventine made his bed. Let him lie in it."

Stephan stifled a snarl and ripped free, tossing one end of the coil off the rampart.

Karl was on it before it hit ground, scrambling down like some simian fiend, short legs kicking, rope zipping through his gauntleted hands. In a blink, he was on the ground, perched atop the ribcage of his new best mate.

"Watch it—" I grunted an instant before I landed atop of the dead guy, bones breaking beneath my feet.

Stephan was beside me on his arse a second later. *"Oooof—"*

"Break your arse?" I hissed down.

"Aye. And if either of you bastards say anything about a crack…"

"Language, young man." I held out a hand.

Karl guffawed as we hoisted Stephan to his feet.

"C'mon." I started along the stable wall toward the Schloss and froze.

Karl seethed by my side, raring to go. But Stephan. Jesus. Hadn't moved. Was just standing there, jaw clenched, shaking his head slowly, back and forth. That look in his eye, the set of his jaw.

"Come on—" I growled.

He shook his head. Just a twitch.

"He's a *dead* man."

"Not yet."

"You *can't* save him."

Stephan shook his head, "I have to try," and bolted toward the maelstrom.

"Odin's eye!" I roared as I gave chase cause he was a stupid-martyr-bastard and all, but when it came down to the few things of this world I gave two shits about, he was nigh on it.

…a cold, haunting beauty, Lady Catherine remains as stunning as ever, even despite the malady gripping her soul. How she has pieced together so much of my family's sordid history lies beyond my ken, but hers is an offer I cannot refuse…

—*Haesken Family Treatise: King Eckhardt Haesken III*

Chapter 58.

EMBERS RIPPED whistling through the gale, coruscating in vortices of orange hail. Heat and by turn freezing rain blasted me as I stumbled on after Stephan, hurtling over bodies, through sucking mud, into the courtyard, toward the bale-fire burning in its midst. The battle engulfed the courtyard. Von Madbury's blackguards fell back to the keep. The Jesuses drove them back but paid in the body and blood for each and every step.

A crippled rictus flashed before me, attached to the body of a starving Jesus, his ribs stark across his torso as he slashed a scourge. I blocked it whipping about my forearm, the end licking my face, and ducked under, gut-punching him with Yolanda's hilt then hurling him aside.

Behind, Karl roared, hacking with his axe.

Ahead, Stephan skidded to a halt, clambered up the scaffold, alongside Eventine. "Mother of God…" Stephan knelt by the massive wheel, by the man, the thing, the detritus of humanity crucified across it. Skin strained taut against broken bone. Eventine screamed as Stephan tried to untangle one of his arms from the spokes. "Judas Priest," Stephan turned, "where do I even start?"

"Ain't about '*start*,' little brother." I gripped my blade, watching his back, head on a swivel.

Eventine's chest glistened with drool and vomit. Bone protruded from his left forearm, a shard of white biting through like the beak of a baby bird. "Who...?" Eventine's eyes were distant, far-seeing, his voice an unearthly warbling peal, *"Dietrick ... please ... no."*

"This ain't your thing," I said.

"No, I ... I'll do it." Stephan stood there, his one hand out toward me, open, waiting.

We stared at each other a moment, insanity swirling.

"Fuck off." I shouldered past, cause even if it were the right thing to do, the only sensible thing to do, it still didn't make it the *easy* thing. "Where's Lady Mary?" I hissed in Eventine's ear.

"Phff..." Eventine's eyes bulged as blackguards slashed past. He struggled to speak, "For..."

"Is she alive?!"

"For..." His eyes rolled as he sneered in pain, lips working, "...get."

Karl set his feet and turned, his grim demeanor as much as his axe an immovable stone cleaving the current amid the river of surging flesh.

"Get *what?* You little prick!?" I grabbed a fistful of Eventine's hair, shook him, screaming, squealing, bleeding. "Is she dead? They kill her? Huh? What about the others?"

"Stop ... please."

"Brother—" Stephan grabbed my shoulder.

"Fuck off!" I shrugged off his paw and ducked as a cadre of bodies flashed past, the spark of steel on steel, Karl haranguing them off. "What of the others? Ruth? The children? Did you kill them?"

"Dietrick, please ... no," Eventine flinched, swallowed, blinking, his tongue working sluggish and imprecise, grey lips contorting, "It was Palatine. To ... to forget..."

A mercenary blasted past, hunted down by a trio of Jesuses latched onto him, bearing him to the mud astride his back, one throttling as the others flogged him rotten.

"You *what?!*" I forced my blade against his throat.

Eventine mouthed the words again, "Forget…"

Eventine never finished, and never thanked me, but I didn't ask for either. I didn't care. I just offered him one last benediction in steel, then shoved Stephan stumbling numb before me, wiping my blade clean on my pant leg.

The Schloss loomed ahead.

...though the younger is a beauty much in line with Lady Catherine, the eldest is staid, strong of body and mind, and thus more apt to withstand the rigors of...
—Haesken Family Treatise: King Eckhardt Haesken III

Chapter 59.

A MAD HOWL erupted within the Schloss. Somewhere distant. Somewhere deep. A mad howl? Nay. Madness indicates some modicum of humanity, however twisted. But this? Shorn completely. I skidded to a halt, freezing as I stared up at the mad tapestry, the demon-king monstrosity crucified across it. "C'mon." I hustled onward, forced open a door to the stairwell as another howl erupted.

"What the fuck was that?" Karl white-knuckled his thane-axe.

"Your mother in town?" I quipped. But I was just talking tough.

"Shhh—" Stephan held up a hand.

Something was pounding below. On metal. Clanging. Hammering. Squealing. Dust drizzled from the ceiling with each stroke. Vibration shivered through the soles of my feet, reverberating up my legs, through my guts, fluttering in my heart.

"The dungeon?" Stephan asked.

"Don't know." I shook my head and loped up the stairs. "Don't want to know."

We found Ruth in her room, splayed across the floor. She hadn't gone quietly. Dried blood smeared from the hearth, across the room to the bed. Scorch marks soiled her dress. Her back'd been broken.

Karl craned his neck past me, offered a growl, which about summed up my thoughts.

"Jesus…" I swallowed. "And we left them."

"Don't have the time," Karl rumbled.

Stephan wiped a tear from his eye then lifted Ruth like a child, setting her in bed next to Abraham.

The hearth was cold, nothing but ashes shifting on the grate. A bowl of cold stew sat on the table.

Stephan laid Ruth's hand in Abraham's, clasped them both, then covered them with a blanket.

"You ready yet?" I asked.

Stephan just gave me a look.

Karl sniffed the old stew, slurped it down, wiped his mouth.

I trudged around the room, searching for something. A clue. A message. A something. An anything that might point to what happened to Lady Mary and the kids. All's I found was Avar, slumped in the corner, cold and grey and full of holes.

I closed his dull eyes.

"He stayed by their side." Stephan crossed himself. "He didn't run."

"Bloody well should have," Karl spat on the floor.

"What of the Queen-Mother?" Stephan asked. "And Palatine?"

"Who gives a shit?" Karl growled.

"Lady Mary?"

"I don't know." I stalked the room, flipped over a table. "She probably took off. She ain't stupid. Took off and hunkered down … I don't know … somewhere." I hoped. Or she was dead. Probably, they were all dead. Slain. Hacked to pieces. Tortured…

Stephan glared out the window at the flames rolling in the courtyard. They'd set the stables afire, and the horses inside were screaming. A few of the mob hammered at the door to no avail.

"What now?" Karl stood grimacing by the door. He wanted to be gone.

I felt his pain. Intensely.

"We stick to the plan," I said. "We get the hell out of here. And we don't look back."

"We can't." Stephan was crawling out of his skin. "We — We can't just fold."

I squared up on him.

Stephan met my glare pound for pound and, being honest, outweighed me on that score by some ten stone of righteous might. But he didn't know what else to do. Where to go. How to find them. If finding them was even an option.

Stephan rose up straight. "We cannot abandon them."

"Forget them, brother," I spat the sour bile taste from my mouth, "just like Eventine said."

"Rose of Sharon—" Stephan's eyes lit up as though he'd seen the Holy Ghost.

...cannot include my father-by-law in the rigors and travails of this ignoble business. And thus, it falls to lesser men to accompany me upon this venture. I know of two such candidates...
—Haesken Family Treatise: King Eckhardt Haesken III

Chapter 60.

SCOURGER AND BLACKGUARD hurled themselves against one another in the great hall, a mad grapple, blades singing, thudding, hammer-fists rising, falling, men screaming, fingers digging into eye sockets, teeth biting, breaking. Amid the madness of slaughter and chant, like a musician conducting an distorted orchestra, the Nazarene towered, whirling a huge flail overhead, striking friend and foe alike. *"Come to me, brothers!"*

Scourgers poured in.

Karl and Stephan hunkered at my back, the three of us huddled behind a cracked door.

The Nazarene grasped one of von Madbury's blackguards — no. Grasp's the wrong word. He reached *into* one of von Madbury's blackguards, his hand gliding into the blackguard's chest as effortlessly as if it were a pool of tepid gruel. The blackguard's teeth shattered as the Nazarene throttled the life from him, pulverizing a fistful of organ and sinew.

"A foul horror doth dwell within!" The Nazarene ripped his hand free, a wet splattering arc, the corpse falling to the ground, just another lump of meat. "And it is we who must eradicate it!" The Nazarene's gaze swept the hall, falling my way as he cast innards aside like ripped fish-guts. "Brother!"

"Back up—" I hissed, pushing back, shoving, tensing,

preparing to do what I did best. Turn tail. Beat feet. Trample Stephan and Karl if need be.

"Krait!" The Nazarene pointed. "Go!"

A crossbow bolt thudded into his throat, blasting matter backward. Unperturbed, the Nazarene lurched toward the shooter.

"Cut the monstrosity down!" von Madbury tore in, tulwar slashing.

"Bastard—" I lunged forth, but Karl yanked me back, growling, "Stifle it, ya bloody fool!"

Lazarus descended upon von Madbury, all gangling like some stick insect, swinging a two-fisted scourge. The knotted wrap of leather and iron spike whipped past von Madbury's head as he ducked forth, whipping his blade out. It arced too fast to follow and cut Lazarus's leg off below the knee, felling him screaming.

The Nazarene and Jesuses whipped around.

Gideon Felmarsh entered the fray, two-handing a broad-blade and crucifying a Jesus with a single swing.

"We gotta move," I grunted.

"No shit," Karl scowled.

"Door's across the hall," Stephan gasped. "There's no other way."

"You sure about this?" I hissed.

"Flee then, brother," Stephan stood poised to dash, "I'll find the path," and took off through the fray.

"Bloody hell—" I grunted, charging after, Karl hounding fast at my heels.

The chanting Jesuses fell swiftly under the blackguards' onslaught, but the Nazarene yet held court, front and center to it all. His cowl fell back, the caved-in ruin of his head revealed horrible in the rippling gloom. Gripping a blackguard by the throat, he bellowed — "Go, brother!" —

his fingers melting through liquid flesh.

"Surround him!" Von Madbury slashed at the Nazarene's tree-trunk legs. "Hack him down!"

Gideon Felmarsh and Brother Miles spread out as more Jesuses poured like a wave through the front door. Von Madbury formed a shield wall with four others and turned to face them.

"Come to me, brothers, sing of the glory of God!" the Nazarene screamed as von Madbury's cohorts descended upon him. "Descend to the depths! Burn free the horror that has taken hold!"

I had no idea what the lunatic was jawing about. Was barely listening, but it was working its way into my brain to the sound of steel hacking into flesh.

"The light!" the Nazarene bellowed, "Yes. *The light!*"

"Shut the fuck up!" someone screamed.

"The light!"

I hurtled out the door behind Stephan, turned and slammed it behind Karl. My last glimpse? The Nazarene borne to the ground, a legion of sword blades thrust into him. Through him. Upon his knees, one arm hacked clean of his body and lying by his side, he bellowed, *"The light, brother! The light!"*

...Catherine must have somehow escaped from the blasted horror, for she harangues the populace during the time of the new moon, spreading discord and terror in much the same manner as the Half-King...
—Haesken Family Treatise: King Eckhardt Haesken III

Chapter 61.

EVENTINE WAS BABBLING," I snarled. "He didn't know where the hell he was. What was going on. All's he knew? His ride was over."

The sound of feet pounding, weapons clanging, bastards screaming, were all but distant echoes muffled above. It was small comfort, though, for now it was the unearthly keen below that froze my step. My blood. My soul. The howls and pounding that above had been thunderheads on a distant horizon down here were a raucous storm.

"Eventine said, *forget them,*'" Stephan huffed. "And you're right, he was nearly gone. Nearly dead. Driven mad by torture. Anguish. Despair. But, what if in his muddled mind by saying *forget them,*' he was alluding to the oubliette?"

"*Oobli*-what?" Karl slunk along behind.

"Just shut up and follow along. Literally, if not figuratively."

"F-Figure...? Eh...? What?" Karl grunted.

"Jesus Christ." I paused at the bottom of the stairs and waited. Listened. Swallowed. The wine cellar lay at the far end of the hall. All beyond lay quiet. I rounded on Stephan. "We're risking our necks down here on word of that dying shit?"

"Where do you put someone you want to forget?" Stephan crept along behind.

"In the ground," Karl rumbled low.

"He ain't wrong," I said.

"Well, yes, I suppose." Stephan nodded in half-hearted agreement. "Or … the oubliette."

"Huh?" Karl hefted his axe.

"A kind of dungeon," I said. "Shaped like a bottle. Entrance and exit through a thin neck up top. A wider chamber below." Not a place for someone you wished to release. To interrogate. To ever see again. And the poor bastards whose job it was to muck it out every century or so…

"So, why're we going to the *oobli … oobli…*" Karl shook his shaggy head. "Bloody bottle dungeon?"

"Cause my idiot brother thinks a dying man was spouting riddles with his last breath." And we were both all-in right beside him. Footsteps pounded, dim and distant. I held up a hand as we reached the heavy wine cellar door. Taking a breath, I turned the door handle and burst in, blade drawn.

Within, the wine racks stood as empty as the room. *Empty,* a beautiful word for once. "Let's be quick."

"Not riddles per se." Stephan followed me in. "But he was confused. Begging for his life. He thought you were von Madbury at first. And at last? I … I don't know. He was having difficulty gathering the strength even to speak." Stephan fixed me an eye. "At the very least, he seemed to genuinely care for Lady Mary, yes?"

I considered, offered a shrug. "Yeah. Sure. In his own shitty way, maybe. He mentioned Palatine, too. Muddled, but—"

"Perhaps they sought to protect her?" Stephan offered. "And perhaps amid all the fight and furor Eventine sought in his own broken way, fighting through fugue and pain, to relay what little he was left privy to."

"So you think he said it in a way that only us *educated* assholes would have the wherewithal to work it out?" I scowled.

"Hrrm," Karl thumbed Stephan's way, "think it was only *this* educated asshole."

"That remains yet to be seen," I said.

Stephan crept past one of the racks, toward the dungeon-door, "Let's just hope it's so."

Cause if it wasn't, we were sticking out necks out for a bunch of corpses, I didn't say.

"Jesus—" I froze.

A mighty crash resounded beyond the dungeon-door, accompanied by the sound of metal squealing in protest, rock shifting, mortar cracking. Then howling. Like some idiot child deprived of its favorite toy.

Stephan grabbed at a rack to steady himself.

"Think I just pissed myself," I breathed.

"I'll etch it on yer tombstone," Karl said.

"And I'll piss on yours."

Stephan paused by the dungeon-door. "Can you feel it?" His hand hovered, trembling above the latch. "What is it?"

"Don't know, brother, but I can feel it, too." I looked to Karl. "Feel something, anyways."

The air was dense. With a palpable greasiness to it, a weight, as if the Schloss above were compressing it somehow, making it thicker, heavier, denser. And there was a reek. A rotten sweetness I couldn't quite place but knew was wrong. All wrong.

The pounding reverberated, waning back to silence.

None of us said anything and despite every intuition, every feeling in my body, my gut, my bones, I started forth.

"Odin's eye," Karl spat. "The Half-King…"

"Shit." I straightened, froze. "Yeah." The feel. The smell. The same as the crypt of the Half-King. The same but … different. A rawer. Heavier. Muskier stench. Like fresh-spawned death. I glared at Karl and he at me. His eyes blared, *We could still just fucking bolt!* And mine were undoubtedly agreeing in full. Signed in triplicate. Notarized — Stephan gripped the latch, tore open the dungeon-door and strode through like Ulysses into the underworld.

"Shit—" Tail between my legs, head down, I scurried after him like someone less.

Four grated cell doors stood off to either side. Each lay empty. Condensed damp dripped from the ceiling, forming shallow pools across uneven floor. A prerequisite, no doubt, for any proper dungeon. I imagined Queen Elona and von Madbury down here, breathing hoarse, whispering, rutting hard in the fetid dark.

"Over here," Karl pointed low with his thane-axe, "two of 'em."

Stephan lifted his lantern.

Two iron trapdoors set into the floor. Both were closed, locked, though the further of the two had seen better days. Its corners were knurled up, bent, as though hammered from within by some mighty force.

"Hrrm…" Karl gripped his thane-axe. "Don't like the looks."

"Yeah." I stepped back. "Me neither. How's that one?"

Stephan set his lantern down. "Looks intact."

"Okay, let's try that one first." And the second one? Never.

"Karl," Stephan held out a hand, "your hand-axe, please."

"Yar. Here." Karl dug it from his belt and tossed it.

Stephan caught it on the fly and hacked at the hasp, wincing at each blow.

I hefted Yolanda. Swallowed. Sweat beaded round my eyes. I nodded down at the deformed trap at Karl's foot. "Be ready to run."

Karl stood over it with his thane-axe raised for a killing blow. He made no smart-ass comment, no grumble, he just adjusted his grip and waited.

Stephan hacked and hacked, grimacing as sparks flew.

"Any progress?"

"Almost…" Stephan brushed hair from his eyes and kept at it.

"Hrm…" Karl shifted his feet. "Something below's pissed."

I glared out the dungeon-door. "Put your back into it."

"Almost…" Stephan grunted, hacked, then hacked again. The rusted hasp finally gave and Stephan slid aside, gripping a ring set in the trapdoor.

I grabbed a second ring. "Ready?"

"Yes."

Together we pulled, bowing our backs, iron hinges groaning, squealing, lifting the hatch open.

A deeper darkness lay beneath, so solid I half-thought if I stepped on it, it'd bear my weight.

"Lady Mary…" I called into the abyss. "Sarah…? Joshua…?"

Nothing at first, my stomach dropping and then, "S-Sir — Sir Luther?" A muted voice, limping up through the darkness. "Is … Is that you? Stephan?"

"Mary!" Stephan lunged headfirst down the chasm.

I caught him by the belt, dead-lifting him up, hauling him dangling back. "Watch it, you damn fool!"

"Stephan!" Lady Mary's voice sounded from below. "Get us out of here. Now. *Rose of Sharon!* Please."

I knelt. "The kids down there with you?"

"Yes. O-Only the children." Her voice seemed distant, muffled, small. "Ruth is … with Abraham. And Avar…"

"Yeah. We know. We're gonna get you out. Judas Priest." Stephan stood, casting about for something, anything, then stripped off his belt. "Lou. Give me your belt. Karl, you too." With his one hand, he started forming a knot, fumbled, froze. "Forget it." Stephan tossed me his. "Here—"

I bound mine to his then added Karl's.

"How long?" Stephan squinted.

"Seven feet, give or take." I yanked on the line, testing my knots. "But we need more. Gotta make a loop."

"Here." Karl tossed me his thane-axe. "Loop it under the beard. Just watch the blade."

I did. "Alright."

Stephan leaned down into the hole. "Get ready." Whispers in the dark as they conferred.

"Ready? Watch your head." Gripping Karl's thane-axe, I stepped in and kicked the makeshift rope into the hole. "Gonna look great with our pants round our ankles."

"Not yer strongest suit." Karl had an axe in each hand.

"It'll still be better than down here," Lady Mary called up.

"You got it?"

I felt a tug.

"Yes."

"Best be quick about it, lad," Karl spat. "Whatever's below's riling hard."

Whatever it was down there was sliding against stone. Like some enormous serpent writhing within. Images of the

Half-King clawed their way ripping through my mind. Long slithering rat-tail appendages. Desiccated flesh. That withered stick tongue scraping furrows through blood. I closed my eyes, shook it off.

"Alright," I opened my eyes, "*heave!*"

I set to it like a demon, gripping the axe haft, trudging backward til I hit wall, then hauling hand-over-hand til a head poked free.

"Sarah!" Stephan snatched her rag-doll arm and pulled her into his embrace.

But I'd already kicked the belt-rope back down, rekindling my effort, ripping hand over hand. Joshua's head emerged an instant later, and Stephan snatched him. He didn't look any better. "Get over with your sister, kid." In a fugue, he didn't move til Sarah gripped his arm, dragging him aside. "Good girl."

The metal trapdoor by Karl's feet started shifting, rising, jangling as something pressed up against it from below. Only the lock held it shut, but the metal hasp was bending, stretching like sinew. For want of some other dumb heavy thing, Karl jumped onto the trapdoor, booted feet slamming it shut.

"Out!" Stephan herded the children through the dungeon-door. "Quickly. Go." He glared back at me. "Lou?"

"Go!" I waved a hand. "I'll get her."

Stephan didn't move. Couldn't move.

Karl's trapdoor squealed as iron failed, the corners knurling up, a nightmare pouring out in length and tendril. A lithe rat-tail appendage slithered out, slapping around like some blind idiot thing finding its way, naked flesh wrapping round Karl's leg, gripping him from ankle to knee. "Odin's Eye!"

The belt-rope was already back down and Lady Mary on it instantly. "What's going on!?"

"No bleeding idea," I grunted and heaved, hand over hand, foot by foot, forcefully not looking Karl's way for fear of shitting myself.

"The children?"

"Get 'em out!" Karl hacked with his hand-axes, slithering appendages flailing about. Squeals and howls erupted as more poured free, sliding, slithering, grasping, wrestling him down to one knee.

Lady Mary's head emerged from the black, and Stephan was at her, grasping her, pulling her free. *Where are the children!* Lady Mary screamed like a banshee.

Wordless, I stepped over the empty hole and snatched Yolanda from the floor as Karl abandoned his hand-axe for a dagger. Teeth bared, he sawed at the tentacle slithering round his thigh as more poured out.

I pointed at the dungeon door, "Get out of here," and marched toward Karl.

The thing had him up to his waist now, squeezing, gripping, constricting.

I raised Yolanda. "Roll to your left."

"Rrrrg—" Karl kicked and squirmed off the trapdoor, gripping at the floor, holding onto the joint-work by fingernails as the rat-tails flexed, bulged, squeezed.

"Don't move—" With a two-handed overhead stroke, I chopped at a tentacle, severing it twitching away like the broken tail of a lizard. Below, a piercing keen ripped out, unearthly, inhuman, the mad screech of Geryon himself. Stones shifted as the monstrosity pressed against the trapdoor, slobbering, keening, working up like puke out a drunkard's throat.

Karl scrambled to his feet, growling, peeling the severed monstrosity from his thigh and flinging it still wriggling across the room. I shoved his thane-axe into his hands as we staggered for the door.

Lady Mary stood dazed, frozen, staggered, as the trapdoor burst into shard, hurling iron and stone. A monstrosity seethed forth, deformed appendages slithering up and out, birthing free, darker than the darkest night.

Lady Mary covered her mouth, "Oh, my dear sweet Lord…"

...made a poor choice in my cohorts, being veritably held hostage by their occult knowledge. I should have known better. I should have ended it myself. I should never have fathered any...
—Haesken Family Treatise: King Eckhardt Haesken III

Chapter 62.

IN THE HALF GLOOM, something birthed up from the trap, something crooked and malformed and willow-thin tall. To my mind's eye, it was the Half-King of the crypt. But then it wasn't. Where the Half-King had been a decrepit thing, a broken desiccated husk of a thing, here stood a thing at its apex, a thing at its prime, a thing full of a malevolent vitality, huffing and squirming and scrabbling up, out, slipping, slavering, free.

"C'mon—" I shoved Lady Mary, gawking, stunned, stutter-stepping woodenly into the wine cellar. *"GO—!"*

Karl stumbled after, skidding to a halt, whirling, slamming the dungeon-door shut, bracing it with his shoulder.

Across the wine cellar, Stephan slammed the keep-door shut and braced it with his back. His eyes wide. Face pale. Teeth bared.

"Open up!" someone roared from beyond the keep-door.

"Mother of fuck," I gasped. "Are you kidding me?"

Stephan's legs locked out straight. "It's von Madbury."

"Least of our bloody worries." Karl wiped his beard, adjusting his feet to gain purchase.

The keep-door shivered at Stephan's back as someone hacked at it with an axe.

Thunk! Thunk! Thunk!

Beyond Karl's door, the horror slid, its rat-tail tentacles and nails grating against wood.

"Hide," I snarled at Lady Mary.

Gawking all round, *"Where!?"* she demanded.

"Jesus Christ—" But she had a point. I pointed toward the empty racks. "I don't know. Jesus. *Somewhere!*"

"Lady Mary!" Sarah's head popped up from behind a pair of barrels.

"Wait for my the signal." I pressed a dagger into her hand and marched to the middle of the chamber.

Lady Mary gripped the dagger. "And what's the signal?"

"Me shitting my pants."

"Right." She scrambled toward the barrels.

"Just get out." I brandished Yolanda. "And keep going. Don't look back." I fixed Stephan a glare then shot Karl one for good measure. "Know where I'm going with this?"

"Straight to hell?" Karl sneered as a board at his back cracked.

"Yeah. Hop aboard."

"Brother—" Stephan's legs shivered with each smash against the door, splinters raining.

"On a three-count," I spread my feet, glaring at Karl, "if you can count that high."

"Are you bloody—" Karl let loose a chain of expletives as the door at his back groaned outward, wood splintering, iron bands squealing.

I turned to Stephan. "Open it."

Stephan unlatched the door and dove aside as it burst open.

Silhouettes stood beyond.

One…

I rose to my full and glorious height. "Gentlemen," I pointed with Yolanda, "I *magnanimously* accept your *unconditional* surrender."

Two...

Von Madbury staggered huffing into the room, a great axe in his two fists as he righted. Gideon Felmarsh slid in behind and along came Brother Miles, a makeshift bandage wrapped round his head. A glut of blackguards wrestled through the doorway behind.

"Lad—" Karl hissed.

Von Madbury wiped a greasy lank of hair from his eyes as he slunk forth, all teeth and murder. "Kill them all."

"Come now, you blackguards!" I stepped forth.

They took the bait whole and ran with it.

Right towards me.

"Three—!" I yelled and launched off to the side, diving through a rack and out the other side.

Behind, a shower of splinters blasted outward. The rack I dove through toppled. I don't know what happened to Karl, but *something* shot past in the gloom, something malformed and hunched and only peripherally man-like. Frozen in terror, a blackguard was instantly engulfed in a tangle of appendages. His screams echoed as bones snapped, popping in quick succession.

"Mother of God!" Brother Miles froze to a halt, turned to run, dropping his mace as the thing descended upon him.

Von Madbury's lone eye blared as he stutter-stepped back.

Brother Miles writhed in chittering madness, squealing as needle-teeth buried into his neck to the sound of slurp and unrepressed ecstasy, his hands flailing, legs kicking, pale face gasping as a long arm slithered into his mouth, thrusting deep, stifling his impotent whimpers. *"Nnng—!"* Brother

Miles kicked and writhed until the thing tore its naked arm free, ripping crimson insides out in a wet pile of slop.

"Holy fuck!" someone yelled.

It might've been me.

Loping under a fallen rack, I struck down a blackguard frozen in terror.

Gideon Felmarsh turned and bolted for the door, and I scrambled after, skewering him through the back. Gasping, screaming, he whirled, Yolanda wrenching from my fist as we both slammed the wall. Felmarsh gained the upper hand and smashed an elbow across my face, shoving me off and clambering up. He was nigh at the door when Stephan cross-tackled him off his feet.

"Go!" Stephan shouted, and Lady Mary bolted into the void, gripping Sarah and Joshua, half-dragging, half-carrying them onward.

The blackguards scrambled.

Something whip-like cracked past my head, knocking me sideways.

The horror from the vault cast Brother Miles's husk aside, just a flaccid sack of skin and bone, and rose to its full height, its head nearly scraping the ceiling, half man and half … *something else.* It was a thing of sinew and manged fur, half trudging, half slithering boneless as it flowed forth. Its face was a cruel parody of Prince Palatine's, contorted, distorted, inhuman. Except for his eyes. Crocodile tears rolled down its face as it snatched up another mercenary, engulfing him, shifting in a quick whirling half-shrug to the sound of dislocating joints. Breaking bones. A trembling squeal.

Then it cast him aside.

Licking his lips, glaring me down, von Madbury inched toward the door as the prince-thing, the monstrosity, the *strigoi,* surged toward Stephan and Felmarsh, struggling on the floor. Gripping a fallen axe, I flung a cut at the monstrosity, shearing through sinew, catching its attention. It whirled instantly.

Lucky. Fucking. Me.

"Stephan!" I dashed for the dungeon-door, freezing as the thing cut me off, looming over like a tidal wave of insanity. "Go!"

Stephan kicked free of Felmarsh and bolted.

Von Madbury dashed, hurdling a noose-like rat-tail, slick as oil, hacking a back-handed slash my way. I ducked it but was on the ground as a tail snagged my leg, wrapping round it, crushing tight. Von Madbury disappeared through the mauled doorway as the *strigoi* drew me close, tearing the axe from my grip.

My fingernails broke off on the flagstone edges. *"No!"*

It peeled me back.

The *strigoi* rose in the dim lantern light, a thing of shadow and mange, black eyes smoldering, glaring down with inhuman curiosity. The thing that was its mouth yawned open, dripping pink, drool coursing, as though trying to form words.

It failed.

Utterly.

Upside down, dangling in the air like the hanged man, tails slithering about my body, I screamed. I screamed senseless. Meaningless. If I'd had a blade, I'd've slit my own throat. The appendages seizing me were snakes of iron, sharp hairs biting into my flesh—

"Thor's hammer!" Karl roared nearby and it cast me across the void, breaking through shelves of felled racks. Next I knew, I was splayed across the ground, seeing double, triple, God, as three monstrosities lurched onward.

A shadow bolted behind it. Short. Squat. Stupid.

"Get up!" Karl set his feet, axe raised. "Run!"

I struggled, arms wobbling, and could do neither.

Thane-axe in hand, Karl hacked at the monstrosity, quick glancing chops, never committing, always moving, never stopping. He drew it back towards the dungeon, leaving me a clear path. *Out.* Jesus. Reality wobbling, I struggled to my knees, my feet, as Karl growled and hacked and ducked and dodged. But the *strigoi* moved with a feral tenacity, an inhuman zeal, quicker than thought, and cut Karl off, cornering him.

"Valhalla!"

Two-handed over his head, Karl hacked into it with a stroke that would've felled an ox, but the *strigoi* barely flinched, taking the blow, engulfing Karl against the far wall. Tentacle and pink appendage poured onto him, over him, sliding across his face and chest, spreading out fluid to all directions.

"Run!" Karl screamed and then didn't as appendages slid over his mouth, consuming his face, choking down his throat.

My head was mush, legs jelly, arms useless. I melted across the floor like some old thing, some broken thing, some useless thing. "Wha—?"

I blinked.

A massive paw thrust into my face.

"Jesus Christ."

And it was. Sort of. Ensconced by a nimbus of rippling torchlight.

"Rise, brother." The Nazarene gripped my hand and shoulder and grunted, hauling me bodily to my feet. He stood before me, his half-head empty, yawning like some crimson chasm, his body thick and massive and hacked nigh on to pieces. His big belly'd been ripped ragged, ropes of innard poured outward in slick glistening loops, trailing behind, thrown across his shoulder. His severed arm was reattached but wrong somehow, off-kilter, backward.

"Jesus. Fucking. Christ."

"Remember we are all brothers against the darkness."

"Yeah! Brothers!" Tears streamed down my face. "Sure! Whatever!"

"Go now, brother!" the Nazarene boomed as he strode toward the monstrosity. "Flee!"

But I didn't run. Couldn't run.

I staggered headfirst toward the wall, using the fallen racks to stay upright, working my way for the door, tripping, falling to one knee, drooling, bleeding over Gideon Felmarsh's twitching corpse. His eyes glared, his teeth fixed in grimace, but he didn't move. Couldn't. And Yolanda lay there, skewered through him neat as you please. Digging a fist beneath him, I seized the hilt, whispered, *"This might hurt,"* then ripped her free.

Crushing tears from my eyes, I turned toward the twin monstrosities closing in upon one another.

"Come to me, brother!" The Nazarene bellowed, his arms up, open.

The *strigoi* turned at that, its green eyes greedy-full with inguinal ecstasy, its one arm still somewhat human slithering out, long and many-jointed and wrong. His other half writhed in an orgy of tail and tentacle, coiling, slithering, twisting.

"Let me sate thine hunger!" the Nazarene bellowed, his thick arms opened, exposing his body, his soul.

The *strigoi* descended, a movement too swift to grasp, too distorted to follow, engulfing the Nazarene in flesh and tendril, wrapping round him in an iron embrace, constrictor snakes surging, all disparate yet acting as one.

Against the wall, forgotten, Karl collapsed, trembling to all fours, eyes blank, gasping, hacking. I didn't say anything, I didn't wait, I just grabbed him by the scruff of the neck and by some force born of desperation and cowardice and tenfold terror, dragged him limp as a sack of drowned kittens.

Behind, the *strigoi* let loose a keen, and I thought he'd finished with the Nazarene.

I was wrong.

The Nazarene, for all his terrible wounds, for all that he was wrapped up in the *strigoi's* legion of appendages, for all that he was buffeted by the slash of the *strigoi's* excoriating force, he was still game. Still on his feet. Still fighting. His thick arms, though twisted askew, grasped the *strigoi's* core, a crushing embrace, his hands disappearing, slipping hidden through hellish flesh.

The *strigoi* keened.

The Nazarene bellowed.

Dust rained from above.

"Brother!" The Nazarene took one single step, grimacing, twisting, bulling the horror before him. Then another. And another. "Show us the light!"

The *strigoi* wailed and gnashed and fought, snatching onto a fallen rack and dragging it behind. But the Nazarene kept moving, slowly, inexorably, step by bloody step towards the dungeon-door. Appendage flailed. The *strigoi* gave up on fighting and latched onto the Nazarene's neck and skull-hole, needle teeth gnashing and gnawing, biting from the inside, sucking blood and bile and unholy ichor, drawing sanity and soul and sustenance, diminishing the Nazarene with each tread of his heavy step.

"The light, brother." Darkness swirled as the Nazarene trudged forth.

Forging onward, I tripped, staggering to a knee.

The barrels of poppy seed oil stood before me. Without thinking, I kicked them onto their sides. Two blows, *Thunk! Thunk!* And I stove in their tops and kicked them rolling across the flagstones.

"Yes, brother!" the Nazarene bellowed, his voice still hale, strong, "Yes!" But in the dungeon darkness, he collapsed to a knee, a husk of bone and desiccated flesh.

I grasped Stephan's lantern.

Gore sluiced from the *strigoi*'s distended maw. It turned, its crippled visage contorting in malice as it came for me, slashing faster than thought, claws distended, half of its mass a slithering orgy of tooth and tail.

Muttering a cacophony of fractured prayer, I clamped my eyes shut, preparing for the onrush of hideous oblivion.

Talons swept past, the fetid kiss of death and decay, the breath of madness and horror as the *strigoi*'s leering masque whined and growled and hissed just shy of murder. I cracked an eye as it slid back a hair.

"What in hell...?"

Behind it, the Nazarene, once so sturdy and monstrous and hale now little more than a skeleton, stood trembling, holding the *strigoi* at bay, pulling it back by his own entrails noosed round the *strigoi*'s throat.

Grimacing, pale lips quavering, the Nazarene held, his gaze locked on mine, his voice a hissing whisper, "The light, brother, show us the—"and I spiked the lantern into the oil.

I didn't stay to watch them burn.

...pray that when that one-eye blackguard's smug scowl meets its end, I am there to bear witness.
—Haesken Family Treatise: King Eckhardt Haesken III

Chapter 63.

A THUNDEROUS COMMOTION lay beyond the Schloss's front door as Karl and I trudged through the great hall. The fume of torch and grease and grime of death and despair shrouded us head to toe.

"Gonna make it?" I asked, gripping Karl's arm across my shoulder, lugging him like a sack-full of shit.

"Rrrg..." Karl was in a rough way. A rough, ugly way. "Don't let me slow you."

Every minute or so, he'd stagger under the bombardment of a coughing jag, nearly turning his insides out hacking up black bile and ... nodules. Polyps. Something...

I shuddered. But he was still on his own two feet. More or less. Still moving under his own volition. Still the most ornery prick I'd ever met.

"Think that thing laid eggs in your belly?" I pondered aloud as we shouldered out the front door.

"I'm gonna lay eggs in your—" Karl gripped the door jamb and froze. "Grimnir's spear..."

The horde had taken the courtyard. Scourgers and townsfolk alike amassed.

Von Madbury stood in their midst, a lone wolf fending off a rabid pack. "Back off, you bloody pissants!"

A circle of carnage lay about him. Bodies. Broken weapons. Churned muck. In one hand, von Madbury bore his curved Mongul blade. In his other, he had Joshua by the hair, on tiptoe, gasping, wincing, wailing, blade pressed against his neck. "Clear a damned path!"

I muscled through the press, shouldering folk aside, gripping Karl.

"Please, Sir Dietrick—" Lady Mary and Stephan stood across the circle. "Don't do this."

Sarah knelt in the muck, sobbing, shaking, wailing.

Von Madbury turned, dragging Joshua. "Tell them to clear a damned path."

"Please, take me instead." Lady Mary licked her lips and straightened. "Let him go."

"Move!" von Madbury snarled.

But the horde deigned not to listen.

Stephan raised his hand. "There's nowhere to go, Sir Dietrick."

"The ship," von Madbury snarled. "I want safe passage down to the docks."

"It's gone." Stephan raised his hands. "It left. Hours ago."

The horde rumbled, grumbled, fingers twitching on weapons. Ugliness. It was coming on swift and strong over the horizon.

Karl's knees buckled as a coughing jag dropped him like a stone. "Go on, lad." He shoved me onward. "Go—"

"Right." I left him and pushed past bodies.

"Fuck yourself!" von Madbury's teeth clenched as the horde rumbled, contracting a hair. His blazing eyes lighted upon me. *"Krait,* you blackguard! Don't you move! Don't you take another step." He gripped his blade. "I'll slit him open. Wide. You know I will!"

"Sure I do," I said because I did.

Joshua whimpered, twitched, winced as von Madbury tore on his hair and slavered in his ear.

The horde shifted as I stepped into the circle. Lianne stood there amongst the press, pitchfork in hand, an eager look in her eye. Her father Giles stood by her side, a bandaged hand pressed to the side of his head. I saw the Tome-Bearer, heard the clink of his chains, the groan of old bones as he slammed his immense burden down across the edge of the scaffold.

"Make them move!" Von Madbury slavered.

"Who the hell am I?" I shrugged. "And why the hell would they listen to me?"

Von Madbury froze. Licked his lips. Swore beneath his breath.

He knew I was right.

"But," I cocked my head toward a shadow rising from the corpse and carnage round the breaking-wheel, "they just might listen to *her*."

Bent and haggard and worn, Elona stood over the corpse of her dead son. She'd unwoven his limbs from the spokes and dragged him free of the wheel, lain him out, smoothed his hair, straightened his shattered limbs. Her arms, up to the elbows, were stained crimson. Wreathed in horror, her eyes met mine. "Palatine?"

I shook my head, *No*.

Lightning struck, her legs wobbled, nigh on felling her, but she gripped the spokes of the breaking-wheel, holding her upright.

"Her? You'd listen to *her?*" Von Madbury sneered as the horde inched in. "You know what her husband did? Your king?" A devil-smirk fixed itself across his face. "For years, he sated that monstrosity, that abomination, that thing, with you and your ilk! Under guise of justice, he'd march them down that tunnel. 'The long walk,' he called it. Your king! He forced them in at sword point. Down into the depths. Into wrack and into ruin."

"Him?" I yelled. "Try *him* and *you* and that fucker, Sir Gustav!"

I didn't know it for truth, but von Madbury's 'long walk' comment sparked something King Eckhardt had said on the Schloss's rooftop weeks past. When I'd asked if von Madbury had leverage on him. And as for Sir Gustav? Well, screw him, either way.

"Shut your gob, *hedge knight,*" von Madbury sneered. "Stranger. Malingerer. No one knows you here. Nor cares what lies your serpent tongue spouts." Von Madbury offered Elona a caustic bow. "And what say you, Your Highness?"

"Eh…? Why should they listen to me?" Still she clutched the breaking-wheel. "Why should *anyone* listen to me? I'm no queen. No ruler. My husband is dead. Slain. Gone. Your king. And what sort of king was he?" She brushed hair from her face, a trail of blood staining in its wake. "You were not far off. The man was weak. Hesitant. Abhorrently cruel when it suited him. And my sons? Everything I hold," she swallowed, *"held* dear? Nay. I bear no right by blood to the Haesken throne. To this town. This realm. I'm naught but a cursed widow wallowing in the ruin of a fallen house."

The horde riled, a grumble running through, rising.

"Did you know?" von Madbury snarled. "Did you know he'd toast wine in the aftermath of the blood sacrifice? Dine to the screams of the fallen?" Von Madbury splayed a hand out. "Whilst they all *starved?"*

"Murderer!" someone yelled.

Elona stood before them, sunken, hollow, broken, waiting on someone to cast the first stone.

My guess?

It wouldn't take long.

Von Madbury laughed, that sharp hyena bark and something changed.

Elona blinked. Glared up. Took a breath. Chin set, a blaze took root in her eye, her heart, her soul.

"I killed the pig." The Queen nodded to herself. "Yes. The swine. Me. I murdered him with his own blade." She laid a hand upon her breast. "My husband. *Your king*. For what he had done. What he did. What he would persist in doing. What Dietrick said is correct. I killed him for it, and I watched him die. It was slow. It was painful. It was necessary." She pushed herself upright off the breaking-wheel. "And it was not nearly enough."

Folk had stones in hand, arms cocked back, but not a one threw.

"And so now you know the truth." The Queen strode to the edge of the scaffold. "The truth of the Haesken line. The truth of your king. And you know the truth of me. So end it here. End it now. End it forever." She raised her arms. "Cast your stones! Strike me down! And I'll thank God for it."

A ripple of chatter tore through the horde.

Followed by a void of silence.

"You are queen!" someone yelled.

Then another, "You are *our* queen!"

A scattering of cheers erupted, barks and clatter, the clash of weapons, the stomp of feet. "You are our queen!" A chant rose through the darkness, from the despair, from the downtrodden and disavowed, avowing once more their faith in divine right.

"Looks like they'll listen." Von Madbury licked his lips, blowing with the wind. "Looks like we can deal."

"Yes." The Queen grew taller as the horde bellowed its chant. "So it would seem."

"So get me out of here."

"Yes," the Queen glared down at her blood-crusted hands, "so it would seem…"

"Order them to move." Von Madbury pressed the blade into Joshua's throat. "To clear a path. *Order them!*"

Queen Elona stood unmoved. "You murdered my son."

"And I'll murder this little shit, too." Von Madbury licked his lips. "Now tell them."

"You think to dictate terms?" The Queen rang blood from her sleeve. "You think me a ruler in the same vein as my son? My husband? Nay." She wiped her hands on her skirts. "Those days are dead. Dead and gone. Withered to dust and blown away."

"I'll—"

"Silence!" the Queen thundered. "And heed this, Dietrick, you snake of a man. You will die tonight. You will die here. You will die now. The only variable is by which means. Release the child and I'll allow you to fall upon your sword." She offered an imperious shrug. "And should you not, you shall suffer the same tender mercies you offered my," her knees wobbled, nigh on buckling, but she maintained, "my son."

Von Madbury tensed like a wolf, hackles risen.

The crowd was ravenous and ready, ready to turn back into a horde, a mob, to enact mob justice. Ready to vent its frustrations. Ready to vent them on the blackguard who'd flogged their sons. Raped their daughters. Knifed their husbands. Forced their kin down for the long walk.

"He cried like a baby." Von Madbury's teeth gleamed between split lips.

427.

"I know it, you fool. I heard it. I watched it." Queen Elona pointed her long slender arm. "Take him!"

"NO!" Lady Mary screamed as Stephan lurched forward, the mob contracting inward, all grasping hands and ill intent.

A quick jerk and Von Madbury kept his word.

He slit Joshua's throat, cast the boy aside and drew back his curved blade as I met him alongside the crush. Through the tangle, Stephan's eyes bulged as his cries choked off. Lady Mary was jostled, shoved aside, trampled, disappearing beneath the surge of body and hatred, their hands reaching for von Madbury, groping at his arms, his legs, tearing his hair, restraining him, ripping his tulwar free, hammering him with fist and stone, wrestling him back and over, kicking and screaming towards the Queen, the scaffold, the breaking-wheel.

Me?

I didn't give a shit. Not as they took him. Not as they carried him. Not as they bound him cruciform, screaming, struggling, roaring, across the spokes.

Joshua was the prize, and I reached him first, shielding him with my body, praying for a flesh wound. Praying it wasn't a vessel. Praying for a miracle. And as always, the Good Lord came through in spades. Joshua lay unconscious, trampled face-first deep into the muck. Bleeding out from the neck, spurting in ragged blasts.

"Jesus." Clamping down on the gash, feeling warm red soak my palms, my sleeves, tasting the copper tang of blood, I scooped mud from his mouth, wiped it on my pant leg. Looked around for something. Someone. Anyone. Anything.

But there was nothing. No one.

A numb buzz entered my ears.

"Abe, I'm sorry…" I squeezed down.

Lady Mary staggered to my side, clutching my shoulder, a wraith in the night, talking, muttering, mumbling. *What the hell was she saying?* Everything, everywhere, heavy, slow, beyond blurry.

"Huh?" I blinked. "What?"

The pounding of a hammer punctuated von Madbury's screams. The scourger chant folded in, melding to the beat.

"Is … Is he—" Lady Mary leaned over my shoulder.

"No. Not yet." I grimaced, pressing down harder, knowing it wouldn't stop, wouldn't slow, wouldn't make one bit of difference.

"Lou!" Beat and battered, Stephan clambered from the mob, clasping Sarah. He hovered over, leaning close, trying to see, trying to help, knowing even with his God-given knack for healing, he was as impotent as me. "Is there anything?"

"I don't know," I lied. Cause I knew. Knew we couldn't slow it. Couldn't stop it. Knew Sarah was gonna have to watch her baby brother die. Knew it was obvious but still didn't have the stones to say it.

"Joshie!" Sarah latched onto him, arms wrapping so hard I nearly lost my grip.

"It's alright, kid," I whispered in Joshua's ear. "Sarah's here. Your sister. She's holding you. With you. Mary and Stephan, too. Just close your eyes. Abe and — your mom and dad'll be there when you open them. It's gonna be … No." The spurting had stopped. "Please." I clamped harder, grimacing, swearing, driving his corpse sinking into the mud. "Come on. Come *the-fuck* on!"

"Brother." Stephan laid a hand on my shoulder. "Lou. He's gone."

I swatted his hand aside and pulled Joshua's eyelid open.

Numb. Glazed. Gone. I needed to hit something. Bite something. Murder something.

"Oy, young feller," a voice cackled from behind. "He's not gone. Close, aye. But not gone. Not yet."

I turned.

The Tome-Bearer stood hunched behind, flab and tendon wobbling on skinny arms, trembling under their shared burden. The slow chant suffusing the air waxed to the sound of von Madbury's begging, pleading, to the sound of his bones broken by hammer.

"What do you mean?" Stephan gripped the Tome-Bearer by the arm.

"Ease up, lad." The Tome-Bearer winced. "I mean, there's still some work what can be done. What can bear him back."

Sarah wailed. Lady Mary took her in her arms, brushing her hair back with a hand, talking, whispering hushed nonsense.

"Then quit jawing and start doing," I barked, still holding pressure.

The old geezer grimaced, showing less teeth than more. "Lad, could ya ease up on my arm?"

"I—I'm sorry." Stephan let go.

"Thing is, young feller, I — *We,* that is," the Tome-Bearer grinned, a sneaky sly-fuck smirk, "need someone. We need a ... what's the word? A nexus."

"Bring him back!" I roared. "Like the Nazarene. Bring him *the-fuck* back!"

"Ya don't ken even half of what ye saw." The old geezer squinted up at the dawn sky. "And you're losing time. Losing it fast."

"Fine. Sure. Yeah." I blinked. "I'll do it."

"Forgive me, young feller, but you won't do." The Tome-Bearer twitched his head toward Stephan. "You now? We could talk about you."

"I'm in." Stephan stepped forth without hesitation. "Just tell me what to do."

"Gotta swear first, boy."

"Swear what?"

"Swear to me." The Tome-Bearer slapped his sunken chest. "Swear yer everything. Everything you have and hold dear and ever will."

"Stephan—" I blurted but it was already too late.

Stephan laid a hand on his heart. "I swear to you my life and my soul. Now tell me."

The shitty old prick cackled with glee, clapping his hands as he dropped the book in the muck and scrabbled through it with grubby paws. "Ya already know, lad."

"I—" Stephan stiffened as though jerked up suddenly by invisible strings, scowling as he hissed some language low and in the shadows. Scourgers slid in, converging, shambling forth like the walking dead, their muted chant shifting, rising, coalescing, filling the air as the horizon pinked in the distance.

Behind, von Madbury squealed raw as a hog being slaughtered.

I didn't know what they were doing to him.

I didn't care.

"Brother, what—?" I said.

"You can let go now, Lou," Stephan said softly, slowly, firmly. "Let go." He peeled my trembling fingers from Joshua's ruined throat. A cut clean down to spine. Like a second mouth. *Jesus Christ.* "Stand aside. Please, brother."

But I couldn't let go. Couldn't move. Couldn't *anything.*

Stephan squeezed my hands, "You've done what you can."

Breathless, I collapsed back in the mud.

The Tome-Bearer clambered atop the open book, pushing it into the mud, pawing it, eyeballing the pages in the waxing dawn, his mouth moving as he lead the chant, as he always lead, a tremble of greed and ecstasy ticking tremors across his squatter's mug.

Stephan knelt over Joshua.

I scrambled aside, trying to see, to watch, to make sense of everything, anything, and knowing I was falling short to all quarters.

Stephan murmured words too soft to hear, words echoing the chant, the hammer, the screams. The very air vibrated with song as he reached up toward the dawn sky, the sun rising just over the horizon, and grasped it in effigy, fingers trembling round it, forming a fist glowing pink from within. He held it there in silent awe. "Rose of Sharon…" he laid the glowing warmth against Joshua's blood-soaked throat, holding it there, pressing it in, blood steaming white. "Please. For the love of God, please…"

When Joshua's leg twitched, I puked in my mouth. Swallowed it back.

Thought it was some artifact of Stephan working. Or Lady Mary moving. Or Sarah. Or me. Or anyone. An earthquake. Something. Anything. Anything but what I saw. But when his leg twitched again, and I heard him draw breath, a slow, labored gurgle, I knew it for truth.

Joshua's next breath was a cough, and he spattered blood across my boots.

"Kid—?"

Eyes bulging in disbelief, Stephan retracted his hand.

Joshua rubbed the blood from his neck and beneath lay a long jagged scar. His mouth moved as he tried to talk, but no sound came.

"Joshie!" Sarah dove atop him.

"Easy." Lady Mary brushed Joshua's hair from his eyes, and Sarah nearly choked him to death in delight.

"I..." Stephan knelt there, pale and shaking, staring at his hand in awe, "I have no words, brother."

"Yeah," I said. "Me neither." And I took him in my arms and clutched him tight, listening all the while to von Madbury screaming in the distance, begging for the end, for death, for his mother, for sweet tender mercy.

It seemed he'd receive none.

Chapter 64.

LADY MARY AND KARL huddled off with Sarah and Joshua, knapsacks shouldered, walking-sticks in hand, anxious glares simmering in their collective eye. They were keen to get moving. Keen to be gone. So was I. The Kriegbad Pass had opened a week ago, and Karl and Joshua were finally hale enough to cross. With any hope.

Queen Elona knelt in the shadow of Saint Wencelaus' Church, praying by the fresh graves of her fallen sons. Her dead father. Her shit-heel of a husband. Her queen's-guard, what were left of them, flanked her. Seven men, the sum total of Husk's vaunted defenses.

"You're still here." She glared up.

I gazed off toward the mountains, muted in blur, far off to the east. "Not for long."

The Queen was ashen, empty, cold as she rose, using Eventine's tombstone to lever herself up. "What is it you want?"

"To warn you," I said. "To thank you. To apologize."

The Queen sighed as though the very act of drawing breath caused her pain. "Which first?"

"The warning." I nodded off toward the Abraxas. "There may be men that come after me. After us. Dangerous men. Men you want no part of."

"I think I am done with the wanting of any part of your species, Sir Luther."

"Fair enough. And I don't blame you. But that won't matter to them. To him."

The Queen raised a hand and her guards edged back a few paces. "And how shall I know this man? This devil? This fiend?"

"You just will."

"Very well," she said. "What would you have me do should he arrive? Cower? Hide? Obfuscate the truth on your behalf?"

"No." I shook my head. "Just tell it to him. The truth. Tell him what happened. Tell him about Abraham and where he's buried. Tell him you hate me. Tell him where I've gone. Tell him everything."

"And what makes you think I wouldn't regardless?"

I glanced over at Lady Mary. "Just a hunch."

"You're going after your brother."

"Through the pass, yeah," I said. "But after that? I don't know. Stephan left with that … that bloody lunatic. And he sold or surrendered or gave away … *something*." A shiver ran down my spine. "So, yeah, best we'd get moving." I shouldered my knapsack, patted Yolanda's hilt, nodded toward the kids. "Find them someplace safe."

I owed Abe and Ruth that. At the very least.

"Next comes the thanks. Then the apology." The Queen crossed her arms. "Please. I fear I shan't stand either. I fear they'd fissure the hate crystalized within me, robbing me of the only strength left privy to me. The sole thing bearing me upright. Yes. I'd rather you forgo them both and simply go."

"Very well." I swallowed, bowed, turned.

"Was there malice in your heart, Sir Luther?"

I paused, straightened. "Malice?"

Her eyes blazed. "When you murdered Eventine?"

"Murder…" I looked down. Away. Shook my head. "No, Your Majesty. Not in the end. In the end there … there was only necessity."

"Necessity?"

"You saw what von Madbury did."

"Yes." The Queen's chin rose. "I saw."

"Then you know it was mercy. Pity. Necessity. I couldn't let him linger like that. Stephan had said it. Had gone after him. To save him. Because that's what he does. But even he…" I sniffed. Swallowed. Shook my head. "Even he knew it was over. That something had to be done. And I didn't want that burdening his soul. He's strong in ways I'm not. But in other ways…"

The rest I left unsaid as I drew my cloak against a mounting breeze, feeling my dagger in hand as I slid it into Eventine's heart, tasting tears as I bore Sir Alaric's body from the Half-King's tomb, hearing the sound of Palatine's inhuman keens as he thrashed, immolating alive. Or dead. Or whatever the hell he was in the end.

"As you say," the Queen said. "And perhaps it was more than most would have done. The Lord knows you could have done less. We can always do less."

I forced a fallow nod. "Sir Alaric… Your father told me a couple things before…" I rubbed my eyes. "Apologies. I'm shite at this."

"Go on. We both of us are," the Queen grimaced. "I wish he'd had the fortitude to tell me himself. Or I he. It's a sin how for granted we take those closest." She cocked her head. "But only when they're alive. Here. In the now. And the moment they've drifted beyond the veil?" Her fingers crumpled into a fist. "A hammer-blow to the temple. A shock of clarity. Sense. Cold and hard. What mattered before seems cheap, tawdry, ephemeral. And who you lost?" She shook her head. "Everything."

I licked my lips. "He said he did it to protect you."

Her eyes narrowed. "Did what?"

"Kill your husband," I said. "Whether it was you or he who murdered King Eckhardt, in the end, I don't know. But your father told me he came upon King Eckhardt in his bedchamber. So imagine him standing before his king. His liege. His lord. The man he'd sworn an oath on his life and soul to protect. And his liege lies dying. Or dead. Or nearly so. I don't know. Foregone, let's say. And your father is torn. Bent. Broken. The castle is bustling. And he has but moments to add to the picture painted. So what's he do? What can he do? With his oath to his liege tolling in his mind?"

I fingered Yolanda's hilt.

"But there are some oaths stronger," I said. "Like those between father and daughter. Man and wife. So he drives King Eckhardt's own blade through him. Then waits to get caught. Red-handed. Cause he figures what I figured the moment I saw the King's corpse."

"And what is it you … figured?" the Queen whispered.

"It's no great magic, Your Majesty." I glanced toward her guards, lowering my voice. "No mystery. No alchemy. Just simple arithmetic." I caught her eye. "You find a wife clipped by violence, you go hounding after her bloke. Find the bloke iced by poison, you go hunting his wife. One of the first maxims my uncle taught me. Way back when but still holds true."

"Poison…?" The Queen licked her lips.

"Yeah. The King's gums were black as coal. Steel through the chest? Won't help with it but won't cause it, yeah?" I shrugged. "And I've heard of it. Manticore's blood. Violet Nightshade mixed with Belladonna and an unhealthy dose of lead and arsenic."

Now it was her turn to offer her guards a glance. "How long have you known?"

"From the start," I said. "Or finish. Choose your poison. Pardon the pun."

"Yet you never said anything?" Her eyes narrowed. "Even though…"

"Even though what? Even though you and I were on the outs? Even though I promised your sons I'd unmask the killer? And already had?" I shrugged. "What was I gonna do? What was I gonna say? Tell the new king his grandfather covered up the murder his mother committed against his father?" I shook my head. "Jesus Christ."

"Perhaps I didn't desire his protection." The Queen drew herself up. "Perhaps I wanted the dice to scatter where they may. Perhaps I courted ruin."

"Like with your confession to the mob?"

"Ruin?" The Queen touched her throat. "Perhaps. Or perhaps, I simply wanted something to change. Needed something. Brought to a head. Cauterized. Burned. At whatever cost. And *that* … Eckhardt." She spat. "He deserved it. He deserved worse. You know it."

I didn't disagree.

She chopped with her hand. "And, yes, I gave no thought to the consequences. No heed to how others might react. Would react. Even," her jaw muscles clenched, "even my own sons."

"Your father figured if he was caught red-handed folk might not notice the King'd been poisoned. Figured folk might not look past the blade he shoved bloody through his lung."

"But they didn't catch him."

"No, they didn't," I said. "Was a lot going on. Murder. Betrayal. Insanity. But even so, he figured when they started looking your way, which they inevitably would, he'd step forth, draw back the curtain, recite some climactic monologue, and take his final bow. And you?" I let it sink in. "You'd be safe. Innocent. Beyond reproach."

"The obtuse machinations of a drunken sot," the Queen scoffed, but a glimmer shivered in her eye.

"Take the intent for the deed and leave it at that," I said. "He was a drunken sot, but a drunken sot who loved you til his dying breath. Just as you'll love him til yours. He tried to protect you. And you tried to protect him. A symmetry some might find beautiful."

Scowling, the Queen shook her head.

"Your confession to the mob," I explained. "If you hated him so much, you could've laid the blame at his feet. Squarely."

"Mere supposition." The Queen ran a hand through her hair.

"You did that with your right hand," I said.

She froze. "And…?"

"Your husband was stabbed in the right side of his chest." I patted my right flank. "Almost certainly by a sinister-handed blackguard. And besides me, your father was the only one in the Schloss."

"And what is all this to you?"

"To me? I'm just trying to balance my books," I said. "I owe your father that much. You, too, I suppose. At the very least. I'm no fan of debts."

"Nor am I."

"He also said he did it to avenge your mother."

"Eh?" The Queen blinked. "To avenge my…?"

"Your mother. Lady Catherine."

"You mentioned oaths, Sir Luther. Oaths between father and daughter. Man and wife. I … I had thought you meant me."

"I did. But not *only* you."

"Please, did," she pursed her lips, "did he explain?"

"No." I scratched my beard. "Those were his last words."

"Lord above…" The Queen bit her lip, whirled, cursing the sky. "Could the fool do nothing right? Could he not even leave a death-bed confession without mucking it up?" The Queen crushed the tears flowing down her cheek. "And so I shall never—"

"No, wait. Look." I held up a hand. "I put it together. Some of it. Enough, I think. Piecemeal maybe, but…" I swallowed. "You remember the night the Grey-Lady—? The night we went out and the Nazarene burned down—" Jesus. "You remember that night?"

"Yes," she said. "My father, despite his initial depths of despondence, took a precipitous fall after. Even from afar it was obvious. Patently so. Painfully. If he was cracked, if he was broken before, he was shattered irrevocably after."

"Understandable, in retrospect," I said. "The man had to suffer through your mother's long illness. Her subsequent disappearance. Of decades of never knowing what happened. Years of guesswork. Wondering. Worrying. Never understanding. Never knowing. Never gaining the closure he'd need to garner some modicum of peace.

"Then one night, out of the blue, he sees her again, but only to watch on helplessly as she's murdered before his very eyes." I rubbed my jaw where he'd struck me. "He attacked me that night. Tried fighting past me. Through me. Would've killed me if he could. I didn't understand. Didn't see. Couldn't see. I thought it was chivalry. Honor. Madness. Save the damsel in distress, and all. But it was more than that. The Grey-Lady *was* Lady Catherine."

"That's—" The Queen stiffened as though struck. "That's absurd. Impossible. It's been almost thirty…"

"One would think," I said. "Except that she wasn't human. Not for the decades since her disappearance. Her long walk. Her rendezvous with the Half-King at your husband's request. Where she became *strigoi*."

"*Strigoi*...?" The Queen followed my gaze off towards the old keep.

"In her last days, your mother made a deal with King Eckhardt," I said. "Times were tough. Lean. The King needed something, *someone* to sate the Half-King. And your mother? She was sick. And knew she was dying. Knew the Haesken Line's dirty secret. And she knew what the King desired. What he needed. So she offered him a deal."

"How ... why?" the Queen stammered. "What did she get out of it?"

"Peace of mind."

"Peace of...?"

"The peace of mind of knowing her eldest daughter'd be taken care of. By a king. And if you were taken care of, so was your sister, Jane. So was your father. So was everyone who came after."

"All of us..." The Queen's muttered. "She traded the last vestiges of her life to..."

"Cement your betrothal. Your future. Your family's future."

"Oh, mother..." The Queen blanched, gasped, swallowed. "She knew about this ... this secret? She knew about the Half-King? The truth?"

"Your father told me all the pieces were there, but he didn't see them. Couldn't see. Or, hell, maybe he just didn't *want* to see them. But your mother...? Jesus, I don't know. She was part of the King's court. And sharp as a stiletto by all accounts. And women see things men don't. Speak truth to power in ways we brave heroes never can. Or never do, anyways."

"B-But you never met her. Never saw her. How could you possibly know this Grey-Lady was she?"

"Cause your father was a damn-fine painter. And your mother? His favorite subject. I didn't put it together, though, not until the night at the *Half-King Tavern.* Von Madbury's ambush. Funny, the things you notice when your life's hanging by a noose. Have you seen her portrait? The one by the stairwell?"

"I don't generally frequent whore-houses."

"It's a tavern, too, but—" I frowned. "She's looking back over her shoulder while standing before a copse of trees. Trees at the height of autumn. All aswirl with red and orange and yellow. Look like they're on fire. Well, that was the last thing I saw the night before the Nazarene…"

"Burned my mother to death," the Queen finished.

The wind blew cold up from the river at our backs.

"Yeah. I'm sorry. I could tell you it was quick. Tell you it was painless. Tell you maybe it wasn't her there at the end." I raised my hands. "And maybe it wasn't. Maybe it was just the *strigoi.* But if I told you I knew it for certain, I'd be lying. And I don't know that hearing any of this shit'll do you any good. But me? Either way? I'd want to know."

The Queen wiped her eyes. "You said you'd pieced it all together … how?"

"Lady Mary and Palatine."

"Palatine…" the Queen choked, her face ashen.

I nodded to Palatine's tombstone. "You saw him?"

"Yes. I saw what he had—" the Queen trembled, "A body. Something. What was left. I could conjure no sense of … of anything. How could it—"

"There was no sense," I cut in. "No meaning. Only curse and murder and madness." I took a breath. "Palatine warned Lady Mary and Ruth of von Madbury's designs. He unlocked them. Set them free, but Ruth in her madness refused to leave Abraham's side. Lady Mary said she ... she just broke. In their flight down through the Schloss, Palatine told Lady Mary what was in the Haesken family treatise. About the curse. Not baldly. Not boldly. Said he read between the lines. But he said it was there."

"Between the lines..." the Queen whispered. "What else did my son say?"

"He said it began two centuries ago. Far to the south. During a war between the Teutonic Knights and some backwater clan-holt. A war that meant nothing. Achieved nothing. Except murder. Said the Teutonics razed the place. Felled a demon. Scourged the populace. Said the last survivor of the clan-holt, a withered old crone, cursed the Haesken line with her dying breath. The first-born heir."

"I-I don't—" The Queen recoiled. "But Eckhardt, he never succumbed to such a curse. Nor his father. Nor his *father's* father."

"Yeah. I don't know. Maybe it'd only affect one at a time. And it had affected one of your husband's ancestors, whichever was the Half-King. Gaston, I believe." I ran a hand through my hair. "And when I killed him. It. Truly killed. The curse passed onto the heir. Which meant that..."

"Yes." Queen Elona sagged, trembling down to one knee, only her dead son's tombstone holding her aloft. "Palatine was the firstborn. The rightful heir. And he knew it, too. Oh, my sweet boy. My sweet, smart, lovely boy. He should have grown to be a man. A king. To be ... something." The Queen shook her head slowly, lips ripping back in a rictus. "Eckhardt thought it best that their birth order be concealed. Reversed. He felt a cripple … oh, what were his words? *'A cripple would diminish our line.'"* She sobbed. "Diminish the line? Lord above."

"Palatine would've made a good king," I said.

"Yes. Better than Eckhardt. Eventine. Far better," the Queen sniffed. "Sir Luther … where is the Haesken Treatise?"

"Palatine told Lady Mary he burned it."

"Pity…" The Queen shook her head. "I wish he hadn't. That I might have garnered some modicum of understanding. Some … connection." She wiped tears from her cheek. "Palatine. You saw him in his last moments…"

"Yeah." I tried hard not seeing Palatine's tortured visage in the darkest corners of my mind.

"Do…" The Queen's nails dug into Palatine's tombstone. A woman lost. Forlorn. Broken. "Do you think he understood? Do you think he understood the peril? Do you think he knew he would bear the brunt of the curse? That should he send you down into the bowels of hell to slay the Half-King, and you were successful, it would mean the casting away of his own life? That he himself would become that … that horror? That thing? That monstrosity? Do you think he knew? Do you think…" She swallowed, licked her lips, her hands trembling. "Do you think he hated his life so much that he would cast it all away?"

"No, Your Majesty," I lied, "of course not."

444.

Dear Reader,

Thank you for reading my work. I truly appreciate it and hope you enjoyed it.

If you would, please take a moment to offer a review of it, I'd greatly appreciate it.

Thanks again,
Kevin Wright

Rock on.
Kevin Wright

ABOUT THE AUTHOR

Kevin Wright studied writing at the University of Massachusetts in Lowell and fully utilized his bachelor's degree by working first as a produce clerk and later as an emergency medical technician and firefighter. His mother is thrilled.

For decades now he has studied a variety of martial arts but steadfastly remains not-tough in any way shape or form. He just likes to pay money to get beat up, apparently.

Kevin Wright peaked intellectually in the seventh grade. Some of his favorite authors and influences are George R.R. Martin, H.P. Lovecraft, Lloyd Alexander, Neil Gaiman, Joe Abercrombie, and Joseph Heller.

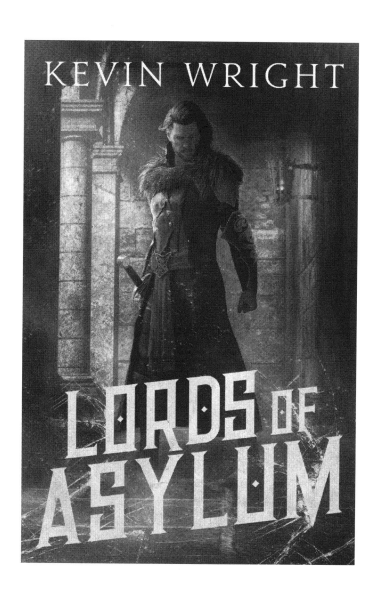

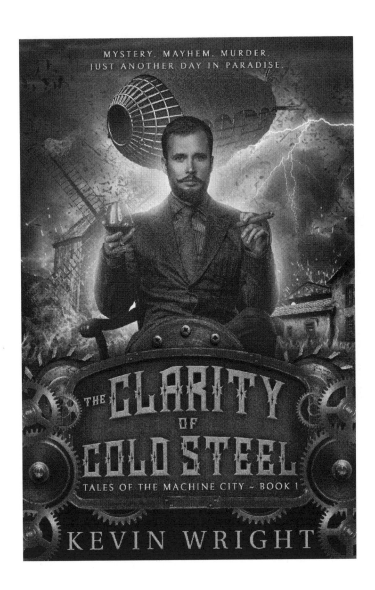

MYSTERY. MAYHEM. MURDER.
JUST ANOTHER DAY IN PARADISE.

THE CLARITY
OF
COLD STEEL

TALES OF THE MACHINE CITY ~ BOOK 1

KEVIN WRIGHT

Enter the Darkness.
Be consumed.
Know fear.

GRIMNOIR

KEVIN WRIGHT

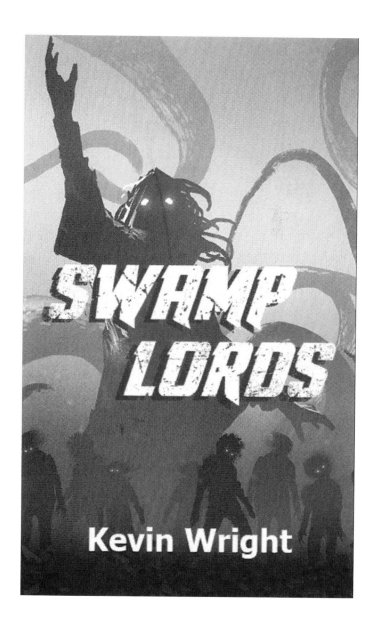

SWAMP LORDS

Kevin Wright

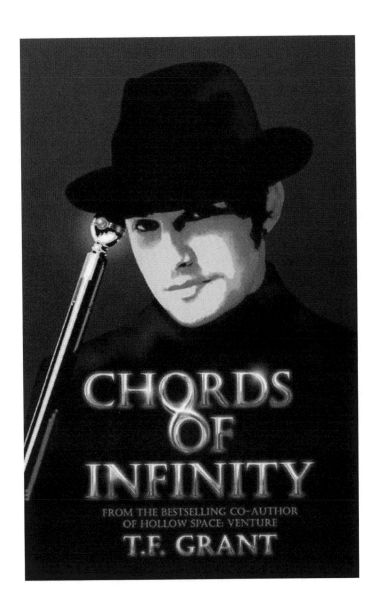

CHORDS OF INFINITY

FROM THE BESTSELLING CO-AUTHOR
OF HOLLOW SPACE: VENTURE

T.F. GRANT

Printed in Great Britain
by Amazon